# Deceit Deserves Revenge

Lucy B. Williams

**Outskirts Press, Inc.**
**Denver, Colorado**

Deceit Deserves Revenge

V4.0



Outskirts Press
http://www.outskirtspress.com

ISBN-10: 0-9770303-2-6
ISBN-13: 978-0-9770303-2-3



Printed in the United States of America

# DEDICATIONS

This book is dedicated to;

**Charles Crawford Williams, Jr.**

Attorney, avid hunter a courageous-splendid man my best friend in this world and the next one to come. He has given me the most important thing in my life, **courage**.

A thank you to;

James Bradley Sides
Jim Jackson
Gary Alan Jackson (singer, entertainer & song writer)
Rex Bolin
James B Williams
Roger Ross
Kamron Lee May

# PRELUDE

As I walked through the house drawing the drapes back and opening the doors, I thought, this is a beautiful day. The willow tree is flowing as if it's about to dance across the yard. The fence is covered in flaming red roses with the morning dew sparkling from the sun.

It's June Fifteenth, Nineteen Eighty-four. Yes, everything was beautiful except my heart and it was about to break. I leaned against the doorframe and thought, yes, just like the big pine tree in the back yard I have bent as far as I can without breaking!

I walked into the kitchen and sat down at the table with my husband, Richard. I looked at him and said, "I can't take anymore. Today I am going to see Dr. Skeet. He is reputed to be the best psychiatrist in Birmingham and my appointment is at two o'clock. Richard, I want you to go with me."

I waited for his answer. Richard never said a word and I sat looking into his hazel eyes and said, "You're handsome Richard. I can't blame others for making over you. It's you!! You just can't control yourself. **It's you!!!** It's you that needs the doctor. Yes, you Richard with Harriet and Percy, my own sister and brother, and you but so do most of the inhabitants of Shady Grove. Dr. Skeet will think I'm a nut, especially when I have to tell him that I grew up hating almost all of my family. What can I say when he asks, why did I move back around them. Why did I move back to Shady Grove?"

Richard asked, "What are you going to tell him?"

I said, "Everything. I'll tell him the truth. I'll tell him I think you're guilty but that you say you're not. I'll tell him you're saying all these things happened, but not for the reasons I think. But one thing is for sure Richard, someone has made my life hell and I want to know who and why. I can't cope with all of this. Look how Percy talks to me. That sawed off little runt I wish I could cut out his lying tongue. And what about Harriet? Richard, you know it was money that made her get mad and keep Brandon away from me. Richard, not you or anyone knows how bad it hurt me. For four years that child had been just like my very own son. I have been with him every day of his life. It's as if my heart is being torn out. If it wasn't for going to jail, I would kill her."

At this point, I began to cry. Then all of a sudden I screamed out at Richard. "I know you want me dead, you want me to kill myself. You'll see, I'll get myself back together and I'll make you pay! **All of you**! You knew better than to let yourself get involved with another woman. You knew better after the first woman!"

Richard started to say something, but I screamed out, "Don't say it. I've heard it before. You think just because you have two heads, you have two brains." At that point, I got up saying, "I'm going to prove to everyone in this world that you are guilty, along with Harriet and Percy. I hate this place, but **Oh No;** you weren't satisfied until you got me back into this **hell hole**!"

As I walked out I said, "You all can kiss my butt from now on."

I was as good as my word. At two o'clock I met with Dr. Skeet. My first impression of him was, that he didn't have enough sense to get a haircut. Without thinking I told Doctor Skeet, Richard would fool him, as sure as I'm living. But he will never fool me.

After the introductions I talked and talked pouring my heart out telling the truth about everything just to hear Dr. Skeet tell me maybe Richard has been set up, maybe he isn't guilty.

I went back week after week, trying to make the doctor understand that I was in danger. I had to prove that Richard was trying to drive me crazy so that I could make him leave. I had to make Richard admit that he and his women were tormenting me. Richard had said that he would get out if I could just prove he had another woman. I knew in my heart that he didn't want to get out. He wanted me dead, but by my own hand. That way it wouldn't cost him a dime. I stressed the fact over and over to Dr. Skeet, Richard will never break me, never!

It was February when I sat hearing the idiot of a doctor tell me in front of Richard that he didn't believe Richard was guilty. I stood up and cursed them both and telling them, if it's not Richard, just who in the hell is it? Thanks for your help doctor, but you and I both know you are an idiot.

The only thing left was for me to fight them all and I knew I would do just that. I didn't go back to see Dr. Skeet. He had said months ago that he didn't know what to do about all of my problems, but for sure there wasn't anything wrong with me mentally. He just didn't have any answers. This left me no choice but to go to the Sheriff's office.

Does my husband Richard want me dead? Does my family resent me so bad that they are helping Richard drive me to suicide? Will I have to take on the whole village? Am I really strong enough to chew iron and spit nails, or will Richard and my family win out?

Will they?

# CHAPTER 1

On October Tenth, Nineteen Eighty-eight while reading his morning paper, Dr. Skeet learned he just might be the **dummy** I said he was.

Canceling all of his appointments, Dr. Skeet unlocked his file cabinet taking out my eight months of tape recorded sessions and began playing one tape after another.

"Drucilla, I can't help you if you don't tell me everything. You say you can't deal with the fact that Harriet is keeping little Brandon from you. You don't understand why Percy has lied about you. You say that Richard has poisoned your coffee and that doesn't bother you as much as the rest."

"Yes sir, I didn't think that my family would ever hurt me again. I keep telling you that I know that Richard has never loved me, so it hasn't been a big surprise. It's just that now he has found a woman he wants and he wants me dead. This doesn't worry me. I can watch Richard. Besides, I'm going to tell the Sheriff the same thing that I'm telling you and Richard will be afraid to kill me.

Don't you worry Dr. Skeet, I'm not going to die and I'm not going to leave my home. I just want to learn to live around them all without letting them hurt me so bad. I just want Richard to leave and give me enough money to pay my utilities and medical costs."

"Okay Drucilla, we'll work on that, but first, tell me everything you can remember about your childhood. And another thing Drucilla, I can't believe you think all men are sorry."

"Believe me, it's not just men. It's ninety-nine and nine-tenths of the human population."

Drucilla let her life roll out as if I had known Dr. Skeet a lifetime in hopes he would help her. She began her story by telling him about DeRoy and her mother, Mama Marselle.

"DeRoy was Mama Marselle's boyfriend before he was my sister, Gertrude's, husband and he sure wouldn't have married Gertrude if Daddy hadn't made him. After DeRoy came to live with us, he took over the house. It was terrible the way he slapped Gertrude around and talked to her. The other children and I had to suffer because of him. He was the boss when Daddy was gone, which was ninety-five percent of the time. When Daddy wasn't at the coalmines, he was in the field trying to raise food.

Gosh, he was big. He is six feet two inches tall and weighing about one hundred eighty-five pounds. Little Gertrude is five foot two inches tall and nothing but bones. It's funny today to think of a **shotgun wedding**, but that's what it was. Mama Marselle wasn't enough for the scumbag. He had to get them both with a baby, but Gertrude didn't know DeRoy had been with Mama Marselle. All this may be hard for you to believe because I'm talking about my mother and brother-in-law but I remember it, as if it were yesterday.

Mama Marselle and DeRoy would send Gertrude to the neighbor's house to call in the grocery order after Daddy would go to work, then they would make all of the kids go outside to play. What they didn't know was that we could see them on the bed!

When Daddy boxed in the porch, he left some boards off around the bottom so that the air could circulate and with the porch being so high off the ground, we could see the furniture on the porch when we looked up. At five years old, I didn't know what they were doing, but I did positively know not to tell anyone. Once when Gertrude came back from calling in the grocery order and I told her that Mama Marselle and DeRoy had been on the bed tickling each other, Mama Marselle said, that's a lie! She was just mashing a blackhead. Everything seemed all right, but later Mama Marselle beat me half to death and told me if I ever told my Daddy or Gertrude anything like that again she would beat me to death. That I was never to tell anyone that she mashed DeRoy's blackheads again.

DeRoy was Mama Marselle's special friend. She let Gertrude go to the Company Store and buy him shinny black shoes and brown khaki clothes. He had plenty of cigarettes to smoke and even more bad jokes to tell. DeRoy always had money. He would stand around jiggling the change in his pockets. He wanted everyone to know he was on a pedestal.

Even when we didn't have anything to eat but bread and gravy, Mama Marselle saw to it that DeRoy had his plate first. Daddy worked the three till eleven shift at the mines. DeRoy didn't have to work. Mama Marselle was taking care of him. He was smart enough to never cause, any trouble when Daddy was home. The scumbag would stay in bed almost all morning and Gertrude or Mama Marselle would carry coffee to him. It was good when he stayed in bed. At least I knew that I wouldn't be beat on by him.

Mama Marselle was only thirty-four years old, but she was sorry when it came to keeping house. We children went without the food we needed and never even had baths like other children. It was terrible the way she sent us to school with dirty clothes and hair so greasy that it hung limp on our shoulders. Even our shoes were pitiful. I guess this was because Mama Marselle was so lazy.

Daddy made good money working in the coalmines, but it was cut out of his paycheck before he even got to see it. It's a fact that DeRoy and Gertrude saw more of his pay than Daddy ever did.

Daddy would get in all the wood and coal to heat the house while DeRoy sat on the porch and watched. Daddy did everything he could to help Mama Marselle. I can still see Daddy going out the door with a sack over his shoulder to beg for food from door-to-door in the winter, when it was too cold to breathe. Daddy was so cowed down. I was ashamed of him.

Mama Marselle wasn't like the other women. They canned and froze food, but not her. All she did was listen to the soaps on the radio and entertain DeRoy. For the life of me, I don't know why Daddy didn't kick her out!

Daddy took me to church one Sunday and this nice looking family came over to where we were seated and introduced themselves. They wanted to know if I could go home with them. They would bring me home later that afternoon. I'm still surprised that Daddy let me go with them. The Baker's home was so clean you could eat off the floor. Mrs. Baker gave me a bath and put the best smelling powder on me. My hair was so pretty and clean. I hated to go back home because it was such a dirty place. Mrs. Baker wouldn't let me take the new things she had given me home, but she taught me how to wash things out by hand. I learned a better way of life and I swore every day that I'd never be like my family. The Baker's told me that some day I would have good things, but I would have to work hard to have them and to keep them. Mrs. Baker was tall and lean. I've never forgotten her. Let me tell you, children don't forget, never!

Then there's Aunt Bessy. I think we all have a **sorry list** and old Aunt Bessy, who lived across the street, was at the top of mine. She was good to the other kids in the neighborhood, but she hated me. She would make clothes for them and give them nice things. The only time she would even let me come around was to wash canning jars or peel tomatoes from water that was so hot it would burn my hands. It never failed that every summer Mama Marselle would make me help her. The only thing the witch ever did for us was telephone the law every time DeRoy would beat the hell out of Gertrude.

Aunt Bessy had a daughter that I hated. She had everything money could buy. With age she turned into a **river rat**, plus being ugly as sin."

"Go ahead Dr. Skeet, laugh, but it's true."

"I was the doll. People would stop Mama Marselle and tell her that I was beautiful. They would come up to the car window to see me, but I was always dirty and in rags. Even though I was young, I was ashamed. I wanted to be clean. I hated everyone around me. All those big people drinking beer, telling dirty jokes and talking so bad, it was horrible.

I thought I would be happy when I started school, but I wasn't. With my birthday being in December, I was seven years old in the first grade and so little the teacher wouldn't let me go to the second grade, saying I was just a baby.

By this time, Mama Marselle had another little girl, Harriet. She's Brandon's mother. Gertrude had her baby and Mama Marselle was sad because DeRoy left hitchhiking with Gertrude and the new baby. I remember standing in the door with tears running down my face as he took Gertrude away. It was pitiful the way she walked along behind him. I didn't know how many times he would beat her before bringing her back. Today, I can't believe that in Nineteen Fifty-one my sister was hitchhiking, but damn if she wasn't!

It didn't take me long to realize that DeRoy would be back as soon as Daddy's strike was over. The coalmines were always on a wildcat strike. I was nine years old when DeRoy and Gertrude came back and their little girl was now two years old. DeRoy acted as if he'd been to Hell taking lessons from the Devil.

I remember the fool kept trying to make their little girl act as if she were six. DeRoy would use the little thing to pick a fight with Gertrude. He'd snatch her up and lock themselves in a room. The child would scream and scream with Gertrude would be pounding on the door, and begging him not to beat her baby and to open the door. I tell you, I hated DeRoy. I would crawl under the bed crying and swearing that I would never have a man in my life.

I couldn't help but hear and see everything because the shack of a house we lived in only had four little rooms, each ten by twelve. Mama Marselle's room had two big beds with Mama, Daddy and the new baby in one and my two brothers and I in the other. It was hard to sleep with all those arms and legs wrapped around me. Some nights I was thankful for the boys because the house was so cold we would freeze. We would sleep in our street clothes and even with all the coats thrown over the bed covers it was still cold.

You can believe me when I say the winters were the worst because we didn't have any food. I cried myself to sleep many nights because I was so hungry. I prayed to die because I knew there wouldn't be any food when I woke up. I will admit I still have a terrible fear of being cold and hungry.

I remember once when Mama Marselle sent me to old Aunt Bessy's, the witch of all witches, to ask for some left over cornbread. She said that she had dinner left over, but it was being saved for her son-in-law. How fast people forget.

My Daddy had sent load after load of vegetables to her home every summer. Yet, that was forgotten in the cold of winter. I don't think it would have killed her to cook us a pan of bread.

My feelings for this Old Lady have never changed. I hated her then and I hate her now! She wasn't any better than my family, just better off.

She had a bastard child by another man before she married money. This daughter grew up and married a drunk that could have passed for DeRoy's twin! Her other child was the **river rat**, living around on a riverbank for months before marrying. She also had to work to support her man. He was no better than DeRoy either.

Well, anyway, Little Baby Harriet was so hungry she was crying and I hated that old witch so bad that I wished she would die. I also hated Daddy, Tommy, my oldest brother, not to mention DeRoy. Tommy was twenty years old and for the life of me I couldn't see how three grown men would let a home go without food.

I could hear the neighbors talking about us saying we were **white trash**. Some said Mama Marselle and Daddy didn't know better and some said they just didn't give a damn. I knew that no one cared.

I tell you Dr. Skeet, I don't know why the people around the neighborhood made themselves out to be so saintly when they were swapping ass as if it were cups of sugar.

I remember DeRoy and Mama Marselle getting into an out-and-out curse fight about Mama Marselle's best friend. DeRoy had said he could prove that the woman was a slut. Lenny was her name. DeRoy told Mama Marselle, just you wait till Friday night when her boys go skating with Jerry and Percy."

Dr. Skeet said, "Wait a minute Drucilla, who are Jerry and Percy?"

"They are my brothers. Jerry is my favorite brother. He's so handsome with cloudy, blue eyes and blond hair. Dr. Skeet, as we go on you'll see why I love him best.

Anyway, Mama Marselle's friend's husband worked nights just like Daddy did, so sure enough the next Friday night, DeRoy, Gertrude and Mama Marselle stood in the back bedroom looking out the window and watched one of the neighborhood men go into Lenny's back door. The houses were back-to-back.

The light in her house never came on. Now, I tell you this was supposed to be a **Miss Goody Two Shoes**, saintly woman, just like old Aunt Bessy. But yet this bunch didn't like my family! I know today they were all sorry.

Isn't it funny Dr. Skeet, how things turn about? I may not be happy, but today I can sure as hell buy those scumbags for what they think they're worth. I hate them all so bad that the only way I'd even go to their funeral is to puke in their dead faces.

Anyway, I was still in the first grade at nine years old because I was only thirty-two inches tall. It didn't matter that I could do the work. I was just too small and no one gave a damn.

Most Mamas' would pack their children a lunch, but not mine. She told me to walk home for lunch, but I knew not to because there wouldn't be anything there to eat. There was a little boy who noticed I never had a lunch and he came up to me one morning with a brown paper bag. He said his Mom sent me a lunch, a peanut butter and raisin sandwich. That little boy gave me a little brown bag all that year. I guess **one** did give a damn.

By this time I was ashamed of my dirty rags and my age. I didn't want to go to school. The other children were laughing about me being too old to be in their room, saying my clothes needed washing and that my Mama didn't love me. But the little boy with the brown bag always had a smile for me. I never saw him after that year, but I will never forget him.

Dr. Skeet, I don't think I'll ever love anyone again. I already know what I need and that's to get away from these people."

"Maybe so Drucilla, but tell me the rest."

"School was out for Christmas, but I knew there was no **Santa Clause** except for the little man from the Methodist Church. Every year he backed his car up to our house and gave us everything from ham to candy. This man made me believe that there must be some good men in the world, plus my brother Jerry. Jerry was a worker. He knew how to hustle. He had a job and had been saying that he had a secret. Lord, he did! When Christmas day came, he gave me the biggest baby doll you ever saw. I can't tell you how much I loved him. Jerry is the only good memory I have. Today he is still so handsome with his blond, curly hair and blue eyes. Believe it or not, I do stop and remember that I did have Jerry.

The Christmas that I was thirteen, Mama Marselle went to the jewelry store and charged DeRoy a watch and Gertrude a ring. The only thing the other kids received came from the church. For the life of me, I didn't know why Daddy was letting Mama Marselle do us children that way. I love my Daddy because he is my Daddy, but I don't respect him. I will never understand why he let our home be taken over by DeRoy.

I couldn't see how Gertrude could live with DeRoy. It looked like she would be scared to death to go in a room with him. I never did know why, but after Christmas, DeRoy had been mad for about a week and one day he put his clothes into a paper bag saying he was going to leave. Gertrude begged and begged him not to go. Then all of a sudden he grabbed her saying, get my clothes ironed and do it right! She had just gotten through ironing them before he stuffed them into the bag. She ironed them again for half a day, but he said she didn't do it right. That scumbag wanted his pants starched so they would stand up on the floor with a perfect crease just so he could sit on the porch and drink coffee. That day they started screaming at each other and he slapped her up against the wall, pulled her around by her hair and kicked her in the ribs. Mama Marselle ran in telling him to stop, but he just picked up a piece of stove wood saying he would knock her brains out. At that same time Tommy came in the door and ran to get Daddy's gun. When he came back into the room to shoot DeRoy, Mama Marselle pushed him to one side and grabbed the gun. Then DeRoy hit Tommy in the mouth. Blood flew from his face and he fell against the heater. The stovepipes on the wood heater came down and soot went everywhere and fire was shooting out of the top of the heater. I heard Tommy say he would kill DeRoy. DeRoy went outside telling Mama Marselle that he was leaving. By the time the police got there, he was gone. Tommy also left and never returned.

It was one thing after another and living from hand to mouth. Daddy had told Mama Marselle that DeRoy had to get a job and get out on his own. But he knew in his heart that Mama Marselle would never let DeRoy go. Mama Marselle would say its okay if they stay and that would be the end of it. Daddy said that even if they don't leave he had to have the car because he had walked to work for the last time. The man he had been riding with told him that he couldn't ride with him anymore because he wore his mining clothes home and they were ruining his car seat. Mama Marselle would take Daddy's car keys while he was sleeping and give them to DeRoy and Daddy would have to walk to work anyway. Mama Marselle didn't care if he walked, lived or died. All she cared about was having enough money to buy beer. It didn't matter that her children were undernourished and abused."

"Now wait a minute Drucilla. I'm not quite clear on your Daddy. Explain that a little more."

"Daddy is small like me. He is five feet two inches tall and weighs about one hundred fifteen pounds, but don't let that fool you.

He walked about five miles through the woods everyday to get to work.

He would go to work sick, unless he was so sick he couldn't stand. One time he went to work sick and the other miners complained to the foreman. They said he should be sent home before the rest of the miners got sick. The foreman refused. So, the next day three men, all about six feet tall, met Daddy in the woods on his way to work. They told him to turn around and go home or they would whip him. He wound up beating the Hell out of all three so bad that they didn't show up for work.

Daddy wasn't afraid of DeRoy or Mama Marselle. That's what I haven't ever figured out. Mama Marselle threatened to beat us if we ever told Daddy about DeRoy, but a blind man could see what was going on.

Dr. Skeet, why is all this necessary for my problems today, all that is over and forgotten."

"Drucilla, it is over, but I promise you it is not forgotten. Go on."

"All right, I want to go back to when I was nine years old. I had gotten so sick that they had to take me to the doctor. The doctor was shocked that I was so small. The doctor told me that I had pinworms, which had stunted my growth and that I had the bones of a three year old. The doctor stressed the fact that if I had a bad fall, my bones would crumble because they were like chalk.

One day, when I was fourteen, Daddy came in saying he could sell this place and build a house in the country. He said there was a spring for water, that the city couldn't cut that off, plenty of land to raise food and no neighbors.

I was so happy. It would be wonderful. I would be away from all the people that had made fun of me.

Mrs. Baker had taught me to keep clean, to change my clothes every day and wash them myself. She said to keep my hair washed and brushed, to brush my teeth morning and night, and to use a biscuit to shine my shoes, even if they did have holes in them so they would be clean. I gathered up pride everywhere I went. I made up my mind to stay away from the others the best I could. I had to pull myself up and away from them.

One good thing happened then, DeRoy left again. He was afraid he would have to help build the house in the country. The bad thing was that the mines had shut down for good and the new house wasn't even half finished. That was fine. It didn't matter if you could see through the floorboards or that there wasn't electricity. At least we were out of the city where the other people couldn't see us.

Here we were, hungry and cold again. But this time we did have water. Daddy couldn't get another job. He couldn't read or write a word. The mines were all he knew. He had worked the mines for forty years. He had started at fourteen years old, but for some reason he didn't draw retirement. Daddy cleared the land for a garden and Jerry brought in whatever he could for us to live on.

The people up the road from us had two big chicken houses and raised hogs. It was as if they hated us from the start. But somehow Jerry started helping the old man and told him we were having a hard time. One morning the old man slipped through the woods and brought Mama Marselle two big hens and a sack of eggs. The old man told Mama Marselle, never tell anyone or the others will have my hide.

By this time I was doing well. I had made me some rollers from the metal bands I had taken from around a meat can. I saved ten pieces and cut them six inches long. I wrapped them with brown paper and used them to roll my hair every night.

One day Jerry came in telling Daddy that there was no other way to make a dime and they would have to make and sell whiskey. The next thing I knew, I was helping to fill five gallon cans and learning to drive.

Percy is younger than Jerry and wasn't good for a damn thing. He wallowed in self-pity and couldn't wipe his butt without smearing it on himself, and this is still Percy today.

At last, we had electricity in the country house. We had one light hanging from the ceiling in each room, and **Glory to God** we had a milk cow. Daddy was bringing in the prettiest feed sacks he could find and I was saving every one of them.

At school it wasn't only the children making fun of me, so were the teachers. It was so unbearable that I just couldn't go back. How could I learn seventh grade work when I didn't know first grade? Going back was a waste of time. The Good Lord knows I was too far behind. I couldn't stand it when the teacher would say. **You're sure dumb**. Deep down in my heart I didn't want to quit, but I knew I would have to teach myself.

By this time I was in the seventh grade, sixteen years old and couldn't read a word. I didn't know my butt from a hole in the ground, so to speak. My math teacher, who was also my home economics teacher, was as nice as Mrs. Baker. She was teaching me how to make my clothes with the feed sacks. But of course at home all the dishes had to be done before I could do anything for myself. It would make me fighting mad when Mama Marselle would make me put the sewing up. God knows sewing things by hand takes forever anyway. I would wipe tears from my eyes while washing dishes every day. She would sit around all day doing nothing and leave the dishes to pile up for me. Believe me washing dishes with a bar of soap is terrible. Have you ever seen pots and pans that have been used on a wood stove? They are soot black and hard for a little girl to wash. I was nothing but a slave in that house.

Mama Marselle's sister gave her an old wringer washer, but the wringers were broken. Even though I was so little, I was made to wash the clothes. It would take me all weekend. Wringing them out by hand, hanging them on the clothes line, taking them off the line as soon as they were dry, and hanging them up in the house. I washed one load after another. You can believe that I was dead tired when night came.

Bringing the water up the hill from the spring was the biggest job, even though Daddy helped and so did Jerry. It was me that did all the housework plus helping Daddy outside. You have to remember that Gertrude was gone, so that left me to do it all. Mama Marselle wasn't going to do anything but cook and little Harriet was too small to do much."

"Drucilla, you hardly mention Percy. What did he do when there was work to do?"

"Dr. Skeet, like I told you before. Percy isn't worth ten cents Daddy found out long ago. Percy wouldn't do anything right and after our run in he stayed away from me.

It was.... it was the summer of Nineteen Fifty-One and I almost worked myself to death. I felt like a punching bag with Percy pushing and shoving me around until one day I warned him to stop and he laughed. The next time he drew back his hand, I kicked him between the legs so hard that he walked straddle-legged for two weeks. You got it. He never touched me again. I didn't know what was wrong with him. He just sat back looking and listening, but he wouldn't get off his tail to work that's for sure. Percy had quit school two years before me."

Dr. Skeet had listened to one tape after another and it was after lunch. He wouldn't be going to lunch today. He was obsessed trying to find what he has missed. He blamed himself for what had happened to Drucilla.

# CHAPTER 2

"Oh Lord, have Mercy! To add to my misery about school, DeRoy and Gertrude were back. This meant we had to give them our room. I could hardly bear the thought of him being in the same house with me. I knew I was not able to wash and clean after them all but, oh my, if you could have seen Mama Marselle. She was one happy woman. It was Drucilla do this and Drucilla do that. It was Jerry that helped me keep my sanity. He was good to me.

Jerry was always bringing in boys that he didn't even let me talk to. He said they were no good. I loved Jerry. He had even fixed the car seat so I could drive the car. Being so short, I had a hard time driving. Jerry taught me all about cars and I could drive as well as anybody. I learned everything about a car from bumper-to-bumper. The boys that came to the house would ask me questions about cars just to see if Jerry was lying about me.

Thinking back, I even loved to go hunting with Daddy. I had to help in the garden and also help him saw firewood. It seemed as if Daddy and Jerry were keeping me busy and away from the house.

I didn't know what Jerry meant when he said if DeRoy ever put his hands on me that he would kill him. Jerry said, you tell me if he ever mistreats you. I was taking up for myself going and coming, but I'm sure everyone knew that I would tell Jerry. Jerry had been taking up for me ever since Gertrude came back with, DeRoy.

He had even told Mama Marselle to make Gertrude do some of the work, that it wasn't my place to do it all.

DeRoy didn't like it very much. The stupid scumbag had little enough sense to pop off at Jerry. Jerry told him he had run over his sisters and brothers the last time and would cut his throat from ear to ear. DeRoy wasn't such a bully after that. I saw then and there that he only bullied the ones who let him. Jerry even gave Mama Marselle a word or two, saying it wouldn't hurt her to do a few things around the house.

It was only a few weeks after that Jerry had to go to jail. He had been caught with a load of moonshine. I cried half the day when Jerry had to leave. It was June of Nineteen Sixty. I couldn't believe he was leaving me there by myself.

After Jerry went to jail, eight Federal men came looking for the whiskey still. They blew up two stills, chopped up barrels and confiscated copper lines and radiators.

Not a word was said to Daddy. I believe the Federal men hated to destroy the stills. As they passed us sitting on the porch, they bowed their heads as if to say, I'm sorry. Everyone knew it was a set-up. There were other neighbors making moonshine and operating cockfights. No one else was bothered and even I knew for a fact that the law in our territory knew about the cockfights and whiskey making.

After that, DeRoy had it in for me and I knew it. I was scared to death of DeRoy because he had already said he was going to get me. I'll be darned, the very next day he caught a lizard to put down my back. The old scumbag chased me all over the woods with me running as fast as I could. I couldn't understand why somebody didn't make him stop. I ran and ran with Mama Marselle and Gertrude laughing from the porch.

When I got so tired I couldn't run any longer, I ran to the house and that's where he caught me. I fainted as he was reaching for me. The next thing I knew, I was crying, saying I was going to tell Daddy, but of course Mama Marselle said she would beat me if I did.

The next day DeRoy pushed me off the porch backwards. I hit the ground on my back, knocking the breath out of myself. I remembered what the doctor had said about my bones. I got up running to the field to find Daddy. I told him I needed the keys to the car that I needed to move it. I ran back to the yard and got into the car just as DeRoy came off the porch asking, where are you going little girl. I screamed for him to stay right where he was so I could run over him. I got into the car and tried to run him down. After I missed him, I was so mad I just drove out and around the road on two wheels. Mama Marselle was on the porch. She thought I was leaving so she sent Percy to find me.

I knew I was too mad to drive, so I just drove out of sight and pulled off the road. I parked until I had cooled off enough to go back. I stopped and picked Percy up on my way back.

As I went up on the porch, Gertrude said that I had caused Mama Marselle to faint when I rounded the curve. I said that I didn't care! I told Gertrude if she didn't keep DeRoy away from me, I would tell Daddy. I asked her what she wanted with DeRoy and told her she was just a fool and that the man wouldn't work tasting pies in a pie house, that I hate his guts and he is the sorriest thing living. I sure don't know what Mama Marselle wants with him. He wouldn't even stay here and help build this house. So why should you come back here to live? DeRoy is sorry. I wouldn't live with a man that wouldn't work if I had to marry twenty, to find one.

Gertrude had said, well, let me tell you little girl, he don't belong to Mama Marselle.

I couldn't help but come back with, you could have fooled me I walked off saying someday I may kill him. Every time he beat Gertrude, it would make me sick. I wanted to kill him.

The next morning DeRoy got up with a smile all over his face. I didn't know what he and Mama Marselle were talking about, but somehow I knew it was about me.

The next day one of the boys that Jerry knew was telling me he would give me a good home. His name was Wayne Gooch and I didn't know anything about him. I did know Jerry had never let me be around him. Mama Marselle said Wayne had told her that he had a good job, plus he would give me anything I asked for.

Mama Marselle sent Daddy with me to the courthouse to sign the papers for us to marry. She told me it was best because he had a job and could feed me. I would have plenty to eat besides all the new clothes that I could have. It sounded so good. Just think I would just have to take care of one person. So, I married him to get away from home.

All I wanted was a home. I knew how to cook and clean. If that is all I had to do, it would be easy. He knew I couldn't do anything else because Mama Marselle had told him that I couldn't even read. He said he would be good to me and that all he wanted was someone to keep house for him. What it really amounted to was DeRoy getting rid of me. Mama Marselle, Gertrude and DeRoy had given me away. This told me for sure that DeRoy was the one that turned Jerry in for hauling whiskey.

I was a little girl, four feet eleven inches tall and weighing about seventy pounds. I didn't know anything about being married. I had slept with my brothers all my life. We had slept in our everyday clothes and they had never put their hands on me. I didn't know what happened when men and women went to bed together. I fought the bastard for a week. I told him that Jerry would kill him if he put his hands on me. All the fighting in the world wouldn't stop the bastard from hurting me.

I know that today it's called rape and an awful thing for a woman to go through. One thing's for sure, it opened my eyes to what Mama Marselle had been doing with DeRoy and Daddy. I knew right then and there where all the babies came from."

"Drucilla, what are you smiling about?"

"Oh, no! Dr. Skeet, you don't want to know. You just think you want to know what I'm smiling about. I just remembered about the blackhead Mama Marselle was mashing.

Anyway, I cried until I made myself sick. I hated all my family and I knew in my heart that they were all sorry. I also knew that I would be good all of my life. I was in a terrible fix, but Jerry would take care of this convict.

Dr. Skeet, I still want revenge. I wish I could pay them all back. I'll tell you one thing, if it wasn't for going to jail, I would get revenge.

The very next Sunday we went to meet his mother for the first time. Mrs. Gooch was short and fat and I do mean **fat**. She dumped a **bomb** in my lap as soon as Wayne went outside. The lady asked me if Wayne had told me that he had just gotten out of prison. I must have turned white. She said, she didn't think he had told me. I knew right then that I would get out of this mess. I just didn't know it would take so long.

It was mid-December and I was sick enough to die everyday. Wayne's mother had a good laugh, saying I was going to have a baby. Those words introduced me to panic attacks. I called the operator and asked for the number for an OBGYN.

One Wednesday, two and one-half months later, Dr. Shane held me while I cried. He said I was a baby having a baby. He said, there's one good thing about being pregnant, you don't have to worry about getting that way.

Dr. Shane was so good to me. He was a big man with a head full of white hair and the warmest smile you have ever seen. There's no way I can tell you or anyone else how much I love him. I hope that maybe someday I can tell him that without him, my life would have been a worse hell than it was.

The next time Jerry saw me, I was as round as I was tall. I could see fire shooting out of his eyes as he said, damn this whole bunch. Jerry went off and got dog drunk. As he lay on the porch, I washed his face and told him I'd be all right and I didn't want him to do anything to them. I told him I wouldn't be able to stand it if he went back to prison. He said he hated what they had done to me and he would never care about Mama Marselle again. It sure changed Jerry. He didn't care if they all died in a pile. I know in my heart that Jerry had made life a little better for me. He is the only good memory I have.

So, you see without a doubt, it was DeRoy's fault that Jerry had to go to prison in the first place.

I had a little girl and I named her Amanda.

I learned a lot about life in the three years that I lived with the Gooch's. Wayne said that DeRoy had told him not to tell Daddy or me that he was seven years older than me and that he had been in prison.

Moving Amanda and I from place to place was one thing, but into his Mom's house, a female DeRoy was all I needed. Mistreating me was one thing but when Amanda would cry she would scream at me to get that crying child out on the porch, that Wayne couldn't sleep. That was more than I could stand.

Knowing I couldn't stay with him any longer, I went to a café and told the lady what kind of mess I was in and that I had to have a job of some kind. She gave me a job working from six a.m. until two p.m. I would leave there and go to a barbecue place and work until eleven p.m. I took Amanda and left. I worked long and hard.

Dr. Skeet, I could relax for the first time in my life. I only had one room, but it was clean and warm. Amanda was the most beautiful child you ever saw. The landlady that kept her while I worked, loved her and was good to us. I only dated two men, to be honest, I was afraid of them all. One thing was for sure, I would look for a clean man that would work.

Jerry had come to the café a few times to see me and to tell me that Mama Marselle wanted me to bring the baby to see them. I told Jerry I tried, but every time I started down that road, a fear took hold of me and I couldn't breathe. Jerry turned to leave and I said, okay, you tell her I'll be there

Sunday because I want to talk to her anyway. Jerry told me, don't be afraid. I'll be there.

A week had never passed so fast before and with every mile I drove down that road, I thought I would die. There was nothing nice about me that day. I was full of hate.

I lit in on Mama Marselle telling her that I would never forgive her as long as I lived for giving me away to Wayne, but most of all for not telling me that the convict would get between my legs! I screamed, Mama, you knew that I didn't know anything about things like that. She screamed back, kids at school talk.

I said, oh yes, but not to me. I was too poor and too dirty for them to talk to me. People don't even believe that I didn't know about sex and it's your fault. You gave me away to a convict to be tormented because you loved mashing DeRoy's blackheads. Mama, I know you love DeRoy. I heard you and DeRoy the day Daddy killed that hog. You and DeRoy were cutting it up and salting it down.

You didn't know I heard you say Daddy should be accidentally shot while on a hunting trip. I have never been so mad, but I went on to say, old woman, you can't ever get rid of my Daddy, because he will rake and scrape to bring you in a bite of food while DeRoy doesn't bring you anything. Do you hear me Mama?

There is no love in me. I hate people like you and DeRoy.

Mama just sat looking at me. She knew Daddy could hear everything I was saying.

Jerry came in telling me to cool down and just try to forget it. I said, hell no, I want her to hear me. I went on. Mama, do you hear me? You made my life a nightmare. I have known from the night you and Daddy were in that fight and you said, old man, I know these kids are mine, but do you know which ones belong to you? I know I don't belong to him because I'm not like you people. I'll tell you something else Mama, giving me away to keep me quiet wasn't as bad as not sending us kids to school everyday. You, old woman, made us brain dead. We don't have anything to offer this world. People like us should be given shots and put to sleep forever. It hurts so bad when people ask me where did I go to school. What college did I attend? All I can be is a housewife. It's so sad, that I'm so good, yet I can't find a respectable man to love Amanda and me because I don't have an education. I live a terrifying life praying that no one will start up a conversation with me because I'm so dumb.

Walking out the door, I told them I wanted them all to go to hell and just maybe something good would happen to me someday and not to ever ask me to come back because I don't have anything good to say to you. I did hug Harriet.

Jerry was waiting for me as I stepped off the porch. He said, crank this car. I think the carburetor needs idling down some. It didn't sound right when you were sitting in the yard. I let him work on the car and told him I loved him before I left. I remember Jerry saying this damn car will sure run, want it Drucilla? I smiled, hearing him say, don't be going fast.

I had a Nineteen Fifty-five hard top, black Ford. It sure would run and just up the road a piece, it dawned on me that there wasn't anything wrong with my carburetor. Jerry had just given me time to cool down.

I wasn't asked to come back and they didn't even ask about Amanda. I didn't see Gertrude or DeRoy. To tell the truth, they didn't even cross my mind. I had to have a good life for Amanda. I couldn't let her go through the hard times that I had seen.

Dr. Skeet, I know now I shouldn't have said anything to the old woman, but I hated them. It's really something to get out in the world and find out that people think that those people who live and have homes in the country are charming. Let me tell you that statement has made me sick many times."

Dr. Skeet had been listening to tapes all day. Here it is near suppertime and he has not found any hint of what he has missed. It had to be there. He would not stop until he found it, what ever it was. He put in another tape.

# CHAPTER 3

"I had been divorced one year, when I was introduced to Richard. I have always tried to second-guess Richard. I tried to stay just two steps ahead of him. That way I felt I wouldn't get walked on, but that statement is a joke."

Dr. Skeet said, "Yes, Drucilla, this is a whole new can of worms."

"You're darn right! Before I get started on that fool, I have one more thing to say. The rows in my Daddy's garden were never so long as the one row Mama Marselle and DeRoy plowed for me. I never dreamed it could be that bad again, but it looks as though I will live in hell until I die.

I also knew that I was the only family member with the pride and caring to help all the young children who were brought into this world by my brothers and sisters. I felt I had to make a better life for them and I have.

Dr. Skeet, I'll tell you now that I'm not sorry that I kicked them all to make them better people. I was raised sorry and I don't want any child to have to live the way I did. I know they hate me because after I helped them get their heads above water, I quit giving them money. They have had to work like crazy to halfway keep up, but I got them on the right track and now that I won't buy their love, they don't want me anymore. It's just that simple!"

"Drucilla, when you married Richard in Nineteen Sixty-five, did you love him?"

"Yes sir, I did."

"Well, let's see if Richard is as bad as the rest."

"Yes sir! I'll tell you about Richard. He hurt me worse than all the rest. I thought he'd been sent from Heaven. You're about to see he's a Devil in disguise.

Richard was so handsome, standing five feet eight inches tall, weighing about one hundred forty pounds and dark skin. He looked as if he had just stepped out of a magazine. Yes, I was in love.

Richard's family was something else. I knew from the first moment we met that my new sister-in-law was the witch of all witches. Hair died so black that she looked like a dead person. I thought living among this bunch of goody-two-shoes is going to be the biggest challenge I'll ever face. I swear to you the woman would have been right at home working in a funeral parlor.

Then, of course, there was Richard's Daddy and stepmother. They had only been married six months and really wanted Richard out of their hair, so false faces were in order.

Wade Hallmark I never did get to know him very well and didn't want to. He said I reminded him of a waitress that he had seen once in a café that was so short that when she walked up to the table he thought she was on her knees. He was a pompous, stuff shirt, worm of a man. No one could get close to him. He kept everyone at arms length. I'm still surprised that Richard did not call him Mr. Hallmark. He was average height, weight and in good shape for a retired truck driver.

As for Mrs. Gladys Hallmark, I didn't see enough of her to know what she was like. She was always just there, never saying a word. I could see the malice in her eyes and thought the pompous old worm deserved her. Richard's brother,

Butch was about the same height and weight as his Daddy. He didn't keep up his looks. He had a potbelly and a sloppy look about him. He was friendly enough in a stupid way. I guess he was trying to be smart and didn't know how. I always say you're a lost cause if you're not smart enough to know how dumb you are.

Butch's wife, Lavita, what can I say. She thought her stuff didn't stink, but she was only one big pile of stuff, so what did she know.

Richard's brother and sister-in-law didn't pull any punches. They let me know right from the start that I was from the wrong side of the tracks.

Take the dinner party for instance. Lavita and Butch really tried to put me down. She set the table with pinto beans, fried potatoes and cornbread with water to drink. She told me that they know that this is what I'm used to having. I just smiled and said pintos are my favorite, thank you. I told myself that I would need the water to help digest this day along with this dinner. Lavita made sure to tell me right out that I wasn't good enough to be a Hallmark before the evening was over!

What a joke these people were. Richard had already told me that Lavita was pregnant before she and Butch were married. He had also told me about the car that brother Butch and Lavita had let Richard take up payments on because they couldn't meet the payments. He had let Lavita keep the car because he had two other cars and really didn't need it until he asked me to marry him. He then took the car from her and gave it to me, as a wedding gift. I feel with all my heart that taking the car from her is why Lavita hated me so much.

Now, speaking of Butchie Boy, darn if I know what kind of living arrangements he had with Lavita because that idiot is gay. The truth of the matter is that I was from a large, poor uneducated family, but I had enough common sense for five people. Richard was so naïve or blind to the facts that he couldn't see what was going on. After a few months of torment, I went to talk to Dr. Shane, who was also my friend and still is.

Dr. Shane laughed and said I sure have gotten myself into a mess this time. Just let my common sense, along with my natural beauty, walk me through life. Learn everything I can as I go through life. What I didn't know, fake it. His people are no better than me and it sounds to him as if they aren't as good. Always remember I didn't marry his people, I married Richard.

I could see that Dr. Shane was deeply concerned and he could tell I was suffering terribly. He said he would always be here to help me. I could call him anytime.

I made up my mind then and there that I would fight them tooth and nail. I thought to myself, I'm proud to be country and good and able to take care of my home. By then I had learned to appreciate what living in the country had taught me. If they wanted a witch, then that's just what I'd give them. I knew that by this time Richard really began to understand how deeply his family had hurt me. He also began to show his true colors. After all, he was furious when I made the announcement of the new baby. He made me feel right at that minute that he had made a mistake, when he married me. We had been married six months and Richard said he didn't have a doubt that the brat belongs to Dan.

Dan was Richard's best friend and I didn't even like the boy. When I began to cry, Richard said, Baby, I'm sorry. I don't know why I would say such a thing. I didn't mean a word of it. But things could never be the same between us again. I had a miscarriage at eight weeks. I didn't know whether to be relieved or give in to misery. It was around this same time that I began to suspect that Richard was screwing around on me.

Richard came home one afternoon undressing as he came through the door. I ask where in the world did you leave your underpants. Richard replied, I accidentally messed in them and by damn I left them on the side of the road.

I said, like hell you did. This is just another slap in the face. Richard was so handsome and lied so convincingly that I let myself believe him. I couldn't bear to lose him. So, I pushed all the hurt to the back of my mind and went on being a loving wife, cooking Richard's favorite meals and keeping him a clean, comfortable home.

One afternoon Richard called and asked me to come and pick him up on the other side of town. He had taken a second job and while driving a paper route, he claimed that the original driver, who was on vacation, had taken the truck away from him and left him stranded.

Now, Dr. Skeet, I know better. By this time I knew my husband couldn't keep his pants on. There was never any money from the job. It was just another one of his lies to be with his woman.

Go ahead and laugh Dr. Skeet. I can see that I'm one patient that you enjoy. But anyway, this incident must have put the fear of God in him. I've always believed that somebody's husband had gotten after him that afternoon. For a long time after that incident, he was a homebody as if he was afraid to show his face in public.

Richard spent a lot of time playing with Amanda. I will admit he has always had his good points as well as bad. He adopted Amanda when he and I first got married. Amanda had only been two and one-half, so Richard was the only Daddy she ever knew.

It was March of Nineteen Sixty-six when Richard got a fantastic new job with the telephone company and bought us a new house just two blocks from the school that Amanda would attend.

It wasn't too long after he bought the new house that he said he was going to cut off my charge account at the gas station. He said that I was costing him too much on gas running back and forth to my Mama's house. I told Richard I was going to see those kids come hell or high water. If that was all I ever cost him, he'll have no reason to be upset. I just thought I had been through hell with Richard so far, but that was before he went to work with the telephone company.

It seemed as though women came out of the woodwork. The telephone company was no place for a whore hopper. It sure kept him hopping and I do mean whore hopping, in one door and out the other. After every hurtful time he would say. It's okay baby. I love you best in the world. I won't hurt you anymore.

I have to hand it to Richard. He bought everything I asked for and more just as long as I didn't make waves. In May of Nineteen Sixty-eight I knew I had made waves the day I told him that I was pregnant again. He ran out of the house and jumping into his truck, he slung gravel for two blocks.

One hot August afternoon in Nineteen Sixty-eight, with me being seven months pregnant and miserable, I sure as Hell was ready to make waves after receiving a bill from a drugstore that I had never been to in my life. I immediately took the bill down to the drug store and told them, I refuse to pay this bill. I've never been in this drugstore before, so how could I possibly have a bill here. If they wanted their money, I'd strongly suggest that they find the other Drucilla Hallmark and not send another bill to my home. On my way home I made up my mind that nothing or no one would take my home apart or come between Richard and me. When I told Richard about the bill, he acted perfectly innocent and said he didn't even know who would do such a thing, but I was not fooled by him in the least. I knew he was up to his old tricks again. This was where the gas charge got cut off for sure...by me! From this day on, I would have cash of my own even though Richard liked giving me money about as much as he enjoys losing his hair.

Richard had said that he would always give me a few dollars if I would let him know the day before I was going off, but he never knew when I had money or how much. I was keeping money out of the grocery money.

Then, one night I tested Richard to see if he would keep his word. I gave him time to get into the bathtub and I went to the bathroom door and asked him if he had a few dollars. He told me no, he don't have a dime. Not believing one word of this, I went to the bedroom and looked in his wallet and find a twenty- dollar bill folded and put to one side. Well, out came that twenty honey, and marching my happy ass back to the bathroom. I waved it in front of his nose, saying see this, now you're not lying. You don't have any money and if you ever lie to me again, I'll go to the bank when I need money and I'll get what I want not just what I need. Richard never said a word.

I do believe that he had x-ray vision. This man has always looked around me, over me, and under me, but never at me. He never hears me unless I am talking about **his** money or hussies."

By now it past ten p.m. Dr. Skeet had been listening to tapes all day. He didn't want to but he would have to stop for tonight. He was obsessed with finding what he was sure he had missed. Something that would have averted what had happened to Drucilla. He was too tired. He couldn't afford to miss the clue again. He would start again first thing in the morning.

# CHAPTER 4

"One afternoon toward the end of September, Richard decided that he had to go to the office to pick up some things and I insisted on going with him. When we got there he evidently forgot that he had left me in the hot car because he was in the office for one and a half hours. I was hot, sick and furious, but Richard didn't care. He said that I should have stayed home. After that I did stay at home. Richard was so wretched and uncaring that it actually seemed to do him good to see me suffer. There I was…eight months pregnant with a man that would hurt me terribly and then say he was sorry about this and that. I knew he didn't want this baby.

Going through my pregnancy, knowing that this time he had found a puss that he couldn't turn loose of was almost more than I could bear. Richard had joined the Union and now it was Union this and Union that. **Union** was a hell of a name for puss, don't you think? More like an excuse to be with his women and tell me he was at the Union Hall."

Dr. Skeet said, "Go on."

"Our so called friends knew what Richard was doing behind my back. At a party one night when I was being shut out by Richard, Bob, a co-worker of Richard's, took me in his arms and told me to just be good and hang in there. Richard has a lot on his mind right now. But I was hurt to the bone by the way Richard was ignoring me. He had never hurt me in front of other people before.

The baby, a beautiful little girl in the very image of Richard, came in October. She became sick and only lived for five days. She died on Halloween morning. Here come all the people putting on their false faces, pouring out their false love. Richard seemed all full of love, but what a joke!

I had to have a caesarean to have my baby. While I was still in the hospital, Richard lied to my sister, Harriet, and lying to her was worse than laying with dogs. He was staying away from home telling her he had flat tires or any excuse he could make up. When Harriet told me that Richard sure must love me the way he was staying at the hospital with me until the wee hours of the morning, I just listened and never let on that he wasn't at the hospital with me.

Dr. Shane had released me from the hospital to go to the Grave Side Service that had been planned for my baby. I was half dead myself and I knew it was going to be an unbearable thing trying to explain to Amanda that God had taken our baby. I think I was so busy getting myself well that Richard not being at the hospital with me had just rolled off my back.

But it all started to make sense. After I was home from the hospital about a week, things got worse and worse. It wasn't bad enough that I had lost my precious baby girl, a couple stopped by to see Richard and said that he had been stopping by the house of one of their relatives and they needed to see him for a minute. Richard wasn't home so I asked whom they were talking about. I didn't recognize the name they told me. They acted stunned that I did not know whom they were talking about. It seemed as though they knew they had gotten Richard in trouble. I thought surely they aren't so dumb. Maybe they were sent here to cause trouble between Richard and me. I wanted to think it was all a mistake, but I knew in my heart he knew what he was doing.

When Richard came home, I was purely pissed off. I confronted him with my fears and demanded to be taken to the house he'd been visiting behind my back or I would go on my own. I wanted to know just who these people were. Richard said he had grown up with her brother and had known her for a long time. I asked if her brother lived there and he said the last he had heard of her brother they were somewhere in the west and besides what difference did it make. He informed me that he could go anywhere, anytime he damn well pleased. I told him he had better be pleased to take me to meet that damn slut tomorrow. Richard said he would but that her husband was a truck driver and he's hardly ever home.

The minute we arrived at the house the next day, the woman had him a glass of tea ready and on the table. I could see through the charade easily. It was a put up job from the word go. I knew darn well that Richard had warned the woman that he was being forced to bring me to meet her. I knew beyond a doubt that they were silently laughing at me. But the last laugh was going to be mine. I informed Richard the minute we drove off that if I ever caught his truck in that darn yard, I would throw gas on it and set it on fire. Richard was mad as Hell at me for giving him an ultimatum to stay away from there. Richard said there's nothing wrong with me going by there for a glass of tea. I remember laughing as I said, it's not the tea that upsets me Richard, it's the puss she serves you for dessert that blows my mind. Richard said he could go anywhere he damn well please once he left me in the morning. He was the property of the telephone company until he came back to me in the evening."

Dr. Skeet said, "Maybe that's his way of making it okay in his mind, but that's a sick way for him to think."

"The slut had four children and she looked to be about thirty-three or thirty-four years old and from what I could find out later, she did not have a husband.

Richard went on to say that it was in my mind and if he screwed every damn woman I accused him of screwing, he'd be dead by now. I told Richard he would be dead if he came home with a bad disease.

Dr. Skeet, you can see how I feel that living with this fool is like having mess rubbed in my face with nothing to wipe it off with and I was in a trap without an education and bad health.

I went to the baby's grave every day and cried myself sick. Even little Amanda had to be taken to the doctor with stomach spasms. She had wanted her little sister so bad. I wanted desperately to give Richard and little Amanda a baby. I thought that Richard's grief was over the loss of his baby daughter. But what was causing grief was Richard being led around by the dick again. I had told Dr. Shane that if the baby was healthy to go ahead and tie my tubes while he was doing the caesarean. The baby didn't get sick until the next day. It was too late! My tubes were tied. I just didn't know that Richard didn't want the baby or any baby by me.

Unaware of his feelings at the time, I went ahead with my plans to go back into the hospital the following August to have my tubes untied so that I could give Richard a baby of his own. The surgery, which was supposed to take only thirty minutes, lasted over four hours. It's true that I put my life on the line for Richard by doing this so that I could give him a child. Dr. Shane told Richard that he ought to be proud of me and that only one woman in a million would have done such a thing. This surgery was a new surgical technique that had not been performed very much at all. It was the first reverse tubal ligation that Dr. Shane had ever performed and he was determined to make it work and he had.

After I came out from under the anesthesia, I expected Richard to be by my side. He wasn't there and he didn't show up for hours. When he finally did arrive he said, he wanted to tell me something. He said, he didn't love me and he didn't want any children by me. He didn't know why he even let me go into the hospital and have this surgery. He turned around and walked out after dropping his bombshell.

I began to cry and then I lost consciousness for two days and nights. When I came to, I was covered in calamine lotion from head to toe. My nerves had been so bad that I had broken out in tiny blisters. Dr. Shane was at my bedside, where he had stayed most of the time. I was crying again and Dr. Shane insisted that I tell him what Richard had said to me to cause this reaction. When I told him what Richard had said to me, Dr. Shane was furious.

Dr. Shane said he would not let the bastard back into this hospital, much less in my room.

I said no, don't do that I just want to get well and go home so I can find out what's wrong. I really believed that only another woman could make a man do such a thing. I knew Richard was sex crazy. I kept thinking, why isn't Harriet coming to see me. Richard's aunt, an old drunk who I didn't like anyway, was staying with me along with people I didn't even know.

Richard finally came back to the hospital. He told me that he didn't know why he said those things to me.

I could only say, I love you Richard.

After I was home from the hospital, I found out that Richard had told Harriet that I didn't want her to come to see me. He was still mad because she had told on him when I was in the hospital the time before.

Richard was always making one excuse or another to leave the house. One night he told me that he was going to get a part for his truck. He was gone for a long time, so I called the service station that he told me he was going to. It was a station that we used a lot, so the people knew us both. The man I spoke with at the station told me that Richard wasn't there and had not even been there. I went out to sit on the porch and wait for him. When he finally came home, he came in from a different direction. I asked him where he had been. Richard said that they didn't have the part that he needed, so he went to another station and they had to order the part because they didn't have it in stock.

The next morning I went to the station where he said he had ordered the part. I approached the attendant and told him, I'm Mrs. Hallmark and I'm here to pick up the part that my husband ordered for his truck. The attendant looked puzzled and said, Mr. Hallmark didn't order a part here Ma'am. Are you sure you've got the right place?

Of course I knew Richard had lied to me. The two men at the other service station had told me that he hadn't been there and now this attendant didn't even know who Richard was.

I confronted Richard when he came home from work. I asked him why he lied to me about the darn part that it makes things worse, lying the way he does. Where was he last night?

Richard said he didn't have to answer to me or anyone else. He was a grown man and could go where he wants and do what he wants and it is no one's business but his own.

I decided to check out the Union meetings he was supposed to be going to. I added one more piece to the puzzle. He was at very few Union meetings. It was all lies, lies and more lies. I asked him what he wanted from me. Why couldn't he love me? Why did he think I was so blind that he thought he could get away with all the lies he kept telling me? He said he's not telling me any darn lies! It's all in my mind. I must be going crazy! If he said this to me one time, he said it twenty.

One day I got a chance to meet and talk with some of the other Union men's wives. It was election time and Bob had said something to her about the Governor being at the Union Hall. So, I made up my mind that the night Richard was supposed to go to the meeting, where the Governor was to be a guest speaker, I was going with him. I didn't let Richard know that I was going until he was ready to go out the door. I dressed as if I were going to meet the President while Richard was in the bath. I knew I was a knockout and there was no way he could tell me to stay home. I meant to put a stop to this Union business once and for all. I knew this was one time Richard would be at the Union meeting. At the Union Hall I was a perfect lady, taking in everything and everyone. Even though I was so mad that I could have taken the place apart, I kept a smile on my face.

I was introduced to Roger, one of Richard's co-workers and his cousin. I asked had he met Richard's cousin? The expression on their faces told me that I had delivered my message. I knew their cousins were their sluts.

The crap hit the fan the next day. I called the President of the Union and told him the darn Union Hall was nothing but a whorehouse. I went on to say **Union Hall**, isn't that a funny name for a whorehouse? I told all the other wives about all the cousins that meet there and I told Richard that he could have me, or the darn Union. I'm going to do everything in my power to put a stop to that Union Hall whorehouse. The end result of my blowing the whistle on the Union business was one divorce and a lot of Hell raised. Richard didn't ever talk Union to me again.

A couple of days later I was at a friend's house for a sewing lesson. The friend asked me why I stayed with Richard knowing what he was doing. I told her that I had Amanda to consider and there was no way I could raise her alone and I didn't have a good enough education to get a decent paying job, but I knew for a fact that if I ever got fed up enough to leave him, I would wind up back home at my Mama and Daddy's house and I just wasn't going to raise Amanda in that hell hole. I just didn't know why he is staying with me if he wanted other women.

As we worked, I kept thinking, if I just had one really good friend that I could confide in. Dr. Shane was the only person I felt comfortable talking to, but if I had one friend who cared enough to help, I knew I could have caught Richard in the act, but I had no help. In reality I had caught him time and time again. I just couldn't catch him with his pants down.

I couldn't help but wonder where he was going and whom he was seeing. I knew he wasn't seeing the truck driver's wife anymore. I didn't know there were two other women and he was still seeing one of them. Later I found out she lived in

Pleasant Grove, where he had moved her to from West End. This affair lasted nineteen months or longer, but I'll tell you more about her later.

He had to be screwing around on me. He hadn't touched me in seven weeks. I tried everything I could think of to entice him, all to no avail. Richard was weird. He would put on the best love act in the world in front of other people, but when we were alone, especially in the bed, he was like a cold stranger. He still kept insisting that there was no other woman.

A few weeks later, I knew for a certainty that I had been right about Richard having another woman. He came in one Saturday with a new fishing license for me. The only problem was that the description on the license sure as hell wasn't mine, blue eyes, brown hair, five feet three inches tall and weighing one hundred thirty pounds. I mean, damn, a blind son-of-a-bitch could see that wasn't me! Just look, Dr. Skeet, I'm four feet eleven inches tall, blond hair, green eyes and I weigh eighty-nine pounds. I couldn't believe my eyes. I just stared at the license for a few minutes...dumfounded. I asked him how in the hell could he be so damn stupid, the sorry son-of-a-bitch. He had that damn bitch on his mind so bad that he couldn't even remember what I looked like. We've been married for two damn years, you would think by now he ought to know what the Hell I look like. Giving him hell, I ripped the license to pieces and threw the pieces in his face. Richard said that wasn't the description he gave the lady. The girl at the hardware store must have made a mistake. You know I love you and I'm not running around on you, so just get that idea right out of your mind."

Dr. Skeet just shook his head and said, "Go on, what happened next?"

"There would be times when Richard would act as if he loved Amanda and me, and then he would do something terrible. One day in June of Nineteen Sixty-seven when Richard came into the house from work, he said that all of those damn flowerpots across the porch railing made people think that an **old lady** lived there. I was so mad at Richard. I thought I'll make him think an **old lady** lives here. I took pride in my yard and it always looked as if it had been manicured. When the flowers were in bloom, the yard was just beautiful. I wanted to mash his mouth, but instead I went out to the porch and dumped out every pot and kicked them in every direction. I told myself that I'd give him a dose of his own medicine that would kill him or cure him. I knew that what I was going to do would look bad to my neighbors and Lord knew what my friends would say, but what had to be, had to be! Richard came out to see what I was doing. I screamed at him and asked him if he was satisfied and did he think I didn't know what he wanted. I told him I knew he wanted me to stay in the house so his damn slut wouldn't see me. I knew Richard couldn't believe his eyes, because he knew how much I loved my flowers. I sat down and began to cry and Richard walked over to me.

I asked him what he was doing to us and that I was too good for a fool like him. I told him that I tried to be the best wife in the world to him and asked him why he continually hurt me. I didn't deserve the treatment that he kept dishing out. Why was he always after me to go out partying? He knew that I didn't like drinking and going out like that. All I wanted was a happy home and a good man, one I didn't have to share, a man that was all mine. When was he ever going to stop whoring around?

Richard swore to me that he didn't have anyone else and he was not doing me wrong. I knew better. Just a week before, he had come home with lipstick on his shirt. When I questioned him about it, he swore that he had gotten it off a telephone he had been working on. I didn't believe anything he said anymore. We argued some more and as the fight got good and hot, Richard said, I wouldn't know the damn truth if it walked up and hit me in the face. I knew I was no fool, no matter what he said. I knew where the damn lipstick had come from and I intended to do my best to make him pay dearly one day. I knew damn well he didn't want me, but he was such a gutless fool that he didn't have the heart or guts to just leave. Besides, he knew it would cost him plenty.

The next morning I went to see my neighbor, Mrs. Jones. I told her exactly what I was planning to do and asked her not to think badly of me no matter what she saw or heard. Mrs. Jones listened to everything I said and then told me that she understood. She was proud that I thought enough of her to tell her what was going on.

Richard wanted to party! Okay, I would party. I hemmed up all of my dresses. Mini-skirts were in style and that was going to really fit in for what I had in mind. I then went to the beauty shop. I knew that by the time Richard got home I was going to be pure dynamite.

Richard was shocked down to his toes when he saw me with the black streak down one side of my blond hair, which I had cut almost as short as his. I told him we were going to Penny's Go-Go House just up the road from the fair grounds. We needed to be there before eight o'clock so that we could get a good table. Richard asked me what in the world had come over me. I smiled and said, anything to please you baby, I do mean anything, if you decide you want a red puss, then by God, I'll get a can of paint and spray mine red! Whatever it takes to please you. If you're going to act like DeRoy, then I'll play Gertrude's part.

At the club that night, one of Richard's friends came to sit at our table and both men turned their backs on me to watch the Go-Go Girls dancing in their cages. For Richard to turn his back on me made me so mad that I could have cheerfully decapitated them both, but this was lesson night! I quietly removed everything from the table. Then, as I stepped up into my chair, I hit Richard's friend on the arm. I stepped up onto the table and began to dance to the chorus of whistles and clapping. When Richard turned around to see what was going on, he turned as white as a sheet at the sight of me on top of the table. The bouncer came across the floor. In his uniform he was so handsome that he took my breath away. He took me by the hand, causing my heart to flutter as he helped me down. He said he wished we had a license for me to dance, but we don't.

Dr. Skeet, to be honest, I was having the time of my life. I laughed out loud thinking to myself Richard really looked like his pants were in a wad. I hadn't believed Richard, when he told me how much fun partying was but he was right. I loved the music and the bright lights, not to mention all the beautiful clothes I could buy to wear partying.

The next week flew by and Friday night I was dressed in pure silk, bell- bottom pants and a backless top. Richard didn't like it at all. I told Richard, that this was what's in style and I would be dressed as well as everyone there. Richard had sure gotten quite. He didn't seem to be as enthusiastic about partying as he had been. We got to the club a little before eight p m Richard was taken aback by the whistles that greeted us as we walked into the room. I didn't have a doubt in my mind that everyone who had been there the previous Friday was back again tonight. I was asked to dance several times, but Richard shook his head no. I laughed and told Richard that maybe I ought to have left him at home. After that Richard and I danced every dance. Then about two o'clock Richard wanted to go home. I told him, hell no. We're going to dance until time for breakfast. I won the battle and Richard was miserable. I reminded Richard that he was warned by my brothers not to take a country girl to party, and then I asked him if he didn't want me, why I couldn't dance with the other men. He reassured me that he did love and want me. I knew he was lying even as he said the words. I sat thinking that I'd already been through too much with him. I knew that he didn't want me, but he couldn't stand the thought of anybody else having me or having to pay child support. All he wanted was a housemaid.

We got home about six-thirty that morning. Even though I was exhausted, I was also exhilarated. I lay awake for the longest time, thinking about the mess my life had become. I had heard all my life that love is like a cancer. It would eat you up slowly. I wished with all my heart that I didn't have to live with Richard. I wished I had a decent education so that I could get a good job that would pay enough to support Amanda and me.

There was one thing for sure, if he wanted out he would have to say it straight out or just pack up and leave. I married him because I loved him, but I had come to the realization that there is a very thin line between love and hate.

Dr. Skeet, I knew Richard didn't love me. He just needed a boarding home, but I wasn't going to give up my new home.

Amanda started to school September of Nineteen Sixty-nine. We were only two blocks from the school and Amanda loved it. To me Amanda's education was the most important thing in the world. I would always tell Amanda, to pay attention and learn everything you can because what you learn is the one thing no one can ever take away from you.

There was no way that I was ever going to give up. I knew what was going on even though Richard thought I was so dumb that I couldn't comprehend what was happening. I have looked over his whore hopping, sacrificing my own happiness for Amanda to have a good life and a decent education. It hadn't seemed to be much of a sacrifice and it wouldn't have been so bad, except for his lies. His attitude toward me was so darn condescending that I had to grit my teeth to keep on going."

"Drucilla, do you mind if I ask Richard about all this?"

"Dr. Skeet, why should I mind? Everything I've said is true.

When I first met him and his goody, goody family, the last thing I would have thought was that he would turn out to be such a darn skirt sniffer, but Richard is addicted to women. He was well experienced in sex. Now it seemed to me that he was trying to bring me down as low as he was. Richard asked me to start wearing make-up and eyeliner on my eyes to make them look larger. The fool that I was, I did as he asked.

Then I noticed that he was calling someone every morning. I asked him whom he was calling and he said, **time service**. The clocks were always right and he was only ten minutes from work. Just more lies.

The intercom buzzed for Dr. Skeet to answer the telephone. He didn't want to but it was an emergency. He picked up the phone and talked to his patient. As soon as he hung up he put another tape in.

# CHAPTER 5

It was August of Nineteen Seventy when the awful phone calls started, with a male voice talking in the morning, then a woman in the afternoon or vise-a-versa, saying Richard didn't want me and wanted out of the marriage, that I should go back to **hick town** with my little girl, that they have had many laughs with Richard about the stupid things I would do and the ignorant way I talked. My friend, Courtney, had answered the phone many times and gave them Hell. Courtney told me not to talk to them, to just hang up, that the sick perverts were enjoying themselves. The calls went on and on.

Courtney had two girls, one was the age of Amanda, and she lived just down the street. She was a doll and truly a good person.

I told Richard the calls had to stop. Between losing the baby and Amanda not feeling well, all this bull crap was too much. If he didn't want me, why couldn't he just be man enough to say so? He said that he hadn't been with the company long enough to get the calls stopped.

I listened, and then told him, I'd get them stopped. I can't take anymore. The witch may have you, but she'll play hell getting your money. I'll get your butt so far in debt that you won't be able to buy toilet paper.

Courtney, Richard and I were the only ones that knew about the tap on the phone. The very day the tap was put on the phone, the calls stopped. Of course Richard put the blame on Courtney. I laughed in his face.

Dr. Shane had told me many times if I ever needed to talk to come to his office and knock on the door, that if there was no answer just to come in and wait and he would come and talk with me as soon as he had time. He had done this many times, but this time he was telling me to spend Richard's money, get out of the house, go shopping, buy anything my heart desired, fix up my house and plant my flowers back. He told me to show Richard that I was going to be happy and make him think I didn't care what he was doing. I will never forget him telling me that his wife loved to square dance and he hated it, but he went anyway. He had told me that it's okay for me to party with Richard, just to pretend that I was having the time of my life.

Dr. Shane also told me that I was learning a lot and I'd be a winner, so don't give up, as long as Richard didn't have the guts to get out, I'd have his money and put his having sex with others out of my mind. He told me to just say to myself, it's okay if he wears out his slut's body. Be thankful that he has someone that's sorry enough to give him that type sex. Be proud that you love yourself too much to give whore service.

I told Dr. Shane that I had taught myself to write checks and mail the bills and now I was making clothes for Amanda and myself. I always felt better after talking to Dr. Shane. He was a joy and one of the finer things in my life. I love him.

The next morning, out came the garden books and I wrote down some of the things I would need. At the store I got everything I needed and more, enough to work for a week.

Boy, did I work. My yard was the nicest around. Richard came home for lunch and I gave him a plate and told him I was on a diet as I went out the door to turn the yard sprinkler off.

I cleaned house and hung all new drapes. I had painted two rooms the day before. Looking around, I made a mental note of what I would get on my next shopping trip, plus a new outfit to wear out with Richard.

I tell you, Richard was looking down in the dumps, but I knew what was wrong. See, Richard couldn't smell and I had been putting perfume on his shirt for his woman to smell so she would claw his butt. This is when he started back having sex with me. I was jumping his bones every night thinking, lets just see if he can take care of two, keeping in mind it was good experience and it sure burns up the calories. Evidently his slut had cut him off because he sure wanted me now!

One hot August day I had worked too hard. I was too tired to cook and when Richard came home from work, I asked him if we could pick-up hamburgers and bring them back to the house to eat. Richard told us to load 'em up and move 'em out. Amanda jumped with joy and ran for the car. Pulling into the hamburger shop, Richard changed all of a sudden. He asked why I couldn't cook. It's always damn hot dogs or hamburgers. He said that this was the last time. He was screaming, do you hear. He went in and got the food, but the joy of the trip was over. I was a nervous wreck, I thought, he must be crazy, because I cook every night.

Richard turned the car around so fast that it threw Amanda across to the other side, and then out on the road he went so fast that it was as if he were trying to wreck us. I asked Richard what was wrong and where was he going. He had turned the wrong way to go home. He made a U-turn in the road and took us home flying. Once we were home, I told him I was sorry that I didn't want him to be upset. After a while he was back to his old self and that's when Richard started refusing to take us anywhere.

What a day I had! Harriet called early that morning crying,

only twelve years old and her life was in an uproar. I hit the floor. I knew what life was like in that hell hole. Once again I had to bring my sister home with me. Harriet and Amanda had just gone out the back door and down the alley to the store to get an ice cream cone when the doorbell rang. Opening the door, the young man asked me to come outside that he needed to talk with me for a minute. I thought how handsome he was and I knew I had seen him before but couldn't place where. I listened as he tried to explain that he had passed my home every day and he said that he had sat across the street watching me work in the yard. He had made it his business to find out everything he could about Richard and I. He could prove to me that Richard had a girlfriend. Girlfriend was his words. I was thinking whores, whores, and more whores. The man said that I could find one of them at a certain café and if Richard could play the game, I could too. He said he would be back in a few days to see me. He suggested that I go to the café and see for myself. I shocked him by telling him that I would check out what he had said. Then I told him if he would come back and ask Richard if I could go out with him, then I would, but until then don't bring your sorry butt back to this house. As he was leaving, I said, **do you get it**. I never said a word to Richard. It just so happened that Richard was off the next Wednesday and I got up early and told him that I wanted him to take me over to the coffee shop for breakfast. That was fine with him. So on the way over, I told Richard about my visitor and what he had said. I told him, I knew that he had told me over and over that there's only old ladies working there and they've been there a long time, but I want to see for myself. Richard sure was quiet as we entered the café. There stood the man that had come to see me. The waitress that came to our table was young and pretty. Richard was slick as a button. The girl took one look at Richard and me and left the table. Then an older woman came with coffee to take our order. Richard asked her if the other girl had just started working there today. The old woman told us she had and went on her way. Richard had just told the old witch what to say. He really thought I was that dumb, but I just chalked up another lie for him.

I didn't know what was going on. What was Richard trying to do to me? By this time I remembered who the man was. He was Lavita's brother. Now I wondered if his family was helping him torment me to death so I would leave and told myself that I wouldn't give up my home if Hell froze over. Richard swore he had never seen the waitress before and he didn't have anything to do with that bastard coming to the house. If he could find out who he was, he would tack his balls to the wall. I laughed to myself because I knew that he knew who the man was. He made love to me that night trying to make me believe him, but it was a waste of time.

Richard believes that sex will make everything better. He tells all my friends that I don't like sex. How would I know? I've been married to him all of my life and for sure, I'd rather be attacked by a mad Pit Bull than have sex with him.

Dr. Skeet, you can feel free to ask Richard about it all. Ask Richard if he's gay. Ask him why he took me to a party where there were only seven young men between twenty-four and twenty-five years old, which was our age at the time.

Richard told me that we had been invited to a party. He never said who or how many. We drove up to a two story white house with only three cars parked outside. When I went in, I was introduced to the boys and I asked if we were early. I was told no, then I asked how many people were coming and I was told that everyone was there.

Fear griped me. I thought what in the hell does Richard mean! The guys seemed nice enough. They never said a word out of the way to me. They just kept me busy dancing or telling me jokes while Richard was off in another part of the house with some of the other guys. I didn't know what they were doing and I had never seen any of them before. Now Dr. Skeet, you know how dumb I was back then so Gays never crossed my mind. Richard has said that I had better never say that he was gay, but one thing is for sure, if there wasn't a woman then there was a man. Anyway, I'll never forget that night. We didn't stay long because I was scared to death and demanded to go home."

By now it was lunch and Dr. Skeet had not eaten since yesterday morning. He would stop for lunch. He grabbed a quick bite and right back to the tapes.

# CHAPTER 6

"The next day the florist delivered a dozen red roses with a note. The note read, a pair of roses for every year for the perfect pair. I thought, pour on the love. I knew he would do something good, which was always his way. He would hurt me terribly, and then he would be kind and good. It looked as if he wanted a divorce, but he wanted it to look as if I was causing it all. If that was what he wanted, he could forget it. I am the best and only raised hell if he gave me a reason.

Just like the time I had planned Percy a birthday party. Getting up that morning to a beautiful snow, I asked Richard if he would go and pick-up Mama Marselle and Daddy because they didn't want to drive in the snow. With a house full of people, I waited and waited for him to return. I called Mama Marselle and Richard had just gotten there. He had been gone two and one-half hours. hell yes, the party went fine and I hid my feelings. My family loved Richard. They thought he was the best man God ever made. He was good about working and he was well mannered. They could see that I didn't want for anything. Everyone enjoyed the party and even I kept a smile on my face, but I was crying in my heart. I knew he had stopped at his woman's house. I would look at Richard and think how I hated him for what he was doing.

I hated God that day. How could He let Richard do this to me? I was good. Why didn't He strike him dead? No one made him marry me.

After everyone left, I asked Richard what he meant by making Mama Marselle and Daddy wait so long and let me worry about them. Damn you Richard. I'll remember that he stopped at his slut's house on Percy's birthday as long as I live."

"How do you know this Drucilla?"

"Because years later, he told me all about it. I tell you Dr. Skeet, Richard is a full-blooded fool. I prayed he would die. He was a whore addict and a two faced liar. I had asked Richard what kind of man was he that kisses me when he comes home and when he leaves every morning tells me he loves me. What is wrong with him that makes him treat me so?"

Dr. Skeet said, "Many great men have written books on that and still we don't know."

"I thought of giving Amanda away so I wouldn't have to live with Richard. I was sick of playing a fool, sick of being hurt. I had rather die than let my family know the real truth. I thought just maybe Richard's Daddy would talk to him. I knew in my heart his Daddy wouldn't help me, but I had to try and, of course, I got my butt kicked.

Richard came in with a hound dog look on his face telling me he wanted me to go to my Daddy's house and stay a week. He had a decision to make and he couldn't make it with me there. I just laughed in his face, telling him it was his decision for him to go to my Daddy's and stay the week. My blood was boiling.

I was thinking what a damn, gutless son-of-a-bitch he was. I let Richard know he could give up. A blind bitch could see that a woman was making him choose. I told him that if he wanted her, go to it and if not go wash it off and behave himself. There again, Richard told me I wouldn't know the truth if it hit me in the face. I told him, oh, hell yes, I knew the truth Richard. I know a woman will tell a man anything to take him away from his family and after she gets him, she's worse than the wife he left behind. Now make your decision, but be damn sure you can live with the one you make.

Dr. Skeet, I know that Richard has a bad problem. Dr. Shane told me one time maybe he's just a **walking phallus**. Dumb me I had to ask what that is? Dr. Shane laughed and said to be honest it's a walking dick, just a man that can't get enough. I told him that he was right and I knew exactly what he needed. He needed to be hooked up to a milking machine and drained dry."

Dr. Skeet laughed and said, "Drucilla, you are a mess."

"After I refused to go to Daddy's house, I guess he made his decision, but the gutless fool never did say. He seemed to be in deep thought. I didn't know what to think. He was being much better to Amanda and me. With Richard you couldn't really tell what was going to happen next. He was hard to understand. If Richard had chosen his honey-pot, Lord, what would I have done?

I asked Richard to talk to me. I had to know what it was all about. What did I do wrong? Why couldn't he love me? Why won't you tell me who your slut is? As always, he would say there is no woman. I told him that is all lies and darn it I wanted the truth. I had rather know for sure it's a woman than to think all this is over a man. The look that came over Richard's face made me cringe. I knew by that look of pure hate that it was another woman. I didn't know whether to run or what when Richard screamed out that I had better never accuse him of being gay or.....I broke in, or what Richard? After all you have put me through, what am I supposed to think? After taking me to that party with only seven men.

Now I tell you Dr. Skeet, he tells me one lie after another. I prove to him that it's a lie, and he tells another lie to back up the first lie.

There's no way I can give him enough to keep him happy. I

guess I should have let him go, but Dr. Skeet, I had to keep Amanda in school and I couldn't bring myself to give up.

The more Richard hurt me the more money I would spend. I had told Richard that Amanda and I wouldn't want for anything and when he got the Master Charge bill, he almost died. After the shock, he just told me to never charge again and that he would take care of the bill.

Richard had lied for nineteen months. When he came in saying he had a decision to make, for me to go to my Daddy's, I wasn't supposed to think anything about it. He may have thought I was crazy, but he had another thought coming. I was sick and tired of all his bull crap. I wanted him to make up his mind. He had shamed me to death with all our friends. He had humiliated me with that hypocrite family of his and he had let them treat me as if I were a dog. I've learned that I'm a much better person than any of the heartless people he has ever introduced me to. I know he found a hotter honey-pot, but he will never find a better wife. I'm the best and my heart will never let me treat anyone the way I've been treated. You can bet I'll survive. I've told Richard that I'll always be good at least one of us will be able to look at ourselves in the mirror. By George, my day will come. When I do get even, it will shock the hell out of him.

It seemed that Richard never listened to me. He just watched T. V. At about seven thirty one night, Amanda ran into the room reminding us not to forget the spaghetti supper at the school the next night. Well, I'm here to tell you Richard sure as hell heard that. He sat straight up on the couch saying he wasn't going. I told him not to say it, that every parent would be there and it was only right that we go, we were still a family, and I already had tickets. For some reason Richard wouldn't fight about these things with me. He would just act mad, but most of the time he would give in to what I wanted.

At the spaghetti supper, Richard and I were invited to a party at one of the children's parents' home and were asked to come over for coffee on Wednesday night. I couldn't wait. I thought we needed to make new friends. Just maybe I can keep Richard busy and if I show him I can be somebody, he will not want other women.

Wednesday came and when Richard and I went to their home, at first we didn't think anyone was at home. There were no lights on and we were trying to decide what to do when the door opened. Amos and Lisa asked us in. I didn't know what to think. The house was lit with candles and I mean candles everywhere. Amanda was sent to play with their two boys in another room. Richard took my hand and followed Amos and Lisa into the kitchen where we were asked if we liked the atmosphere. Richard kept quite, but I said yes. It was so cozy. I did love it.

Amos explained the way their party worked. One couple would have a party at their house each week inviting a different couple. Everyone would meet at a certain place to follow each other so no one would get lost, all party houses would be lit only by candles and no one was allowed to turn on a light. Lisa asked me what kind of perfume I liked and what drink did I prefer. Looking at Richard I thought, what in the hell have I gotten us into! Amos was asking Richard about his job and even asked about his income. Then right back on to the party. Amos told us that they now have fifteen couples and no one could come without a mate. Richard drank his coffee and listened. Once he winked at me. My heart stopped! Oh, how I wished he could love me.

To tell the truth Dr. Skeet, I couldn't believe it when Amos told us how it worked. When you get to the house where the party is being held, everyone takes a different partner and goes about their business anywhere in the house they please. You can't have the same partner each week. You must surely have a different partner to keep things fair. Richard took me by the hand and stood up telling Amos he was sure the parties were fun, but we weren't interested at all. Calling for Amanda to come to him, Richard told them thanks for the coffee and we left. For the first time in my life, I didn't have a thing to say. I was in shock.

As we drove off, I asked, what in the hell is this address. I want to avoid it. Richard, are they for real? Richard said, hell, I guess baby, but don't have anything to do with that woman. She's not playing with a full deck. We both laughed. I couldn't believe he had called me baby and held my hand. I hoped it was to let me know not to be afraid that he would protect me. I've always felt safe with Richard, except when he was having one of his puss fits.

Somehow he seemed different, as if he felt better. At the dinner table the next night, Amanda told us that at school that day little Andy, one of Amos' boys, told her his Daddy was in love with her Mama. I couldn't look at Richard without laughing and almost choked on the tea I was drinking. Amanda must have thought we were nuts.

One thing about Richard and me, we never fought where Amanda could hear us. One of the weekends that we went out, Amanda got to stay at Grandma's house with Harriet.

I tell you, going back to Shady Grove got easier as life got better for me.

I can't explain it, but something in me wanted desperately to teach the children there's a better way. I didn't want Richard to know how bad they had treated me. To be honest, it was mostly for Harriet that I started going back. Every time they got on her bad, she would call me to come get her. After a few times, my feelings about them got better.

In the spring of Nineteen Seventy-one, I had made a beautiful garden at my Daddy's house and before I knew it, I was teaching Amanda and Richard all about gardening. At least I hoped I was teaching Richard. He had bought me an upright freezer. Richard didn't say a word about the gas it took to go back and forth to work with the vegetables.

When fall came, I also surprised Richard and Amanda when I told them I was going to work Monday at a sewing factory. I had to work three p.m. until eleven p.m. I would be running a quilting machine. Richard didn't believe me until he came home and found me gone I left a note saying, don't forget to pick-up Amanda. After about three months, I was training other people to run my machine and I was happy for the first time in months. I knew now I could make it on my own if I was forced to.

I remember one Friday at work a very nice girl was sent to me to train. The girl reminded me of myself, so I was especially good to her. She told me that she had to have a job. I knew I would teach her everything I knew. Mary was her name. She told me her husband was going to pick her up and take her to eat and she wished I would stop and eat with them. It never crossed my mind that Richard would come looking for me if I was a few minutes late, much less be worried about me.

The café where we stopped was only five minutes from my home. After placing our order, Mary went to the bathroom leaving her husband to talk with me. She had just returned to the table when Richard stormed into the place wearing only a tee shirt with a snub nose revolver stuck in the belt of his pants, no socks, hair a mess, and the strangest look on his face I had ever seen. I have often wondered if Mary's husband and I had been at the table alone would he have killed me. I have always been thankful that Mary had come back, because I do believe Richard is crazy as hell. When he walked up to our table, it scared the hell out of me. He told me he would see me when I got home. I didn't have any business being late. I didn't know what to say to Richard, so I asked him to sit down and have some tea with us. I went on to say that I didn't mean for him to worry that I was only fifteen minutes late and besides he was always asleep when I came home. Richard stayed for some tea, but I knew I would have to talk to him when we got home.

Going in the door, Richard told me good night as hateful as he could. I said, **whoa, good night hell!!!** I shouted, don't you ever embarrass me again. Do you hear me? You treat me like a dog and laugh in my face with all the lies I've let you get away with. What's wrong? Do you think I might pay you back for what you have been doing to me? Believe me, you have taught me well Richard. I didn't know men would be so sorry. I didn't know people wore two faces, but I learn fast. I'm telling you now, don't dish out things to me that you don't want dished back. I looked up and the fool was pretending to be asleep. I went over and shook him saying, **damn you**. He got up and went to the couch.

Dr. Skeet, I was sick to death of all this. No one made him marry me. He said he loved me and I believed he did until that false face family brainwashed him. At first he was good to me, and then he started treating me like a dog. Now he gets mad and crazy because I'm fifteen damn minutes late. I'll tell you what he wanted then and now. What he wanted was a darn boarding house, a maid, but he can forget it. I don't give a darn anymore. I tell you I was so mad and ready for the fight of my life. I followed Richard to the living room and started again. He listened for a while and then he asked if I was through because he needed to go to sleep, that he had to work tomorrow. I took my purse and ran out the door to the car. He really thought I didn't deserve any better. I remember him saying, I give you good treatment and I don't do you wrong. I wonder what that fool calls bad treatment.

It's true. He is at home most of the time. He does his whore hopping in the daytime while he's supposed to be working. He gives me money to run the house and pay the bills. But puts what he wants into savings so he can take his bankcard and withdraw money for a room or whatever at his convenience.

Dr. Skeet, we both know money doesn't replace man or woman. It's the things he does to me. I don't understand him. He's driving me nuts.

Anyway, I drove around maybe ten minutes then I went home. The fool didn't miss me. I had been so hurt and I still have a hard time letting him put his hands on me. When he reaches across the bed, I want to vomit. It's just the thought of him hating me so bad and the way he continues to degrade me like he does. He even came home one day with a picture of a girl riding a big pig and gave me the picture. He also gave me a miniature plastic pig. The picture had been torn from a magazine and Richard had put my name on it. He said he had been told that I enjoyed riding the pigs around the yard. He put the picture and plastic pig beside my bed and told me he thought it was funny. I silently cried. It was a cruel joke. How could he love me and do such a thing?

I knew that some day Amanda would have a good life. That and only that would make all this worth it. Just for Amanda would I live in this and wiping tears from my face I wrote this song."

**HE WASN'T MADE TO MARRY ME**

Where is the smile that belongs on my face?
What am I doing in this dreadful place?
Feeling so unloved, I know I should leave
I want to know what's wrong,
He wasn't made to marry me...............

"That's a good song Drucilla, just maybe you have talent you don't know about."

"Oh yes, I know about it, but again my education stands in the way."

Just as the tape ended Dr. Skeet's secretary buzzed in, his one o' clock was here. He expected to be through by now. He told her to make his excesses and cancel all his appointments for the rest of the week. He put in another tape.

# CHAPTER 7

"I had realized that Richard was putting up a front with everyone about loving me. I also knew I would have to continue to play dumb and continue to look over his lies for Amanda. I wanted to know more than anything in the world what had changed Richard's mind. What had happened to make him think so little of me? What made him think I deserved such a degrading thing? I have asked myself this over and over. I had to know. I was obsessed by it. I would know if it was the last thing I ever did.

The next day I was off work. While I was sitting at the kitchen table wondering what to do, the doorbell went nuts. I ran toward the door and Gail had the door open yelling for me to get out there. She had something to tell me. Crazy Carl had been caught whoring around on the job and the company had fired him that morning.

Gail is Bob's wife. You remember Bob, I mentioned him before. He's Richard's co-worker. Carl is another co-worker and it seems another whore hopper, just like Richard.

I shouted hallelujah to Gail. I hope they catch Richard. They will fire him, but I don't care. Gail gave me the low down on what had happened. Carl had been going to the same house for months. Some of the neighbors started asking questions. They knew no one worked for the telephone company in that certain house. Someone turned him in to the company and security jumped him like a duck on a June bug. After watching him for weeks, they brought Carl in and had him to write a confession. That's not the worst of it, they made a copy of the confession and hand delivered it to his wife. She was eight months pregnant.

Richard came home for lunch and I asked him if he had heard about Carl. He looked like a sheep killing dog. When I said what he needed was someone to turn him in and I might just be that someone, he took me into his arms and told me to go ahead. He said that maybe then I'd see that he wasn't doing anything, it was just my imagination and besides, it's not a tool that can be worn out, and then he laughed! I told him that if that was true, I could have sex with others and he would never miss it. I told him that the man at the shoe store said, **you would never miss it**. I didn't believe him, but I guess I was wrong. I put a dumb founded look on my face and walked off. I thought to myself, let the fool wonder if I'll get smart and start selling man's favorite dish. Dr. Skeet, just to keep the record straight, I never did and I never will."

"Drucilla, I'm not here to condemn people for their actions."

"As weeks went by Richard came home more often. He even built me two more brick flower beds out in front of the new house. But like I said before, he is a strange person. I kept telling myself there's one thing for sure, I would stay two steps ahead of Richard so he couldn't walk all over me. But sure enough, he has. But he never fooled me for long, because I could always read between the lines.

Richard and the other men that he worked with had decided they would all take turns giving beer parties. I told Richard it was our turn to give a party, but I wanted to know that he would at least act happy. He said that he would, but all these parties were getting old. I loved them because they were wonderful. I told Richard that we'd have a good time, he'd see. I didn't start the parties, but I did love them.

Boy, did I have a good time. I opened the door wearing a green satin dress and green shoes to match. There were three couples. The men took their wives' coats and I led them to the bedroom to put the coats away. Turning to leave out of the room, all three stretched out their arms and backed me up against the end of the bed. The one in the middle, Tim, did the talking. He asked me didn't I know Italians made the best lovers. While kissing me on the forehead, he lifted my chin saying my dress was beautiful and it brought out my green eyes.

I was dumb founded. Looking into his eyes my voice wouldn't work. Finally I said, thank you, but don't you think we need to get to the party? Turning around Tim and I could see fire shooting from his wife's eyes. I walked toward Pam, that's Tim's wife, telling her, let's party Pam, darn men are nuts. I whispered to her, when you get him home, beat him up. Just smile at Tim every once in a while and that will make him wonder what you're thinking. Now let's party. Four more couples showed up that night. I had a wonderful time, but I could see that Pam was miserable.

Living among Richard's friends, not to mention the people I worked with, had taught me a lot. I may not have much book learning, but I could read these people like I was a college graduate. Dr. Shane was so right. My beauty is my best asset. Many times I've said, thank you Dear Lord for Dr. Shane. I know I will make it now. Now I know how. I began turning the tables on Richard. I had learned to turn on the charm that I didn't know I had. A lot of my new friends had said I was beautiful and they could tell I had been watching my weight. Gail had told me to swing my hips when I walked, keep a smile on and to hold my shoulders back. People will notice you. Was she ever right especially, the men. It just convinced me that all men were just alike. They'll drop their pants for any smile. I knew very well Richard would. He had! But I would never let it go that far. I will not dirty myself.

Gail was the laugh of the party and full of jokes. Everyone loved her. She was older than me and had three children, so when she talked I listened.

Once when Gail came by for a cup of coffee, she could see that I had been crying. She insisted that I tell her what was wrong. I told her that Richard was a whore hopper. Gail laughed out loud saying men that act like that had been pushed away all their life. They have to stay busy constructively building up their ego. Worst of all, this type hasn't been taught that there is no real love in that way of life, so they will never love. They will spend their life looking for women to stroke their ego. If this is the real Richard, you may as well give up now because you'll only know hurt with a man like that. Gail told me that there's one thing people would learn about love and that's we can learn to love anyone that loves us back. To remember that if you let someone else love you, it would make the hurt from Richard go away. If it's true, don't mope around this house. Get out of here and let someone work on your ego.

Two weeks later I knew that Gail practiced what she preached. I always knew when it was Gail at the door because she rang the doorbell over and over as fast as she could. I never had time to get to the door. Gail stormed in saying I need the phone. She looked upset so Richard and I left the room, but not before we heard Gail curse her husband, Bob, calling him everything but a white man. I went to the bathroom after a washcloth to wipe my face. I was so upset. I didn't know what had happened, but one thing was for sure, Bob wasn't at fault.

I knew that Bob was the finest man I have or would ever meet. He gave his three children a bath every night and put them to bed. He was always at home and took care of all the heavy housework. He was a handsome man, clean and just the best.

I was hurt to hear Gail talk to him in such an awful way. The truth came out a few days later. Gail had been running a whorehouse and Bob had caught her. It seems that Gail and Richard were a lot alike. I wished I could have had Bob, but also hoped he would be all right because I knew what a broken heart was. I was convinced that Gail was crazy. I told Richard that anyone who'll give up their home and tear their children's lives apart needed to be done away with. What Gail needed was to have turpentine poured up her puss once a week. Richard laughed. I said for him to go ahead and laugh because when you die. I'll have you castrated so when you come back you'll be a female puss.

Dr. Skeet, so help me, I wish he would come back as a puss on four legs with every dog in the city chasing him.

Bob came by to see me. He told me that I was the best wife he had ever seen and if I loved Richard, stay the same and just maybe he would wake up. I wanted to tell Bob that I would divorce Richard and help him raise his children because I knew I could love him. I couldn't bring myself to say it. Even a few days later when Bob called to say Gail had signed the divorce papers, he wanted me to keep him up-to-date with what was happening at school. Bob loved his children and home. I hated myself. I was so good and Richard couldn't love me. Bob was so mistreated and unloved by Gail. What's fair in this world?

It all but killed me the day that Courtney called saying Dan was moving her to Pleasant Grove. I remember saying, I'm feeling paranoid as if everyone is out to make me miserable. Gail's gone nuts, Harriet's afraid to live at home, and Courtney's upset because Dan didn't consider her feelings about moving. Dan, her supposed to be husband, bought a house without her even knowing about it until it was time to move.

I couldn't stand the thought of Courtney and her two girls moving. Courtney was the first person I had let myself get close to. She and I are a lot alike. We liked and cooked the same types of food. Courtney couldn't drive so I drove us to the store and we would take the children to Kiddieland Park and we sure had some good times at Oak Mountain State Park.

We played hard, but we worked hard. We cooked a many a meal and halved it. We painted our house inside and out. I think that if it had not been for Courtney's family, I think I would have gone crazy.

I went to the sewing room. There I could keep my mind off others.

Picking up a piece of print that I knew was large enough to make Amanda and Harriet shorts and tops, I cut out several outfits. One thing was for sure little Amanda didn't cause me a minute's trouble. I sewed until I knew I would die when I hit the bed.

Waking up the next morning, I couldn't get Gail off my mind. City people, uptown, fast living people, all they were good for was to make people like me unhappy. It was beyond me why I couldn't find people in this world who lived good and if they couldn't help you, they sure wouldn't hurt you. It seemed to me that no one in this God forsaken place was happy and they didn't want anyone else to be happy. They sure worked day and night at being miserable.

It was for sure Amanda was happy. Her grades were good and she loved school and wouldn't miss a day. She was up and dressed before I turned over every morning. I looked into my child's big brown eyes and thought, you're worth it baby. Just for you I live in this Hell. God only knows how much I suffered.

I had made Amanda some of the prettiest dresses and pant suits that anyone had ever seen. Amanda had never worn the same outfit to school twice. I had sworn to myself that Amanda would have the best of everything regardless of what happened. I made up my mind that I would marry twenty men to give Amanda a good life. I couldn't stand the thought of her being raised in the country because the country life I had was unbearable. I did teach her country ways. If you have a country heart, you will be the best, but most of all you will be a survivor.

Amanda had been taught well. She would save her

allowance to buy expensive things to decorate her room or put them on lay-a-way and pay them out. She was never without money of her own.

Once I had let Harriet and Amanda go shopping and when they returned, Amanda was smiling ear to ear. As she came toward me with a bag in her outstretched hand, she said, here Mama, this is for you. Looking into the bag, a knot came up in my throat. Amanda had bought us both a pair of matching sandals. No gift would ever mean as much as this gift from Amanda. As I fought back the tears, I knew I had given Amanda that country heart. I knew that Amanda would always consider other people and she would be a wonderful person.

There was only one thing that bothered me. I knew that Amanda loved me, but she didn't mind telling everyone that she loved her Daddy best. It upset me a little because I knew Richard didn't love my child. That, I could plainly see. So, I gave Amanda enough love for us both and gave my daughter money saying it was from Daddy so she wouldn't know the truth.

A month went by, and I didn't fight with Richard. It was party, party, party. I was having the time of my life. I would flirt and carry on, maybe tell a joke or two. Richard accused me of not having a sense of humor, but he was wrong about a lot of things. Living with him proved I had a sense of humor.

When I told Richard about one of his friends asking me for a date, it was him that didn't have a sense of humor. I laughed telling him not to worry, he's worse than you. When the flowers were delivered from his friend and the card read that his home needed my beauty and charm and that he would put Amanda and me on a pedestal, I showed the card to Richard. He didn't say a word, so I took this as him not giving a darn. Yet, I never let his friend know that I even got his flowers.

Dr. Skeet, that is what I don't understand. One day he cares and the next he doesn't.

I refused to go to one of the parties saying I couldn't get my false face to fit right that day, so I just as soon stay home.

Richard could see I was beginning to slow down. I had already told him to get the hell away from me and do whatever made him happy. I said he could stop worrying about me. You see I knew I could get someone else and it didn't matter if Richard didn't love me, not anymore.

I had ignored Richard for weeks. I kept Amanda busy and out of his way, telling her that Daddy needed space and he needed for us to be quiet, letting her think I needed her help so she would stay close by.

Amanda was no dummy. When Richard asked what was wrong, she said, what's wrong is you don't want us. He walked out the door where he piddled in the yard for hours.

After getting in bed, he took me in his arms and asked me to forgive him. He didn't know what had been wrong. He loved Amanda and me. He would make everything up to us and to please just hold him and love him. The change that came over him was unreal. He helped with the house, with the washing, took care of the yard, took Amanda and I shopping, buying everything we asked for. I was a nervous wreck. This was too good to be true. I waited for the other side to appear again.

Weeks turned into months and Richard was still as good to us as he could be. Several weekends we went to Gulf Shores taking Harriet with us. Amanda and I loved the ocean. Amanda had been swimming since the age of four and now Harriet was learning how. It was doubtful that I would ever learn. I was so afraid of the water. It was impossible to get me out deeper than my waist. Amanda would beg, please Mom, I'll help you finally I told her to shut-up about it. I would actually stop breathing when the water gets above my waist. I told Amanda to let me stay here and read my book or I wouldn't bring her back. Amanda was mad and screamed out, all you do is read I was laughing at them, thinking someday I'll tell her why I was doing all that reading.

I had just gotten to where I could read well enough to enjoy the books I had picked up so many times. Reading was a miracle and A Star Fell From Heaven was the most wonderful story. I found myself hugging the book and thanking God that He had let me learn to read. Someday I would remind Amanda of the reading records that were bought for her to teach her to read and while she was learning the fundamentals so she could sound out the words, I was learning right along with her and she never knew it. I had a lot of time to make up for.

Now that I could read, I was learning a lot. A lot about life, children and men, I was hungry for knowledge. Amanda was right I did have my head stuck in a book with every free moment I could find.

Looking out over the ocean, I knew this was where I belonged. I said out loud, I was born to have sand under my feet. Richard had asked me what I had said. Then it dawned on me that Richard was sitting there. I said, I belong here and I know this is where I need to live. I'm happy here. I will never gripe about the sand. I love the Gulf. It's my dream place.

I jumped up and ran to throw water on Amanda and Harriet saying, come on and help me build a castle. I want one big enough that I can live in. Then you can leave me here. Amanda said, no, Mama, you'll have to wait till we get a real castle that's big enough for us all. I cried while packing for home. I vowed that someday I would never leave here."

Dr. Skeet asked, "Drucilla, did you ever ask Richard to move there permanent?"

"Dr. Skeet, he wouldn't even discuss it!"

# CHAPTER 8

"We had no more pulled back into the yard and unlocked the house until the phone was ringing. Running fast as her little legs would go Amanda answered the phone and told Richard it was Pa-Pa. Richard talked to my Daddy for a long time. The children had unloaded the car and were putting things away. I was ordering the girls to take the dirty clothes bag to the washroom as Richard called me to the kitchen."

"Drucilla, were you mad at the girls for some reason?"

"No, Dr. Skeet, it's just that every time I have to leave the Gulf, I dread coming back to Birmingham so bad that I get hateful. I just don't know the Gulf is so peaceful I can just forget everything, but just let me get back home and my stomach knots up. Someday I'll gather enough guts to leave this place and never come back....someday.

I asked Richard if something was wrong or had anything happened at Shady Grove. Then he dropped the bomb. He asked if I wanted to move to the country. I told Richard he was crazy. Yes sir, this set me on fire! We no more than get back in this damn place until he starts in on me again. If he doesn't want us damn it, he can get out.

Richard told me to wait a minute, that it was my Daddy's idea. He had found a house that we could buy for four hundred dollars. He told Richard that he would give us some land and help us get it ready. We would have to move the house onto the lot. Richard said it would be a lot of work, but we wouldn't have a house payment. He said, just think about it, no house payment. I didn't have to think about it, that's what he wanted. I told him, oh yes, move me down into those woods so you can tell your people and your honey-pots that I couldn't wait to get back to riding the hogs. Then all of a sudden Amanda asked, Mama, did you ride a hog? I told her no that was something that her Daddy had made up one day when he needed something to laugh about. Richard didn't like the country, so I asked him why he would want to move there. That stupid brother of Richard's told him **hicks** only come out at night. That stupid fool doesn't even know what a hick is.

Boy, did I laugh when Amanda asked me what a hick was. I told Amanda that it's a city person that doesn't know how dumb they really are and that city people call country people hicks to make fun of them. That's why I had to stop saying ah shaw and start saying ah crap. You have to spell it out for the city people. They're smart in one subject and dumb as hell in everything else.

Harriet was so happy when she heard. She hugged Amanda and then ran to me, begging me please move and then she could live with me all the time. I knew the child would be the happiest in the world, but I would have to think about the move. First, I would have to sell my house.

Richard called the next day to ask if I was going to look at the house. I told him not until he could go. But Richard insisted that I go see for myself and tell him what could and couldn't be done to make it livable. I asked him about the water. He said he would have to have a well drilled and get butane gas to heat the house. He reminded me that my garden spot was there and if we were there he could help me. I could teach him how to make a garden then and he also promised to buy a tractor. He would fix the house any way I wanted it. Richard was pleading. He had it all figured out, but I still didn't know.

The two girls talked and talked all day and before the day was over Amanda had a pony and Harriet could be her sister.

My Daddy called again and said I had to let him know. The house had to be moved before June and it was September fifteenth. I told Richard there was no way I could do that and besides Daddy wouldn't give me a clear deed. I didn't want the land without a clear deed. Everybody was against me. Daddy said he would give me a clear deed, the men at work said they would help Richard move the house, and my brothers said, yes sir, they would do whatever they could.

Richard's Daddy wasn't trying to help me. He told Richard he knew he couldn't do it because he didn't know how. He thought Richard was stupid. Everything Richard mentioned to him, he only discouraged him. I can hear him now saying, son, you don't know how to do that. This only made Richard want to show his Daddy that he could. Richard didn't like his Daddy, but he had an obsession to prove himself to the old fool.

I asked Richard why he cared what his Daddy thought. I told him his Daddy couldn't do anything but drive a truck. It's not because you can't do the work, it's because you're with me and all my people live there. I reminded him of what his Daddy said about my people. I asked Richard, what does he know about people in general other than to entice women? Richard said, no, in his eyes I've always been a dip shit.

I knew my life was going to hell, sure, fire hell! I cried for two weeks. Cursing God, asking Him where are you? I couldn't understand why in the hell He was letting this happen to me. God knew I didn't want to be there. I knew it was too hard. I can still hear myself say, I just can't. Yet, I was moving!

Richard came home with fruit trees and the four hundred

dollars to pay for the house. Like a fool, I put my house up for sale. The ad wasn't in the paper a week and it sold and the paperwork taken care of in only three days.

Richard had looked at the house saying it was fine and he had called about insurance for moving it. It was only two hundred dollars for six hours. County regulations require you to start at midnight and be off the road by six a.m. Once you set the date with the insurance company, you can't change it. Once you commit yourself, you have to go through with it.

I was sure of one thing, either Richard was in a hurry to get rid of me or he wasn't afraid of work. He started on that house and had it ready to move in a month. He rented the equipment and everyone was ready. The insurance was paid, but Richard was waiting until the last minute to notify the company of the date. The weather bureau predicted snow the weekend Richard wanted to move the house, so he called the move off. That very weekend it came the biggest snow of the year. Richard walked the floor all the next week, listening to the weather. The weather was going to be fine the coming weekend and Richard set it up again and called the insurance company.

Finally, it was Saturday, February of Nineteen Eighty-one and time to get the house on the road. Twelve midnight everything was ready except for the truck. Then, all of a sudden the rain came. It rained so hard you couldn't see a thing. I started to cry and told Richard it wasn't meant to be. The rain stopped just long enough to get the truck hooked to the house. Richard said he would pay the men if he had to, but the house had to go rain or no rain. He had already been told that the house would be bulldozed off the land if it wasn't moved that weekend. He was determined to go with it and he did. It took all of the six hours to move the house. It had rained so much that Richard couldn't get the house as far off the road as he wanted. He told me it was the best he could do and I cried my eyes out.

I cried off and on for months. My heart was broken. No one knew how it hurt me to clean that house. The black coal dust from where the chimney had been torn out sent me home filthy for weeks. I wiped down wood, scrubbed floors, cleaned windows and worked in the yard planting trees, bushes, roses and the vegetable garden. Arriving home after a day in that filth, I ran from the car into the back door so no one could see me. I was so ashamed. When asked about my new place, I would change the subject and I never would give anyone directions to find the new house. I had told myself I couldn't bear for my friends to see the house. It didn't have any underpinning or plumbing, it was a shack, and awful shack!

Looking around I could see why the flies and mosquitoes were so bad.

The other women threw their dirty dishwater out the back door and the garbage was piled so close to their houses that by the time the dogs got through with it, it looked like one big garbage dump, plus no one had water in their homes, which meant no plumbing. The bathroom was behind any tree you chose. To some, a bath on Saturday was a joke, but to these people it was real. They brought their water home in gallon jars and five, gallon cans. On Saturday after washing clothes, they took a bath in a number three washtub using the rinse water and then using the same water to scrub off the porches.

As I stood in my new yard and watched the small children play, I promised myself that I would help them to be better people. Show them a better way to live.

Dr. Skeet, looking back at all that poverty, it was awful to live through, but it made us all stronger and taught us how to survive in this world. It's really funny now, when I watch television, the news blames poverty for all drug users and peddlers, thieves and low life, when in reality the government had destroyed our people with the free give away programs. They have made living so easy that it has turned what should have been real men into wimps. I believe there are a lot of people out there that think as I do, but are afraid to say it out loud. Only the workingmen can change the mind of government. Welfare, food stamps, free, this and that was the cause. Give man the opportunity to work, but don't pay him not to work. I despise the free loading retards the government has created."

"Drucilla, you are right, but you can't tell people. Half are bleeding hearts and the other half get mad because you do speak out because they are afraid to. Now, let's get back to you."

"I wondered what I did wrong to deserve being back in Shady Grove. I asked God why He sent me back to the hell hole I hated so bad. The life I had left behind so long ago. I asked Richard what I had done wrong. Why did he want to get rid of me so bad as to put me back in this God forsaken place? I had tears streaming down my face. Seeing my Daddy unload the water jugs from the car made me sick. This life was unbearable, but I would survive it somehow. Daddy was the only one with an outside toilet and by now the spring had gone bad.

June first of Nineteen Eighty-two we moved into the middle of hell. Our well was drilled and a kitchen and bath were added to the little four rooms. Richard had promised to draw the water for the house and to empty the potty every morning and for sure he would hurry up and finish the plumbing. Moving from my beautiful home into the shack at Shady Grove was a nightmare. The floors were bare really bare, just plywood, no rug at all, no cabinets, no sink, no bath fixtures. I swear Dr. Skeet; I knew I must be, paying for Mama Marselle's sins.

Dr. Skeet said, "Or, maybe it's to show them a better way of life."

"I silently cried as I took my first bath in the number three washtub that night. While silently talking to myself about how I hated everyone, I knew there was no God and no one need ever try to tell me that garbage again.

I could hear Richard in the other room. I hated him. Oh, no, he didn't think I was good enough to be uptown with the fancy people. He couldn't let anybody see what he had married. So the whore hopper had brought me back where he thought I belonged. I began to laugh. Just maybe I should have invited all his friends and family to a hog riding party, but I knew I had too much pride to do a thing like that. The sorry fool may never love me, but I loved myself too much to bring shame my way. No, I wouldn't even let my friends find me at home, until my home was nice and the surroundings clean.

Richard did draw the water from the well and empty the potty every morning. He knew darn well I wasn't going to do those things. You can believe Hell would freeze over first.

Summer flew by with me working myself to death. I had canned everything I could get my hands on and worked in the yard until I was dead at night. Little Amanda had made new friends and was happy. Harriet worked helping me do everything. She hardly ever left my side. Mama Marselle was raising Hell about her loving me so much. I loved Harriet as though she were my own.

By October you could hear the wind blowing through the house and the heat went right up through the top. There was no insulation in the house. The heating bill was two hundred dollars a month after it got cold. I asked Richard how I was supposed to have money to work on this place if I had to pay out everything he made just to live. Wiping my face, I told Richard I would make it. And Amanda wouldn't be cold or hungry. I did make it somehow. I got my mind off Richard's whore hopping butt because I didn't have time to worry about him and I knew I had to shield Amanda from the way the others lived around her.

One morning I begged Richard to please borrow the money to fix the house. No way would Richard do that oh, no, he wouldn't because he didn't have to be there all day because he was at work, he only slept there. He didn't give a damn that it was awful for Amanda and me. He didn't care how we felt. I knew there was a Devil building inside me. I knew I would fight Richard. I had diagnosed him a long time ago and knew the right kind of medicine he needed.

When Friday morning came, I told him we were going out

that night so don't be late. Richard said we couldn't afford to go out. I told him we couldn't afford not to go out. I wasn't staying in those woods any longer, now he could go or stay, but I was going. I tell you I came home so happy and full of life, it seemed as if I didn't have a care in the world.

Saturday morning Richard worked on the house all day. He built me a wooden back porch. I walked out to see the finished porch and he put his arm around me telling me that I had hurt his feelings when I told everyone that he had moved me to the woods and was building me a house just so he could get rid of me with a clear conscious. When he said I knew it wasn't true, I pulled away from him. I told Richard he couldn't fool me anymore. Smiling at him, I told him just get the house livable. I know all I've ever been to Richard is the keeper of the boarding house. I wasn't about to be fooled by him.

I didn't just have Richard to put up with I had Mama Marselle and Daddy. Who were firm believers in their own religion. They were going to a nearby church, but it was for sure that I hadn't read in my Bible what these people believed. Besides, I was too busy to put up with a bunch of bull and you can believe it was getting deeper and deeper.

The first time my Daddy came out to the yard where I was working and asked me to come to church, I told him maybe when I had time. He knew I spent all my time working at that God forsaken place. It didn't stop Daddy. He came back every Saturday, not to help me with my work, but to give me a message from his preacher. The message was that I was a living Devil, my hair being cut short and bleached was sending me to hell. My jewelry, I must give up. To wear jewelry was a sin. Next time it was my clothes, but that was the last straw. I was fed up with his messages.

Getting off my knees where I had been pulling the dirt to a rose bush, I looked my Daddy in the face and told him that I had a message for the preacher today, and I would deliver it myself. With mud and dirt on my jeans and shoes, I got into my car and drove the five miles to see the preacher. Brother

Romar was his name. Telling the lady at the door that I must see the Preacher for just a minute, the lady turned up her nose, but she let me in and pointed to a door down the hall. The Preacher stood up as I came in and put out his hand then drew it back after seeing the dirt on my hands. As I was introducing myself, he stopped me saying that he knew who I was. That's when I told him I had never laid eyes on him in my life, but if he had known me, he would have known not to send me any more messages. I wanted this false face fool to leave me alone. So, I told him to take off his jewelry and tell his wife to take off her fake hairpiece and tell her that make-up is make-up. It doesn't matter if it's light or dark and that nail polish is still nail polish even if it's clear. I told him to get a Volkswagen to drive instead of burning up his congregation's money to run back and forth to do what ever it was he did in his Cadillac. I was not one of his people. I had not signed his book saying I would live by his rules and I never would. Just looking at him, I thought he had a full time job worrying about himself and getting his own butt to heaven. I told him he wasn't God and he couldn't see what's in my heart or on my mind and for him not to send any more messages to me.

By this time he had slumped back into his chair looking as if someone had slapped his face. Turning to leave from the room, there stood Daddy, DeRoy and Percy with their mouths open. I said hello as I left the room.

Daddy didn't speak to me for a month and the preacher didn't ever again send me a message. The next time I saw him on the road, he was driving a Volkswagen instead of his Cadillac. I remember saying to myself, I'll be darn."

"Drucilla, do you think that was the right thing to do?"

"Hell yes, Dr. Skeet, remember the Volkswagen, it must have hit home."

# CHAPTER 9

"I worked like a slave. My garden was coming in and I was in the fields early and out by nine a.m. with the most beautiful vegetables you ever saw. That year alone I put up over two hundred and seventy-five quarts of food. I froze corn on the cob, okra and peas as well. There wasn't an empty jar or a spot in the freezer to be found. I had and still have anything you would want to eat. Even old Mr. Hallmark couldn't believe the heads of lettuce that I grew. I was so proud of my new pressure cooker. I would work all day getting things ready for the cooker and after dinner, Richard would help me. He knew I was afraid it might blow up. Many nights we worked until two o'clock in the morning. I would think, he may leave me, but I won't go hungry, after a few times, I wasn't afraid of the cooker. I tell you, I worked and before the summer was over, I had everybody in Shady Grove working except for DeRoy and Gertrude, they had moved to New Orleans.

It was the seventeenth of July and I was working in the yard when a brown truck pulled up. The happiest, friendliest face came toward me. He said he thought he'd come look things over. He wanted to see my house. I told him I was so ashamed I could die. Mr. Cork told me not to worry about it, that I would make it. Looking around in the kitchen, he said he was going to make me some cabinets. I couldn't believe what I heard. He took out a ruler and measured the room up one side and down the other. Mr. Cork left saying he'd be back one day.

On his way to the truck, Richard's dog walked over to him and with me telling Mr. Cork the dog didn't bite, you won't believe it, that darn dog jumped up taking a bite out of Mr. Cork's butt. I could have killed that dog, but Mr. Cork said to think nothing of it, that he would be seeing me soon.

In two weeks Mr. Cork was back and he backed his truck up to my back door. I said, oh, my goodness! I was crying with happiness. I had never seen so many cabinets in my life. He had a helper with him and they measured the room. It was seventeen by seventeen. Bringing the cabinets in and standing them against the wall, they worked hard pushing and pulling getting them just where Mr. Cork wanted them to be. They were beautiful. I told him I loved them and how could I ever thank him. As Mr. Cork drove off, I burst out crying and ran back inside to look at my new cabinets. I was thinking, oh Lord, he's got to be the best person on this earth and he loves me.

Mr. Cork was back in no time with the other cabinets. Happy as he could be, telling me that he was glad he was through and that it had been a big job. I thanked him and told him I loved him for what he had done for me. It was better than Christmas Day. I got busy and stained them. Lord, they were beautiful and no one knew how much I loved Mr. Cork.

I tell you Dr. Skeet, then and today, I love Mr. Cork. He is a wonderful person.

When Richard came in, he couldn't believe his eyes. He opened the doors looking the cabinets over.

Richard asked me why is Mr. Cork helping us. I said, **not us**, Richard, **Me**. He's doing this for me. Mr. Cork knows I don't belong here, but I am here and he cares so he is helping me make the best of it. I'll always love him. He will always be my best friend.

Richard had told me to order the blocks to underpin the house and he would stop on his way home and get the cement. The next Saturday he got up telling me to get myself dressed to go with him to buy insulation for the attic. I looked at him as if he had gone nuts, wondering what had come over him. He had been working his tail off around the house lately. I almost fainted when he said I could have sixteen hundred dollars to get carpet and other things for the house.

I knew he was making better money because Richard had taken a better job with the company. What I couldn't understand was if he was going to leave me, then why was he being so good to me and fixing the house up better than I thought he would.

Then it dawned on me what had happened. Mr. Cork! It was Mr. Cork. Mr. Cork had shamed Richard by making the cabinets. He had showed Richard that I deserved better than what he had moved me into. I knew then that Mr. Cork knew what he was doing all the time. I knew he was the best friend that I could ever have.

Richard would come from work and start working on the house and work until dark, plus every weekend. Percy was more like Richard's brother than mine.

He worked along beside of Richard as if it was his home. I wanted to tell Percy that Richard would leave me when the house was finished, but I didn't have the heart. Besides, Percy wouldn't believe it anyway. By this time Richard had them all fooled. They all thought he worshiped me. It was always baby this and baby that. To top it all, I had never known Percy to work as hard in his life.

A year had gone by, but a year of pulling water and bathing in a washtub was enough to last Richard a lifetime. I couldn't understand what kept him here. It was for sure Richard had never lived like this or worked so hard in all his life. He really didn't seem to mind. The day he finished the plumbing and hooked up the hot water was without a doubt the happiest day of my life. It didn't seem like a big thing to Richard.

I had gotten an antique bathtub with crowfeet. It was big and deep. I had talked Richard into building a platform about six inches high all the way across the short end of the bathroom, which was ten by seventeen feet. The bathroom was red, black and gold when I finished it. It was beautiful. The house was looking good.

Richard had put a house trailer on a rental lot at the river where he went fishing. It was just something else to worry me. I finally talked Richard into selling the trailer and using the money to build a fireplace in the house. I put an ad in the paper and the trailer was sold in two days. I called the man who was going to install my fireplace and told him to get started and to hurry before Richard changed his mind.

Many times Richard and I talked about the front two rooms. I told him I couldn't breathe in them and that I was going to take out the wall and make one big room. Richard said the roof would fall in if the wall was torn down. I didn't argue with him. I told him okay while telling myself, so be it. When my feet hit the floor the next day, the wall came down. By the time Richard came home that night, the wall was in the yard. He was shaking his head as he came in. I just knew I would catch hell, but I didn't. He just said he would have to go up in the attic and brace the roof. He did and boy was he mad!

The fireplace was built and the carpet was put in and the room was beautiful. One wall was mirrored with a hanging chair in one corner of the room and half the wall around the fireplace was bricked. The room would take your breath away. I was beginning to be proud of my house. It seemed as if life might be getting better."

"Were you any happier with Richard at this time, Drucilla?"

"Gosh no!!! I knew Richard would never change, but I felt more secure and my nerves had calmed down some.

That is until Harriet came in telling about her new

boyfriend. She had gotten a job at a hamburger stand and now she thought she was grown, but talking boy talk was nuts. Harriet said she wanted to bring him home to meet me. She did just that and when I saw him, I almost threw up. He had to be the bottom of the barrel! I tell you this put a fit on me. I ranted and raved, raising hell like no one had ever seen before, telling Harriet that she was pretty and could find many boyfriends and not to bring him back. Amanda was laughing telling me that Harriet skated with him all the time and was always holding his hand. I was screaming now, telling Harriet she had better sense than to screw up her life. Harriet was crying by then and was saying she liked him and Mama Marselle had said she could date him. I was sick over Harriet and didn't fail to tell the whole family. Hell yes! Mama Marselle doesn't care. She gave me away when I was a child too. She wanted the house empty so DeRoy could move back to stay. She didn't give a care what I said. Harriet was in love.

I was so proud of Amanda. She was a champion skater by the age of thirteen. She won trophy after trophy and she was happy in the country. She got another pony, which made two, plus she loved to ride her trail bike in the woods with all her new friends, especially the two boys down the road.

I wasn't very fond of either of them and before the day was over, it was a day to remember. Mr. Adcock hadn't meant to set the woods on fire. He had worked all day picking up brush and raking leaves to burn. The wind came up all of a sudden and the old man tried to keep the fire under control, but the wind took it across the road. It was bad by the time help came, everyone was watching the fire, but not me I was watching the boys.

I knew the brats would pay me back for running them away from the fire, but the fire was burning bad and out of control. The boys had cursed and kicked when I sent them home. They screamed at me and I screamed right back.

The boys belong to my friend and neighbor and I knew Pamela Jo would want me to keep them safe. I also knew the boys didn't want me to boss them. They said they were big enough to help and tried to slip out to the woods, but I was too smart for them. The fire fighter had the fire out by four o'clock that afternoon. Pamela Jo was home and very thankful that her boys were safe. I knew the boys were mean as the Devil and would do anything they thought they could get away with. To be honest, I was a little afraid of them.

Strange things started happening around the house after that. The oldest boy was Joe. He had eyes for Amanda. He was fifteen and I didn't think he was playing with a full deck. He was at our house more often than Johnny, who was twelve and a little on the quite side. Joe was a bad influence on Johnny. You could tell Johnny wasn't a happy child.

One day the boys had come to play games with Amanda and a fifty-five dollar cake plate was broken. All at once Johnny jumped up and said he must go home. Joe stayed until after dark, laughing and playing. The next morning I went to finish the flowerbed that I had been working on the day before. I couldn't believe my eyes. Plants had been pulled up all over the yard. All my new plants I had worked so hard on. I screamed that I'd kill the little scoundrels. Then, I remembered the cake plate and Johnny leaving so early and now the plants. I had to work fast to get everything back into the ground and watered. I just hoped the plants would live.

The weekend before all this took place, Joe had been driving Richard's truck and had run into the side of my car. He said the brakes on Richard's truck didn't work. Richard let him get away with it because he was the nut that had let him drive.

Amanda finally came into the yard. I joked with her about the boys being sweet on her. It had been a long day, so after dinner and after talking to Richard for a while I went to bed. I was so tired that I didn't hear Amanda come into the bedroom to tell her Daddy that someone was at her window. All at once I heard shots. I ran from the bedroom to find Amanda crying and Richard outside where he had fired several times at someone you could still hear running through the kudzu field. I knew who it was all right, but he was so young. I knew I would have to talk to Amanda about that young man. I wanted him to stay away from Amanda.

Mr. Adcock was back the next day. He needed to use the truck and some tools. Now that his nerves were better, he could finish his job of cleaning his land off. After talking for a minute, I went on about my business, plus giving Amanda a job to do. She was mad but there would be no bike riding today. I would not give in. She had work to do and that was that.

The day went by so fast that I forgot to take the meat out of the freezer for dinner. I called Harriet to see if she would ride to the grocery store with me. I picked her up laughing and talking about the day. Then all at once I got quiet and slowed down. Telling Harriet not to be afraid, but I had to go back to the service station where there were lights. With a nervous voice, I told that something cold just went across my foot. I was scared to death, not knowing if it was a snake or not. I was turning around when the cold thing began to touch my neck. Going as fast as I could, I pulled into the service station letting my window down and called for two young men to come over to the car. I told them what was wrong. Harriet was so frightened she couldn't say a word. One of the men backed up, but the other man slowly opened the car door. At that time the biggest frog in this world jumped over to my arm and out the door it went. I asked Harriet if she was okay and she said, yes, thank the Lord we could have had a wreck and been hurt. I said I was sorry and let's just go back home.

I knew the boys had put that frog in my car. They had said they would get me back the day of the fire and they did! After the tearful fear had gone, I was mad, so mad that I called Joe and Johnny. Pamela Jo didn't know what to think. Even Amanda was upset. When they came in, I told them to find a seat and decide who's going to tell me the truth. Which one of them put the frog in my car? They could have caused me to wreck. When I asked about the cake plate and the plants,

Johnny ran out the door saying he hadn't done anything and was going to get his Daddy. That left Joe to face me. I told him what a childish thing he had done and to stay away from Amanda's window as well. He may not be so lucky the next time. I told him I knew Johnny did not do any of those things. Telling Joe he knew better than to break the cake plate and pull up plants, he would be punished before he could come back to my house and he had to talk to Richard about being at Amanda's window.

Joe got mad. He let it all out, telling me I could stop bossing him. He was big enough to help with the fire and I had no right to send him away. I told him to get out of my house and not to ever come back until he grew up. Amanda and Johnny needed more mature playmates, to set better examples for them. I told him to talk to his Mom because I was going to tell her about Amanda's window.

Dr. Skeet, I guess you can see I can't stand kids that won't mind. There were seventeen kids in Shady Grove with sorry parents.

Well, anyway, Mr. Adcock came by the next day and said he was grateful for all the help and thankful no one had gotten hurt by the fire.

Amanda sure pulls down the shades on her windows and I will always look in the car before leaving. The young man at the service station has always laughed about the frog, but to me the frog will never be funny.

After several weeks, Joe got around to apologizing, but all the kids around town knew that I would pull out their hair if they were ever caught around my car."

# CHAPTER 10

"I was skinning a lot of heads. The families, I made them clean their yards and their houses, even Mama Marselle and Daddy. It got so bad people began to tease me about being the boss. Hell, I was the **boss**! It wasn't hard. Anybody with a little money to wave around could make them jump. I wanted them to be clean. All eleven families living in Shady Grove lived just like junk people.

I told Richard about an old man and woman who had been by to ask if they could have a few pieces of scrap iron. Their names were Mr. and Mrs. White and they were from Ensley. They were hungry and needed money. I took them out to a field where my brothers, Jerry and Percy, had dumped old cars. They had also cleaned out a warehouse and just dumped this and that all over the place. I told the people to take it all. What about the cars, the old man asked I said if you can take them, take them. I just want it all cleaned up. I told my brothers that I had given it all away and they didn't say a word, but my Daddy walked the yard ranting and raving mad as the Devil. I raised the Devil right back. I was making enemies left and right. I sure didn't have time to worry about that. The place had to be cleaned up and I kept telling myself that someday they would all love me for making things better.

The old man and woman were back at six o'clock the next morning with a full grown grandson and a burning torch. They worked for two weeks, hauling out seven loads a day on a pick-up truck with sideboards piled as high as possible. I was thrilled to death. Now I would have a bigger garden spot. I sang and danced around the house, even helped the old woman when I could. On their way out with their last load, Mrs. White stopped to tell me thanks and that God would bless me for all I had given them. I hugged her as I said, God blessed me by sending you to clean that spot up for me.

Daddy and I fought like cats and dogs. He would say if I wanted the city I should have stayed in the city. Evidently, he had never seen me mad, because when I got started on him, he didn't know what to say. I told him he was a crazy, old and brain dead at that, because it was his idea for me to leave the city.

The next day as Daddy was loading old stoves and refrigerators on his truck. Mama Marselle told me I must have set a fire under that old man. He told Mama Marselle he was going to help the other kids pick up their yards. In a way, I loved Mama Marselle and Daddy. They had been good to Richard and me. I knew they wanted things cleaned up, but they didn't want to be the ones to cause the fight and get it done. I had told my Daddy he must be afraid of his own boys, saying, it's you that believes in the Bible. Don't you believe in cleanliness? It only takes a little work. Didn't that Bible say, a man that won't work shouldn't be allowed to eat?

I tell you Dr. Skeet, even the mail carrier called me a **workaholic**. Richard would get on my case about being so hard on everyone. He would say, you can't change people, just leave them alone. Let them live like they want to. That would start a fight. Oh yes, he'd like that. He'd like for me to be so ashamed that I'd never tell any of my friends where we lived. I told Richard he was dreaming if that's what he wanted. I said, yes they'll change. You'll see.

All the while Richard was adding porches, a driveway and a sidewalk to the house. I was still cleaning up the scenery. I had bought two of the old dilapidated houses and torn them down with the help of several teenagers. I burned and raked the lots clean.

I began to get tired easy and my stomach began to swell. It had gotten bigger and bigger. I knew I would have to go see Dr. Shane. He said I had ovarian cysts, but it wouldn't keep me down long and I needed the rest.

Dr. Shane asked about Richard, was he being better to me. I said ever since we had made the move he had been better. The only thing wrong with Richard was his hemorrhoids. He was the one that needed to see a doctor.

I was just getting over my surgery for ovarian cysts when Harriet came in with that terrible boyfriend of hers again. Harriet said they were getting married. **What**!!! I asked. I thought for sure she was joking. But, I said, you're crazy, little girl you're not marrying anybody. Boy, did she let me know that no one had to sign for her to get married. She was eighteen years old. I screamed at her to get out of my house and not to come back until Richard came home. Lord only knows I had to have time to think. I told Richard he had to do something. We couldn't let Harriet end up with that boy that he would never give her a thing. Richard talked to her, telling her he would buy her a new car or send her to California to live with his Auntie that she just needed time to find someone that could afford her.

Someone who could afford to take her places and buy her nice things. Richard told her this boy couldn't give her a thing. All Harriet would say is but I love him. That's when I came into the room and told Richard to let her see for herself.

The very next weekend Harriet came in with an engagement ring. I was so mad I could have killed the two of them. I screamed, Lord Almighty you dumb girl, I need a magnifying glass to see the diamonds if there is any. This sent Harriet out the door with that nut on her heels. I went through the house crying. My heart was broken. I can't understand why there is never any happiness. All I have ever had is heartache and hard work. After kicking the idea of a wedding around a time or two, I told Richard we might as well give in and give Harriet a wedding. When a girl gets it in her head, she isn't satisfied until she gets it in her ass.

Arthur was his name. He was just tall enough for Harriet. He had been sheltered all of his life. He was going from one job to another.

I used to watch him when I knew he was looking for an unemployment check in the mail. When the mail lady came, he would run out to the mailbox.

He would look at the mail and if the check wasn't there, he would throw all the mail straight up in the air and walk off stomping his feet and cursing. I would die laughing. Harriet would have to go to the mailbox and pick up the mail off the ground.

I met his Mother and was told his Dad had passed away. I loved his Mom. Her name was Betty and she was a precious person. She was a short, stocky, elderly lady. Even when she would get mad, she was always the perfect lady.

I set in on making Harriet's wedding gown and a dress for Amanda. Harriet's wedding gown was beautiful. The date had been set, flowers ordered and the party planned. I knew it would be a pretty wedding. I paid the florist to decorate the church and prayed that nothing would go wrong.

Five days before the wedding, Richard's hemorrhoids started bleeding. His doctor put him into the hospital to do the surgery, which was scheduled for the day before the wedding. I told Richard he could have waited, that it was his way of getting away from the wedding because he couldn't stand weddings.

The wedding went fine and the two kids went to the hospital in their wedding clothes to see Richard.

Dr. Skeet, Richard had my whole family fooled and they loved him. They couldn't believe how good he was to everyone and they knew if I said I wanted something, it was there in two or three days. They called me everyday to ask about him telling me to take care of him and to be good to him. I had been good to Richard for the past few years because he had been good to me or maybe I had been too busy to worry about his whoring around. Richard's doctor said he would be out of the hospital in three days and off work for six weeks.

Amanda was sad now that Harriet was married and that she and Arthur were moving out of town. Amanda told Richard he had better hurry up and get well because he had to take her skating. She was fourteen years old now, going on twenty. I didn't know where the years had gone. I said for Amanda not to worry, Harriet would be back in no time but that we would see that she didn't miss out on anything and the Good Lord knows she didn't. She had almost driven me nuts with the noisy motorcycle and the two crazy boys that were always under her feet. I told Amanda her Daddy was coming home from the hospital and I wanted things to be quiet for a few days.

Dr. Skeet's secretary buzzed in and told him she was going home. He told her not to come in tomorrow that he would be listening to tapes all day."

# CHAPTER 11

"The other Hallmarks didn't bother us much anymore. Even Richard's Daddy hasn't been to see him in months and that visit was to change clothes for his aunt's funeral. Richard had words with that idiot brother of his. I don't know what Richard said to him, but something had caused him to start calling us every time he got drunk. The strange thing was he called during day before Richard came home from work. So he called one day catching me in a bad mood and I told him not to call my house again. This just set him off. He called me a barfly, said he would jack my jaws and box my ears. If I could have pulled him through the phone that day, I would have killed him.

I told Butchie boy that I would start doing my shopping on his side of town and I would beat the mess out of that slut he called a wife every time I saw her. Asking him if he understood me, I hung up. I waited a minute or two then called his house. Lavita answered the phone. I asked her if she could hear me loud and clear. When she said she could, I told her if Butchie ever dialed my number again I would have him arrested.

It wasn't long after that until Mr. Hallmark came to visit and he acted as if he had his butt on his shoulders. He told me that the filter in the air conditioner needed to be cleaned. So I asked him if he knew how to clean it. He looked at me funny and said, yes. I said, you clean it yourself and anything else you see that's not clean enough for you. Butchie boy didn't call back and Wade Hallmark hasn't been back either.

Richard was home but didn't complain about anything. He stayed in bed until time for his sits baths. Amanda had made a get well card and I cooked special foods and babied him. I had him watching the soap operas on television every day.

Main Street Hospital was on and I have to watch this one almost every day. On that particular day, one of the leading men was confessing to his wife about being unfaithful. I said, Richard, why can't you be as brave as that guy and tell me who that woman was. I know everything except her name.

I tell you Dr. Skeet the fool started talking and told me what the bitch's name was and where she lived in Pleasant Grove. He knew I had known all of the time. You see this is why I hate him. Lies and more lies. Why did he keep lying when he knew I was right all of the time? Just look how many years he had lied and had protected his women. The years he made me suffer and the hurt he caused me! The awful lies and the things he had said to hurt me! It took sixteen years just to get her name. This is the slut that he had for nineteen months. The slut that was the reason he didn't want his own baby that had died!

Everything flashed before my eyes. I had screamed at him, **for sixteen years**! Sixteen years! I remember thinking, this started in Nineteen Sixty-eight and here it was Nineteen Eighty-four. Dr. Skeet, I hated him. I wanted him to die, not leave, not make a move, just die! I had known hate before, but not like this.

I screamed at him, **damn you! You, low-life son-of-a-bitch!** You and that whore caused me to lose my baby. You have put me through sixteen years of pure hell!

In a daze I went to the kitchen and picked up the phone book. Her name was Faye. I found Faye's number and called. Her Mama answered. I told her I was Faye's friend and would like to speak to her, that I had been out of town and out of touch with her. She told me where Faye worked and gave me the number to the paint store. Without a word to Richard, I got my keys and bag and went out the door.

I went over to my friend Courtney's. She took one look at me and ask, Child what is wrong? You look sick. Shaking my head, I sat down and cried my heart out. She didn't know what to say so she just listened. I told her I didn't know why I was so hurt. I knew it all the time even when he would say it was just in my mind, that I was just crazy I knew I hated him, I hated his guts. He slept with that woman the whole time that I carried my baby and for months after. He let his people, treat Amanda and me like dogs and laugh at us. I wish I could kill him. She asked me why did I live with him and let him lie, the way he did."

"Drucilla, I would like you to answer that."

"Doctor, it's because I had to give Amanda a home and I loved him. He was handsome, clean and worked so hard. I wanted to be wrong."

"Drucilla, you wanted to be wrong, remember that."

"Dr. Skeet, I wanted the hurt to go away. It'll never go away and he'll never be clean.

I told Courtney that I was going to see that bitch, just to see if she looked any better than me. I just didn't want Richard to know. He could have her. I knew I would put him out. He had called Amanda a watchdog and even left her in the car while he went in to see her."

"What do you mean Drucilla? He left Amanda in the car."

"One night I was helping Amanda get ready for bed and her eyes were all red and I asked her if she had been crying. She said, yes Mama. Tonight when I went off with Daddy, he left me outside in the car in front of a big, white house with a screened in porch. He was gone a long, long time and I was afraid. Richard and I had a fight about this, but like everything else, he lied about it saying Amanda must have dreamed it.

As sick as he was, he came to find me. It was just after dark. The sorry dog wasn't supposed to be out of bed and here he was. I went home thinking, hell yes I'm going home. It's my home, but I'll put him out. As we walked back into the house, I told him to get his ass out of my life. I didn't want to ever look at him again as long as I lived, **damn you**. Richard was saying, Drucilla, please don't talk that way. He begged me saying he was sorry and he wouldn't ever hurt me again. Every time I looked at him I saw DeRoy. I said, you're damn right about that. You get out and know you are a dog and I will always see you as a dog. Do you hear me? I want you to die. If I can get my hands on that two-bit slut, I'll kill her myself. I had screamed at him until my throat hurt. I wanted to kill him, but I didn't want to go to jail or go to hell.

Nobody could be a better wife than I had been. I wanted to be the best at everything, but he wanted a whore and that I couldn't be. There wasn't going to be any kinky stuff, that was for the whores and if that's what I had to do to keep a man, I wouldn't have one. It shouldn't be against the law to kill a whore hopper.

Richard knew that I was a good woman. The night we had married and made love the first time, it was as if I was a virgin again. He knew I hadn't been with anyone. Now look how sorry he's been because of sex. He is an addict! He had to have it morning, and night. Now he could go to it. I would do everything in my power to get him well, if only he would get out. All of my family and all of my friends that had envied me to death should have been in my shoes. The ones that wanted to find him in their Christmas stocking should have him. Hell no, they couldn't see through all that fake love he was pouring out in front of them. Damn him then and now! He has me back in hick town. Maybe he's been pretending that I'd hitch up Pa's old big hog to ride around. Maybe he's been pretending that I've been his whore for the past few years.

Dr. Skeet, this has got to stop. I have to get this off my mind. He knew my heart was hurting. Most of my trouble is shame. I am so ashamed that I have lived with him after all he has done to me. I have to make myself get rid of him and never have anything to do with him again."

"That is what we are doing Drucilla, by talking it out this way."

"The next day after he told me who she was, I couldn't say two words to Richard. It made me sick to look at him. His medicine was on the bedside table. He had water and I brought his food to the bed. He tried to talk to me, but I was just too hurt to care for him. Things would flash before my eyes, like the drugstore bill. It was his slut pretending to be me.

I didn't want to sleep with him, but I wasn't going to give my bed up either. I didn't go to bed that night until I was so sleepy I couldn't hold my eyes open and wouldn't dare say a word to him. About one o'clock I woke up. Richard was sitting up on the side of the bed. I didn't know what woke me up. I asked him what in the world was wrong with him. Why was he up? I moved over and turned on the light and there were tears running down Richard's face. I asked him if he was hurting or just crazy. He looked at me and said he just didn't want to live if he couldn't have Amanda and me and that we were all he had. I told Richard, he should have thought about that when he was having fun with Faye and all the others.

I was looking around to see what was really wrong. Then, I saw what was wrong. He had taken all of the medicine in the house. I got Percy on the phone and told him to get to my house in a hurry. I didn't know that Richard had put his thirty-eight caliber pistol under his pillow. Percy came in and I told him I'd be right back and out the back door I ran. I was back in a split second with Jerry. Meanwhile, Richard pulled the gun out from under his pillow and Percy had wrestled the gun away from him. I told Richard we were taking him to the hospital and he began fighting Jerry and Percy. The two of them got him outside, but when they got him to the car, he took hold of the handle. They almost never got his hands loose. Percy made him a promise that I would not leave him. Three miles down the road I couldn't find a pulse. I was so mad I slapped his face saying **wake up damn you!** You live so that I can make you sorry for what you've done to me. While the doctors worked with him, I had to talk to the police.

When I saw whom the policeman was, my blood boiled. The old fool was a smart aleck I had known all of my life. Tom wasn't a good cop. He wasn't good for a thing. He asked what made Richard do such a thing. I told him that he had surgery a few days ago and that he had been hurting so bad he just took more medicine than he thought and he was so drowsy that it scared me, so I brought him to the hospital. This was the same thing I told the doctor. I was walking across the room when Tom said I know you caused that boy to take an overdose. I told him, he was crazy as hell I didn't cause him to do a damn thing. I screamed it's just like I said now take it or leave it. But don't try to push me around tonight. I've been through enough. He went out the door and drove off. The doctor came out and said to take him home but not to let him go to sleep until seven in the morning. Make him drink coffee, one cup after another until seven. Do not let him go to sleep. Percy helped me all night. I had to tell Percy what had caused him to do this. Percy didn't say a word he just shook the crap out of Richard asking him if he knew what he was doing. Richard said he was not living without me.

Dr. Skeet, even today I could kick my own self. Why didn't I just go back to bed and go to sleep so the crazy fool could just die. By ten o'clock the next morning, I hated him more.

I knocked on Dr. Shane's office door, no answer. I sat down to wait. Then Dr. Shane came in. He always told to come on in and sit down if he didn't answer the door. He took one look at me and shook his head. What's wrong baby, Dr. Shane asked. I told him everything, but not crying like I had done in the past. He said, you know that hate will kill you don't you? Yes sir, let's not talk about that. Remember my last checkup.

You said that if the spotting didn't stop that you may have to give me a complete hysterectomy. I want you to do it now. I want you to take everything out. I told Dr. Shane that I wouldn't give Richard a child for all the money this world has to offer. Dr. Shane said you're mad right now Drucilla so wait six months. I told him No! I'll go to another doctor if you won't do it now.

Dr. Shane told me he didn't blame me for the way I feel. I've gone through hell for him even he knew that. Dr. Shane said you must have loved him a lot when you went through with the tubal ligation. I did, but that was yesterday. Dr. Shane said, you knew what he was doing all the time. Yes, I knew. I loved him so much I thought I could take it, but I can't and I hate myself for living with him.

I told Dr. Shane, if the crazy fool killed himself his darn people would say it was because of the hick family he had married into and he just couldn't take it. Dr. Shane told me I might be right, but I would have to stop worrying about what other people think. The hell with what they think. You have to start thinking about what's good for you. You don't have to have sex with him. Tell him you'll live with him, but he'll have to have a whore because you don't want him.

**No, hell no!** I wanted the surgery I don't want a baby ever. Not by anybody. I asked, Dr. Shane, hasn't he heard me. He said, okay Drucilla have it your way.

I went on to tell him if Richard ever got me pregnant I would have an abortion and I think he knew that. Dr. Shane said, yes, he knew I had a strong will. He has never met anyone like me, but it's helped me to survive.

You can believe me Dr. Skeet, I was a lot happier. I couldn't have his kids. I hated him. Damn him! Dr. Shane said he would set a time for the surgery.

The very next week I went into the hospital. I didn't tell anybody that I was going. I got Harriet to take care of Amanda and I asked Courtney to stay with me at the hospital after the surgery. I hated Richard so much that I didn't want him around me. He knew what I was doing and he knew the whys. I had asked Dr. Shane if he would get me into the operating room early and get me out before Richard came to see me at lunchtime. He said he would.

I told everyone but Courtney that my surgery would be on Thursday when it was really going to be on Tuesday. Tuesday came and when Richard came in to see me at lunch, I was out like a light. He was mad at Courtney and she told him that she had done what I asked her to do and that it was his own fault that I didn't love him. Richard never said a word about the hysterectomy."

"Drucilla, do you need a minute to compose yourself?"

"No, I'll be alright. The more I think about Richard the more I hate him.

I wiped tears saying damn Richard. **Damn you, Richard**! No, I don't want him to die. I want to kill him myself. I hate his guts. I hate his damn Daddy and his whole false faced family. They'll never hurt me again. I had made up my mind that I'd tell them the next time in words they could understand.

Every time I came home, Richard has a worried look on his face. Asking where I had been and that he was worried to death about me. I laughed at the bastard, you worried about me Richard, you, love me Richard. I don't want you to love me anymore and you had better be worried. Worried that I might bring you in a bad disease. He had hurt me so bad that all I wanted was to make those bastards hurt…the way I had hurt."

# CHAPTER 12

"It was on a Monday in March of Nineteen Eighty-four when I called Courtney. We had been friends for a long time and she was one of the best people in the world. I asked her to go with me to the paint store. Swearing, I just wanted to get a look at his slut. I just had to see what she looked like. Courtney said she would go but that I had better not get us into trouble. All the way there I was thinking that I'd get a can of red paint and throw it all over the bitch.

We arrived at the store at nine o'clock and as we walked around the store, I picked up a pint can of red paint and began looking for something to open it with. The next thing I knew I was asking the woman if she knew Richard and if she knew me. With a frightened look on her face she said, yes. I had looked around but there was no way to get to her. I remember saying, the first thing I've got to say to you is, my ass would make you a Sunday face and you're so damn ugly you'd snag lightning and triple thunder. The slut looking bitch started to cry. By that time I had thrown the red paint in her face and told her that if I caught her outside of that damn place I'd run over her with the car.

Then, before I knew what was happening, three men had come from behind Courtney and had gotten hold of both of us and escorted us outside. They forced us into my car telling me that I had better never be caught around Bessemer again or they would have me arrested. I screamed out and told them that I would be back and that sooner or later I would get her. My tires squalled for half a block, without me saying another word.

Pulling into the driveway at Courtney's house, she said, damn you Drucilla, I'll never go off with you again. I told her to shut up and open the damn door. If I'd thought about it, I would have taken the damn gun out of my purse and put a bullet between her ugly eyes.

The very next morning, I walked straight to the phone and called she wasn't there. I called every day until I got her. You remember all the calls you made to my home? How does it feel to be called what you are? You'll know because I'm going to call you every day. After seeing you, I know why you screw married men. You're so ugly they can't take you anywhere but to bed.

I called her every day that rolled around. I called that thing everything but a Nun. I tried everything to get her to meet me. Oh no she was a nice girl. She didn't cuss or fight. Once I told her that I had forgotten that Richard did tell me that she went to church. I let her know how funny it sounded to hear someone talk about going to church when they lay with married men, mostly giving oral sex.

Now Dr. Skeet, for the life of me I don't know what makes her so **Saintly**. I don't know why the damn church didn't fall in when she entered it. I even called her Mama and told her what a slut she had raised and if it wasn't for going to jail, I would burn their damn house down with them in it and I might do it anyway.

Two months passed and I didn't let up. I hated Richard. I begged him to make a date with her. I told him if he loved me he would get her out so I could get my hands on her. No way. Richard wouldn't hear of it. I would scream at him telling him to go ahead and protect her fat puss and that I would hate him even after I was dead twenty years. Richard knew better than to get her out because he knew what I'd do. He knew I would kill her.

One night the phone rang and Richard picked it up. The look on his face made me jump up and run for the other phone just in time to hear the slut say, you've got to make her stop. She's got to leave me alone or I'll lose my job. That's when I screamed out, hang up that damn phone Richard! You listen to me. He can't make me do a thing. I control this mind, soul and body and I'm going to get you if it's the last thing I do. I went on to tell her not to call my house that if I wanted to talk to her, I would call her. I left the house on two wheels looking for her, but she must have been invisible. I couldn't find her anywhere. Believe me, no one came from her house. I even watched her Mama's house. She never came there either."

"Drucilla, why don't you call this woman by her name?"

"What are you talking about, **Bitch** is her name!

This is when I began to party again, but this time I was having a good time for real. I had eased up on her and Richard a little, but just a little. For the life of me, I don't know why Richard was staying with Amanda and me. Amanda was the only thing keeping me sane. I couldn't bring shame to Amanda. I had to keep her safe and I had to take time to let her know that I loved her best in the world regardless of what was happening. I would look at Amanda and think of her as a model and thank God that's what she wanted to be. She was beautiful and thank God she was doing fine in school making A's and B's.

I would fill my days making clothes or shopping. Amanda and I didn't want for a thing. Richard never said a word about what I did or didn't do. One thing was for sure the house had turned into a doll house. I even bought paint for Percy's house and helped him paint it. I helped all my family, but they didn't care for me and I knew it. The only time they cared was when I was giving out money to get things done, but that was getting old with me too. I made up my mind that if they didn't like me, they didn't like my money.

Harriet had moved back from Mississippi, but she sure didn't know the Drucilla she came home to. One Friday I asked Harriet and Amanda to go shopping at the mall with me. I wanted something new and silky to wear that night.

I no sooner got in the mall until I spotted the outfit I wanted. The sales lady helped me look for the right size but said she was sorry all the size five's had been sold. I said, Ma'am, the mannequin has on a size five and I want that one. The lady said she was sorry but she couldn't get that one for me and walked off. You could see the blood drain from Harriet as I stepped over the rail and onto the platform.

I undressed the mannequin and took the outfit to the sales lady telling her to ring it up. The sales lady was visibly mad saying she would have to get the manager. I said, **no lady!** This has a price tag on it. Now you ring it up. About that time the manager walked up asking if there was a problem and I said, not that I can see. Sir, I wanted this outfit and it has a price tag. It's the only one in my size. I asked the lady to take it off the mannequin and she refused. So, I got it myself. The manager rang up the outfit and said he was sorry for the inconvenience. As the girls and I walked out, I was telling Harriet not to be upset, that I was just not going to be run over anymore. I said you'll learn people will walk on you if you don't stay two steps ahead of them then some do it anyway.

Harriet had been gone a year or so. She had left right after her wedding. Her new brother-in-law had gotten him a job at a tire company and the job had played out, so they came back. Mama had bought them a trailer and had it set up and waiting. Her husband got a job in Birmingham, where he still works.

I was ready to party when Richard came home. I told Richard that we were going out to eat and then for a ride before we went to the club. Richard didn't know that his bitch had moved, so when I pulled up at her apartment and said this is where you get out, he didn't know what to think. He said, woman you've got to be nuts. I'm not getting out and if you're going to raise Hell tonight let's just go home. I told Richard this was where his cow had moved. Dr. Skeet, Richard wouldn't get out."

"You didn't really expect him to, did you?"

"No! I was still driving a new car, and it would run like crazy. I topped the hill from her apartment and saw a red car. I asked Richard, if he saw the red car. That's her car isn't it? Richard stuttered, yes, it looks like it. Her car had a dented fender. The woman in the car had a little girl with her that looked about the same age as Amanda and a woman that looked like her Mama. I ran that little red car off the side of the road and got out. I was going to kill her. Walking up to the window I stopped, saying to myself, it's not them. I said I'm sorry lady. You're not the person I'm looking for. I got back into my car and left.

Richard never said a word. He was hurt and sorry for what he had done. He didn't want to loose me, but he didn't know what to do. He said do what you have to do to get it out of your system.

Dr. Skeet, here it is Nineteen Eighty-four and I've told you a lot, but I can tell you I will have to be brain dead to forget the hurt that Richard has caused me. It took a long time for it to dawn on me that I wasn't married to his slut. It was Richard that had hurt me.

"There are ways Drucilla, tell me the rest."

"It was payback time and damn it if Richard was so in love with me now, I would show him what it's like to have heartache."

It was now late at night. Dr. Skeet had listened to tapes for two days now. He was too tired to continue. He would have to start again tomorrow.

# CHAPTER 13

"As I went into the club, the music sounded different, better than ever before. I walked in as if I owned the place and sat at the front table. The drummer winked, I thought, wow he's a doll. He was singing Satin Sheets and I didn't take my eyes off of him for a second. It was as if he had me hypnotized. Even while dancing, I would look straight into his coal, black eyes. **Hell No!** I didn't want to go home. Home was a miserable place to be. I couldn't get the baby off my mind. That woman and Richard had tormented me to death, causing my baby to die. I hated them, but the music seemed to make it all go away.

I had read a book about the Catholic religion and it said that when someone had a problem, they would go to their Priest. I thought to myself, I don't have anything to lose. I opened the phone book, found the church listing and closing my eyes I put my finger on one. I came up with Father Andrew. I called Father Andrew and explained my situation to him and he told me to come see him. Father Andrew and I talked many times after that day.

Talking to Father Andrew had helped some, but I had to

have answers. I had to know why Richard was living with me and why he lied. Father Andrew said for me to ask Richard if he would come over and talk to him and me. I told Richard that we had an appointment to see Father Andrew. We went to see Father Andrew and we talked for three hours.

He said, today we'll put the blame where it belongs Drucilla. You are not married to any man. You are married to Richard. He is the one that has done all this to you, so you must deal with Richard. Father Andrew lit in on Richard with the third degree. Richard admitted he had told the woman the phone was bugged and that she had picked him up at work and left his truck so I would think he was working. He also admitted spending Percy's birthday with that woman and laughing about me being his **hick wife**. It was all true. Father Andrew asked why Richard, why did you do this to Drucilla? What's wrong with Drucilla? Is she clean? Yes. Do you love her? Yes. What's wrong with her? Not one thing. Richard told Father Andrew. She is perfection in every way. Are you sure Richard? Yes Sir. Are you ever going to do her wrong again? I remember Richard saying, No sir. What do you tell your women Richard? Whatever they want to hear. But Richard had gotten mad the night before and told me he didn't want her because she was just like me. Now even though he had answered Father Andrew and my mind was settled with a lot of things, I had sworn I'd never forgive him.

On the way home I thought, yes Richard, you will protect your butt and your women. You think I will take my life. You know I'm afraid to stay by myself at night. You know I'm ashamed to tell what you've done to me, but most of all you know my health won't let me hold down a job and you say if I make you leave you won't give me a dime.

You're right Richard, the only thing I can do is be quiet and live with you or take my life and get out of it all.

In a day or two, Father Andrew called me to tell me that it was alright to put Richard out. He told me that he and the Lord knew that I was a good wife and that the Lord would make a way for me, a way for me not to fight with Richard but to tell him that I couldn't deal with this and that I was turning it over to the Lord and that the Lord would take care of things. I listened and cried. I knew there was no Lord. What I needed was the Mafia.

I tell you Dr. Skeet, I'm not like his slut, but I wanted to be worse. I wanted to hurt Richard.

Father Andrew had made me promise to leave that woman alone. He was sure the woman had sent Richard home or he wouldn't still be there. Father Andrew said my best bet is to get him out of my life. I was torn all to pieces and needed time to think. I needed peace and quiet.

I went into a deep depression for months. I wanted to be left alone. The house was kept quiet and dark and all I did was read and sleep. I called Father Andrew telling him the only way out was to die. I couldn't live with Richard. I had rather be dead. Yet, I promised him I'd go out to eat Friday and go see my doctor.

I tell you, Dr. Shane was a sight to see. I loved the old man and wished I could go home with him. He had been like a father to me. I just needed someone to keep me safe, but that couldn't be.

You know as well as I do that when it comes down to it other people don't give a darn about someone else's problems."

"That's not always the case Drucilla."

"Besides I had Amanda. She was a beautiful young lady. I knew I had to get back on my feet. I couldn't let the son-of-a-bitch do this to me.

Dr. Shane said, Richard always has and always will as long as you have him, because he knows you aren't going to do anything about it. Now, pull yourself together and fight.

I left Dr. Shane's telling myself that I would be better. The only thing that would make me feel better would be to go to the club. The music would make me forget it all.

Another three or four months had passed with Richard and

me going out every Friday and sometimes Saturday nights.

I was on the dance floor, but this time I winked at the drummer. Richard and I danced every weekend. I was going out like it or not and Richard wasn't liking it very much. He had made up his mind that he wasn't going to the club the next weekend. He was tired of going out. I told him not me, you better get your self in gear or I'll leave you at home. I'm going out! Richard said, no you're not Drucilla! This has got to stop. The fight started when I said, the hell you say. You! You wanted a party girl. **Now here she is**. Richard told me that all I wanted was that drummer and I couldn't have them both. I calmly walked to the bathroom door where Richard was.

I said, I'm going now and if you make me choose, I'm afraid it'll be the drummer. Don't start telling me what to do after what you've done to me. I came in at two o'clock that next morning.

I want you to know Dr. Skeet that I had two hundred tomato plants to get out that morning and I was up at six o'clock, but I was happy."

"Drucilla, does keeping busy help the hurt go away?"

"No! It just keeps him off my mind.

The next Friday night I was at the Club alone. Richard had refused to go. Fritzie, the drummer, came to my table asking where I had left my husband. Fritzie saw I was mad at Richard. He said, Drucilla, I know you don't belong in this place. Do you see the girl at that second table? She's here to be picked up. Is that what you want people to think about you? Fritzie told me that he wished I would leave so that he wouldn't have to worry about me. I gave him a Devilish smile and told him to mind his own business. But every time a man came to my table, darn if Fritzie didn't hit his drums so hard everyone looked up to see him shaking his head no at me. The man would walk away without asking me to dance. I knew Fritzie was protecting me and when his break came he asked me to have lunch with him the next day.

The lunch date Fritzie and I had turned into an all day talk.

He told me that most men have a whore at one time in their life. It seemed as if we had known each other for years. I felt safe with him. He was a good person. He sat quietly and listened as I told him that I didn't believe Richard loved me and that I was nothing more than a maid. Then he said I'll tell you what, we'll just see if he loves you. Fritzie would call me just to see what was on my mind or ask me to call and get him up at a certain time. He had a small child and I loved little Joel as if he were my own. The child's mom was nice enough. Her name was Midge. She and Fritzie were divorced because she was so jealous of Fritzie she couldn't live with him. Whenever she'd leave, I would be called to pick the child up. By now Fritzie had become my best friend.

It bothered Richard, but as long as I didn't make waves about his sluts he was happy. He let me go and do anything I pleased. I thought that Richard would be jealous of Fritzie Rogue, and it did seem like he was at first, but thinking back, it's as if he was relieved. He just wanted me to leave him alone. Fritzie had made me feel much better about Richard even though I was hurt. Richard didn't care if I had lunch with Fritzie or make clothes for the band. Many times Fritzie told me that Richard loved me and that he did have a good job. Just give everything time to heal. Fritzie thought I loved Richard, but I had been hurt to the core and I didn't love him anymore.

Months had gone by and making Richard jealous hadn't worked. I was sick of hearing about how Richard loved me. I told Fritzie to stop saying it. I screamed at him once. It's just bull crap and I don't want to hear that! Actions speak louder than words and I want a man that needs no one but me. I want to be loved first. I wanted to hurt Richard and I wanted him to suffer.

Yet, Dr. Skeet I was realizing that I was hurting myself. I was learning a lot about life, but Amanda and my house needed to come first. I thought if I could just stay busy, I would forget all the hurt and I couldn't let myself be scared. I made up my mind to stay home more and just talk to Fritzie on the phone. I asked him one day if he had E. S. P. It seemed as if every time I was feeling low he would call. He jokingly told me that I was his rainy day woman. After that I asked him to never sing that song when I was at the club. I didn't want to be a rainy day woman. He said he wouldn't and to my knowledge, he never sang it again.

It gave me strength just to look in Fritzie's eyes. Richard and I didn't fight much anymore and while cooking dinner one afternoon I began to sing.

**I FELL IN LOVE WITH A DRUMMER BOY**

My baby and I were in a fight
So he took me out one Friday night.
Now we don't fight anymore,
Cause I fell in love with the drummer boy.
Now we don't fight anymore………..

I knew Fritzie was a wonderful person and that he would never try to put the make on me. Even though we were together two and three times a week, he would call me to come to the jam sessions and introduced me to everyone. It wasn't long until Fritzie's ex-wife, Midge came back and they called me to have lunch with them and little Joel. Fritzie had to leave us saying that he'd see me Friday, but he said not a word to Midge. I knew he didn't love her. He couldn't. She griped night and day about him being gone all the time. She couldn't understand that he had to mix and mingle with the people at the club to keep them coming back. It was his way of making a living and he was the best entertainer in town.

Trying to unwind, Fritzie and the boys would play pool after leaving the club, but he also played golf about three days a week. Midge told me that Fritzie had promised to remarry her, but she didn't think he ever would. Neither did I, and so help me I said so before I even thought. I went on to tell her she was so ate up with jealously that all she could do was raise hell every time she got near him. That it was no wonder he stayed away from her. I let her know he wasn't running around and there wasn't any whoring on the golf course at any time. I asked her why couldn't she just spend his money, take care of his child and help make him a good home. He had told me that the girls at the club made him sick. I left her thinking how sorry I felt for them both.

Fritzie and I got into an awful fight about a yellow shirt I had made for him just a few days before. Making clothes to please him wasn't easy. I cursed him and threw the shirt in his face and told him to wipe himself on it. The next thing I knew, Fritzie's contract was up and he was moving out of town. That would mean, one lonely me. Once before when he left, I cried for three days. Even though I could go to see him, it wasn't like having him nearby. Richard would go with me sometimes except when I was mad at him, and then I would just leave a note saying, see you Sunday.

Fritzie had been gone for two years. One Friday morning he called me asking me if I was coming to see him that weekend. I told him that it was just too cold and I was afraid I would get snowed in. He laughed, saying it would be wonderful if I did, but that he was just across town. Fritzie said, now come on over and I'll pray for the snow. I had a lump in my throat with tears running down my face. When I saw him, he took my face in his hands and said I see me in your eyes. It was like Christmas day. I picked up my Joel swinging him around and around telling him I came after him and he could visit with Amanda.

At the club that night, Fritzie came straight to my table. He bent over and lightly kissed my lips and said hello to Richard. Then turning back to me he asked would you like a Hawaiian punch. If you're buying, I said. He laughed and drew back his fist to punch me and we all had a big laugh. When Fritzie had walked off, Richard told me that all this wasn't going to start again and for me to tell Fritzie not to kiss me anymore.

A few days later I did tell Fritzie. He laughed about it and told me not to worry, so I forgot about it until the next weekend. So help me Fritzie was on stage saying, this next song is for a special friend. Then he sang, I won't just kiss her once, next time I'll kiss her all over. When I looked at Richard, we both burst out laughing.

I loved Fritzie. I couldn't help myself. When everyone was kicking me around, he pulled me up by petting and pampering me as if I were special. Yet, he made me strong telling me I could survive this or that.

I tell you Dr. Skeet sometimes I did draw my strength from Fritzie. I wasn't afraid to go to his club by myself. If he didn't walk me to the car, he would have one of the other boys in his band walk me to my car, to make sure that I was safe. After the kiss incident, it seemed as if Fritzie had a grudge against Richard. He called me more often just to see about me."

"How did you feel about that Drucilla?"

"Mostly confused. I just hurt.

Fritzie started to pour on the love. He would come to our table and tell me my hair looked good or my perfume smelled delicious. If he had time to talk a minute, he would pull his chair next to me and sing, Hello Darling, don't let it be so long."

# CHAPTER 14

Richard had taken me on vacation and we fought like cats and dogs. I would not give Fritzie up. He was the only true friend I ever had and I felt safe with him. He was the brother I should have had. With all Richard's threats, I didn't call Fritzie when I returned nor did I go to the club. After what seemed like a month of Sundays, Fritzie called. If I didn't come to see him, he would come to me. I broke down and cried telling him Richard wouldn't let me. He said he'd leave me. This made Fritzie furious. He said then let him go. Fritzie convinced me to get dressed and go shopping with him. Being with Fritzie I would forget all that Richard had done to me. I would laugh out loud and be myself with him.

That day Fritzie asked me where did a girl like me come from. Who made me like I am? He'd met a lot of women in his line of work, but not one like me. He said, Richard's a damn fool and I can't feel sorry for him any longer.

Fritzie stopped me as I was about to get out of the car saying, he needed to talk a minute more if I have time. I was shocked to hear what he was saying. Fritzes poured his heart out, telling me Joel needed me and so did he.

He swore he wouldn't ever mistreat me, or Amanda. He said that I wouldn't ever want for a thing. I remember so well. He said, Drucilla, I know you don't love me like you've loved Richard, but you will in time. I love you enough to take care of us both and I will if you'll let me. By this time tears were dropping from my face. I said Fritzie, I think you're nuts. We have known each other for years and you're just now saying this to me. I asked him why he had let me stay with Richard if he loved me so much.

He was so serious when he told me that at first he was just mad at Richard and he knew I was hurt and he wanted to help me, and Richard. Hell, he didn't know how it happened. As time went by, he got to know me better. He couldn't see how Richard could hurt me in the first place. He had looked at me and listened to me and even asked questions about me. He knew I was the best. Then Fritzie hesitated and said let's not talk anymore now Drucilla. He told me that he would have to leave again in six months and wanted my answer then and that six months should give me enough time to make my decision.

I didn't know what to say to him except to say, Fritzie, you have never been anything but my friend. I will always hear him say, yes Drucilla, and I'll always be your friend regardless of what your answer is. I'll never stop loving you.

I went home, picked up a good book and didn't put it down until two-thirty that morning. I went to the club every chance I got. I didn't talk to Fritzie or anyone else about what he had said to me, but I saw him in a different way. I would ask myself what if this or what if that. I was sure about only one thing. I would never love anyone as much as I had loved Richard when I married him, but I would love myself best in the world and do what was best for Amanda and me.

I told myself, the hell with men's love. I had kicked that kind of love in the butt. From now on love would be Amanda, old people and little children. It seemed as if everyone had gone crazy.

Two weeks after Fritzie had sprung his surprise on me, Midge called to spring her surprise. She said that she was coming over, so I told her I would put on a pot of coffee for us. Before the day was over, I was wishing for a bottle of Black Velvet. The asinine idiot had told me she would let me adopt little Joel if I would divorce Richard and marry Fritzie. I let her know I didn't want Fritzie or the child for my own. I was just their friend. I loved all three of them. She insisted that Fritzie loved and respected me beyond anything she had seen. She told me that he talked about me with a feeling that he'd never talked about anyone, how self-sufficient, perfect and beautiful I was. I was fed up with all of her bull crap and said so. Hell girl, you are all those things, I told her. The only thing wrong with you is that you make Fritzie crazy with that jealously of yours. Why can't you keep yourself at home and take care of your baby instead of running off every other week. All Fritzie wants is a home, a real home. Can't you see that? You're just his ex-wife, but he lets you move in and out anytime you take a notion. Why can't you be satisfied with a home for Joel or get the hell away from Fritzie? There's no need in making him miserable. Can't you see, its Joel that is being hurt the child never knows when his Mom might get mad for no reason and take off. Make up your mind, who is the most important, you or Joel. Stop trying to give the little fellow away. He needs his Mom and Dad. He needs to know you're going to be there always. If you love him, get yourself a job and stop dragging him from place to place. There's one darn thing for sure, you can rest assured I don't want Fritzie for a husband. I love Richard and I don't think he will ever hurt me again.

Midge left. She really left, packed up everything leaving Fritzie without a glass to drink out of and left a note saying she was going back to her Mama's.

Fritzie called me and asked. What in the hell did you say to Midge?

I told Fritzie that all I said was for her to just grow up and take you like you are or get the hell away from here. What about it, I asked. Poor Fritzie said, Drucilla, the letter will be on the table for you to read. She said I could have Joel. She has no way of taking care of him. I didn't know what to say. What could I say but hell yes Fritzie, I'll be there in forty-five minutes, but you are going to have to find someone to take care of Joel there. It's not fair to run him from one family to another.

I didn't know what Fritzie the drummer was thinking, but one thing was for sure, I was between a rock and a hard place. Some of the hurt had gone away and Richard was being good to me. He told me that I'd never have to worry about another woman again. I believed him even though I knew there had been more than one.

I weighed the faults of both men and then the good in them, but after months and months I couldn't give up the security. He was so clean, handsome, rich looking and so sophisticated. I had to have him for myself. Even though he had put me through hell, I had security for Amanda.

The six months were up and when Fritzie left he didn't even call me until he had bought a house and his new club was doing well. He called asking me to come to Atlanta. I let him know that Richard would be with me and I didn't want any trouble. My heart broke when he said there wouldn't be any trouble and that he was going to marry Midge so Joel would have a home. I hated him in one way but loved him in another. With a knot in my throat I said I was happy for them and I would try to come there for the weekend. After Richard heard the news, he went back to rolling his eyes at what he called my uneducated remarks while looking at me with a smug smile on his face. I thought what an idiot he was. He just thought I didn't know him. I'd been reading between his lines for most of my life.

I remained friends with Fritzie. I would always be thankful for all he had done for me. Richard and I spent a lot of weekends traveling to his new club to dance to Fritzie's music. I knew Fritzie's new marriage wouldn't last long. I had told Richard that Midge was a whiner and that she would never be good for Fritzie.

Fritzie was back in Birmingham in eight months. He said he loved Joel, but that he couldn't live with her whining. He saw that I was getting on with my life and didn't tempt me. He did tell me I would be the only woman he would ever love even if he couldn't have me. I didn't see him very often. I was trying to keep Richard happy. I was studying everything I could get my hands on. I couldn't let Richard be ashamed of me. I was determined to be the best.

I picked up two tickets for a makeup class. The class was from eight until ten at a large hotel downtown. The makeup artist was well known. I felt lucky to get the tickets and I just had to see if my makeup was right for me. About thirty minutes into the class, a ghost of a woman was standing in the door looking straight at Richard and me. The woman had a pale complexion, long, stringy, white hair and no makeup. I asked Richard who she was and did he know her. He said he didn't know her, but in a split second he was going to the bar to get a drink. He said he would be back in a minute. I watched him stand in the doorway and talk to the Ghost Woman. When he returned, I asked him did he find out who she was and he said, no baby, I didn't. I knew he was lying and I hated his guts.

I was so ashamed I had believed all his lies. The hurt was unbearable. I was too ashamed to tell Fritzie. I would just have to put on a false face for everyone. I didn't even let on to Richard how hurt I was, but I did ask him time and time again about the Ghost Woman. It was weeks later when I had to pick him up at work that I saw the Ghost Woman. This low life son-of-a-bitch had this woman working right there at the Telephone Company with him in the same building all this time.

When I confronted him with the facts, he said just because she worked where he did, didn't mean that he knew her. I wondered how long this one had been his whore and wished he would die and be out of my life once and for all. I had wished that many times. For Amanda, I knew I would have to live with him.

Here I was living in the woods with very little education, a broken heart and a child. How I hated myself for being dumb. I knew Richard would never love me, but why did he insist that he did? Why did he continue to tell all the lies?

Dr. Skeet can't you see I've been in this trap for years and can't get out. I don't have the guts and it takes money."

Dr. Skeet said, "Go on Drucilla."

"I tried to put Richard out of my mind when he was at work. I even got a job making shrouds and worked for a while, but I couldn't make enough money to take care of Amanda and run the house.

I fought City Hall to get water put in for all the families. Everyone had a bathroom. There wasn't room for stupidity around me. I had come too far. I knew what people could do for themselves and I didn't put up with whiners."

"Drucilla, I think you're saying you took your frustration out on everyone except Richard. You never told Fritzie about your education did you Drucilla?"

"No!  I'm surprised that I've even told you.

I worked in the garden. My home meant more to me than anything. Amanda was a beauty. I saw to it that she had everything a young girl could want. For her sixteenth birthday she got a car, a nineteen sixty-five Mustang. I wanted her to love me. God only knows how many times I had wanted to run away, but Amanda has kept me here.

We both know that money is freedom and you can bet if I had money, I'd never live with him.

I insisted that Amanda learn to do everything and I couldn't stand to see anyone sitting around if there was work to be done. I didn't realize I was working myself to death just to keep Richard off my mind, plus causing all my family to hate me more and more.

I wanted to tell Fritzie so bad, but I just couldn't bring myself to do it. I knew he wasn't a challenge to Richard anymore because Richard knew I didn't want Fritzie's kind of life either. I had a roof over my head and I couldn't let it get away from me. Richard had turned me into a coldhearted person that just wanted to die.

I knew all the signals and I could tell when Richard was hot for a woman because he always treated me so much better, plus his entire dressing code would change shined boots and all. I tried to tell him he was sick and needed a doctor, that it wasn't normal for a man to be so sex crazy.

He would be so good, but I knew he was sick. I just didn't know what to do. No way would I let Richard's family know anything about us and I wanted his family to stay away and leave me alone.

My heart was full of pain and things would be bottled up inside me so bad that the least little thing could set me off. All hell would break loose and I would feel better for a few days. I would sit for hours writing songs, pouring my heart out on paper. I would sing to the top of my voice. It's no wonder most of the family thought I was crazy. Sometimes I even think I am.

I did ask Fritzie to let me sing one night at the club. He said sure, come over Saturday and we will practice. He told me that I could sing two songs and assured me that I would be great. The next Friday night I was ready. I started with,

**Sixteen Again**

Sixteen again, sixteen again and know what I know today.
I'd love 'em, deceive 'em, cheat 'em, and leave 'em
if I were sixteen again.

The crowd loved it. They kept hollering for more so I went on to sing.

**I Sorta Melt**

I'm a married woman and you a married man.
I sorta melt at the touch of your hand.
I know that you're married and I'm married too
But I love you, yes I love you.

Richard was so mad because I had sung at the club.

I thought maybe it was time to tell Amanda everything. I did, ending with I didn't know why I was put here on earth, but it wasn't to be run over by a man for the rest of my life. I told Amanda some of what had happened in her life, how Richard had hurt me, and how I thought Richard had killed all the love I had for him.

Dr. Skeet, evidently I still love him or his whore hopping wouldn't hurt me so bad. Don't you think?"

Dr. Skeet said, "It doesn't matter what I think. It's what you think that matters."

"I told Amanda that I didn't know what we would do for money, but I may have to divorce Richard. Amanda looked sad for days. It had broken her heart. I had never let the child know what was going on. Always before a fight with Richard, I would send Amanda to Mama Marselle's.

I had made up my mind that Richard would tell me who the Ghostly Woman was. Richard wouldn't talk about the Ghost Woman, but he said he was going to put a stop to it all. He would just leave. He said he had all of the bitching he could stand and what he did away from home was none of my business. I laughed and said to him, Richard you can't stop whoring and you don't want to party. You want that good girl back and that's too bad. She's gone for good. You made me what I am. He told me that he wanted me to grow up now and he was sorry for all he had done and said. He screamed at me, do you think I can't see? All the men go crazy when you walk into a place. How do you think I feel? I screamed right back I don't give a damn how you feel. You've got just what you wanted. Fritzie out of your way so you think I'm in a trap that I can't get out of, but you'll see. He said, go to hell, I'm leaving. He ran through the house to pack.

I got out the ironing board. He had three shirts that had to be ironed. I told him it would take a few minutes and he wasn't leaving home without them being ironed. That damned two-faced family of his couldn't say I had not taken care of him. I can still hear Richard say, I don't have time to wait. I got madder by the minute and told him that he had better not go out that door without the shirts, because when you leave I don't want you to show your face around here again. He didn't hear a word I said. He grabbed up his old duffel bag and threw it over his shoulder as he was going out the door.

I stepped to the corner of the room and picked up the rifle he had given me on our first Christmas together. The gun was loaded with sixteen bullets. When I reached the end of the porch, I told Richard if the truck moved I'd shoot his tires. Evidently he didn't think I would. That's when he was introduced to the new me in a matter of seconds. When the truck started to roll I started firing. All sixteen shots went into the back of his truck flattening both tires. Richard came out of the truck kicking and cursing. He screamed, damn you! Don't you know you could have hit my gas tank and blown this truck up? I was reloading the gun saying, yes Richard, and if you move that truck, I will hit the tank. He didn't leave that night, but now I knew I would divorce him as soon as I could, plus now he knew that I would fight back. I had said I would shoot his ass off a damn telephone pole if I had to and that I'd kill him if I found out he was whoring around again.

I had told Harriet I would kill him if I knew for sure and I was going to watch him like a hawk if he stayed. I didn't know how I could love him and hate him at the same time, but one thing was for sure the money outweighed the hate. Yet, I wasn't going to be pushed around for his money anymore.

Harriet didn't know what to think. After seeing what the shooting was about, she took herself back across the road. She had told me that the whole family was mad about the way I was treating Richard. I just shook my head.

Richard was saying my drummer boy and me had paid him back for all he had done to me. Oh hell no I thought, but some day revenge will be mine.

The hospital scene couldn't be undone. My baby couldn't be brought back and I knew nothing would ever take the hurt away until he was dead. Then, maybe I could get over what he had done to me. Months went by and we had tolerated each other without a fight.

Amanda came into my bedroom pouting telling me, Richard was going to give her a whipping. I came out of my bed like a mad mother hen ready to scratch his eyes out. I said, oh no you're not Richard. She is a young lady now and you're not to touch her again. Richard, while I'm up I'll tell you I am going to have my ears pierced today. I know you said not to, but I want them done. He was mad about Amanda and said, go ahead, do whatever it takes to make you happy. Okay, I said, I'll do that too and while I'm at it tell Chappell I said good morning."

# CHAPTER 15

"At nine o'clock the next morning, I had my ears pierced. At ten o'clock I was in the lawyer's office telling him to get me a divorce that day. I told him to have the papers ready by twelve-thirty for Richard to sign them. I picked up the phone on his desk and called Richard telling him to be at the lawyer's office at twelve thirty. Richard went to the lawyer's office and when he signed the papers, he was so mad that he didn't take time to read them and by three o'clock that afternoon, we were divorced. Richard was shocked along with many others after all of those years of hell he had put me through. It was over.

I still had to listen to my family. All the blame was put on me. No one would believe that hard working Richard had done anything wrong. It was one more slap in the face, only this time it was my own family. I didn't think I could be shocked again, but I was. The family had been much better to me in the past few years. Doc, money talks and bullshit walks you know.

The next Saturday, after the divorce, Richard took Amanda to visit his Daddy. It was a good two-hour drive for the weekend trip. Late that same night, I heard a car and then a car door shut. Amanda was coming into the house. She told me that Richard had gone home and was hurt. I asked why?

Why had the two of them come back home that night. She was supposed to stay the weekend at Papa Hallmark. Amanda told me, you should have heard the way Papa Hallmark talked to Daddy. That old man asked him what he had come there for saying that he didn't have anything for Daddy. He hurt my Daddy bad and I hate him. Daddy told him that he was only there to visit. Amanda had asked if she could stay the following week. After they had talked for a while, Papa said Dean, Butch's son, had stayed all thc week before and that Amanda couldn't stay that week because of what the neighbor's might think. Richard asked him what did he mean, why would the neighbors say anything about his own granddaughter staying there. The old man said she's not my granddaughter. That's when Richard brought Amanda home. After Amanda told me her story, I was shocked that Richard's Daddy had said what he did. Even though I knew how his whole family felt about Amanda and me, evidently Richard didn't.

I thought that they would take Richard back with open arms. He was free of **the hick**, but I guess bringing Amanda with him made the difference. Now he could have that educated, steak and potato girl they wanted him to have. I thought they would be happy. Damn that bastard! The more I thought about it, the madder I got. I told myself that it may not help anybody but me, but I'd give that old man a piece of my mind. It had never dawned on me just how much I hated his family.

I called the old man and when he answered the phone, I didn't let him get a word in edgewise. Telling him he had half-assed raised Richard and even though he was a whore hopper, he was still a credit to him. I told him that Richard didn't come there for a thing and that he didn't have anything Richard needed. Richard had as much as he did and furthermore, if he ever hurt him again, I'd come there and personally blow his brains out. Hanging up the phone, I still wasn't satisfied. I sat down and wrote a three-page business like letter telling him just how sorry his whole bunch had been to Amanda and me. He called Richard and asked him if he knew about the letter. Richard told him he did and it was all true.

Those very words won me back for him. He had told his Daddy he would marry me back if I would have him. The old man said he wouldn't know me if he met me on the street. That was okay with me. It just meant I had put a pair of shoes on him that he couldn't take off. I felt better that I had put them in their place. Now I knew I'd never be bothered with any of them.

Richard called Mama Marselle and told her that he had caused the divorce and he didn't want anyone mistreating me.

After two months and two bottles of champagne, I married Richard again. He promised that with the job he now had that he didn't have to go into any buildings and he didn't have to deal with any women for anything. Richard told me he worshipped me, and that he would never hurt me again and he was sorry for all he had done. He also told me that he had been young and stupid, that he would never sit, stand or be around any women, and that he would never touch anybody as long as he lived. He told me that he would never give me any cause to worry. Even though I raised most of my food, made my clothes, and loved to be at home taking care of my house and yard, I was scared to death not having health insurance. I knew at least with Richard, I would have security.

I had the appropriate legal document drawn up stating that if I ever wanted a divorce, Richard would give it to me without any trouble and that he would leave without a thing. The document also stated that he would give me half of the overtime he earned, because he always saved that money, the house, land, furniture and sign for me a new car every three years. I talked to Amanda and Harriet and told them that I believed Richard loved me or he wouldn't sign such a document. The only thing that worried me was my lawyer, Mr.

Williams. He advised me not to marry Richard again because he had a bad feeling about him. I remember smiling at him and saying that I would be okay and that I thought Richard had finally grown up.

Here I was, divorced for two months and didn't leave the house. In my heart I knew I should have found myself a Mafia Man to cut down everybody that had ever hurt me, because that's sure what I wanted and I made myself a promise that if Richard ever hurt me again, I would marry the Devil himself to get back at him. I would have his balls in a jar one way or another. I had talked long and hard to Richard and he had admitted that in the past he would have screwed a squirrel if he could have caught one. Now, I had done my best to forget all he had done to me and as long as he was good to me, I would stay away from the nightclubs. To reassure him, I even turned off the radios that were played all day at the house. I put all the songs and poems I had written into the fireplace. We would start over, loving no one but each other.

My dream had been to have my very own racecar, so Richard built me a beauty. Now this was happiness! It took me thirty-five years to know real happiness. I was so excited I couldn't stand myself. The round track was three quarters of a mile. I raced against seventeen men and I wasn't afraid of anything that wore shoe leather. When I crawled through that car window and into that car seat and drove out into the lineup, it was the happiest night of my life. The car wasn't fast enough. I came in seventh place and the officials said I was as good a driver as anyone on the track, even better than some of them because I wasn't afraid. I didn't dare tell the other drivers that at the age of fifteen I had run seventy-five gallons of moonshine ten miles two times a week in a matter of twelve minutes, and that was taking time to throw it out of the car. As I sat with all the engines roaring around me, I looked up through the smoke and said thanks, maybe, just maybe, there's a God after all.

In all of my years of sorrow…the hell, crying and other

women I lived through, the shame that Richard had given me, the young years of my life that had been thrown away…now looking in the mirror, I was saying thanks. I had prayed for better days.

Richard was wonderful now and it was a joyful night, but I didn't let him know that I had hurt myself. The seat belt had pulled something in my stomach. I loved my race car and I couldn't let anything be wrong. Besides, Richard and I were happy and for the first time in my life, I was happy with him and I believed he was all mine. The fear of losing him was gone.

A day or two had gone by and my stomach was still hurting and swollen. I knew then that it wasn't going to get better. At the race track a few weekends later, I couldn't make myself drive. I knew what the seat belt would do to me, so I backed out and brought my car home that night. I was sick at heart and afraid I had let Richard down, even more afraid of facing Dr. Shane after marrying Richard again. Dr. Shane had said that he would skin me if I remarried him. I think I had almost rather die than to face him, so I waited…until I had to be taken to the emergency room. Surgery was done to remove two large tumors. My racing was over. My world fell apart again.

Dr. Skeet, you know very well that doctors can't leave you alone. They always come up with more and more. My chest X-rays were so bad that in six weeks, I had to have lung surgery.

Doctor Shane's son, Doctor Bob, was my doctor this time. He told me that smoking was killing me and if I didn't stop, I would die. The young doctor scared me to death. I was going to die. I told my family and went about making plans. My health got worse, but so did my smoking.

Doctor Bob sent me to a lung specialist. Doctor Tim was a doll about five feet seven inches tall with green eyes. He was about forty-two years old, but all business. Lord, I was sick. I coughed eighteen hours a day, sometimes until I just passed out from exhaustion. Doctor Tim tried everything, but most of the medication just made me sicker. Finally, he gave me something that stopped the cough.

By this time my family and friends didn't come around. It didn't take long for me to see that people don't want you if you're sick. I was half nuts. I would scream out in my mind, **why now?** I had killed myself for a pretty home and a good family. Damn it to hell. Where are you Lord? Do you need me to point out the trash that needs to be taken off the face of this earth? Why me? I've been good all of my life. You know I'm as close to being a Saint as anyone can get. Why let me be sick?

Richard was good to me. He and Amanda waited on me hand and foot.

One look at Amanda and you could see that she was meant to be a New York model. She had promised me that one day her face would be on the cover of the best magazine and she would work hard and be the best.

Being sick all year, I had lived in my rocker with a security blanket wrapped around me. When it was cold, I didn't take my eyes off the fireplace. When the weather was warm, I still lived in my rocker. I had not left the house for over a year. I couldn't be around smoke. I couldn't be too hot or too cold, nor could I be around anyone else that was sick because my lungs were so weak.

It was the Fifteenth of December Nineteen Eighty-six and I'll never forget it. I had gotten up crying that morning. All I had on my mind was death. I called Father Andrew and he told me to come to see him. I told him that I didn't think I could come by myself and that Richard would have to bring me. Father Andrew said, oh no he doesn't. You get into your car and bring yourself. Lord only knew how nauseated I was, but I managed to get there.

I poured my heart out to him telling him that if my life was going to continue to be like this then I wanted to die now. I didn't want a long, drawn out ordeal with death. I told him that Amanda wasn't herself either. Something was wrong and my sister, Harriet, had a baby, three and one-half pounds of pure love. Harriet had let me name him Brandon. I asked Father Andrew what I could do. I didn't want to die. I wanted my family. I had to help take care of the children and to see that they went to school. I knew for sure they couldn't take care of themselves. Father Andrew listened and then he said to me, Drucilla, I want you to do just like I say, but above all, remember…you can sit in that rocker and tell yourself that you are going to die and you will, or you can stay out of it saying you don't have time to die and you'll get better. Dress yourself up every morning, make yourself go somewhere, get involved with whatever Amanda's doing, and help Harriet with the new baby. He will need you to set a better example in his life. Children have a hard time in today's world. Some just like you did years ago. Don't just sit around feeling sorry for yourself. I'm here if you need to bring Richard back to see me. Tell him I'm prepared to skin his head. One other thing, Drucilla, the family and friends that have left you alone are in worse shape than you. They didn't know how to love and care for you because they're not as strong as you. I want you to look in the mirror every morning and say, I love you today and I'm going to do something good for you today. Always love yourself best Drucilla, put yourself first. Make yourself get well.

With a promise of doing what Father Andrew had said, I went home. I was very fond of the old priest and we talked many times after that day.

Once I had confessed that having Amanda had made life harder for me and had made me make Amanda grow up fast and a matter-of-fact person. Father Andrew told me that I had done the best I knew how and Amanda would be fine but to tell her why I raised her the way I had, tell her that I was a child raising a child and that I was sorry that I had made life all work and no play. He told me she would understand that she was my life and regardless of how hard I was about her schooling, I did put her ahead of my own life.

I felt really good after talking with Father Andrew. I folded my blanket and put it away. It was amazing how much better I was, how well I looked and how much better I began to feel as time passed. I was back on my feet with a smile on my face when Amanda informed us she was going to New York.

God had never been very good to me, but He sure smiled down on Amanda. She had graduated from modeling school a month before graduating from high school. She entered a beauty contest at the Galleria. She won first place plus a contract with a New York modeling agency. A beauty and modeling consultant out of Forestdale had taken Amanda under her wings and turned a wonderful daughter into a superb model.

Her airline tickets were for Saturday morning. I was so happy that I was beside myself. My very own Amanda had a modeling job in New York. I told her that I would help her pack and get everything ready. She was going to share a room with another young girl. Amanda gave me the address and phone number where she would be staying. I talked to Amanda and told her that she had made all my hard times not seem so bad. She knew I wanted her to have the best of everything, but most of all, I wanted her to love herself. Before Amanda left, I stressed the fact that she must love herself best in the world always.

Amanda knew that I would be fine, especially since Harriet had brought the new baby home. I was thrilled to see Brandon. When Harriet came home from the hospital, she came straight to my house and handed the four and one-half pound baby boy to me saying, here's you something to live for.

For two months I lived and breathed for no one else, just for little Brandon. He was and is my heart and soul. It was as if the child had possessed me. Richard and I shopped buying him everything. I kept him in my arms singing to him or rocking him to sleep. I put him in the tub with me to have his bath when he was three months old. We had bubble bath suds up to our neck. I would hold him in my lap and soap him singing, Give me that jam between your fingers, give me that jam between you toes. We will save it for Mama's rolls.

When Amanda called home she couldn't believe I was doing so well. It was little Brandon this and little Brandon that. I told Amanda to come home so she could see him. He was seven months old now and when I give him his bath, he almost drowns me. Amanda promised me she would come home soon and that she had something important to tell me.

Amanda wanted to talk to Harriet, so I handed the phone to her. I could only hear one side of the conversation, but that was enough. I heard Harriet telling Amanda that I thought Brandon belonged to me and that I made her bring Brandon to my house every day, but that was going to stop.

Dr. Skeet, you know what I thought when I heard that? **Bull! Just bull!** Yet, I think I knew she would hurt me someday over Brandon.

Amanda was coming home for Christmas and Harriet said she would be there with Brandon. I had never been so happy. Richard let me shop until it was a shame. Amanda had been gone a year. It would be Brandon's first Christmas. The tree was piled high and Santa was bringing Brandon everything money could buy. I cooked for a week and decorated the house inside and out.

Everything was fine until I was told that all the family was mad because I was teaching Brandon to call me Mam Maw and Richard Papa. I told Richard to look over what was said because Brandon belonged to me and that the whole bunch could kiss off.

I swear Dr. Skeet, I don't know what came over me, but I was ready to take on everyone that got in my way.

I told Mama Marselle, all you did was have Harriet. It was me that raised her. I feel like Harriet belongs to me and Brandon is mine, like it or not. You all sound as if this child won't have enough love for everyone. He will. He will be the best. I'll see to that. I couldn't understand why everyone couldn't be happy. It was Christmas and no one was going to put a damper on my happiness.

On Christmas Eve Amanda called saying, Mother, I can't come home now but without fail, I'll be there for New Year's. When I hung the phone up, I screamed, **Damn this whole world.** Making myself a cup of coffee, I wouldn't even talk to Richard. I was so mad at Amanda and besides Richard had back slid on all his promises. I was sick to death as I picked up on all of his whoring signals. I told myself to smile and put it all on a shelf until after New Year's. I walked over to Richard telling him how much I loved him.

I wanted to go to the club for thc holiday parties, but Richard said no. **Hell No! No!** That was nothing new…it was always no!

Brandon and I had a good Christmas and I didn't give a damn about anyone else. The child loved me as if I was his Mom and, by damn, that would never change. Brandon would know I loved him best."

# CHAPTER 16

"Amanda didn't even call. She had rented a little blue sports car and drove up honking the horn. I ran for the yard with Brandon. I was thrilled to see Amanda, and I knew Amanda would want to see the baby. I knew Amanda would love him, but when I saw that Amanda had brought that egotistical low life Jeff, home with her, I could have died. Amanda told me she and Jeff had gotten married during Christmas.

That's when I turned around calling for Harriet to come and take Brandon. I gave the baby to Harriet telling her to take him home and I would call her later.

Dr. Skeet, you would have to know this boy to really hate him. He's the type that thinks the world exists just for his wants and needs. Amanda started dating him before she went to New York. I loved him at first, and then the real Jeff came out, which didn't take long. I ran him off and thought I had seen the last of him."

Dr. Skeet said, "You realize that you don't have to live with him don't you?"

"Yes, and she won't either if I can help it. I looked Amanda in the eyes with all the hate I could muster, I told her that I believed that she had better get a flight out that night that she knew this hair brain wasn't welcome here and I couldn't believe she had done this to me.

Amanda is as hot headed as I am, so she left on two wheels. Richard came out wanting to know what had happened and where was Amanda. I couldn't even talk to him. I felt as if my heart would burst and wished it would. I did not see how it was possible to take anymore. It was just hell and more hell. My life wasn't worth living.

Dr. Skeet, all the things that I'm telling you are true and Richard is guilty, I don't care what he may say, he is guilty!

The next day I took all of Richard's signals off the shelf and as I did, I began taking a good look at them. He had three pair of boots that he kept shined. He had asked that I buy him all new underwear and he replaced his jeans with brown Khakis. He was a walking doll when he left for work. I did buy the new underwear. His drawer was packed full.

One day half of his tee shirts, briefs and socks were gone. Richard had said someone must have come into the house and gotten them because he sure didn't take them off. I knew well it had to be him or Harriet because I swear no one but the three of us had been in that house.

After months of the same old thing, I told him not to worry about me and that if he wanted someone else, go to it and not to put me through what he had before. Richard would swear that he wasn't doing anything. I wanted to believe him, but things started to happen.

Harriet was in the hospital for fourteen days and Richard refused to go to see about her on his lunch hour, which was very unusual because he had always gone to spend that hour with anyone he knew that was in the hospital. Besides, he was supposed to love Harriet. I asked him every night for fourteen nights if he had gone to see her just to hear him say no. I asked him to go because he knew I couldn't. I had to take care of Brandon. Richard would just say he didn't want to. No, he was with his honey pot. I was crushed. I couldn't believe he was doing this to me again. I was worried to death about Harriet because she was real sick.

I was even more shocked when I found the note on the table that I had put into Richard's lunch. When I asked why he took it out, he told me that he had read it and didn't see any need in leaving it in there. He told me that if it was going to make me mad then not to put any more notes in his lunch.

It was a week or so later when Richard told me not to call him at work anymore because his boss said he wasn't going to give out messages to the husbands. I asked him to tell me why.

I didn't call the plant, besides I already knew why. Richard knew if I called and he didn't answer his radio, the boss would go hunting him and he was afraid of being found. We had begun to fight about all this and Richard said for me to ask the boss. When I asked him, he said he didn't tell Richard that and he didn't know why he would say such a thing. Weeks later Richard took me to the plant and told his boss that he did say it right in front of me.

Chicken bosses were born everyday and this retard was new born. I knew he was full of it when he said he knew where his men were every minute of the day. That was a laugh because he didn't know his butt from a hole in the ground. What more can I say…he was a coward.

I was so lonesome and hurt. I didn't have a soul and Richard wouldn't even take me to the mall to shop. Week after week, I sat alone. Harriet and all the other family were mad because of the way I had done Amanda. I couldn't help that, I wouldn't give in I knew that someday Amanda would wake up and come to her senses. I was worried about myself. I was too worried to be worried about Amanda or anyone. That's why I'm here in this mess. I know what Richard is doing. He is pushing me into a depression so I will take my life. He has me right where he wants me. I would never tell anyone about the mess that I'm in again and he is doing everything he can to hurt me.

Even though he would take me to the gulf for a weekend, he would mess up every picture he took of me while we were there and then laugh, shrug his shoulders and tell me that he just wasn't a picture taker.

Months went by. Harriet had stopped me from seeing Brandon and it was killing me."

Dr. Skeet asked, "Why did Harriet stop you from seeing Brandon?"

"I asked her if she had taken the food and this was the fight of all fights. She stormed out of the house swearing that she wouldn't let me see Brandon again. Sure enough, she didn't and for a year the wench made the child lie down in the car seat so I couldn't see him when they passed my house.

No one knows how hard it was having Brandon living across the road from me and not be able to share his life. Harriet was so cold and cruel and I knew that little Brandon didn't understand what was going on and he was surely as hurt as I. Can you believe that she would make the child lie down in the seat of the car when they passed my house so that I wouldn't see him? He was also made to play in his back yard.

As usual days turned into weeks and weeks into months. Months and months had passed and I was half crazy, but I was not going to let Brandon think that I didn't love him.

Brandon's birthday was coming and I was so sad that I could have died. I thought and thought. What could I do to let him know that I loved him and that I would never stop loving him? Then I had a brainstorm!

I went to the lumberyard and got a four by eight sheet of plywood, two pieces of two by fours and staples for a staple gun. This was about three days after Thanksgiving. I worked pulling that plywood over the fence. I nailed the two by fours onto the plywood for legs and turned it over and stapled a set of large Christmas lights around the plywood. With spray paint I wrote Happy Birthday and Merry, Merry Christmas Baby I love you best. I stood it up against the fence facing Brandon's house. I lit it up at dark every night and left it on until midnight.

I had shopped for his Christmas just like I had for the past seven years. I can't say what came over me, but the week before Christmas I hated Harriet so bad that I just wanted to bash her face in. I was worried to death about Brandon. Harriet is an ill-humored woman, a violent woman. It tears me all to pieces when I hear her screaming at Brandon. I knew she was stupid, but I hoped and prayed that she wouldn't make me turn into a savage and hurt her.

By the time school turned out for the Christmas holidays, I had made up my mind that I would talk to Brandon. So I watched and waited for her to drive around the road and I ran out of the house right in front of her car. I told her that she was going to stop hurting Brandon and if she didn't I was prepared to take her to Court. I thought about this many times, but I was afraid the Court would take him away until they could make a decision. Believe me, it's damned if you do and damned if you don't. Anyway, talking to her worked. She told me many things that Percy had said about me, lies, but knowing Harriet I didn't know whether to believe half of what she said.

I now had to find out what was going on with Richard. Either I was going crazy or Richard had another slut. We had fought every night since Harriet was in the hospital. It was February and one day he came in with an odor on his face that smelled like dead fish. Turning my head as he bent down to kiss me, I told him to go wash his face. His reply was that he hoped the other men didn't smell him. He continued to say that the smell was from the paper towels that he was using at work. I got my hand on some of the very same paper towels that he was using and it doesn't matter what you did with those paper towels, they did not smell like that. I knew it must be that nasty fat ass slut and Richard screamed back at me that the bitch wasn't fat and that she was all muscle.

I had it all figured out. He was spending his time with that slut at the garage where all the telephone trucks were repaired. That's why he had stopped using sugar and cream in his coffee. It would be hard to keep the goodies at that place. When

Richard lied about knowing where the garage was, I knew I was right. If he was eating her up in a damn telephone truck, there would be no place to wash his face.

Just like his first slut. It was one thing after another as if I didn't have good sense. I didn't know what to do. He was hurting me with all the lies. He had been giving the Boy Scouts twenty five dollars a month and just like the coffee without sugar and cream, I didn't know about it.

I hadn't been getting up with Richard in the mornings until I found out that my home canned food had disappeared.

Richard had always emptied the ice in an ice bucket for me, but one morning I got up and there he was, taking the ice on the back porch. He was making sure I didn't wake up and find him taking my food for his slut. I knew I should make him leave, but I had to know who the slut was. I talked and talked. I followed him to and from work and caught him in one lie after another.

Let me tell you about my books! Richard said he didn't take them either, but when books were as thick as those, you couldn't take one out and not help but see they were gone. I tell you, he was trying to drive me crazy and he wanted me to believe Harriet or someone else was doing these things so that I wouldn't let anyone come into the house. He knew I would just get more depressed. There were only one or two other people in my home and I never left, so how did the house key end up in my desk drawer.

I had come in from the mailbox one day and opened the desk drawer to find and old house key lying on the white envelopes. Now, I knew darn well that Richard had put that key in the drawer just to blame it on Harriet. I knew him like a book. He was a snake. I remembered well about the sex, the ice, don't call the plant, and don't put notes in his lunch. Hell, I remembered it all. I knew he was trying to put the blame off on Harriet, but at the same time he was telling me not to plan anything for Friday's because his boss would make him work.

It was pitiful. I was in prison and I had been so naïve that he had just told me anything and I had let it go as if I were a zombie. I couldn't believe he was doing this to me again. Worry had taken me over. I was sick at heart and the worse sick a person can be. Richard would swear that he loved me and that I was wrong about it all. I would ask, Richard what about my books. My family didn't take my books out of this house.

I tell you Dr. Skeet, you may not believe this, but half the towels and washcloths plus a bath mat disappeared. Of course, Richard didn't take them either. I knew he took them. I was looking and listening to anything and everything.

When Richard started talking about a finance company, I asked him how many girls did they have working for them. He said not a one, just an old man in a little cubby hole.

The next day I called the **cubby hole** to find a sweet little Lisa and another lie for Richard. How many more lies did I need before I would know the truth?

One day Richard came in telling me to give him a check and he would buy a new pair of shoes. What a laugh. When the bank statement came, I looked for the check he had asked for to buy the shoes. There was no check for the shoes. The shoes were old and worn, even the sack that he had the shoes in was old and worn. A fool could see the shoes had been worn a lot. I knew the shoes had been used to change from his boots when he met his slut for lunch. I couldn't prove a thing, but one thing was for sure, Richard didn't lose a dime, yet money was missing every payday and he was saying that he didn't know what happened to it. He guessed I spent it.

I tell you Dr. Skeet I hate him for whore hopping, but mostly for lying about it, the same Richard just a rerun of yesteryears.

Richard would call me from work. I would answer the phone just to hear Richard say, I've got to go. I would bury my head in my hands and cry. He would call several times a day and do the same thing. I knew he was just trying to make me more depressed. I had told him time and again that if I could prove he was fooling around on me that I would sue them both. I knew I just needed to prove it to my lawyer and others.

Finally, at the end of February, a woman called and told me she wanted Richard and all Richard felt for me was pity. He wanted out but he felt sorry for me. I knew it was true, but I told her to come to our home at five-thirty and tell me in front of Richard and I would put his butt out the door and that no one was making him come back to this house every night. More calls came. Then a white car started coming by the house. I had seen that car or cars just like it at the Telephone Company. It was lunchtime and the slut had come down to see where Richard lived. I went to the Telephone Company garage and there were the cars the very same ones.

I made up my mind to sell quilts and that way I could advertise them at the Telephone Company. I worked as fast as I could. I told Richard the papers for advertising the sale of my quilts were ready to put on the bulletin board and he would have to take me to the company building. He didn't say a word. He just went with me and tacked up the advertisement for the quilts. He had said he didn't ever go in or around those buildings. But when I insisted on going in the front, he began to look frightened. The bulletin boards were at the elevator and when a lady walked up, Richard looked at her scared to death. I knew he was afraid someone was going to see him with me. That was the purpose of taking him there. I had been told that Richard lied about going in those buildings, but I couldn't imagine him having a hussy at each of those places. It was only a few days later that I was told all the advertisements had been taken down. I didn't get the first call.

One other thing that I couldn't understand was the experience with the C.B. radio. One day after coming home from work he said he needed to go back to the plant to pick something up. Without a word I walked out with him and got into the truck. This was in his personal truck. Richard and I were going down the road and the C.B. made a noise. Richard grabbed it up saying Wade and then hung it up and cut it off.

Wade is his Daddy's name. I asked what in the world that was all about and he said, they asked if we knew a truck driver, so I said Wade. I told him that he was full of it and that no one had said that at all and why would he say a word. Wade had been retired for years. I asked him why he lied because he knew darn well it was his way of giving a message to someone. I said for him to take the darn C.B. out of that truck and I never wanted to see it again. That night he took the C.B. out and put it up. I couldn't understand it.

Why was he doing things to please me, yet torment me and all at the same time?"

"Drucilla, only Richard can answer that."

"The slut didn't call back and things died down some, but one day on my way to the beauty shop, I stopped at the mailbox and took out a plain white envelope with no writing on it. Walking to the car, I opened it to find a tape of sad songs. Thinking one of the family, had given it to me I put it in the tape player. After returning home, I asked who had given it to me and no one had.

Dr. Skeet, I hope you can remember all this. Better yet, I hope you can come up with the guilty party.

Anyway, Richard had been bad to talk in his sleep and one night he said what sounded like Fran. The next day I asked Richard who she was. He was at work at the time and he said he didn't know what I was talking about. That night at the dinner table he said he had remembered and that he had trouble on Fran's line, so to be able to find the trouble he talked to her so he could hear the noise on her phone. He had asked her if she was going out that weekend and just bull crap to keep her on the line long enough to clear the trouble. I knew better, but I listened. I asked was she black or white. Richard said, Hell, he didn't know she was on the other end of the phone line. I asked him how he knew her name and he said it was on her desk, but he had already told me he had only talked to her on the phone that one time and now he knew her name was Frances Williams and he had been in her office. More lies. Every time I got him to talking, he would get all mixed up and catch his, own self in a lie. I would get on his butt hot and heavy telling him to get out and that I couldn't live with him if he didn't tell me the truth. He wouldn't make a move to leave or to answer my questions.

Then children started to call saying to tell Richard to come to see them and asking if Richard were home. I would tell them no, but he would be home at five-thirty. Once a little boy said, when he gets there, put him up your ass and pull him out your nose. It was past time to put a stop to it all. I insisted that Richard give me the big boss's telephone number. The calls stopped.

After a week or so, I began to feel sick every morning as if I were pregnant. I would be so nauseated and dizzy that I couldn't stand up. Richard didn't say a word. He just went about living as if I didn't exist, but he was making my coffee every morning. He would have it ready for me to drink before he got me out of bed.

Now Dr. Skeet, this is when it dawned on me that Richard was poisoning my coffee. I started leaving the coffee and pouring it out after he had gone to work. I began to get better, but I was still dizzy.

Richard had left me crying two or three mornings. I begged him to stay home and take care of me, to help me find out what was wrong. I wanted him to take me to the doctor. He didn't give a damn! He would just say, yes, it's all happening, but not for the reasons you think. I would ask him what were the reasons and he would always come back with, I don't know because I don't have anything to do with it.

By this time I was so sick that I would have to hold on to something just to get around the kitchen even though I took just one drink of the coffee. Then, there it was. The little green pellet…rat poison! The little tiny pieces were lying beside the coffee maker. I was in a daze and went to find the container. I found it…one-fourth empty! He had been putting it in my coffee. He was trying to kill me. I didn't know what to do.

Percy had told me I was crazy and that the change of life was making me nuts. I was afraid the family would laugh at me. I wouldn't drink anything that Richard gave me. I told him that I knew what he was doing, but it wasn't going to work.

After my nerves calmed down, I drank many glasses of water trying to get my system cleaned out. I started eating better and wouldn't touch anything that Richard prepared. After I got to feeling better, I called Dr. Shane and asked him if my estrogen was strong enough. I told him how sick I was, but I didn't want to tell him or anyone what I was thinking about Richard. He had me come in for some tests telling me that I was getting enough estrogen.

He sent me to the lab for blood tests and other tests. The test results came back, but he couldn't find anything wrong with me.

You see Dr. Skeet I didn't tell him what to look for.

On my way out I stopped to see Dr. Tim, my lung specialist. I told him everything, including my thoughts about Richard and the poison. I knew he would help me plus keep his mouth shut. He tried to make me put Richard out, but just like before, I had to know why and who.

Richard had even broken down and cried saying he didn't know anything about what was happening. I would just shake my head. His tears came too easy and his lies came fast and with a straight face.

I knew I must stay busy. I had friends in for lunch and I went shopping. I had to get suicide off my mind. I wasn't going to let him kill me and I wasn't going to take my life for him. I deserved to live and be happy just as much as anyone.

Dr. Tim had opened my eyes. He told me, girl, can't you see that if you die, Richard won't have to give up all he's worked for all these years? If you divorce him, he will lose it all, but he will be in fine shape if you die one way or another. What woman would want him if he has to give up everything? You had better put his ass out before he kills you. Dr. Tim has taken my file out and wrote on the front of it to be sure to perform an autopsy if anything should happen to me. It was for sure Richard wouldn't get away with murdering me."

# CHAPTER 17

"When Richard came home, I started asking questions and he got good and mad. I asked him why he called me three and four times a day. He said that it was to help clear trouble off the telephone lines. I said, **Bullshit!** You have new equipment and other ways to do that. He screamed, yes I do, but all the phones ringing gave her a headache. That was a slip of the tongue. I said, yes, I'm sure it was because where I come from a slip of the tongue is something we didn't mean to say. I asked him how he knew it gave her a headache and why in the Hell did he care. The bitch was getting paid to do her job.

He's just a damn whore hopper and he's right back where he used to be, not giving a damn how much I suffer, just as long as his dick gets satisfied.

Richard didn't even speak a word. I screamed out at him, I know Richard, that dick of yours has a mind of its own.

Dr. Skeet, you see, now he was making me think this woman worked on the test board, but it looks as if there was more than one.

I can remember when Richard told me that I didn't make

tea right and that I was only good for once a week. When Brandon would come to the house, I would have to call Richard down for trying to hurt him. I knew he didn't love Brandon. He had his new puss's kids to love. I told myself that hurting me was one thing, but if he hurts Brandon, I'll kill him. I would kill him for sure.

It's go to jail, go to hell, or put him out. I tell you Dr. Skeet, every time one thing happens all of it comes flashing before my eyes.

I would work some on my house and try to decide what to do about Richard. Dr. Tim had said that with the evidence that I had I could have him hospitalized or go to the law, but I had better do one or the other before I go to my grave. I had to think about it.

I took out the phone book and found a bricklayer. I hired him and he was working on a flowerbed in the front yard. I had a guest for lunch and we had just sat down at the table when I had to answer the doorbell.

The bricklayer asked me if I knew the woman standing at the end of the sidewalk. I said no and asked where she came from. He said he didn't know that she had just walked out of the woods. I stepped to the end of the porch and she looked like the one in the white car that had driven past my house on two different days between twelve and one o'clock. I asked her if she was lost and the girl said no. Then I asked, what are you doing down this road, it's a dead end and where did you come from? She told me she came from the projects.

The girl was about five feet, six inches tall and weighed about one hundred sixty pounds. She was a big person with shorts up to her butt and wearing white tennis shoes. Her dark hair was to her shoulders, curly as Hell and looked wet as if she had just washed it and picked it out with a comb.

I told her there weren't any projects around there within walking distance unless she was talking about the Indian Creek apartments. She said, no. She asked me if I had any children and I told her no. Then she told me that I had a pretty house and walked out to the road and left.

I asked the bricklayer what did she say to him. He said she just ask for a light, but he never did see a cigarette. He told her he didn't have one, but the lady in the house may have one. The girl told him she didn't want to see the lady in the house.

I shrugged my shoulders and went back to my guest. It was just a minute or two when the white car came flying in the driveway and back out again. I caught just a glimpse of the driver and I knew it was the same girl. It didn't dawn on me that the girl may have been there to do harm to me. I remembered what Richard had said about the garage girl being big and strong and that someone had taken pictures of them talking, once in the parking lot. He said that he didn't give a damn to let them take pictures. When I told Richard about the girl, I also told him I would shoot any of his honey pots that tried to hurt me and that he had better tell her to stay away from my house.

Another thing I remember is Richard brought home a watch saying that one of the men at work gave it to him. Now you know that is pure bull crap!

He brought home some plastic letters that spelled his name and a shoulder patch to put on his jacket. I knew these little things were from this slut's kids because these things were childish.

Now, I'm here for you to help me get the truth out of him. So what are we going to do?"

"Drucilla, just keep talking and let me listen and think."

"Richard had forgotten that he told me about how some of the men were taking turns with the garage girl and how he got a kick out of her telling him and Sam about Bones being white as a sheet when she got through with him. How Bones' dream was to do it dog style. I believe the garage girl was fulfilling all the son-of-a-bitch's dreams. One thing was for sure, whoever Richard's woman was, she had to be hungry to eat another woman's home canned food and half of mine disappeared and with the kids calling me and him paying money out to the Boy

Scouts. She had kids and Richard must be playing with her kids because he sure as Hell wasn't playing with Brandon like he had been.

I told Richard if I could find this slut and her bastards, I would kill his ass. After what he had put me through, there wasn't a Judge in the world that would punish me for getting rid of his sorry ass.

You can see Dr. Skeet I've been half crazy. I didn't know what to do and it didn't matter what I said or what happened, Richard would not leave."

"Drucilla, let me set you straight right now. You wouldn't get off on my testimony because you are not crazy."

"Darn what am I to do. Three brothers and two sisters I have given to, done for and worked myself to death to make life better for them, yet here I am…alone.

At the beauty shop the girls would laugh and joke about my sisters coming in and telling everyone that the change of life had made me sick and that I needed to be prayed for because I had bad problems. The joke was on the family and Richard because everyone knew that I was the best. They knew there wasn't anything wrong with me except I was terribly unhappy. Richard had hurt me bad.

I remember on Mother's Day in Nineteen Eighty-four. I'm going back now, I had told Richard not to get me anything. I wanted to forget about Amanda, but oh no! Here he comes in with a Mother's Day poem book. One more bad fight. I told him the only way I would believe him would be for him to put me up a billboard with our picture on it on the side of the road going into town advertising my quilts. It would sure tell everyone that he was married to me. Richard screamed, **hell no!** It's a waste of money. Hell no! Richard doesn't want anyone to see that he was happy with a wife. He took me in his arms and told me how much he loved me and he would do anything to keep me and that I was all he had. **Bullshit! Just more bullshit.** Too much has happened. I will never believe him.

I will never love Harriet after she has left me to deal with this all alone and saying that all of this mess was my fault and to take care of myself. Yes, Hell! Old ironsides can make it. No one wants to be involved. All the cowards looked suspicious. One darn thing was for sure, somebody had done all these things and if Richard didn't, then who did?

I knew for sure Richard had lied about seven things so far. I was watching and listening for any clue I might pick up.

The calls were unbearable. The more I thought about Harriet, the more I wanted to believe Richard. He had said the smell on his face was the towels and that the company gave them the towels to wipe their faces. I didn't believe it. That was in February and he wouldn't be wiping his face. It was a damn whore smell and no matter how hard I tried to believe different, proving it or not, he was the one that had done it all.

It was in May on a Sunday afternoon after Richard and I had washed my car, inside and out. That night Richard told me, go on and cry, ring your hands and get bent out of shape. Let the phone calls do this to you. Believe all this instead of what I say. I said, Richard you are slowly killing me. You married me back with a pack of lies and you have always had to have women and more women. I don't want you anymore. All I want is to know the names of these women.

I had made up my mind to have him investigated. The investigator told me it was impossible to get information from the telephone people. They were all afraid of being fired. They won't talk against each other, but he would do his best. The company teaches their people that a lie isn't a lie unless you can prove it's a lie. I know that because Richard has said it many times. I was sick of hearing, I'll tell you seven different ways before I'll lie to you baby. The investigator said Richard was in and out of the phone buildings downtown hopping from one place to another.

Oh. Damn him, I said, with ten operators flashing before my eyes. Look what I have been through just to live and now to worry about AIDS."

# CHAPTER 18

"Amanda came flying in the door one day. Mother, why haven't you answered my letters and why wouldn't you take my calls? I stood my ground saying I told her not to come back as long as she was with that son-of-a-bitch. I didn't raise her to live like that and I wouldn't see her live with him. Amanda was saying, Mama, I divorced him a month ago, but I couldn't tell you. Now listen to me Mama, I understand why Daddy wouldn't tell you who the witch is. I feel sorry for Daddy. You can't see how really mean you are. You scare the hell out of people. When you say you'll do something, you do it. Whatever comes to your mind comes out your mouth. You don't care who it hurts.

I spoke up saying, the best thing you can do little girl is load'em up and move'em out. Don't come in here telling me how to take care or your Daddy. If he didn't lie and whore hop, he wouldn't have to fear me. Besides, why should anybody fear me? I don't have a private little graveyard to bury the people I kill. He could tell what part he did play in all this and then I could deal with that brain dead family of mine. I told

Amanda to go back to New York. I didn't want her in this. I hadn't seen Brandon in a year and I hated them all. I would survive somehow, I always had.

Just knowing she was away from that hair brain low life made me feel better. I didn't have to worry about her.

I asked what was it you said about me one time Amanda? My Mom tells everyone…love yourself, know who you are, what you are, be as good as you can everyday and be proud that you are good. Amanda hugged me saying, you are a good Mom. You are a beautiful peacock surrounded by a bunch of turkeys. I began to cry telling Amanda that I loved her. Amanda only stayed a week, but it was good for me.

Mr. Cork came by one day. What a dear friend. He could talk to me about most everything. Today he said I know you love your place, but you need to move from here. You'll never be happy. I told Mr. Cork that I would never give up my house that it wasn't given to me and I had worked like Hell for what I had and besides, I loved my kitchen. I told him that I could never thank him enough and I never went into my kitchen without thinking of him.

As we sat talking, I thought how beautiful my kitchen was. Half country and half the most up-to-date money could buy. The whole house was like turning the pages of a magazine. The rooms sparkled with brass and lead crystal. I had done my decorating and the accessories were perfect, right down to the elegant Fantasia dinnerware collection I had for my own use.

I'm here to stay Mr. Cork. I'll never let them run me off. Mr. Cork is a good person and he always tells me when he leaves, call if you need me.

I sat looking around after Mr. Cork left. I counted five chandeliers. The families living around me ask why I want those things living in the woods. I just smile and say, I don't live in the woods, I live in this house and they're for me.

Dr. Skeet, I'm not young anymore, but I am wise. I

can't let them get the best of me. I love life and I'll get even with them so help me God.

I went to the Sheriff's office last week and came out mad as hell. They said I had to have proof, but I tell you someone is going to pay for what has been done to me.

I loved Richard, but he couldn't keep his pants up. Why did I have to end up with him? And I do ask myself why I can't leave it alone. He's good in all other ways. I don't think he will try to harm me again. He knows now the Sheriff would get his butt. I have to get proof and that's underway. Just any day now the truth will come out. Did Richard try to kill me? I knew in my heart he did. This time he must have found a woman he couldn't live without, one that he would kill me for.

I had spent an hour and forty-five minutes at the Sheriff's office. I told them everything. I told the Sheriff that I must stress the fact that I feared for my life, that either someone was trying to drive me crazy or drive me into suicide. I answered their questions and went over everything.

The Sheriff was in his late fifties and was well versed in his work. He was a nice man, five feet eleven inches tall and weighing one hundred seventy-five pounds with blond, wavy hair and deep blue eyes.

He talked to me for a long time. He told me that in today's world people are jealous of what each other have and that your close friends will cause trouble if they're jealous over your cars or jewelry. Sometimes things can go too far and people can get hurt just like you are now. By the time I got through talking about Richard, I was nervous and mad. The Sheriff said for me not to talk to anyone about the problem that they were as close as the phone.

Dr. Skeet, it was too late to tell me that because I had already told everyone and I was as nervous as a cocked gun all day.

I almost never went to sleep that night and when I did, it was one dream after another. Once I woke up because the dreams were so bad. I was afraid to go back to sleep. I had dreamed that Richard was doing the calling and that he would call just to see if I was there and hang up as soon as I answered. Then he would call saying, hello, I've got to go and hang up before I had a chance to say a word. Other times he would laugh and say, it's me, it's me and hang up. Finally, I was asleep, but this time I had a nightmare. This time he was in the woods, where he had taken me once before to see about some firewood. At least that's what he told me, but I was afraid he had taken me there to kill me. In the dream I could see his truck and hear the noise as I walked closer and closer. There they were…naked…

His honey pot was on top of him and Richard was holding her buttocks jogging her up and down as fast as he could and his grunting got louder and louder.

When I awoke the next morning, I hated him. I begged him to please stay home and take me somewhere, just to please get me away from that place that I couldn't take anymore. Richard screamed at me, **no! no! no!** Why can't you leave me alone? I have to go to work. That same day this woman called and laughed into the phone. It always happened the very next day after a nightmare. No one but Richard knew how bad the dreams were or even about the dreams. He knew she was calling.

I didn't tell Richard about my eight o'clock call from Phillip Jimez, the detective from the Sheriff's office, to meet him at three o'clock. When I met Phillip, he automatically called me Drucilla. He was a young and very handsome man about five feet nine inches tall, sandy hair and beautiful teeth. He said that he was really worried about me, especially after I told him that I was so upset about the phone calls that I had told Richard that I wished I were dead and I needed to blow my brains out and get out of it all. I told Phillip that I was still in the bed crying and Richard started to leave for work, he reached up to the top of the dresser and took down a Three Fifty-seven Magnum, cocked the hammer and laid it back down as if to say…here it is, go ahead!

Phillip said he didn't want to see any harm come to me and that he would see to it that the calls would stop he only wished I had come to him months ago. He then made a list of all the things that had happened and all the people I thought may have a grudge against me. He wanted to see the layout of my house and he had put a tap on my telephone line. I knew what to do.

I told Richard and he said, now maybe you'll catch the bastards. I thought, yes, just maybe it would have been you if I hadn't told you about the tap. I knew I shouldn't have told him, of all people, not Richard! Phillip sat at the table and went over everything with me.

I had hope for the first time. I was sick of all this. Where was Francis Williams? Just in his mind. Did he steal my food, my books and my towels? Were he and his woman doing the calling? Did she leave her panties in his truck and the cassette tape in our mailbox? Why did he lie about the shoes he bought? Why did he stop me from putting love notes in his lunch? Why did he call and say hello and good-bye in the same breath? Why did he answer the C.B. and say his name was Wade? Why did he make remarks about being a, has been? Where is the garage girl that he said he couldn't find? Who were the girls in the white car? Who was the bitch that came to the house asking questions? Why did he lie about the finance company? There is no way he will ever convince me that smell on his face wasn't pure skunk puss.

Phillip joked with me a little after seeing how mad I got from just talking about it all, but I wasn't in a joking mood. I told him to take me seriously. He did. Much more than I realized. He made me promise to call him every other day and always when I was going off.

We talked some about my family and friends. I told Phillip all about Amanda and Jeff. I knew I was on Jeff's list. I told him that for the life of me I didn't know why Percy had lied the way he did and that when Harriet told the family that I had stopped at the Sheriff's office, Gertrude had gotten mad as hell for some reason saying it was family business and I shouldn't have gone to see them at all. I had told Harriet to be sure and tell them that someone was going to pay for what has happened to me.

Before Phillip left he told me that he had talked to my Dr. Shane and he said that you were fine and dandy and sweet as candy and that he loved you and we better not let anything happen to you. You have some good friends that think the world of you. We want you to stay calm so you can help us, but whatever you do, don't leave this house without calling me.

The first week the tap was on the phone there were no calls. Phillip said to give them time that the calls would start back. All this may have been done to separate you and Richard, but don't let your guard down. After what has already been done to you and knowing it didn't separate you and Richard, you can believe their tricks will get worse.

Phillip told me to get out and about with Richard and make everyone think I was happy. If it wasn't Richard making the calls, then maybe they would keep on and they would catch them.

Dr. Skeet, I tell you, it was Richard, but anyway….

Phillip said that he would be there to listen and he wanted me to tell him more, hoping he could eliminate one or two.

I talked and talked and finally getting around to Percy. I didn't have the slightest idea that Percy resented me until then. I believe it was because of his new wife. The girl was so jealous of Richard's money that she could tell you how many hours of overtime he worked each week.

I think it was July. Richard and Percy had been working on the house all day and Percy had heard me giving Richard hell. So jokingly, he asked, what's going on boy? She catch you with you pants down? Richard just ignored the question. Everyone knew I was mad as hell because I was ranting and raving. I came out in the yard and asked Percy if he was the one who threw the soda pop bottle with the cigarette pack in it into the back of Richard's camper shell. Percy said, what if I did? He went on to tell me that if he saw Richard in the bed with a lover, he'd swear Richard had stumbled over something and fell in it. Percy shouted at me that I must be going crazy or through the change of life like Mama Marselle did. Then he told me to get in the house and keep my mouth shut.

Percy had been talking bad to me for sometime now. I was taking it all in and knew I would have to talk to Percy when no one was around. I asked him to find time to talk to me. The next Saturday he came over to my house and I told him about all the things and begged him to help me saying that there was more to this than meets the eye. I wasn't prepared for what he said to me and couldn't imagine a brother hurting me so bad. Percy told me I was just getting paid back for getting rid of my first husband and all the whoring around that I had done.

That just floored me, but I just let him talk. Then it made me mad and I wanted to see just how far he would go. After he raked me over the coals, he left with that satisfied smile on his face. I'm sure he felt like a big boy. I had good reason to get rid of that convict and sure as hell I have never messed with anyone. A whore gets paid, and I didn't have any money. I couldn't get Percy off my mind. How could he have the guts to talk to me this way? Even if he didn't love me, he should have respected me. Hearing him say, you're sick, you're damn sick was enough to make me cringe.

I remember thinking after he left, well, old boy, I have good sense now because I just had a rude awakening. I had been a whore in his eyes, but he didn't mind taking all my good deeds. I had helped him pay for a burial, paid many furniture notes, given his new wife a wedding shower and paid for a beautiful wedding, never asking a dime because I loved him. I wanted him to be happy.

When he came to me and said the trailer he was trying to finance didn't go through, I said I would take care of it. I did and two days later a big three, bedroom trailer was delivered. I had never kept track of the money I had let him have because I loved him and it didn't matter. I thought he would always be there if I needed him. I felt sorry for Percy now he had cut off his nose to spite his face.

Months went by and I didn't speak to him and he didn't bother to come back. Then one day Harriet told me that Percy had told her something I was supposed to have said about Brandon. I couldn't believe my ears. I knew Percy was a complete idiot, but I couldn't believe he would tell such a lie. Everyone knew Brandon was my heart and soul. He kept me sane in this insane world. I picked up the phone with my heart pounding and dialed Percy's number. When he answered, I asked him if he had told Harriet that I had said I would give up Brandon only if I could get Amanda to come back home.

Dr. Skeet, this was before Amanda went to New York."

"You haven't said too much about Amanda, Drucilla. I take it she hurt you and left home."

"Yes, Jeff talked her into getting an apartment of her own, but that's another story.

Percy said that he sure as hell did tell Harriet and I asked him what made him tell an ungodly lie like that. I asked him how could he lie on me and hurt me so bad. I had always been good to him. Why was he doing me this way? He knew I didn't say anything like that and that I would give up everybody on the face of this earth before I'd give Brandon up. I let Percy know that it was his fault that Harriet had kept Brandon away from me and I would get him back and let him know he just lost the best friend he would ever have. I won't ever get over his lies or what he has said to me. I feel sorry for Percy and will pity him forever."

"Drucilla, would you get back at him if you could?"

"You're damn right I would!"

"I note hostility Drucilla. I have listened to your every word. What I hear is someone that you have loved doesn't love you back. I see a very hurt and bitter person. You are harming yourself, not anyone else. I can see it's revenge you want. We could talk until the cows come home and it wouldn't help you. You have to forgive these people and get on with your life."

"Listen Mr.! I think you're full of **bullshit**. I don't think you have heard a word I have said. We have talked about people that have actually tried to get rid of me and you want me to **forget!!** I know one thing, there are people that are crazy and know it, you're crazy and don't know it, if you think I'm going to forgive and let this bunch get by with what they have done to me!!"

"But Drucilla, what about God getting revenge? Do you believe in God? You don't have to answer these questions if you had rather not, but it would help me to understand you better."

"Now, Dr. Skeet, how many people are there that can answer that question with an honest heart? I can say this I have taken time to smell the roses. I've watched the seasons come and go and I've watched new life enter this world and old life leave it. I love scientist, but for sure I'm a realist. The only way I can answer you is to say if He does exist He must have had so many children in Nineteen Forty-four that He forgot about me. I was put into the Devil's Day Care Center where I was brought up half naked, nasty, snotty nose, cold and hungry.

So, being in this situation for the first twenty-two years of my life didn't help me to believe there's someone that can snap their finger and turn you from rags to riches. If there is a God, then why are some of the most precious people suffering the most? Just take a walk through Children's Hospital or visit the nursing homes. Take a look at our babies dying and the old folks that are helpless and being mistreated, and then take a walk back through the forty-three years of my life. Dr. Skeet, I have been the best and I did believe at one time.

Take for instance after I married Richard back, then in a matter of months that was shot to hell. So while you are judging me, remember I am a realist. But to answer your question, I believe that when we get old enough to fend for ourselves, we make our own Heaven and hell right here under our feet. I believe if there had been a God, He wouldn't have let me suffer so badly."

"But Drucilla!"

"**No!** Dr. Skeet, don't say it. We both know its money.

Money is freedom and those that have it are in Heaven and just don't know it. The one's that don't have it suffer in hell.

What I would like is for someone to tell me what's right about us suffering here on earth for years and more years, mentally and physically. Children and the old people and lots of people in between are going hungry to pay their tithes while suffering and praying their hearts out hoping for a better place, hoping their soul is going to a fine golden place where there will be only happiness. I'm no expert Dr. Skeet, but we have preachers on television healing the sick. I wish I could walk through the Children's Ward watching them heal the little children and even though I know the old must die, I'd like for them to have a little peace before they go. I'm afraid you will have to conjure up Job from the Bible and talk to him about God, because I wasn't sent to the land of milk and honey. Remember, I was sent to the Devil's Day Care Center and I tell you it has a high fence. You can have the best behavior, but without money you will not have freedom.

Dr. Skeet, if there is a God, I wish He would take the helpless to Heaven, make the children well, and send the sorry to hell. He could do this instead of letting men at the rate of ten thousand a year be turned into Pussies and women being turned into men, just let them disintegrate and then let me win the biggest lottery so I can buy some land build me a little world of my own. I'll tell you **THEN** I would believe. I would be in Heaven. It's hard to believe when I have had forty-three years of bruises and know in my heart that I have been the best person I could be. I will tell you that I never met a true Christian and I know I'll never be one because I want revenge so bad for the deceit that has been dished out to me. So, really you could say, it doesn't make a damn if there is a God or not and if so, just maybe I'll have time to get forgiveness when I'm through.

Mama Marselle didn't believe me either. I had gone to see Mama Marselle and asked her why she didn't believe me and that she knew Percy and Harriet had lied and hurt me by keeping Brandon away from me.

I told her to just look at the things that had happened to me. Why were she and Daddy staying away from me? A bitch dog will eat you up over her puppies and a hen will scratch your eyes out over her chicks, but not her! I told her that I had never cost her a dime and asked her if I ever lied to her. Mama Marselle said, no. I asked her why she wouldn't go to see Dr. Shane and why she wouldn't go to the Sheriff's office with me so she could talk to Phillip. I had told her that I knew Richard didn't do all the things that had been done to me, but I was going to find out who did and why.

Harriet was keeping Brandon away because of Percy's lies and I cut her money off and maybe she knew Brandon loved me best. Percy hates me because I have money. Gertrude and DeRoy hated me because I knew too much. All three of them live in fear that I'll talk and I thought I just might. I wanted revenge now and they knew I wouldn't stop until I got it. Somehow I had to know the answers.

Phillip Jimez came by last week and told me that I should leave before I get hurt. I told him there was no way I could leave. I couldn't make enough money to live on and Richard had told me that he wouldn't give me a dime. Why should I leave anyway? This is my home and I'm not leaving. I don't know what to think anymore, but one thing is for sure, Richard has lied and hurt me more than I can bear. I would bet my life that Richard wants me dead. He has done so many things…trying to kill me didn't work so he had to drive me into a depression hoping I would take my own life. As you can see, I almost did before I went to see Phillip. I just wanted out of it all.

One day I went to the hardware store and bought a flexible black drainpipe to run from the tail pipe of my car into the window. I knew it would be an easy way to die. In my heart I knew Richard didn't want me, but he didn't want to give up all he had worked for in the past twenty-three years and have to give me money to live on. This is just a boarding house for him and the only time he knows that I exist is when I'm raising hell.

Phillip told me that he had seen what part of my trouble was, that I am a very out-spoken person and a truthful person. People don't like that in today's world. Most people are sorry. They won't work, yet they're so jealous of what others have that they cause them trouble. It's easy to see I don't belong here and I will always have trouble here. He could see that all the women around here are lazy. I make them look bad to their husbands. He could even see something new I've done every time he came here. What Richard gives me make their husbands look bad to them. This makes them all mad at me. Don't you see that it's jealousy? It looks like Richard is guilty of a lot, but someone besides him is out to get me. As he was leaving, Phillip said, don't forget to call me and keep those doors locked.

I had to call Phillip again. I was so upset about the harassing phone calls. It was in the middle of the week when the calls started again. The following Monday morning Phillip called me to say the tap was on the phone but that I was not to tell Richard or anyone. I was so happy. Phillip called to say that they got one call, and then he let the air out of the balloon. The phone company wouldn't turn the telephone number over to him. It's their policy and they have to have two calls from the same number before they will release it for prosecution. I was so mad that I wanted to know where that damn call came from I was so close to knowing who the bastards were. Phillip didn't want me to be upset, and he said they would leave the tap on the line and just maybe they would call back. The week was over and they didn't call again. I admitted to Phillip that I had gotten into a fight with Richard and told him about the tap. I was sorry now, but sorry didn't help.

I had talked to the Security Department at the telephone company thinking they would catch Richard if he was whoring around on the job. I didn't give a damn if he got fired. I just wanted to know the truth. Truth hell, the woman's name is all I needed to know!"

"Calm down Drucilla, and go on."

"Dr. Skeet, with God as my witness, the very day the tap was put on the phone, Richard came up with his very own phone pager. This woman didn't have to call him at home anymore. I love Richard for what he has given Amanda and me, but I hate him for what he has done to me.

I go about my work just as if there is nothing wrong. I cook Richard the best meals and stay as busy as I can. The calls have stopped for a while and my nerves have been better. If I could just forget that it all happened, but of course my mind would have to be wiped out to forget."

"Drucilla, I can't find a way to help you. You don't have medical problems and it's hard for me to believe that Richard is guilty."

"How in the hell can you say that? I tell you he is and if you would get him in here and make him mad, he would tell you the truth."

"Calm down, Drucilla, if you can get Richard to come in here, I guarantee you I will know if he's lying or not."

"You're damn right he's lying. Not one person is allowed in the house. Now I ask you, is that anyway to live? That's one way to know if anything else happens I will know its Richard. Richard has changed all the locks on the doors and I had the phone number changed and unlisted. Phillip has recommended all this, plus for me to get an answering machine for the telephone. It has all been taken care of."

"Drucilla, we can do a number of things. We can wait to see what happens, let the Sheriff put Richard out and end it all, or bring him in here and let me talk to him. Let me know what you decide."

# CHAPTER 19

"Hello Drucilla, how have you been since our last visit? Are you sleeping well? If not, I can give you something to help you rest."

"No sir, I won't let you give me anything. I want to keep what little sense I have. Darn drugs are killing everybody. I don't think you believe what I say, but I came here for your help and I am telling you the truth I do want you to talk to Richard, he's waiting outside. Tell him he must tell me the truth. Believe me, once I hear him say her name, I can let him out of my life with no feeling whatsoever. I know it looks as if it's me that's crazy, but only Richard and I know the truth, right? But Dr. Skeet there is one thing you should keep in mind. It's me that came to you for help. I didn't come here to lie to you. I want the truth. If I just wanted Richard out that would be easy, I'd just divorce him. What I want is for him to admit he has another woman so I can make him pay me support to live on. I will also sue his honey pot. Richard knows all this, that's why he will never tell. Besides, he will lose everything he has worked for in the last twenty-three years. Damn, Dr. Skeet!! Would you want to face me with the truth about all this? I sat here time and time again and told you that Dr. Shane has known me all my life and you don' t believe me. If you ask Dr. Shane, he'll tell you I'm the most honest person he knows. All I have heard out of you is that you don't think Richard is guilty. While you're sitting on your butt thinking, he could have me dead. Now get him in here and make him tell you the truth. It's you that is supposed to have the **know how** to get the truth out of him."

"Drucilla, please calm down, get a hold of yourself. I'll talk to Richard, but you're too upset. I think you should wait outside. I'll get Richard now."

Dr. Skeet escorted Drucilla to the waiting room. Dr. Skeet turned to Richard and asked, "Would you please come in now."

Drucilla said, "This would be a waste of time. The lying bastard would never tell."

Dr. Skeet said, "Richard, I have called you in to ask you what you think of the situation Drucilla thinks she's in."

"Dr. Skeet, I know all these things have happened, but I didn't do any of them."

"Okay Richard, lets say you didn't take any of the things from the house. Now what about all these personal things that has happened just between you and Drucilla? We are talking about your new dress code from head to toe, never taking her anywhere, the bad odor on your face and saying your boss made you work overtime every Friday night. I'll tell you Richard, Drucilla has proved that is not true. She tells me you say you don't know why all this has happened. You tell Drucilla that you don't remember this and that. How about telling me."

"Dr. Skeet, Drucilla won't accept any answer except an admission of guilt. If she didn't like my answer, she would tell me that I didn't answer the question. The dress code, well that's simple. The blue jeans I used to wear would be tight around the waist and I have been complaining about it for a long time, I finally had enough and changed. I don't harp on things, I just say they hurt me and drop it, but Drucilla didn't pay any attention to me. Now she doesn't remember me ever complaining about it. The odor on my face…that was a hard one I didn't smell it so I didn't know it was there. After she complained about it so much, I asked the other boys at work, if their wives complained about a bad smell. Sure enough the old paper towels we used to wipe our hands on were causing the stink. If the towels were wet and sit overnight, they would sour. The next day I used the same towel to dry my hands and sometimes wiped my face. As for the Friday nights, what a mess, you see I have an idiot for a boss. At that time nobody wanted any overtime. It seemed like everybody was passing the buck down to our department, so they could get off for the weekend. My boss would make the low man on the overtime list stay and work. I told Drucilla not to plan anything on Friday nights because I never knew when I might have to work. She got it into her head that I worked more than I really did and to top things off, she asked my boss how many times he made me stay and work. The idiot lied about it, said he didn't have to make his men stay. The idiot also lied about forcing me to work a Saturday before I was scheduled a week's vacation. There has been so much happening that I can't keep it straight. I can't even believe some of what has happened."

"Let me tell you Richard, Drucilla can state years, months, days and times. If I were you I'd come up with some answers that she will believe. If Drucilla can prove you, in fact, did have this woman you just might be facing an attempted murder charge. Now Richard, I can't find one thing mentally wrong with Drucilla. I can say all this has made her a living Devil and I for one wouldn't want to be on her list. I'm sure she will not take much more. I'll let you leave now with this thought in mind. You say all these things did happen. If she were my wife, I'd be finding out why they happened and who made them happen if not for her, then for myself. Tell Drucilla I'll see her next at our next appointment. We have used up all the time for today."

"Hello Doc, this has been a long couple of months."

"Yes, Drucilla, and are you still sleeping well?"

"Yes sir, and don't ask me again! I'm not about to let you dope me up and those damn people are not going to make me lose sleep.

Phillip called me day before yesterday, telling me that he had called Richard at work to come by the Sheriff's office he was giving him a polygraph test. Phillip asked me if I was sure I wanted to know the truth. If not, this was the time to say it. This test will tell us the truth. Richard's mind won't let him lie to the machine. At least Phillip can see through Richard. He told me it sure looks as if he's guilty. He also said to be honest, he was almost certain of Richard's guilt. Phillip said if Richard failed the test that I would have to make him leave. He also said I should think about having Richard arrested for attempted murder. He asked again was I sure I wanted to give him the test and I told him yes. He told me to stay home and he would call me the minute Richard left.

I walked the floor. It seemed as if time had stopped. I wondered if he would let them give him the test and just how reliable the test was. I knew if anyone could pass it, Richard could. He has told me some of the most God awful lies with the straightest face. Maybe that is because he didn't love me and not because he is a good liar. I hoped with all my heart that he wouldn't be able to pass the test. I don't want to die. I'm afraid if I don't find someone to love and take care of me I won't be able to fight them much longer. I hoped it would end that night and I was sure it would. If Richard couldn't pass the polygraph test, I would make him leave. Phillip would put him out once and for all. I was in deep thought when the phone rang. It was Phillip.

He told me that I knew he was a specialist when it comes to this machine. He teaches it and he has given the test to the worst of criminals. He assured me he knew this machine and he didn't think Richard could have passed the test if he had been guilty. We both didn't know how Richard could be innocent, but the polygraph says he was. I was quiet for so long that Phillip asked if I was still there. Finally, I told Phillip that he knew darn well Richard was guilty. Phillip told me he would have to think this over before we did anything else. Then he said if I had asked Richard these questions over and over, then maybe he is immune to them and if he really doesn't love me, it may be possible. If he is sick enough to think he is right about what he is doing, then that way his mind would be lying to the machine. He wanted to think about this and for me to give him a call tomorrow.

Dr. Skeet, I had hoped this machine would bring the truth out."

"Are you sure it didn't, Drucilla? Like I told you, I don't think Richard is guilty"

"**Hell yes I'm sure!** That was a stupid question. But any way, Dr. Skeet, when Richard came in he was happy as hell saying, see it wasn't me now stay off my ass. He wasn't going to listen to any more of my, so-called, bullshit. It's that damn family of mine. They've caused him too much trouble and he wanted them to stay the hell away from him.

I'm scared to death of Richard, but after he said if I made him leave he wouldn't give me any money to live on, I don't know what to do. I don't have any family to help me and my health wouldn't let me hold down a job even if I could find one. My nerves are all to pieces. I tell you, I don't know what to do. I have to get some rest. I have to find someone to help me, someone to believe me.

I made up my mind to call Fritzie yesterday. Thinking surely he would help me. I told him everything that had happened and began to cry. I told Fritzie my life was in danger. I needed him to help me. Richard has passed the polygraph test because he didn't love me not because he was innocent. He almost killed me and now he's trying to make me kill myself. Why couldn't he help me stop them? Help me get the truth out. Fritzie had promised me that he would never let anything come between our friendship. Fritzie said maybe things aren't as bad as I thought. I asked Fritzie what happened to all that love, how could he call himself my friend. Now he is going to leave me to fight them all without anyone to help me. Fritzie told me that Richard had said that maybe I was going through the change of life. I cut the fool off. I told him that's not true. There is nothing wrong with me mentally or physically. Richard is at the root of all this and someone living right around me is helping him drive me nuts. I told Fritzie that he was hurting me. He had told me I could always come to him and that he would always love me.

But that's okay. Let them mistreat me with their lies and maybe even take my life. It will be him and a lot more that pay dearly for doing me wrong. I told him he was just like the rest, nothing but sorry. Fritzie tried to explain that what he meant was he didn't think it was anybody but Richard and I wouldn't put him out. Hanging up the phone, I became nauseated.

Dr. Skeet, I can't understand why everyone is against me. All you have told me time and time again is that this is just jealously, but that is hard for me to believe. I cried, with tears running down my face. I was thinking. I just couldn't get over Fritzie acting like he loved me best in the world and now telling me to go to hell. I can still hear Fritzie saying, that's bad family trouble I can't get involved. He knew darn well Richard was as guilty as a dog in the hen house with feathers in his mouth. This has made me so darn hellish he knew that anything could happen. Fritzie said that if Richard were out of the picture he would be there but…**But hell!** I cut him off. I said forget Richard and forget me to.

I made up my mind then and there to live the best I could and never love anyone else as long as I lived. I would kill Richard if he hurt me again. I would get busy, clean house, go shopping and to the beauty shop. I had been down in the dumps long enough. I would never mix and mingle with that bunch of white trash again. Hell, let them be jealous. I don't give a darn. Let Richard screw every woman in town, I'll stop having sex with him."

"Drucilla, I don't think you should go to extremes. Think about all this and we'll discuss it next time."

"Think about it hell! Dr. Skeet, I just thought I was full of hate. I didn't know what hate was until I got home last Wednesday."

"Tell me what happened."

"I came home last Wednesday and found my pearls broken into five different parts. I could have killed everybody in sight. I just sat there and looked at Richard. I wanted him dead. I wanted to collect his insurance. I could have killed him with my own hands. Why is he doing this? Some how some way, I had to find out who his honey pot is. I will survive. I know I have to. I will show them all.

To top it all, when we went to bed Wednesday night, the bed was so hot I couldn't sleep in it. We have a waterbed and it has two heaters with dual controls. The one on my side of the bed was turned up full blast. I was so mad I wouldn't let Richard sleep either. I cussed Richard all night. I told Richard over and over again that he turned the waterbed up and pulled my pearls apart.

Why in the hell didn't he just get out of my life? He's going to keep on until someone gets hurt and the next time it might not be me. Richard said he didn't know who broke my pearls, but it sure wasn't him. I screamed out at him that hell yes, it was him. He and I were the only ones that had been in the house. It had to be him, if not why wasn't he mad about someone else coming into his house and doing this to me. These son-of-a-bitches have called and done this and that and it doesn't upset him at all. Joke. Ha. I know damn well he's guilty. But now I don't give a damn. I'm going to live and somehow I'm going to be happy.

Dr. Sheet, tomorrow morning I'm going to have my pearls restrung and then I'm going to the Gulf for a few days. It's always nice at the beach in October. You know that's when they have the Shrimp Festival."

"Call me if you need me, Drucilla."

"Yes sir. I need a long vacation."

But the next time Dr. Skeet heard from Drucilla Hallmark was what he read in the paper and heard from Phillip Jimez.

He had listened to all the tapes and still couldn't find the answer to his questions.

# CHAPTER 20

I was back from the jewelers packing to leave for the Gulf. It had cost me plenty to get my pearls restrung. Richard didn't want me to go by myself and I certainly didn't want Richard to go with me.

"You're not going by yourself, Drucilla!"

"Why Richard? Are you afraid I'll find someone to replace you? Why can't I go by myself? I am over twenty-one. I'll just sit on the beach and write a song or two."

"I'll take a few days off and go with you."

I didn't want Richard to go, but I was in such a hurry to get away from that place, I didn't want to argue. Richard left in the van to gas up and check the tires. I called Amanda to let her know I was going to the Gulf but didn't get an answer. I went about my packing and remembered I had left my favorite towels in the dryer out back. As I came back into the house, I heard a noise at the other end of the house. I stopped in my tracks. I knew Richard had not come back with the van. Drawers were opening and closing. Somebody was searching the house. Whoever it was must have thought I was in the van with Richard. My heart was pounding so hard that I thought they might hear it and that only made it beat harder. There was a gun in every room of the house. I couldn't remember where it was in this room. I could hear whomever it was tearing up my bedroom. I tiptoed through the house to the library.

With a gun in every room of the house, all I could find was a twelve-gauge shotgun. It was a Christmas present from my Uncle Slim. I can still hear him saying, you're so little you need a big gun. I had been afraid to shoot it. Now I would have to. Now I would take care of this devious bastard once and for all. I put the gun to my shoulder.

I screamed, "**Richard! Richard**! Richard, if you came back to scare me, it's not so funny."

Things got quite and the phone started to ring. I couldn't pick it up. I screamed, "Come out of there!" I couldn't hear anything but my own heart pounding. I screamed, "What do you want from me? Why are you doing this to me? **Damn you!!!** Come out of there. For months you have tormented me."

I knew I had to shoot whoever it was. I couldn't let them get away. I had to end it now, right now. When he came though the bedroom door, he was smiling at me. I felt my heart stop. He was so big I couldn't miss. Now I was smiling. I had waited a long time for this moment. Still smiling he started to take a step.

I screamed out, "What have I ever done to you? No wonder Mama Marselle wouldn't help me, it was you all the time."

I heard the sound of a car. It sounded like more than one. What the hell I thought, they'll just pass me by, but it would do them good to see the mess I'm in. Then all of a sudden he threw my newly strung pearls across the room in pieces and started to run. I pulled the trigger and sat his ass up against the wall.

Richard and Harriet burst in one door, and then Amanda and Phillip came through the back. Phillip was the first to reach me. He knelt down beside me and asked, "Are you alright?"

I didn't answer him. Phillip looked over at the man on the

floor. Even from here he could tell that the man was dead. I had shot him full in the throat, almost tore his head off.

Phillip said, “It’s over now. DeRoy is dead.”

I said, “Maybe but he has hit me with something.”

I had turned to run and heard what sounded like a door slam shut, then my knees gave way.

Someone I didn’t know had walked up and was talking to Phillip. I couldn’t overhear what they were saying, but I could hear Harriet telling Richard something about what had been said at dinner the night before and that Amanda had read between the lines. Harriet said she couldn’t stay at work, so at lunch she picked up Amanda and started to my house, stopping off at the Sheriff’s office to see Phillip. He said he knew I was leaving for the Gulf but not until two o’clock. He dialed my number and began to worry when I didn’t answer because I always did exactly what I told him. Phillip said I never left the house without calling him first. It was lucky for me that I had missed Phillip’s call. I was out back putting clothes into the washing machine and couldn’t hear the phone. Amanda has called again on her cell phone as she entered the driveway.

Richard was just standing there shaking his head and Amanda was crying. The person Phillip was talking to had left and he was kneeling at my side.

He slipped his hand under my back and brought it back with blood on his fingers. “Yes, Phillip said, DeRoy has hit you with something. We’ve called for an ambulance.”

I wouldn’t let Phillip leave my side. I asked him, “Will you get all these people out of my house and make sure the house is locked before you leave?”

“Drucilla, don’t you worry. I’ll take care of everything.”

When Phillip came speeding up with the red lights flashing, all of my enemies had come out to see what was going on. I told Phillip that they could look from the road. I wouldn’t have them in my house. Damn them all. Where are they all coming from? The bastards don’t even like me.

I couldn’t help thinking how I had begged my people to

help me, just to have my ass kicked and now look here they are, coming to see if I'm dead. Just as Phillip ordered everyone out, in came Percy. Falling on his knees asking what could he do? I tried to laugh out loud, but I couldn't.

I said, "Get the hell out of my face. I never begged anyone in life, but I did beg you, but no you couldn't help me. I needed you then, I don't need you now, so get the hell out."

The firemen and paramedics were the first to respond to the 911 call. One of the firemen said, "Everybody move, the ambulance is backing up to the door."

Amanda walked over to me with a bottle of lotion in her hand. She took my rings off and gave them to Richard.

The house was quiet as the ambulance attendants lifted me onto the stretcher. I could feel myself fading away as they rolled me out the door and off the porch. I was sure I had died and gone to hell. On my porch stood the very person that I despised most in the whole world. I was thinking that the slut was so big if someone could build a porch on her and put a roof over her head she could be sold as a mobile home....eyes for windows and a mouth big enough for a door.

The ambulance attendant was a handsome young man with a worried look on his face. He turned to Richard as he stepped up into the ambulance saying, "Mr. Hallmark, you will have to ride up front because we need the room to work."

Richard bent down to kiss me just to hear me say, "I hope you are satisfied now. You got just what you wanted and I sure pray that I never have to come back to Shady Grove again."

Richard stepped back saying, "I'm sorry."

I knew the young man was talking to a doctor at the hospital. He was slapping my hand so hard it hurt. He kept saying, "I'm sorry Mrs. Hallmark, I'm trying to get a vein up."

He kept saying no pulse, no blood pressure she's falling, falling and how sorry he was about the bumpy road that we would be at the emergency room in a minute.

We're here now. I could feel them taking me out and someone said, "Okay Mrs. Hallmark, we are going into the trauma unit now."

I was thinking, Oh no!! I've got to go to Gulf Shores. I don't have time for this. I could feel the anger building.

I was screaming, "You, hey you, get Dr. Bob. Where is Dr. Bob? What are you doing? I don't feel any pain, get Dr. Bob."

Someone said, "We have to do what has to be done and do it now."

They were making me crazy asking questions. "Yes, I have had ten operations. **Yes, hell yes!** Yes, I did have a tetanus shot about two weeks ago. Hell yes, why don't you call for my chart and leave me alone. I have a chart in the hospital, why don't you get it. **Hey you!** This damn table is spinning around. No! I'm going to the Gulf."

I heard that angry voice again. "Let's go! We're losing her! Damn, son-of-a-bitch, we can't lose her! We can't! I won't let her die!"

Phillip sat in the I.C.U. waiting room making out his report. Phillip sat holding the file in his hand. He wanted my doctor to read the report. He wanted them to know the real Drucilla. Phillip liked me and would make sure the doctors knew that I was worth the extra mile, if it came to it.

**Personal report Phillip Jimez**
**For the File of Drucilla Hallmark**

It's my personal belief and I'm proud to say Drucilla is as perfect as anyone will ever be. When you first meet Drucilla, you get the impression of a tough bitch with strong opinions and a strict way of living. The truth is she's as mean as you make her and as good as you let her be.

One thing's for sure, she will tell you where to stick it if you're trying to stick it in the wrong place. She wants men to be real men, not pussies when there's a problem. She can't stand a wimp. She knows only you, yourself, can make your life better. Drucilla can't stand lazy people and won't help those who won't help themselves. No one asks her opinion anymore, because they can't stand her answers. She has put all of her older brothers and sisters to shame. It was done with just one thing, work. If just one of her people had looked past her surface to see the soft, warm and good heart inside, they would have to love her.

Drucilla would take a poem book off the shelf and read for hours. I have read stacks of songs she has written even though she was sad. She loves the old people and makes them her friend. Loving everyone's children until her little nephew, Brandon was taken away from her by her sister, Harriet. I think someday Brandon will go to Drucilla. He will always know she loved him best. Drucilla has always been the child's Mam Maw. She loves this child better than life.

Her people will never get to know her. They'll never take the time. They seem happy just the way they are. The good that Drucilla has done, was resented by them all the food, money and other good things she has done for them, all fourteen mostly a cleaner way of life.

She never gave a second thought to giving Richard's money away to help others. She just knew she worked equally as hard as Richard did for what they had. I can still hear her say, as long as she works like a dog, she will do as she pleases.

The only problem she had was Richard and her family. She wants to be loved, but I know she will have to give up and get the Hell away. The kind of love her people have has almost killed her.

I now wonder if a new Drucilla will come through this. I will always hear her say, I have loved so many that didn't love me back. I have seen some mistreated people let God get revenge but some were afraid that God would take too long.

Drucilla isn't a spur of the moment person and not a predictable person. Will she wait for God's revenge or not? I will sit back and wait to hear from Drucilla Hallmark.

# CHAPTER 21

Everything was white. The sun was shining in my face and the sand was hot. Digging my feet into the sand, I was singing a song while thinking of Richard and Fritzie. I had begun to sing.

**ANGELS DO CRY**

You may think Angels on earth don't cry
Well let me tell you they do
I've been an Angel and you made me cry
You've broke my heart into
Angels do cry you know I wouldn't tell a lie
I've been an Angel always
How could you hurt me this way..............

I was thinking hard. I had to find someone to buy my songs. I didn't know how to go about it, but I would learn. My mind was made up. I'm going back home and get rid of Richard, plus shake off all the leeches, whether they are friend or family.

All of a sudden I heard a child scream, I was on my feet

running. Blood was pouring from the child's foot. I couldn't believe some fool had left a broken bottle on the beach. Snatching the sweatband from my head, I tied the child's foot tight to stop the bleeding. The child had stopped crying. His hair and eyes were coal black and his skin was so tan that, the sun made him look as though he had been dipped in gold.

My concentration was broken as the child said, "Father, I stepped on this bottle and cut my foot." The child held the bottle for his father to see.

As I stood up, the father's coal black hair and yes he took my breath away. I thought this has got to be the most handsome man in the world. We both laughed as the child said, "Father, this lady would make the best Mom."

The handsome man smiled and said, "Anthony is always looking for a Mother. Thank you for helping my son." Saying that he picked his child up and walked away.

That same afternoon I was lying down resting, when I heard someone knocking at the motel door. Richard answered the door and was handed a basket with two dozen miniature pink roses mixed with babies breath, a bottle of champagne and a note saying, I'll be seeing you, you would make a great Mom and it was signed Tony Tortomasi.

Richard and I never said a word on our way back from Gulf Shores. Two weeks had passed and no one had come to visit. I was singing to the top of my voice while sweeping off the pool deck. Looking up I saw a new Lamborghini drive up. Lord! He was walking toward me. I couldn't breathe. Time was standing still. Oh my! He's a golden God. I couldn't hear him. What? What did you say? Looking into his eyes, I had lost all my senses. I could barely hear him talking.

"No!" I said, "I don't love Richard. Yes, he has hurt me so many times.

Kill them all. No, I want Richard to be saved for last."

The ringing of the doorbell woke me from my dream. My hands were curled as if I were holding a broom. I went to the door and looked out the peephole. I saw it a new white

Lamborghini. I didn't want to open the door. I sure didn't take him serious when he said he would be seeing me. Besides that, how did he find me? Surely Phillip didn't tell anyone that I wanted to know about him. No one but Phillip and I knew that I wanted to see him again. I sure can't let him just stand there.

Opening the door I said, "Hello Mr. Tortomasi, come on in. What brings you to the country? Is little Anthony's foot better? You're a long way from the gulf."

I rattled on and on. I was so nervous I couldn't help myself. "Oh yes, I haven't taken the time to send you a thank you note. So, thank you. The pink roses were lovely and the champagne was divine."

I stopped talking. He was smiling at me. I couldn't do anything but stare. Finally I asked, "Would you like to have a glass of wine Mr. Tortomasi?"

He surprised me by saying, "Yes and I wish you would be quiet so I can talk to you." Following me into the kitchen he said, "I wish you would call me Tony, Dru."

"If you don't mind, Tony, I would rather sit out by the pool." He followed me through the French doors to the pool deck.

"I want you to listen to me Dru. I know you're not happy here. You have been between a rock and a hard place for sometime now. It's time for a change. I know I'm ten years older than you, but I can't see where that makes any difference. Anthony needs a mother and I've got to bring you home. You will be the best, remember."

I was stunned. I never expected anything like this.

"Dru, are you listening to me?"

That brought me back. "Yes, I am, but I don't know what to say. You must know I'm married."

Tony pulled his chair right up in front of me. Taking my hand in his he said, "I know you have had maybe seven good years out of twenty-three. I think you have always been married, but Richard has just used you. You deserve better and that's what I'm here for. Besides, I do love you. I've looked from one end of the world to the other. No one has ever affected me the way you do. We both know there is nothing here for you, Dru. You have been ridiculed by, people that are bad to the bone, look around you, all you have ever known is misery. I'm offering you a whole new world."

I was fighting that darn knot. It was hung in my throat again, bringing tears to my eyes. I got up saying, "You're right Tony, but if you know so much, you know this place is all I have in the world. It's the only security I have. I'm afraid to leave here."

"I won't leave you here, Dru. Richard has told you so many trumped up stories. He was born with a forked tongue."

"I don't care what you think, but…."

"But hell girl! Haven't you ever heard of a counterfeit man? Deception is lurking from behind every bush. It's beyond me how you've lived with this decaying bunch.

I've been told your story is a mystery. But Dru, there's no mystery here. Look around you. You're dealing with a bunch of barefaced liars. Just this morning, I was told that Richard takes advantage of your goodness. You've let him get away with so much he thinks you're gullible. He said you couldn't comprehend what's right before your face. Didn't he say that?"

Taking an envelope from his pocket he handed it to me. He took my hands in his and said, "Never doubt me Dru. I'm your freedom. I'm your way out of here. Pack what you can't live without and call the movers. Everyone at the house is expecting you."

"Tony, you've got to be nuts. I'm not an easy person to live with by any means. I'm not happy and I sure as hell have a broken heart. As a matter of fact, I'm down right good for nothing."

"Damn you woman, I'm not going to beg and I've got to go. Now get your butt in gear and get out of this hell hole." He turned and walked off the pool deck heading for his car.

I tore the envelope open dumping the contents out on the table. I counted it over and over again five thousand dollars in cash plus a bank receipt for one hundred thousand dollars, with just my name on the receipt. I didn't realize I was talking out loud to myself.

"Good Lord! This man's not whistling Dixie. He's as serious as AIDS!"

I went straight to the bathroom and ran the tub full of water. I had to think about all this and the tub is my favorite place to think. Even with money, I'm not a spur of the moment person. The minute I stretched out in the tub I said to myself, I've been waiting for a proposition like this all my life. I know I must leave here. Breathing a sigh of relief for the first time in my life, I felt free. Laughing and crying at the same time, I had never been so happy. Oh God, Thank you! This man is a real man.

The doorbell rang. It scared me to death. Jumping out of the tub, I wrapped a towel around my head then one around my body as I ran to answer the door. I just knew it would be Harriet, but I was fooled. Standing before me was Tony.

I just stood there looking at him thinking how handsome he was, until he said, "Please let me come in."

I stepped aside as he looked me up and down he said, "Good Lord Girl, didn't anyone ever tell you to always look your best because you never know when you might meet your next husband."

We both laughed. I said, "You're so right Tony. Maybe I shouldn't have opened the door."

"Oh yes you should have. I have to wait for someone. I thought I might as well wait here. Can I have a hug?"

"No!" I began to back away. "Not until I'm free."

"O K don't just stand there, go finish your bath. I want you free before dark."

I went to the phone and called my lawyer's office. His secretary answered the phone. I said, "This is Drucilla Hallmark tell Williams I'll be there in forty-five minutes. I want a divorce and I want it today."

I hung up the phone. Turning back to Tony I said, "Now

you listen. I'll be free today, but you have to keep your hands off me until you marry me. Do you understand that?"

He didn't answer that in a hurry. Finally he said, "I guess so."

"Tony, I don't know what you came back for, but I'm glad you did. I must tell you that I'm afraid to love any man. I've been so hurt by Richard. I must be honest. I've never loved anyone but him and now I don't love him. Right now the only thing I love is money."

Tony had been looking at me so serious, but when I said I loved money, he burst out laughing. He said, "Maybe so, but you will love me."

It had to be the fastest bath on record for me. I was out and dressed in ten minutes. Asking him if he would be waiting here for me to return. Hearing him say yes, I told him to make himself at home. I would be back in a flash and out the door I went. Just up the road I passed a moving van. I smiled thinking yes in just sixty days I'll call a moving van to get me out of here.

Tony Tortomasi was God sent. Looking into the rear view mirror, I could see dollar signs in my eyes. I would use his money to make them all pay. Shaking my head, I told myself, stop this way of thinking. I must love Tony and Anthony. Not to mention now I could have Brandon back.

I all but ran into Williams' law office. I told his receptionist to tell him I was in a hurry.

He came through the door with a big smile and said, "What can I do for you Drucilla? What's wrong? You look to happy for much to be wrong."

My eyes were out sparkling my diamonds. I said, "There's nothing wrong, I just want a divorce today. If you'll get the papers ready, I'll get a hold of Richard."

I called Richard's pager number and within two minutes he called back. Mr. Williams explained that I was there filing for a divorce and he would have to come by the law office by two-thirty to sign the papers. It could be taken care of that afternoon if Richard could get there.

Hanging up the phone, Mr. Williams looked at me saying, "He's on his way now."

Mr. Williams told me that Richard said that, hell yes he would sign the papers. He knew someday I would leave him. That it might as well be today as tomorrow.

I said, "That's good. The fool never loved me, but I'll make him wish he had."

"What?" Asked Mr. Williams with an ear cocked, waiting for an answer.

Mr. Williams gave his secretary orders to hurry.

I said, "I don't want to be here when Richard gets here. Just let me sign the papers and go. I want you to get me the same agreement as before, but seven hundred a month until I marry and have Richard send the money to you and you send the money to Brandon. You can do that can't you? Remember, Richard gets his personal belongings and that is all."

It just hit me..... I didn't just dislike Richard. I despised him for what he had done to me.

Mr. Williams said, "Talk Drucilla. Tell me why today? Why right now? You know in Nineteen Seventy-seven, I told you not to marry Richard again. But you did anyway, so why today?"

"Yes sir, I know you did. I had to, I couldn't get a job and besides, I thought he had learned his lesson. But, I know now he'll never learn. I can't handle his whore hopping any longer. I'm sick of hearing that I'm the one with the problem, I have to accept things, that when he leaves the house for work, he's no longer my business until he comes home at night. I have never lied to you and I won't start now. I will marry Tony Tortomasi in sixty-one days from today."

Mr. Williams jumped to his feet and grabbed the morning paper. "Are you talking about The Tortomasi from Gulf Shores, Alabama?"

"Yes sir, that's where I met him."

"Do you know who he is? Not to mention what he is."

"Yes sir, he is head of the mafia in Gulf Shores. Let me ask you a question Mr. Williams. Do you believe in prayer? The Good Lord sent Tony to me. I've been kicked around for forty-four years, but today is the end of that. So don't hand me any bull crap just hand me a divorce."

"I guess you do know." He mashed a button and his secretary walked in showing me where to sign.

On my way back home, I passed the moving van again. I thought that was fast, maybe my time will be next. I wouldn't be driving back down this road many more times. Getting out of my car, I looked all around. This place has been hell from day one.

Then it hit me. I froze. What am I doing? He's a gangster, a harden criminal. How can I marry him when I don't have the guts to just walk away from here? A little voice started saying, calm down girl. You're marrying his money. You're sick of this place and lets be honest, you despise everyone here except little Brandon. I smiled at the thought of Brandon's name. Yes, I can leave. I should have gone years ago.

Tony opened the door saying, "Well?"

"Well, Tony, I'll be yours in sixty-one days. Do you know what's wrong with this world Tony? Too many of us allow ourselves to get wrapped up in our personal problems. Walking blindly past our loved ones not realizing that a few words of encouragement or just a few minutes of our time might save them from days, week, months or maybe even years of pure hell. I'll never be that busy again, Tony. I'll never be so busy or uncaring that I can't get involved in the troubles of those I love. I will always remember when I desperately needed someone to help me, someone did. I also know what it's like to be sick at heart. It's the worst sick of all."

Tony always tried to read between the lines of a tearful tale. It may be even more sad, than spoken.

We went into the house and when I took a look around, the room was empty. My mouth flew wide open. "Heavens Tony, did you let my sister in this house? If she sells my things in a garage sale, I'll kill her with my bare hands. I should have told you Tony. Sister Harriet will sell her last pair of panties at a garage sale. Did you give her my things?"

"No, I had the movers to come and pack it up and it's on its way."

"Tony, how did the movers know what to pack?"

"That's easy Dru, one look at you says it all, glass, brass and ass."

"This is no laughing matter Tony. I want all my antiques, then I want this place burned to the ground, but I don't ever want this land sold. I don't ever want anyone to live here again. This is the center of hell."

"Dru, let's go now. I will take care of this place later."

"Yes Tony, but give me a minute to call Phillip. He's the only best friend I ever had here. I can't leave without telling him bye."

I thanked Phillip for being my friend and made him promise to bring his family to the gulf for a visit.

Picking up a box of Kleenex I said, "Let's go before I change my mind."

I was still crying when we reached Alabaster. That was thirty miles out of town and forty-five minutes later.

"Dru, I don't know what to think about you. What can I do? Tell me and just let me deal with it."

"I'll be okay Tony. It just hurts to give up, because I still don't have all the answers."

"But that's okay Dru. I'll get even for you, you'll see. I'll make Richard wish he had been a Saint, along with Percy and Harriet."

"Tony, I'm glad I'm away from there. Maybe just maybe, I won't have any more nightmares or bad phone calls."

"Take my hand Dru, I promise to always keep you safe."

Having pulled out of my yard and away from my home I knew I didn't deserve Tony. Now I was the evil one. I was the one filled with a want --- and a need for revenge.

"I'll need time, Tony. I love the Gulf and I will be happy

there, but you need to give me time to rest and to get to know my new family. Even though living with you. Is what I want to do. It's still scary not knowing what lies ahead of me."

"That's the reason for the money I gave you. It's yours to do with as you please. It's your security blanket. You take the next two months to quiet your nerves and if you still want me, I'm yours. If not, take the money and see if you can find happiness.

You've talked of depression Dru. I know very well what depression is. I have seen little Anthony grieve over his mother until he was sick. Now you're all he talks about. He will be happy to see you. I promised to let him show you around town. I don't want you to worry. I know you will be fine.

I have a brother, Michael, who is giving you his home to live in until everything is settled with you and me. He will live at my house. His place is down at Fort Morgan, it's nice and private. I'm sure you will love it."

"But Tony, I don't want to inconvenience him."

"Believe me Dru, you're not, he stays at my house more than he stays at home. I'm beginning to think he's lonely. Michael is thirty-four and he has been in love so many times I've lost count. He tells them all that he will marry and as sure as one starts talking marriage, he drops her flat. I don't know why. Maybe he hasn't found the right one. You will be happy at his place Dru. I assure you he doesn't mind.

Dru, take this little red book, you will find everything you need in here. I won't call you for a few days. Just take all the time you need to adjust to what has happened, but if you need me, call."

Pulling into the yard it was everything I had imagined it would be. Walking in, I found the most luxurious bachelor pad.

"Come on in Dru, and let me show you your room. I know this has been a long day and you need to rest."

Trying not to show my emotions, I looked away from Tony. Looking around I noticed all my personal belongings were here. Suitcases, my trunks and even my make-up had been set out.

Tony said, "Dru, I've opened the curtains and the sliding glass door to let the breeze blow in."

Walking out on the deck, a peace came over me like never before, a peace of knowing that this is where I belonged. Kicking off my shoes, I took Tony's hand saying, "Run, I want to feel the water and sand. I want to make sure this is not a dream."

When we arrived at the water I took him in my arms saying, "No Tony, it's not a dream, it's a miracle. I'm fine now. I know I will be fine. Can you bring Anthony to see me tomorrow? Tony, I won't let you down and you will never be sorry that you chose me to be his mother."

"I didn't choose you to be his Mother, Dru, he did. I chose you to be my wife. Anthony reminded me the other day that he saw you first. I can't help it if it took me a few days to see that he has good judgment, but from now on, I will listen to his opinion.

Dru, it surprises me to see the change that has come over you. It is as though someone has plugged you into electricity. You've come alive."

"Tony, I will learn my responsibilities fast. Whether you know it or not I've been in a war for forty-four years. I'm well decorated and I'm brave. I just pray that you won't be disappointed in me."

Tony kissed me like I had never been kissed before. "Dru, I could never be disappointed in you."

We walked along not saying a word, just soaking up the sun, wind and each other. Tony said, "Let's go back to the house. Someone just closed the door."

When we got back to the house, we found on the kitchen table two dishes of fruit, mostly watermelon. I ate as if I was starved to death.

Tony said, "I'm sure it is not just wishful thinking on my part, the change is there. I know I've got myself a live wire. Little girl you are special, much more than I had hoped for."

He was smiling at me, but it was a puzzled smile. I asked

him what he was thinking. About that same time the maid walked in saying, “I hope both of you had a good trip. Could I get anything for you?”

Tony said, “Dru, I would like you to meet Sandra. She will take care of you. If you need anything, just let her know. She is here around the clock.”

I said, “Sandra, maybe we can talk after while. Tony is about to leave.

Come on Tony, I will walk you to the door.”

At the door I told Tony, “Don’t worry about me, I’ll be fine.”

After my bath, I talked to Sandra telling her what to do with my clothes and what I needed for the next day. She talked on and on telling me that little Anthony had described me to a tee and that the little man sure fell in love with me and that I was all he had talked about.

# CHAPTER 22

I was up at daybreak calling Harriet on the telephone and telling her where I was and that I would never be back. There was one thing that we did agree on though and that was Brandon's happiness. When I told her I wanted him here for my wedding, she asked if it had been a secret. I told her it all happened so fast and that I didn't know myself until yesterday. But, I was sure I would be happy. Harriet told me that Mama Marselle said I could never come back to her house.

That was nothing new to me. If I could dig DeRoy up and kill him over again, I sure as hell would. If Harriet didn't want to bring Brandon, I would send someone to get him. I made that clear!

I went back to the beach with my hair in rollers and no make-up on. I could have died when I saw little Anthony running toward me. Tony wasn't far behind and had stopped just to watch Anthony. When I could see little Anthony's smile, I started running as fast as I could to pick him up.

He said over and over again, "I knew you would come to live with me."

I didn't know what to say. Here was a little boy that really loved and needed me. The only person that ever loved me was Brandon. Two little boys, one here and one had to be left behind. Just the thought of Brandon brought tears to my eyes.

Anthony said, "Are you really going to live with me forever?"

"Yes I am Anthony and I also have a nephew that's just about your age who might come live with us too."

"When can he come? When can he come? I need someone to play with!"

"Soon Anthony, I promise you, soon."

Tony walked up and I said, "Tony I now have two boys that love me, maybe three."

The weeks went by so fast with Tony and little Anthony, playing, shopping, and going here and there. There was no deceit in my new family. No deception whatsoever. I knew that for the first time in my life, I didn't have to worry about what was going to happen next. I knew because I was planning it.

Harriet was first on my list of plans after I had gotten everything ready for my wedding. Tony was spoiling me by giving me beautiful gifts of jewelry and the house always had fresh cut flowers. Tony had introduced me to everyone, but I didn't know half the people that knew me. I couldn't help but remember Charlie. He seemed to be everywhere I looked. I remembered the afternoon that I beat Tony, playing golf. I was so nervous about beating him in front of his friends. I just knew it would shame him and he would be mad. It seemed as though he were in deep thought. He was so quiet.

Walking into the Club House Tony took off his hat and said, "Okay boys payoff! You're alright Charlie, you're the only one with good sense or the only one that has had the chance to play against her."

I was amazed to see the hat full of money. Then I started joking with them. I said, "Don't you boys know to always bet on a sure thing?"

As I kissed Tony to leave, he gave me the money and said, "Here baby, you won this. Now take it and have a good afternoon."

I did. I went straight to the post office and mailed it to Brandon. I couldn't believe it, fourteen hundred dollars in two and a half hours!

I had to hurry. The dressmaker was to be at the house at three o'clock. Good Lord I thought, just two more weeks until the wedding. I had just walked in the door when Ms. Hinkle, the dressmaker rang the doorbell. My dress was pink. Everything would be pink and white. I wasn't disappointed. The dress was the most beautiful thing I had ever seen.

I said, "Ms. Hinkle, this is not the dress you were supposed to make for me."

"Yes, Ms. Drucilla, it is except Mr. Tony said to add the diamonds to it. Now let's see if it will fit. Step in front of the mirror when you get it on."

Looking in the mirror I was so proud. I was beautiful. My wheat colored hair and dark tan with the pink was wonderful. Then I panicked. I thought Oh God! I hope this is not a dream. Please let me be happy. Please let me be good to Tony. He really seems to love me. I smiled at myself thinking, this is not a daydream Drucilla.

I said, "Ms. Hinkle, this dress is perfect."

Sandra came in and said, "Ms. Drucilla, Mr. Tony is on the phone and wants to know if you can meet him at 8:00 p.m.?"

"Tell him no, Sandra. I'll see him tomorrow."

Sandra left, as I began to think about the pink dress, it made me sad.

I walked out to the pool hoping the breeze would clear my head. The second time I married Richard, my dress was pink. I had loved him so much, I was sick that I didn't give him his freedom years ago. I'll never stop hating him and somehow I had to make him pay. I will! Maybe that will satisfy me. Just maybe I would be able to get him off my mind. If Tony hadn't put the diamonds on the dress, I could change the color, but it was too late now. I can't believe how my life has changed. I left hell behind, but I still can't forget him. Just two more weeks and Tony will take all the hurt away.

Sandra came back and said, "Ms. Drucilla, Mr. Tombrello is here to see you."

"Tell him to come out here Sandra, and bring us some lemonade."

"Max, what can I do for you?"

"That was my question to you Ms. Drucilla. Mr. Tony said we will be having a new little boy coming to visit and I need to know a few things about him. Tell me, when will he arrive?"

"The little boy's name is Brandon and he belongs to my sister Harriet. He will arrive here next weekend. He is nine years old and about the size of Anthony. If I have my way, he will always be with us. I love him as if he was my own and he matters more to me than life itself. But, I don't want any difference shown in the two boys. I want you to talk to Anthony and ask him to be good to Brandon and learn to love him like a brother.

Max, I want the boys to have flying, dance and guitar lessons. Keep them busy learning. I want them to grow into men. Teach them to fish and hunt. Teach them a little about everything.

Brandon is a wonderful child but as you will see, he's behind in his learning. Not because he can't learn, but because of how he has to live and with whom he has to live. He loves me and I know he will be happy here."

"That's half the battle, Ms. Drucilla, now don't you worry, I will take care of him for you. Is there anything else you need to talk about?"

"No Max, I'll be fine, why?"

"Ms. Drucilla, when I first came out here, you seemed a little sad. I'll help you in any way I can."

"I know you would Max, but maybe time will take yesterday away and that's all I need. If not, I'll let you know. ..... Max, would you teach me how to swim?"

"Yes, Ms. Drucilla, anytime you want to start."

"I want to learn now if that's okay with you, but let me tell you, I'm scared to death of water. I want to swim so bad that I can't stand it. When the water gets above my waist, I stop breathing. I think it's because I've always been afraid of the people around me. I wouldn't let them teach me. I don't think you would let me drown and I'm not afraid of you. What about it? Are you ready?"

"Sure Ms. Drucilla, I'll be back in a minute."

I knew that Max was special. He had been good to me. He was strict with Anthony but in a nice way. It was easy to see that Anthony loved him. I knew Max had been with them since the child was born and was his constant companion. I knew he would take care of Brandon.

I put on my swimsuit and told Sandra to let no one know I was taking swimming lessons, just in case I couldn't do it. While in the pool, I was thinking how surprised Brandon would be that I would be able to swim with him. Boy, will I be surprised myself!

Max returned, dove into the water and began to swim toward me. "Are you ready, Ms. Drucilla? Come on take your feet off the bottom. I'll help you."

Max put his hand on my stomach and lifted me up telling me how to move my arms and legs.

"You're doing fine, Ms. Drucilla, just fine. Don't be afraid, I won't turn you loose. We will work until you get too tired to go on."

After working for about two hours, I began to tire. I asked Max if he could come back the next day at four o'clock. He said that would be fine and disappeared into the house. A few minutes later I heard his car leave.

I laid out on a lounge chair to read and rest for a while, but to no avail. I couldn't get Richard out of my mind. Wondering what he was doing now that I was out of his life. If he had only told me the truth, I wouldn't have left him. Why was I lying here feeling sorry for myself? Now, I have everything. Besides, he never loved me anyway. Face it and send him a piece or two that he can't wash off. I'll do just that, as soon as I take care of Harriet and Percy. First, I have to show Tony that I'm going to be happy.

I went back into the house and told Sandra to call Tony and tell him that I had changed my mind and that I would be there at eight o'clock. I dressed up in a white sundress with my hair up high. I put on all my gold chains and diamonds. Oh yes, I will stay with Tony tonight until he makes me come home. I will smile until my face hurts and besides I have to brag about my golf game. Tomorrow I would call Courtney just maybe she can come to the wedding.

Tony and I stayed at the supper club until two-thirty in the morning. I didn't have to pretend to have a good time because I did. I loved everybody at the gulf. They didn't seem to have any troubles. They were all happy, fun loving people. Dancing with Tony was like floating on a cloud. He had to make me come home.

I told myself I've got too much to do. I can't get used to sleeping all day! I woke early, had breakfast and messed around until eight o'clock then I dialed Courtney's number. I could just see Courtney answering so sleepy that her eyes were crossed. I was ready to be bawled out for not calling before now. When she answered, I told her the news and asked her to come to the wedding.

Courtney said, "Oh God yes! You know I'll be there, Drucilla. I'll be there three days before the wedding so I can get some sun."

After talking for about forty-five minutes, Courtney began talking about what happened with DeRoy. "Drucilla, I read all about DeRoy in the newspaper and that it was very smart of Amanda to make Harriet go with her to have dinner at DeRoy's house just to hear what they would say about you. The paper said that you didn't even know that Amanda was in town until the night before it all broke loose."

"That's right Courtney, but let's not talk about it now. By

the way, Courtney, do you still have that newspaper?"

"Yes Drucilla, I'll bring it to you when I come."

Hanging up the phone, I went down to the beach and sat in the sand. I was thinking about the last time Courtney and I lay in the sun trying to get a tan. Courtney gave me hell. She told me that she didn't care what anyone said, all men are just alike. She told me the story about finding a waitress' apron in Dan's car and it still had the bitch's tips in it. Men will do anything, she said.

I had only told Courtney what Amanda had said about Richard. I knew the child didn't lie. I was mad at myself because Amanda could have been kidnapped. Courtney had said I had better not let Amanda go off with Richard again. Even though this happened in Nineteen Sixty-nine, it seemed like yesterday. Richard had been telling me I was just so jealous that it was making me nuts. That it was just my imagination. It wasn't just my imagination the day little Amanda wanted to go with Richard to the plant. He got mad saying she couldn't go and he didn't need a watchdog. Amanda cried so. I told him to take her or stay home. Later that night while helping Amanda with her bath she asked, why did Daddy leave me in the car today? She was scared to death. He was gone so long Amanda thought he had forgotten her. She asked Daddy doesn't love me does he?

I had asked Amanda where he went. I listened as my child told about the house with a screened in front porch. It was big and scary. She didn't want to go with him anymore and Richard talked so mean to her. I told Amanda I was sorry and not to think about it, that she and I would go shopping tomorrow. I could still hear Courtney saying, don't you let Amanda go off with him again. Of course, Richard lied like a dog about leaving Amanda in the car. I was so mad. Hurting me was one thing, but to hurt Amanda! I hated him. I told him what to do with his blue eyeliner and his need for big blue eyes. Saying one more thing before I walked off, **I hate you Richard**. I think he had been pretending that I was his honey pot. I think he sees one of his sluts every time he looked at me. Lord! I know why people say love is like cancer. It will eat you up if you let it. I'll put that on the shelf for now. His day will come.

Even then I wanted to tell him he was a lot like DeRoy, but I couldn't bring myself to think that bad of him, yet.

Courtney was the best person I had ever known. Courtney has had a hard life and knew the value of a dollar. Courtney has two beautiful girls that I love. I love Courtney like a sister. Courtney had moved away first, then I moved to the country. Even though we had remained friends for twenty years, I couldn't tell her what I was going through. I found myself remembering, laughing and crying as I wrote Tony's name in the sand saying out loud, "Courtney, how many times did I tell you that some day I'd marry a Mafia Man? You'll see me do it in a few days."

The next day, I knew I had to swim. It was so important to be able to swim in the pool with my boys. Just think in a few days, Brandon, Amanda, Courtney and Harriet would be here. After my swimming lesson, I began making a grocery list of things Sandra would need to pick up for my friends visit. Sandra came in as I was finishing the list.

I said, "Sandra, I'll help you cook. We will have plenty of food and I want my friends to have a good time, so try to help them in any way you can. You know that I'll be so nervous that I won't be able to think straight.

Sandra, while you are out, would you please stop by the hairdresser and pick up some conditioner for me. My hair is a little dry from the sun. One more thing, I want all baths to have everything. We don't want the girls to have anything to complain about."

For the next few days I had Sandra busy cleaning and baking. The poor girl couldn't sleep at night. She had never worked so hard in her life. I asked if she would come and live with Tony and myself after we were married. I also knew I would have to ask Michael if it would be all right. The boys needed a good cook. Sandra never answered my question but slowly walked away with her shoulders bent. I thought I sure am glad the girl isn't as lazy as she acts.

The wedding announcement came out in the Sunday newspaper with full pictures of Tony and me. We are to be married at the Mayor's home and then leave for the Bahamas. No one but Max knew that the two boys were going with us. He had been getting the boys things together and came by to show me the new luggage he had picked up for Brandon.

Max also told me that he was going to take Brandon shopping to fill his luggage. Max was thrilled to be going shopping with the boys.

After Max had left, Tony began telling me how Max had lost his parents in a car accident and he had taken Max in. But, Max had paid for his raising. He had stuck with the family like glue. He helps with everything. When little Anthony lost his Mom, Max had automatically became his guardian. Now it looked as if he had added Brandon and me to his list.

Tony said, "Max is infatuated with you, Dru."

"You said that for a joke, Tony, but a blind person could see that he really is. I would never hurt Max.

Tony, I'm late for an appointment. I would like for Max and Anthony to have dinner with us tonight. If that is all right with you?"

"I think that would be a wonderful idea, Dru. Anthony would love that."

"I'll tell Sandra on my way out."

As soon as I left the room I was hollering, "Sandra! Sandra! We have to have dinner for the family tonight because my guests will be here tomorrow. You know after that, we won't have a quiet meal."

I hurried as fast as I dared to make my appointment, knowing I would be late anyway. I was meeting with the Mayor's wife, Sally, to talk over all of the arrangements for the wedding. We talked all afternoon. All I was expected to do for the wedding was to show up with Tony. I knew I could handle that. Once we were finished, I headed for home.

When I got home Tony met me in the yard before I even had a chance to get out of the car. I ran to him throwing my arms around him.

"Tony, are you ready to marry me?"

"You sure got that right, baby."

As I walked into the house I heard little Anthony run into the room with arms out stretched. He said, "Mama, where have you been?"

Turning, I winked at Tony, and then gave my new son a tight hug. I said,

"I've been to Sally's house taking care of last minute wedding plans. Soon I can live at your house. If you would like, Anthony, since tomorrow is Saturday, I will spend the afternoon with you on the beach."

That day on the beach while building sand castles, we talked about his Mother, cartoons and Brandon, but mostly about Brandon.

I said, "Brandon will be here tonight Anthony. I hope you will treat him as a brother."

"Mama, I hope he can live with us forever!"

"When we go back to the house I will get the picture album of Brandon and tell you all about him."

After we returned to the house, as I had promised, I got the picture album and began showing Anthony the pictures of Brandon and telling him everything he would need to know about him. Then Anthony looked up at me with a sad face and asked, "Do you love him more than me?"

I thought for a second, you know I'm not a liar and you know that I love Brandon more than life. What must I say?

I said, "No my boy, I will love you both the same, but I love you better than Tony cause you loved me first."

This brightened up his eyes and I said, "Let's sing that little song I taught you the other day."

**LITTLE RAYS OF SUNSHINE**

I love you deeper than the ocean and deeper than the sea.
Higher than the stars above the mountains and the trees
You're my little rays of sunshine that lighten every day
Even when the days are blue, those little rays come shining through …………

Tony had heard us singing and had come in to listen.

I said, "Tony, one thing's for sure, little Anthony belongs on stage! I have never heard a child sing the way Anthony does. You should see him, he pours out his heart, mind and soul into his singing."

Tony said, "He does sound good, but right now it's time to wash up for supper."

I said, "Tony, I know Anthony isn't worried about Brandon anymore. Just think one hour and my boy will be here."

# CHAPTER 23

I knew I would have to have a long talk with Brandon about Richard. The child loved Richard. He followed him around like a shadow. I'm going to tell him the truth, that I had to leave or die. Max came by to drop Anthony off on his way to the airport and it seemed as if I would burst with excitement.

Tony stayed with me and Anthony was watching TV in another room.

"Sit down Dru they won't get here any faster if you walk the soles off your shoes."

"Tony, I should have gone with Max."

I no sooner said that when I heard the car doors shut. Brandon came running in and I was crying as I hugged him.

"Oh Boy, Mam-Maw has missed you."

"Mam-Maw, you won't let her take me back, will you?"

Whispering back I said, "No man, I won't."

I stood up to see Amanda and Courtney smiling. Sandra and Max came in with food and drinks. The two boys were off to play as if they had been together all their lives. I had forgotten about Harriet, who was slumped in a chair, acting like the dead until Sandra asked her if she would like a drink.

Harriet said, "No thank you, I just need to lie down."

I knew that's what she was going to say. Those were her famous words. I cocked a thumb at Max, which meant get her out of here.

Before the night was over the house was full. Harriet didn't show her face. Courtney and I talked. Lord, did we have hundreds of things to talk about. After a while I looked around the room. I noticed that Amanda wasn't there.

I asked, "Tony, where is Amanda?"

"Don't worry Dru she and Michael have gone for a walk."

The next morning when Sandra came in to wake me, it seemed as though I had just lay down to go to sleep.

Sandra said, "Miss Drucilla, get up."

I said, "Get up hell! Get your butt out of here."

Then, I remembered Courtney. Looking at the clock, I knew that Courtney had drunk a pot of coffee by now. I ran for the bathroom snatching on my swimsuit.

I said, "Sandra, you had better stay out of Amanda's room. If you wake her, you'll have hell to pay. But if she or Harriet do come alive, tell them where to find us."

When I got out to the pool, I was surprised to see Tony and the two boys as well as Courtney.

Tony said, "Dru, what are you doing to me? Anthony was up at daylight."

I said, "Well, mister, you should have left him here last night. Anyway, where's Max?"

Tony winked at me saying, "Taking care of business."

"What business, Tony?"

"That's a none-ya."

I looked at Courtney, "Do you know what that means?"

Courtney said, "It means none of your darn business."

I said, "That's no way to start a marriage. But I'm sure I'll have things that will be none of your business. Do you get that?"

Tony jumped up to grab me, but I was too fast for him. I was all ready on the other side of the pool when he said, "Your business will always be mine."

Courtney planned to get a super tan today. I told her not to over do it. But before the day was over, everything was burned about her except her two headlights and her tail pipe.

We went back to the lounge chairs so Courtney could get out of the sun. We overheard Tony tell Amanda that she was the most beautiful daughter a man could ask for.

Courtney asked me, "Have you ever noticed how much Amanda looks like Tony?"

Before I could answer Michael walked up and asked, "How long have you known Tony?"

I said, "Why do you ask me that Michael? You already know the answer."

Courtney said, "I know what you mean Michael, but it's just her brown eyes and that dark tan."

Michael took me by the shoulders, looking me dead in the eye he asked, "Do you care if I ask Amanda out?"

"No, Michael, I don't mind, but I think most of your dolls have been to dress, undress and play with. You best remember that this doll better not be touched until she's bought with a heart of gold. Do you know what I mean?"

My stare had never moved from his eyes.

He kissed me and said, "Yes, I do know."

He walked over and talked to Amanda and Tony for a minute and then he and Amanda went for a walk on the beach. I got up and was walking along side the pool when I just fell in.

Courtney screamed scaring Brandon. Tony jumped up, grabbed Brandon and kept asking, "What's wrong? What's wrong?"

I was swimming around in the pool when Courtney realized that I wasn't drowning, it put her in a cursing fit.

Courtney said, "Drucilla, why didn't you tell me you had learned to swim?"

I was laughing so hard I couldn't answer her.

Courtney said, "I'll pay you back for that. The last time I saw you, the thought of water scared you to death."

Later that night we all laughed about it. Amanda said so

seriously, "I am proud of you, Mama and I sure am glad you found someone to love you."

Tony said, "Not to break up a good time, but I need to talk to my bride-to-be. We're going for a ride."

He turned to me and said, "You do remember that tomorrow is the big day?"

We drove around and talked. Mostly about the boys and how well they got along. Tony pulled into the parking lot of the supper club.

"Let's get a drink, Dru."

Going in the door I said, "My Lord Tony, everybody's here. Look in that corner, all the boys are at that table."

Tony had a table waiting for us. As we were sitting down Tony said, "Dru, before Papa Perricotti asks you to dance, I must tell you that he has a wedding gift and he insists on giving it to you on the dance floor so everyone will see. It will shock you because it even shocked me, but don't turn him down."

About that time Papa Perricotti walked up to our table. Taking my hand I was on my feet walking toward the dance floor before I knew what was happening. In the middle of a song, we stopped dancing the band stopped playing and as I was looking around…all eyes were on us. Papa Perricotti pulled a ring out of his pocket and in a voice that everyone could hear he said, "Drucilla, I give you this out of love, from the whole family."

As he slipped the ring on my finger, he bent to kiss me whispering, "Let them all see that you are my favorite, because you are."

The band started up and we were the only couple on the floor. Tears rolled down my face as I danced with Papa Perricotti. Looking at my new solitary eight- carat diamond I said to myself, Lord I have made it, I really made it. I am one of them. Tony came out of his seat as the band started playing another song Papa handed me to Tony, and the party started.

I will never forget the night that Papa tried to buy me from Tony. I was to meet Tony at the Love Club, not knowing there would be nine others at the table with him. As I walked up to the table all nine men stood up with Papa.

The old man told me to come over there beside him. I liked the old man because he had guts. I knew he would smile at your face while driving a knife in your gut if he had a reason. Papa asked me to dance. I looked at Tony not knowing what to say. Tony nodded yes. I walked with Papa Perricotti to the dance floor. We danced a few minutes in silence, and then he broke the silence with a bang. He said I will make you an offer. If you'll come live with me, I'll give you a blank check. You can fill in any amount you want. I wanted to laugh but… I didn't dare. I told Papa, I knew he was old, but he was not senile and I knew he was smart enough to know that I will never trade Tony. You knew that Tony had delivered me from the pits of hell. Even now, if we didn't get back to the table Tony may have Charlie to jack his jaws.

Papa said I like you girl. You know who butters your bread. I told Papa he could be my best friend if he wanted to.

I had only been here a few days when that happened. Now I can see he was just trying me out to see if I would be a good wife for Tony.

I said, "Tony, I'll be back in a minute."

I left Tony on the dance floor to say thanks to Papa, one more time. As I took his hand and went to the dance floor, everybody sat down. The band played as hard as Papa and I danced. We danced all over the place.

When the music stopped, I kissed him saying, "I love you best Papa."

I had never in all my life felt so loved. With everyone telling us they would see us at the wedding, Tony and I left for home.

I said, "Thank you Tony. It was a lovely night, not to mention this ring. You and Papa are the best. Tony, I wish I had been with you all my life."

"You are very welcome Dru. I wish you had been here always too."

Courtney was still up when I got home. We talked while

doing our nails and she promised to bring the girls back to visit next time.

I said, "If you don't I'll have Max throw you into the trunk of the car for the five hour trip back to get the girls."

Courtney said, "Damn you, you would do that, wouldn't you?"

I laughed and said, "I'm going to bed. Tomorrow is my big day."

The florist had worked overtime. The house was full of flowers.

The next morning Sandra knocked on my bedroom door and came on in before I could answer.

"Ms. Drucilla, there are lots of flowers, but these are the only ones with a note. I thought you might like to see them now."

Sandra handed me the note along with two, dozen pink roses. The note read:

You are like a Morning Star.
You shine so bright and clear.
You are like a Christmas morning.
You make me so happy dear.
You are beautiful like flowers in spring.
You are warm and tender like a summer breeze.
You are natural like the leaves in the fall.
You are pure as the snow in the winter.
You are someone special with a heart of gold.
And now you are mine forever more.
I'll call you at four see you at eight.
All My Love,
Tony

Holding Tony's note in my hand I fell asleep. I woke up at eleven as Amanda jumped upon my bed. She said, "Mom, wake up! What the hell are you doing sleeping with flowers in your arms?"

"How the hell can I sleep with everybody running in and out."

"Mom, we have to talk and half the day is gone. Do you

have any qualms about marrying Tony?"

"I sat up looking around. Amanda did you wake me up without having me some coffee?"

A knock at the door answered that. Sandra came in carrying a tray with a coffee pot and two cups on it. She walked with her head down and not saying a word. She put the tray down and turned to leave the room.

I asked, "Sandra, what's wrong with you this morning? Are you not happy for me?"

"Yes ma'am, Ms. Drucilla, but it's going to be lonely here when you go with Mr. Tony."

"You won't be lonely Sandra, because you are going with me. I have already asked Michael."

The expression that came over Sandra's face told it all. She danced out of the room.

I looked at Amanda and said, " Well I guess I forgot to tell Sandra that Michael said she could go with me. Now Amanda, it took you a long time to see what was happening to me before. No one has to tell you that I'm a survivor. They almost destroyed me."

"Mom!! This time we're not talking about deceitful people. Mom, we're talking about the gang. Do you get my meaning?"

"I never want you to insinuate that I'm gullible again. Amanda, I was never fooled by your father and I'm not fooled by Tony. So what if they are the gang, as you put it. This gang has given me more love in three months than I've had in forty-four years. Look around you, are you disappointed?"

"No Mother, that's not what I was talking about."

"Amanda, you must have confidence in yourself, not the people around you. No matter what your surroundings are, it won't influence you unless you are weak. I'm not weak nor am I blind. I know full well what I'm doing, you'll see!"

"Mother, I just don't want you to be caught in something that you can't get out of."

"Don't worry about me. I feel sorry for the ones we left behind and even sorrier for the ones that hurt us. I hope I can persuade you to go on with your life, trust in me, confide in me, and most of all be my own very best friend. We haven't been that close, but I hope that will change."

"I hope so too, Mom, I really do."

"Amanda, I hope you can shake Jeff from your mind because he's poison just like Richard. Wipe the slate clean and find what you want and go after it."

"I have put Jeff in the past. If only he'll leave me alone. Mom, I'm glad we had this talk."

"Amanda, I need you to do something about Harriet. All she does is pout. Remind her that she is being paid to let Brandon go with me so I don't want any hell raised when the time comes. If she doesn't want to come to my wedding, she can leave now. Tell her I'll call her when we get back, but I wish she would straighten her face and have a good time."

"I will and one more question Mom? Does Tony know how bad tempered and bitchy you are, early in the mornings?"

Throwing a pillow at Amanda, I said, "I'm sure he will know today at the rate your jaws are running.  Now get out of here."

Amanda ran out laughing. The day flew by. Everyone was so busy. I stayed in my room most all of the day. I made a call to Max. I had to see Brandon. It was a serious talk for a nine year old. I had to know that he understood what was going on and that my love for him would never change. With a promise that he was happy that I was marrying Uncle Tony, I let him go back to play.

Bob Tosti, a friend of Tony's called. He couldn't get back from his trip in time for our wedding but he wished us well and a lifetime of love. I couldn't believe all the calls and gifts from people I hardly knew.

But of course they were Tony's friends. I would sure have to get better at remembering names.

Brandon came running down the hall yelling, "We got to go, Papa Perricotti has sent the limousine."

As the doors began to open, I stood back to see what

Amanda had chosen to wear. As of last night she still hadn't made up her mind. There she was, dressed in a pale yellow and white dress with pale yellow satin shoes. She was as beautiful as I ever wanted her to be. Coming up the hall you could tell she was happy by the spring in her step and her beautiful smile.

As always, Courtney was complaining about her hair even though she had the best head of hair in town. It was piled high with a curl hanging loose here and there. Her burgundy and pink gown was long and slinky.

Amanda said, "Courtney, with that figure you could be a model. Why do you stay hid under all those clothes you wear?"

Courtney and Papa Perricotti were the only ones in the ceremony. Courtney is Maid of Honor and Papa is giving the bride away. I thought, Lord, just wait until Papa sees Courtney. His eyes will pop out and knock his glasses off. I didn't know I was laughing out loud.

Amanda asked, "What's so funny?"

I said, "Not one thing. Let's go."

Brandon asked, "Where is Mama?"

We all three turned around just in time to see Harriet come out of the door. I shook my head hoping it would clear my eyes. Slowly walking toward us was a purple five foot tall, two hundred pound Harriet. Jogging suit bagging around her ankles. Her shoes were lavender flip-flops and her hair was standing up as if someone had scared the hell out of her.

Brandon, while laughing and jumping up and down said, "Mama, you look so funny."

I said, "Brandon, be quiet and go find Max."

Amanda was in shock, but not Courtney. She ran to Harriet.

Courtney said, "What the hell do you mean. I helped you lay your clothes out last night." Courtney got quiet, "My word Drucilla, she's loop legged."

I laughingly said, "Oh Harriet, you have made my day. Every time I think about you drinking, I remember you saying, all the alcohol you drink goes right between your legs."

I was bent double with laughter as Max ran in.

Max said, "What's wrong, Ms. Drucilla?"

I said, "Not one thing Max, but Harriet wants to be locked in her room with two bottles of champagne. Then see to it that she gets home tomorrow."

Courtney and Amanda already had Brandon in the limousine. I pulled myself together. I knew this would be the last time Harriet screwed things up.

Her fat ass had never been nothing but trouble, a trouble making, bitch for as long as I could remember. As we pulled away I mumbled to myself, "You just wait Miss Harriet, I'll put your turd cutter through the change of life just as soon as I get back. You won't shame Brandon anymore."

Amanda asked, "What did you say Mom?"

Courtney laughingly said, "Turd cutter! Where did you get that?"

It was only a short drive to the Mayor's house. I said, "Thank God we're here. Don't any of you look at me because if I think of Harriet, I'll laugh."

Sally let us in at the rose garden doors. The scent of orchards filled the air. I looked down into the ballroom, thinking how beautiful my wedding was going to be. The music was softly playing. One thing is for sure Italians know how to do things right. There were no strangers, everybody danced and laughed having the time of their lives.

At the top of the stairs, I stood counting the steps, wondering if my knees would give away to nervousness, then Tony appeared at the bottom. As he lifted his arm to welcome me, all nervousness was forgotten. I slowly walked down with Tony stepping up the last few steps as he reached me. The cameras began to flash and all doubts went away as I remembered what Tony's money was going to do for me.

Standing before the Priest, I couldn't get my mind off of Harriet, Percy, Richard and Brandon. Lord, little Brandon can't go back to Shady Grove. Tony was holding me, kissing me, all of a sudden, I was terror stricken. I couldn't remember a thing the Priest had said and yet the ceremony was over. How had I made it through the ceremony without saying a word?

I heard everything from congratulations, bravo, well done, and best wishes, in every way that could be said. Not a person was neglected. It was fabulous. This is like being in a Fairy Land. In all my imagination, I couldn't imagine a wedding so grand. Expensive wasn't the right word for it. This is the life I loved, but a far cry from the life I knew. The best thing about all these people is no false-faces. If they don't love you or you don't love them, it's okay no love wasted.

Max and Papa Perricotti walked up breaking my train of thought. Papa said, "It's time to leave for the airport, Miss Drucilla."

Papa walked with Tony and me up the stairs and out the rose garden door where Max was already waiting at the limousine with Courtney and the boys. I'll always wonder how Max had beat us to the car.

Amanda ran around the corner saying, "Thank God, I'm not too late."

I said, "To late for what, Amanda?"

Amanda said, "To go with the boys of course, Tony, tell Mom so we can go. The plane will leave us."

Tony said, "Dru, I have changed our plans. I am letting Amanda and Courtney take our place with the boys. They will be going to Disney World. It will be safer for us if we stay here. No one will know where any of us will be."

Amanda said, "Mom, I beg you, go home so we can go."

Papa Perricotti said, "Load 'em up and move 'em out."

I said, "Damn you Tony, I don't like this!"

Tony said, "You will Dru, I promise you."

With Papa Perricotti laughing, Max drove away. If all the sweet talk had turned to syrup, we would have drowned in the car. By the time the new bride and groom drove into the basement, it was a real honeymoon.

# CHAPTER 24

The house was beautiful. I was proud of Tony. He had thought of everything. For two weeks the one and only call we received was from Papa Perricotti. Time passed fast and everything was back to normal. The boys were running wild and having the time of their lives.

I received an anonymous telephone call. The caller said Percy was running his mouth to Harriet about giving Brandon away. I had been the perfect wife, so cool and calm until I received this phone call and it sent a tornado through my bloodstream. Throwing the telephone across the room, I cursed a blue streak. That son-of-a-bitch must have had a sex change. He wags his tongue like a gossiping old woman. Here I am hundreds of miles away and that fool burns my blood. I'll burn his ass!

I caught a glimpse of Sandra standing in the doorway looking at me.

I screamed, "What the hell are you looking at? Get out of here and find Max. Tell him to get Tony home! **Get out!"**

They'll never leave me alone. They'll never let me be happy until I give them some trouble of their own to take up their time. Tony had never seen me mad. He talked and talked but he couldn't calm me down. I couldn't even sleep, but I already knew what I would do to Percy.

One thing is for sure. Percy didn't know too much about Harriet or he would surely have known that she was too busy to worry about Brandon. I already had the wheels rolling on her case.

It was on the first of April Nineteen Eighty-nine. Bob Tosti moved into a big house in Shady Grove and set out to find Harriet.

I knew he would get the job done. Besides, he was perfect for Harriet. Bob was five feet seven inches tall, one hundred thirty pounds and red headed. I had received the pink roses and a note saying, Tupperware. That was prearranged to let me know he had found her and had set the plan into motion. I laughed out loud saying, hell fire tupperware parties must be the oldest line in the world.

Bob called to give me an update and while we were talking Bob asked, why was I so mad at her about that little boy?

I assure you it's because I fear for him. She is hurting him mentally and physically. I'll tell you why Bob. It is one hundred and seventy-five feet from my house to theirs and many times I saw her jerk him around and I couldn't keep my mouth shut.

Bob, I have seen Harriet fight Gertrude, bruising her face and would have hurt Gertrude worse, but Jerry came in and pulled Harriet off of her. Then there was another girl, I don't remember her name or why they were fighting, but Harriet busted her in the mouth. Plus things like Harriet going to one of my friend's home and cursing her so bad and so loud that all her neighbors came out to see what was going on. My friend was seven months pregnant. I tell you what really made me see that she is really evil and that was the time she threw a pop bottle at Arthur, hitting him in the head. I tell you the man cried. Now this was before Brandon was born and with them living so close to me, I could see and hear everything. It hurt me and I think she needs the fear of God put into her.

A few days before I moved, Harriet and I had a bad fight over Brandon. I was sitting at my kitchen table with the door closed and I heard Harriet screaming at Brandon. Jumping up, I went out into the back porch, and then I began to run. I burst into her front door and saw the child was shaking from head to toe. He had marks around his neck and his eyes were red from crying. I took Brandon in my arms and held him until he stopped shaking. Harriet told Brandon to go to his room and for me to go home. Quietly I told her I would, but if I ever heard her scream at Brandon again I would call the child abuse center on her. That started the worse fight we had ever had. She kept screaming at me, screaming, that she had brought him into this world and she could take him out. She said she would keep him away from me and never let me see him again. It was my time to scream now, but Brandon had come back into the room and Harriet took him by his little shoulders and said that he knew she had born him into this world and she could take him out. I stood there until she sent Brandon to the car. As soon as the child went out the door, I got her by the hair like a crazy person shaking her and screaming that I'd fight her in court to stop her from hurting him. She got loose from me and ran to the car. So you see Bob, Harriet has a bad problem and I can't sit back and let her hurt Brandon. Bob assured he could solve her problem, permanently.

I told Bob no, not now anyway. I even feel sorry for Arthur, he leaves for work at five-thirty in the morning and gets home at four sometimes as late as six o'clock p.m. He still has to wash dishes every night plus dry all the clothes once a week. Oh, and he does cut the grass. I don't know why she does him this way. He is a good man and he has never drank liqueur, smoked, or caused anyone a minutes trouble. I feel sorry for him. He wasn't raised to deal with the likes of her. What she needs is a man that will put her in her place.

I hope Bob understood. Tony didn't just save me he is saving Brandon also. I didn't want to call the abuse center or take her to court. I just want to kill her for hurting him. She is sorry and I want Brandon away from Shady Grove. She is the world's worst to get mad at someone else and take it out on someone smaller than her, so Brandon gets hell.

One day I went over to the house and there she was…mad because he had forgotten part of a message that Mama Marselle had told the child to tell her. I want you to work on her, Bob I never want Brandon to go back there.

On the third Friday, Harriet called to say that Brandon could stay a little longer. Planting a big kiss on my little angel, I thought boy, Harriet fell hook, line and sinker. Now if the medication will start the headaches. Bob and I had gone over every little detail. He knew I'd have his butt if he let me down. This had to work and to my surprise, Bob didn't have a minutes trouble. He rented the other house.

It was a three week job putting fake bathrooms in it. His bus ride to the next town gave him time to sleep for the drive back with the U-Haul. It didn't take Bob as long as he thought it would, he had looked at his watch, it was 3:00 a.m. Bob was sure that no one saw him unload the bathroom fixtures. He had worked fast so he could get the truck back and get himself back to his apartment.

At two fifteen that afternoon, Bob was on the telephone talking to Harriet, pouring syrup through the lines. Bob was asking Harriet about her husband. Harriet said he is a village idiot. You can call me anytime and if he is here, I'll just say you have the wrong number. I myself knew that Harriet was hot to trot!

Bob had told Harriet that he would meet her at the bar to have a drink before dinner. Hanging up, Bob went to bed. He had to get some sleep. He had been working on the house until dawn. But boy, oh boy, tonight is the night! Bob had done well. The house was ready for his mission.

Bob said that he sure hoped Harriet had a good heart or that damn house would kill her instead of scaring the hell out of her.

Artificial blood was placed all over every bathroom with a long sharp knife stuck in the back of the showers. Each knife had blood running off. I knew that being stabbed in the shower was the worst fear Harriet had ever had. Tonight would be the night for real nightmares.

I had the medication tested and sent to Bob. He knew it would only put Harriet out for ten minutes. That would give him just enough time to get her into the other room. Everything was ready. It was a must that he get Harriet into his bed tonight.

She was waiting and all smiles. It didn't take long. Bob handed her a drink as she lay back against the pillow and he silently wished her sweet dreams. She was out in a flash, so he rolled her off the bed and onto a rug so he could pull her into the other room. Bob lay her up against one of the big tubs and tip toed out the door to wait.

Harriet sat up wiping her eyes and calling Bob's name. She could hear him saying, here I am. She slowly stood up, stumbling around the room, and then she saw it. Letting out a blood curdling scream she ran to the next room. One look at all the blood and she was throwing up, but still trying to get out. She had turned white after she fell and got blood on her hands. She ran from one room after another until finally she fainted.

Bob knew she was exhausted, he ran helping her up and out the door. Bob got Harriet back in his bed and gave her a shot and had just finished washing the blood off her when she woke up screaming.

Hugging her up close to him he said, "Baby, what's wrong with you? You dozed off and started screaming."

Harriet said, "Where am I?"

Looking around, she began to cry and said, "Bob, I have to go and I'm sorry I went to sleep."

"Harriet, can I drive you or call you a cab?"

"No, I'll be fine."

Bob drove her home. The next afternoon, Bob called Harriet. She was sick and still in the bed.

Bob asked, "Harriet what is wrong."

Harriet said, "That damn dream, it scared me half to death. I tell you it was so real. I don't know what made me dream it anyway. I haven't even had knives on my mind."

Bob ask, "What did you dream?"

Harriet said, "I woke up looking for you. I could hear you calling, so I got up and that's when I saw it! The bathrooms were covered in blood and someone had left the knives stuck in the back of the shower, all bloody. I tell you Bob, I was so sick that when I got home, I just bathed off in the kitchen sink."

Bob was laughing his butt off, trying hard not to let her hear him. She said, "I think it was real! Maybe it was a warning or maybe I'm psychic. If I were you, I would not live there. One thing's for sure, I'm scared to death of being stabbed in the shower! Are you laughing Bob?"

"No, I'm sorry you're so upset baby. Can I see you Friday night?"

Harriet said, "Sure, call me!"

The next day Harriet called me. She was having terrible headaches and wanted to know if Brandon could just stay a little longer. I told her sure, smiling all the while. He's having the time of his life.

Then Harriet told me about the dream. She said, "It was so real, I'm beginning to think it was!"

I said, "Bullcrap, Harriet, what you need is to get out and have some fun."

When I got off the phone with her, I called the florist and sent her a love bouquet. The card read, Sweet dreams baby! Its working I thought, before I'm through with her, she will be crazy.

Bob turned on the love he didn't know he had. Harriet was eating out of his hands. He had taken her shopping, spending money left and right.

Waking up from the last trip to the bloody bathrooms. Bob had to give her a shot with a tranquilizing gun after she had gotten hysterical. She didn't faint she just sat in the floor and screamed.

Harriet was in bed when Bob called the next day. She was

just too sick to get up. She said, "Bob, I can't get back in your bed again and maybe not see you anymore. Maybe I have been in that house! Maybe all that was real, maybe I'm just remembering."

"No way, Harriet, It's just bad dreams!"

"I don't know Bob. That's not the only thing that's happened to me. I've got to where I can't remember things and I have these severe headaches."

He laughed out loud and said, "How old did you say you are? Just maybe you're going through the change of life! You know some women go crazy during this time in their lives."

This shut Harriet up. She said, "I'll call you later, Bob."

Bob called Charlie to come to town. He was ready for him to do his thing. Charles Perricotti was mean as hell. He would do anything for me and this wasn't half bad. Bob had given Harriet basketball tickets for her hubby, telling her to get his ass out of that house so she could meet him. This gave Charlie the time he needed to fix Harriet's bathroom. You can bet your bottom dollar this looked as real as real could get. Charlie had used real blood and used one of Harriet's knives.

Charles leaned back and smiled, picking up his flashlight, he sat on the sofa to wait. Bob said he would have her back before the ball game would be over. Bob had seen to it that Harriet had too much to drink. Knowing she wasn't about to go to sleep he said that he was tired and needed to get into the bed early.

She was ready to go home. Bob went to the bathroom and called Charlie.

Charlie was waiting by the phone. Hearing Bob say, "She is on her way." Charlie reached into his back pocket and took out the tranquilizing gun. As soon as she got home Harriet went straight for the bathroom. She let out a "No, No, I'm not crazy. **I'm not!"**

Charlie came up behind her shooting her in the back of her arm. In a split second she was out. He put her to bed and cleaned up the bathroom.

The next day, Harriet signed herself into the hospital saying over and over, I'm not crazy.

After a two, week stay, she came home still half nuts telling some of the wildest tales anyone had ever heard. Now everyone thought she had gone crazy. Someone was going to kill her. Someone had put blood all over her bathroom. Even the knife was gone and it was her favorite knife. Now all her friends were backing away and the family didn't go around her. She sure had a problem.

Sure the knife was gone. Charlie had brought it back with him as a souvenir for me.

Harriet called and begged Bob to help her. Bob said, "Harriet, I'm sorry, I can't, I must be moving on. I have another construction job waiting for me. Get yourself well Harriet and come down to see me sometime. I will show you the town."

Crying, Harriet hung up. She said, "Damn them all. I'll call Drucilla she will understand."

Harriet called but I was saying, "I don't have time for your bullcrap Harriet. All you need is to stay busy, now get out of the house! Isn't that what you told me one time or was it call the doctor to give me some medication. Its just life! Is that not what you told me Harriet."

By this time Harriet was screaming in the phone. "I can't live like this**. I'd rather be dead!"**

I said, "Whatever you want, Harriet. You can call me when you feel better. You know darn well all those things are just dreams!"

**"No!** Drucilla, they're not dreams. Not everything, you don't know it all."

"No Harriet, I don't want to know it all. It's your problem. Harriet, isn't that what you said to me, that it was all in my mind?"

A few days later hubby Arthur called to say he had to put Harriet in the mental hospital. She had gotten to the point he just couldn't live with her. Oh my, I thought he must be the village idiot, because when he came in from the basketball game and found Harriet crying he didn't know what to do. Harriet had said that he was just a fool, that he should find some way to help her. Arthur said that he knew no one was trying to kill her so he didn't have any choice but to put her into the hospital. Arthur went on to say that we would have to keep Brandon until Harriet got well enough to come home.

# CHAPTER 25

Some how I knew it was the right time to work on Percy. I couldn't sleep for thinking about him. Jumping out of bed, I rang Max's room telling him to meet me in the kitchen in ten minutes.

Max came in rubbing his eyes. "Woman, do you know it's two o'clock in the morning!"

Calmly I handed him a cup of coffee and the telephone. I said, "Max, I want two guys to go to Birmingham, so get them over here!"

It took only twenty minutes for Gervase Topaz and Sam Arturo to quietly come in the back door. I was afraid they would laugh because these boys were not used to petty jobs. But I went right into telling them about Percy and why I wanted him yanked around.

For some reason he doesn't want me to have Brandon. He has continued to stay on Harriet's butt and as you already know Max, he's the very one that lied and caused her to take him away from me before. Now, I don't want you to kill anybody, but I want Percy to know what chill out means!

I went on to tell the guys about Percy's first wife. How she had almost gone crazy when he had met her for lunch one day telling her not to come back home that he had rented her an apartment in North Birmingham and had moved all of her things.

Her name is Judy Clay. Take this address and find her. Tell her that Percy has sent you to pick her up and bring her home. You won't have any trouble because she still loves him. She's been saying he would wake up someday, but I promise you, Percy hates her.

Percy goes fishing before daylight every Saturday morning and he doesn't have any neighbors so you won't be seen. Take his new Tush to the basement. Gag her and lock her in the laundry room. Be sure to have everything you need to lock all the doors so Percy can't get in that house. Lock all the windows on the outside. I know he'll go in from the basement. Tell Judy that Percy, won't be home until late, but he guarantees her a night she won't forget.

Boy's we are talking about a woman that goes crazy when she gets mad and when Percy comes home to find her taking his new Tush's place. He will be fit to be tied! Now on your way to Percy's house with Judy, stop at the liquor store and get her some fine wine, but knowing Judy, she will have a sack full of goodies. Anyway, I know she'll be half drunk when Percy gets there.

Gervase wanted to know about the other broad. What kind of fit is she going to have? None, every time I think about her I laugh. She'll do what ever you say, and I do not want her hurt. She can't help what Percy does.

I began to burst out laughing. Max said, "Tell us what's so funny?"

I said, "All right, I'll tell you. For months and months after Percy married his new Tush. He was acting like a bully in front of her.

He would talk for hours about how he was going to rob a bank. That he knew he could get away with it. Tush would listen to him and believe everything he said. So one day there was a news flash, a Southside bank had been robbed. I told Harriet to be quiet while I talked. When Tush answered the phone, I told her

I was Mrs. Sides from the Birmingham Jail and that we had Percy in jail for robbing a bank and that he would call her as soon as he got through talking to his lawyer. I'll never forget it. Tush said, thank you for calling me and hung up. I laughed so hard I was almost sick. Every time Harriet looked at me I would burst out laughing.

Percy lived next door to me and that day it came up a bad storm and Mama Marselle came to my house to see if we could get Tush to be with us before the storm came. Mama Marselle always wants everybody together during a storm. I will never forget the way Mama Marselle looked as she said, Tush is crying, someone called her about Percy robbing that Southside bank and she won't come out until Percy calls her! When Mama said that, Harriet got in the floor and rolled with laughter. Mama Marselle threw her arms up in the air saying, Damn you Drucilla, you are the one that called that girl. Mama left so mad she could have killed us both. Harriet said that Percy would kill me when he got home. So I waited and watched for him. At four o'clock, I dialed the phone and when Percy answered, I asked if he had counted his money yet. Before he could say a word I told him he shouldn't tell that girl he was going to rob banks or any other stupid thing. Well boys, she is the same today. Tush is good but she is just another village idiot."

I got up saying, "Let Max know, if you need anything, but leave today."

I then told Max that I was going for a walk on the beach and that if Tony woke up to tell him where to find me. It was just breaking day and the breeze was wonderful. I loved the beach. I could forget Shady Grove while listening to the waves. It was as if I were in another world with leaches holding on in the name of revenge. Here I was in a beautiful place with revenge never leaving my mind. As I walked I thought that I must start making plans for Richard. I had put him out of my mind long enough. I would send him a piece of ass in a few days, a piece he would never get rid of. No! I don't have time for Richard, there was too much going on with Harriet and besides, Tonnymacker should send me word any minute about the Hallmarks. One thing's for sure, that bunch will be smoked bacon when he's through with them.

The Hallmark house was surrounded with fire from the ground to the roof when the speaker came on. Throughout the house you could hear over and over, Drucilla is here, your hick daughter-in-law has arrived. I have a surprise for you. All the wires have been cut from the house. There is no electricity or telephones. The speakers are playing on battery!

Tonnymacker was in the trees fifty feet away and he could hear the screams. He waited until the house had burned to the grass roots knowing damn well that I would reward him if he left nothing standing. He was anxious to let me know that the job had been taken care of. So as soon as he could he went to the florist and wired me two, dozen miniature pink roses with white baby's breath.

Oh! How I had planned and waited! For Thanksgiving, I knew all the Hallmarks would be together. Papa Wade was an old man now and Butchie boy was kissing his ass. How else could he be number one bastard?

At nine thirty, I was crawling across the king size water bed with two glasses and a bottle of champagne saying, "Tony, Tony, wake up."

Tony turned over while I was straddling him. Even half asleep he could see I had been up to my eyeballs in mischief. He always knew because I was happy from head to toe.

I said, "Just one glass Tony, come on, just one to help me celebrate!"

"It's so damn early, Dru. First tell me what we're celebrating. Money, I want to drink to money. It will buy anything. I love it! Now drink up and Tony, I love you. You're so good to me. Go back to sleep baby, I'll be back after my bath."

As Tony turned over he said, “How can I sleep with bath water running.”

There I was singing as loud as I could, happy as hell! Tony jumped out of bed and came running into the bathroom. He said, “The curiosity is killing me. You now have my full attention, so talk.”

I said, “Okay…shave Tony. Amanda is flying in today and I’m so happy, I can’t stand myself.”

Tony looked at me smiling.

I said, “Money…Money is wonderful, Tony.”

He grabbed me by one arm and one leg pulling me out of the tub and back to bed. Looking across the bed at me Tony said, “Girl you have a big heart for those you love and a lot of hate packed inside such a little body for those you left behind. I’ll never let you down, Dru. It is a mystery to me why you were born into that decaying bunch. But now the only worry I have is all the hate that you have let build up until it won’t go away.”

Tony had every confidential file that existed on me even the things that had been put under the seal of secrecy. There’s no mystery of how Tony gets what he wants it just takes money.

I will never forget how surprised I was the night Tony took me downstairs to meet my wedding presents. Looking around the room, I didn’t see a thing but four young handsome men. This is what you said you have wished for all your life Dru, and they are my very best. They know to do whatever you ask. I only ask you one thing, don’t ever bite off more than you can chew!

Tony introduced them one by one, here you have, Max Tombrello, Roger Tonnymacker, Charles Perricotti and Michael Tortomasi.

Tony had broken my silence by saying your eyes are sparkling like never before. I wish I could read your mind.

Now Tony, this is the most unusual gift I’ve ever heard of, but I love them all! I know Tony I must be the strangest puzzle you have ever had to put together.

# CHAPTER 26

I wanted everything money could buy and more, but I also wanted privacy. Tony sure couldn't understand why I didn't want anyone but Sandra and myself in the kitchen. I wanted to do most of the cooking. Tony would say for the life of me, I don't know why. Just look. You have maids to take care of it all. Then Tony would stop and look at me smiling and say, whatever makes you happy.

I had lay in bed thinking about too much. Looking at the clock, I said, "Tony, get up!"

One look at his watch got him out of bed. He said, "I have a day planned with Anthony and Brandon, but I will be back in early."

The two boys knew about the new house. They also knew better than to tell me. It was the biggest surprise they had ever known about and they were sure to keep it a secret.

The big Oak trees on Wolf Creek were beautiful and Tony had said he would build the boys a tree house on one condition, that they wouldn't ever disturb the moss that hung from the trees because I loved it best of all. The house was a big split-level. The room that Tony was the most proud of was the big private room…just for me. If you didn't know about the secret room, you would never know by just walking into the bedroom that it was even there. It just looked like mirrored sliding doors for a closet. The large bedroom had a beautiful rock fireplace surrounded with bookcases. The entrance is the mirrored door but there is a button on the right inside door facing which opens the back wall. The room was all finished with a kitchen that was complete and my very own antiques. The big, white Southern Home Comfort, cooking range that looked like new, but so did the big, white cabinet. The oak table and chairs were shinning like glass. Looking around he was so proud. I would have my kitchen that didn't need electricity. This kitchen had another surprise, for just off to the left was another set of doors and behind them are a portable washer and dryer with a new electric range sitting beside it. Closing all the doors, Tony walked out of the bedroom and sat down by the new pool.

The boys ran up asking, "Can we tell Mom now?"

"No way. Not until it's ready to move into and that will be soon!" Walking back to the car, Tony said, "Boys we were lucky to find these twelve acres. I thought it would be impossible. Don't you think Wolf Creek is a perfect place?"

Tony reached over to mess up Brandon's hair just as Brandon said, "Yes sir. My Mam-Maw is always saying she can hear the gulf calling her. Now she can live here forever and just get in her car and drive to the ocean everyday."

"That's right, my little man. Now we just have to find a way to keep you here."

I was waiting with open arms as all three came in looking as if they had done something wrong. I said, "Where have you all been?"

The boys had a funny look on their faces but then Tony saved them by saying, "We spent the afternoon at the water park."

I said, "Okay boys. Max is waiting for you, so hurry and get a bath. Do you boys remember that Amanda will be here soon?"

Brandon turned and asked, "Mam-Maw, when is my Mom coming down?"

With a nervous voice, I said, "I don't know man."

Brandon hesitated and then said, "I wish she could be here."

Now I could hear my heart pounding. I would never hurt Brandon. I ran falling to my knees in front of him and holding him in my arms, I said, "I will go see your Mom next week. Don't you worry about her. Maybe I can get her to come here. Now we must get ready for dinner."

I looked up when I heard the car horn. Everyone jumped at the same time. Anthony and Brandon were out the door in a flash. We heard Brandon squeal out, "Mam-Maw, its Amanda."

As Tony and I walked out, I could feel the tears coming.

Tony said, "You can be proud Dru. She is a beauty."

Amanda's hair was frosted and bouncing around her shoulders as she walked toward us. Her pink satin suit was gorgeous and fit like a glove. Going straight for Tony, Amanda gave him a big hug and said, "Thanks for the car!"

Tony said, "Don't thank me baby. It was Michael's idea. He said that he couldn't get here before you and he wanted you to have a car of your own."

Amanda said, "I'll sure have to thank him."

Amanda was hugging me and laughing at the boys that were trying to bring her luggage into the house. I said, "Amanda, Michael asked us to wait for him. He will be here in time for dinner. Your room is the first on the right at the top of the stairs."

Amanda helped the boys with the small luggage while Max got the rest. Amanda was back down stairs pacing the room. "Mom, I'm starving to death. The only time I get to eat is when I come home."

About that time Michael came in. Tony was on his feet, "Come on Amanda, your Mom is the best cook in town."

Sitting at the table, I looked at my new family and thought

how lucky I am. I knew Amanda would marry Michael when he asked her. How lucky they both would be. I knew it wouldn't be long. Michael looked at Amanda with the most loving eyes and tender smile. I had told him that Amanda had been hurt once and I didn't want her fooled again. I advised him not to play with her heart. I could hear Amanda asking about the new club. Tony told Amanda that I had found the land to build it on so it wouldn't be long now. When dinner was over everyone disappeared. The boys went to their room to watch a movie on the VCR and Michael and Amanda went to the disco.

Tony stood up. Taking my hand he said, "Let's talk. I think I know someone you may remember."

"I doubt that, but whom?"

"You're Uncle Louie. I met him just after he spent time for killing that man in Chicago."

"Not many knew about my Uncle Louie. He had always been my favorite. He is my mother's brother."

Tony laughed, "I know all about your Uncle. He also had older friends that knew him well. That's why the gang loves you so much. You're so much like him. You do have his gumption Dru. I know you've known all of your life that you and Louie were not like the rest of your family. We know that there was no man living with more guts than Louie King."

Jokingly Tony asked, "Haven't you ever wondered where your Grandma was when she got pregnant with Louie?"

"Sure I wondered. He was the only one in the entire family that would do what he had to do to your face."

Tony went on to say, "Louie had lived out most of his life in New Orleans. That is, of course, when he wasn't in jail or prison."

"Why Tony, did you know him?"

Tears ran down my face as I remembered Uncle Louie. I know for a fact that he was the only one in the family that ever loved me besides Jerry. He would have killed DeRoy if it hadn't been for Mama Marselle begging him not to.

Once he came into town for a visit and DeRoy was raising hell. One word led to another and like a flash of lightning, DeRoy was out cold on the floor. Uncle Louie grabbed up a chain saw that was next to the wood stove and one pull on it and it fired off. I can still hear DeRoy screaming out as Uncle Louie stepped on DeRoy's neck telling him he would stick the saw down his throat. That's when Mama Marselle ran in pulling him away from DeRoy begging him to leave DeRoy alone. Uncle Louie let him go and DeRoy didn't want anymore so he crawled out the back door and ran for the outside toilet. I don't remember how he got back into the house, but I think he came back through the bedroom window. Uncle Louie told Mama Marselle that she had better keep DeRoy under her coattail because if he ever crossed his path, she'd never see the bastard again.

Telling Tony the story I said, "Tony, I know it's not funny to some, but to me it's always been hilarious. The way he could send all five grownups with a half dozen kids running with their bed cover under their arms to our house in the middle of the night. Mama Marselle's sister's family would make pallets all over our floor. This happened more times than I can count. It's funny now that you've got me to thinking about it. I didn't realize what Daddy meant when he was telling Mama Marselle that I was born with Uncle Louie's tendencies. Daddy was right and I'm proud."

"I'll have to agree with your Daddy. That's why I love you."

"Tony, I did some crazy things to be so little. When Amanda was about three months old and I had to move back into the house with Mama Marselle until I could find a place to rent, Jerry had married a Go Go Dancer and was living with us as well. I hated her beyond words. Most of all, I hated being there. Every morning for a week and a half, Mama Marselle told Jerry's new wife not to come to her table without washing her hands. The girl just ignored Mama Marselle. I swear to you Tony, I don't know what came over me. I just jumped up and had a knife at her throat before I knew what I was doing. Jerry came in so I let her go. It made her mad as the Devil in hell when Jerry laughed saying that next time she may not be so lucky. Come to think of it, I didn't have to deal with her anymore until Richard and I moved to the country. Then she put her little girl up to telling Amanda that Richard wasn't her real Daddy. All hell broke loose. I gave her one- week to move. That was on Sunday and they were gone Wednesday. I even bought their house from Jerry to assure myself that she'd never move back.

Even Harriet used to say that the family secretly hated me and was afraid of me because I was like Uncle Louie. Oh! Tony, I can laugh now. Remember how they used to say, it's the change of life."

"That just goes to show how love mellows us."

"What do you mean?"

"Look back Dru? You didn't give into or up, on your family until they changed their way of living. Even though these same people gave you a terrible childhood and you didn't want to love them. I gave you better things and some of the hurt eased up in you. You wanted your people to have better because it would make them better people. Your love for them mellowed you, but they will never see that. All that they'll ever see, is you being tough like Uncle Louie, making them do this or that."

"You don't know what you're talking about Tony. After I found out that Richard was whoring around on me, I wasn't mellow. I just didn't want to go to jail and I knew what my family had done. It was as if Richard was playing football and one of the family members took the ball and ran for a touch down. They knew he was doing a fine job of making me sick, so they set in to help him put me away one way or another. If I had been mellow, they would have put me away and you know that. Can't you see I couldn't do anything! I had nineteen reasons why I should make Richard leave and I tried. We fought for months. He just wouldn't go on his own. I was afraid the courts wouldn't give me a dime to live on. I couldn't prove he was doing any of the things even though I knew for sure he did. The Sheriff knew. The Priest knew. But they couldn't give me proof and I didn't have the money to hire a detective. I was between a rock and a hard place. Not a way in the world to make a dime of my own. Amanda was gone and Harriet was siding with the rest of the family saying I was crazy."

"You damn better believe it's called tough."

"Tony, a mellow person couldn't live through what I did. I'm no fool! I knew from the way Richard was insisting that he had to have new work clothes and he had three pair of boots that he kept shined making sure he had a clean pair for every day. He told me not to put notes in his lunch anymore and not to call the plant asking for him. And working, if he worked all the hours he was gone, he would be dead.

Every Friday night for more than a year he was out saying his boss was making him work. For the first time in his life, there was money coming up missing. He just didn't know what happened to it and he wasn't going to give an account for the money he spent. He said it wasn't supposed to be any of my business anyway. It was his money. He worked for it. Richard worked two and three hours overtime every night…for sure on Friday and there wasn't any overtime money.

Now Tony, the thing that upset me the most is Richard talked for weeks about a loan company downtown saying he went in there a lot to talk to the old-man that ran the place. So one day I looked up the number and called just to hear a girl say this is Lisa, may I help you.

Keep in mind that Richard had said there wasn't anyone working in this office except an old man. I wanted to see for myself what was there. I walked right up to Lisa handing her a picture of Richard asking her if she knew this man.

I said he works for the telephone company and I'm told that he hangs out here a lot. Lisa said he does look familiar. Then in walked what is supposed to be that old man a very handsome thirty-eight year old man. He asked if he could help me. I said yes sir if you can tell me if you know this man. He said, yes I do. But your trouble isn't here it is with that floozy he rides with. I could tell by the way they frolicked around that they were involved. She is your trouble.

He also took me into an office opening what looked like a closet, but inside were large gray boxes of telephone wires, which must have taken care of more than that one building. Richard had lied again. He had told me that if I would marry him back that he would never ride or work with a female.

I confronted Richard once again. Oh, was he mad and did he ever lie. And to tell you the truth, it wasn't the women this time that had set me into a tailspin. It was the fact that upstairs from this place was a gay club. I didn't want to believe this, but I was half crazy and he had insisted that there was no woman. All I knew was things were happening to us that I didn't understand. Like he said he had to have new underclothes and then half of them came up missing. So did a lot of towels and a bath mat. Did he have a home away from home? Now when I saw that my food was gone, I sure raised some hell. Then to my surprise, I found a key in my desk drawer that went to the house. There it lay on top of all the white envelopes. Richard said that Harriet brought it back and Harriet put it there.

Then the Sheriff said that it came off of Richard's key chain. I know very well it was Richard and he tried to make it look like Harriet had done it all. I'll tell you Tony, if it hadn't been for my doctors and the Sheriff's Office. I would have been crazy, if not dead. I was crazy anyway for living with him and crazy for being alone so much.

Why don't you just say it Tony? I'm not as tough as Uncle Louie or I wouldn't have cared for going to jail. I would have taken care of Richard and all the rest. Look at me! I'm not but four feet eleven inches tall. What can I do about anything? As you well know, it takes money. I've done the best I could. Richard kept saying he wasn't guilty of any of it and the fool that I was I wanted to believe him. But in my heart, I knew! I knew the family was helping him hurt me. I couldn't do any more than I did. The only way was to die or continue to take it."

Tony was on his feet, "I'm sorry Dru. We were just talking. I didn't mean to send you into a whirlwind. It's all over. You're with me now!"

As I pulled away from Tony, I said, "That's where you're wrong Tony. It won't be over until they pay for what they did to me!"

I walked over to my desk and took out two letters and handed them to

Tony, "Read these. One was sent to Mama Marselle from a friend. The other letter was sent to Percy from Richard. It will show you that Richard tried to help me get the family off my back."

Tony opened the letter to Mama Marselle first and began to read:

Dear Marselle,

I'm just a friend, but I have to say what's on my mind. Because of pure jealousy, your whole family has turned on Drucilla. You need to take a good look at her. She has always been the backbone of your family. She has brought you from the ghetto to a modern way of living. She and Richard have given her sisters and brothers everything to make their life better. And Harriet, what did she mean by taking Brandon away from Drucilla? She has loved that boy better than life. We don't know why you people can't love her. She is the best you people have. Do you ever look at her and think about what she has done?

Drucilla has a garden every year canning and freezing most all of her food. Bakes and out cooks anybody we know. Quilts, makes her clothes, and makes candy of all kinds. This girl loves life. I could go on and on. She dances and races cars, but first of all, she puts others first. What do your other children do? Just name one thing. Have they come as far as Drucilla? Do they have as much as her? Who made her what she is?

She is a wonderful person a joy to be around. No one can believe that Percy could have done what he has to her. But you, you're her Mother you should have put a stop to it all. Drucilla has friends that love her.

We will take care of her the best we can, but you may wait around until it's too late and she may never forgive you for the part you're playing in all of this. In all truth, Drucilla should have been going to school instead of killing herself taking care of all of you.

Tony looked up at me saying, "People never understand unless they know the whole story Dru. I'm sure a lot more friends would have stood by you if they had known."

I laughed at Tony saying, "That's what you think baby. Many of my, so called friends did know, but said right off that they couldn't get involved in family matters. I got sick of hearing church and prayer. But most of all I got sick of hearing the change of life. I hope I never hear that ever again."

Tony had never laughed as hard as he did when I told him what brought on the change in a woman. "See Tony, when a man hits his early forties, he gets scared that he's losing it, so he starts whoring around with younger women to prove he's still got it. By this time everyone thinks he's the best family man in town. Then, all of a sudden, his wife finds out and all hell breaks loose. People say there's no way! Not him. He wouldn't do anything like that. All the family and neighbors stand around shaking their heads and saying, poor little thing. She's just going through the change of life.

You can believe that after giving a man all the young years of your life, being clean, good and saving herself for him, it will change your life alright. Plus making me want to rearrange his face. Most women just keep quite, but I was too hurt. One thing is for sure, if Uncle Louie had been alive, this is one time I would have asked him to kill Richard."

"Dru, you're a mess. I have never heard it put like that before."

"I couldn't believe Harriet was lying about so much. It was things that I knew for sure she was lying about. Little things just kept building up and up. Like, I had been giving Brandon money every Friday to go shopping until Harriet came in saying Brandon wanted a toy that cost twenty-five dollars. It was only four days after Christmas, so I said, no way. I told her that I had bought him everything in the world and I didn't believe he needed another toy. I felt like Harriet was pulling one over on me. No joke. The next day I stopped in at the toy store. Can you believe that toy was only four dollars and ninety-nine cents! I bought it, but I told her she had lied to me her last time. Harriet was just using Brandon to strip me of every dime she could get. Maybe I should be immune to hurt by now, but I'm not. I have bought ninety percent of everything the child has ever had. Don't get me wrong the money I spent on him was out of love for Brandon.

Tony, I know Brandon belongs to her, but I love him as if he is my own son. Harriet knew that the worst thing that she could do to me was to keep him away from me. I had never been away from him more than two days when she got mad and kept him away for three weeks. It was at this same time that I let it be known that Richard was whoring around again. Harriet just laughed in my face when I begged her not to keep Brandon from me. I told her that I couldn't take much more. I had loved this child for seven years. I could stand anything, but not her taking Brandon from me.

After a week and a half, I was so sick and dizzy that I had to hold onto the furniture just to get around the house. Tony, this is when I noticed that the coffee was making me sick. After about two drinks, I would be so nauseated that I couldn't hold my head up. I thought at first it was just my nerves, and then I found the little green pellets of rat poison lying to the side of the coffee maker. I knew that no one would believe that Richard was poisoning me, so I just stopped drinking the coffee he had waiting for me every morning. After he would leave for work, I would pour it out. By the time I was able to go to the doctor, it was all out of my blood. But I do know that he tried to kill me with that rat poison! When I confronted him about it, he didn't say two words. He just got up and got the container of rat poison and went outside. When he came back, I asked him what did he do with it and he said he poured it under the floor so the rats could eat it.

All the evidence was gone. He never said another word about it and neither did I, but I didn't eat or drink anything he made for me after that.

To my surprise, Harriet let Brandon come back but she talked to me as if I were a dog. She said that she would show me what it was like not to have a dollar someday."

"How long did she keep Brandon away?"

"Oh! I well remember. This was the first time she took him from me. It was from June fifteenth until the middle of July. During that time Harriet had told so many lies and talked so bad to me that when the food and other things came up missing, I didn't know which one had done what.

But one thing was for sure it looked like both of them were trying to force me into suicide. Harriet and Richard were the only two people in my house for over a year. Yet everything that was happening to me was right there in the house.

Tony, I did come back from a few days vacation to find the doors open and everything searched through. I knew Richard didn't do it because he was with me. What I didn't know was…what if Richard had given his honey pot a key to my house! I had found panties and slips in the house that didn't belong to me. Not to mention the panties that I found in the truck. Anyway, after Richard took the polygraph test, I told Harriet she was next. That's when she said she wished that I were dead and yes she would take the test. It wouldn't prove a thing. What she didn't know is that the test was going to cost me a hundred dollars and I didn't have the money, so I told her that she wasn't worth the time but one thing was for sure that I would survive her and Richard no matter what. I swear to you Tony, if it wasn't for Brandon, I wouldn't let her come within fifty miles of me.

Hell! You know what happened next. The winch took Brandon away from me for a whole year. Phillip Jimez was mad as hell. He said it looked like she was sure helping Richard especially after taking Brandon away the second time.

I had begged her to help me find out who was tormenting me to death. But when she wasn't saying it was just in my mind, she was saying that I knew it was Richard. I made her pay. She did not get away with what she has done to me. Her first Richard next! I loved her Tony, as if she belonged to me, but not anymore. Keeping Brandon away from me just made me hate her.

Then there's good old Percy. I bet he wishes he were dead because he knows it's me. I didn't want to kill him, but I wanted him to pay for lying like he did."

Tony took me in his arms and said, "Dru, its true isn't it?"

"What Tony?"

"You will never rest until you get revenge on them all."

"Don't you worry Tony, I'll get revenge. I was born with a forgiving heart, but I don't forgive the same person over and over. You know the old saying don't you. The first time you hurt me, its shame on you. The next time you hurt me, its shame on me for giving you a second chance. Let's not talk anymore Tony. I'm ready to go to bed."

"Okay, but I haven't read the letter to Percy. Just give me a minute."

I stretched out on the sofa saying, "You read Tony, but I don't want to talk about it anymore. I'll tell you one more thing Tony, Richard sure tried to make that letter sound like he wasn't guilty and that he loved me."

"By all means let me read it then."

Percy, For one thing, I'm too upset and mad to talk to you about this, but I sure as Hell have things to say. So you can tell yourself and everyone else that you run your mouth to.

Drucilla does not need a doctor. It's one thing to hurt me with your lies. But you've hurt Brandon and yes, this hurt Brandon most of all and that's why Drucilla tried so hard to find the ones that caused all this trouble. It hurt to know that you played a part in it. Why did you cause us trouble instead of helping us? Was it you that killed the trees in my yard? Was it you that put the panties in my truck? Who left that tape in my mail- box? Who did all these things plus others that almost took my home apart? Why do you hate Drucilla so bad? How could you tell Harriet those awful lies?

I'm well aware of what has been going on in and around my house. My wife has not seen a doctor in fourteen months because the doctor has said she is sane and never needed a doctor in the first place. She just needed to be taught to live around her family as if they were neighbors. That way she would not have to worry about what they needed or didn't have. I personally cannot believe that you would talk to Drucilla the way you did or make up so many lies. You must be dreaming. Drucilla did not and would not ever say that she would get rid of Brandon for anybody. Why you would lie about this is beyond me. But you did lie. I can tell you or anyone else that Drucilla has not lied about any of this. Drucilla and myself have been knee deep into this at the Sheriff's Office. We do not know who did this to us, but someday we will. I will find out myself. Furthermore, Drucilla is not a whore and has never been. It wasn't me that tried my shoes on before I bought them. You best not call her out of her name again. You, Percy, sat at my table and said that I make more money than the rest of the family and I should give them what they need. Now you say that you didn't say that. You did! That's a fact. I heard you. Why did you say anything at all to hurt Drucilla or me?

You of all people know how much I love Brandon. You also know it's a fact that Harriet did get mad at Drucilla and I. She kept Brandon away from us from June fifteenth until sometime in July of Nineteen Eighty-eight. I live here too. You know that I know what goes on here. What in the hell has happened to the truth with you people? There is nothing wrong with Drucilla except she has been hurt to the bone with lies and more lies. You of all people should have come running when Drucilla needed you. It was she who bent over backwards to help you over the years. You can rest assured it was my money, but it was her love that helped you. When you were taking the nerve medication, were you going through the change of life? Drucilla's psychiatrist said she didn't need any and that she didn't even need a doctor.

Do you get that!

P.S. I want you to read and re-read this until you understand how we feel.

Even now because of your lies, Harriet is mistreating Drucilla and Drucilla is giving me a bad time. Why did you have to hurt us?

Tony would look at the letter and then look at me. He said, "Dru, you have been used and abused for the last time."

Tony put the letter back into the desk and came to the sofa. Taking me into his arms, he carried me to our room and turned on my bath water. I was watching him. He wasn't like any gangster I had ever read about. Tony was more like a dream come true. He said for me to relax in my bath that he would be back soon.

# CHAPTER 27

What I didn't know was that Topaze and Arturo had to get permission from Papa Perricotti to go to Birmingham. Papa had already told Tony that I had given them orders to go and that was fine until reading the letters. After telling Max to bring the car around, he got on the phone with Topaze saying he was going with them to deal with Percy. Topaze and Arturo were to wait for Tony and forget about what I had said. He would do this job right.

Coming back into the room, Tony said, "I have to go help Papa Perricotti with a job. I won't be back until about two o'clock tomorrow afternoon."

Tony hurried out of the room telling Max he should have shut Percy up when I got the phone call saying Percy had been running his mouth about me having Brandon.

When the plane landed at the Jasper Airport, Topaze and Arturo had planned ahead to have a rental car waiting for them. At two-thirty a.m., there were only three cars on the highway all the way to Shady Grove. Luck stayed with them. Not a single person was seen as they drove into Percy's yard. Jumping out of the car, all four men were at the door at the same time.

Tony said, “Kick that damn door in boys.”

With splinters flying everywhere, Percy was out of bed naked and yelling, “What in the hell’s happening?”

Tony said, “Just do it boys.”

Percy’s new Tush started to run, but Arturo grabbed her legs pulling her back. Max and Topaze had given Percy two broken legs.

Tony said, “One leg is for Brandon and one is for Dru.”

Yanking his arm up, popping it half into Tony said, “This one’s for me! If you ever open your mouth about my family again, it’ll be your last. Do you get it?”

Max dragged Percy over to the basement stairs and rolled him down them. Tony got a hand full of Tush’s hair and said, “You had better forget all you have seen or I will personally pluck your eyes out.”

By four a.m. their plane was back in the air heading home. When they got back to the gulf, they went to Papa Perricotti’s house.

Tony said, “It was a job well done. But now I have to stay at your house. Dru doesn’t expect me back until this afternoon. She thinks I’m helping you. Now Max, you had better beat it back to the house. You know Dru is going after Harriet today. She doesn’t want Brandon sad or suspicious about his Mom, so she is bringing her home.”

Sam Arturo spoke up, “Tony, I need a woman. Maybe Mrs. Tony will let me come around to see Harriet. Didn’t I hear someone say that her husband had divorced her?”

Tony said, “That’s right Sam. But as you know, Brandon doesn’t go with the deal. If you want to know what Dru will do to you over Brandon, just ask Percy.”

They all rocked with laughter.

Doctor Skeet was trying to be my friend after DeRoy’s death. It had taken him weeks to get me to forgive him for not seeing through Richard and DeRoy. Now he visits me every time he comes to the gulf. This time was to give me some tips on how to deal with Harriet. Doctor Skeet asked if there was anything I needed, but a soft smile told him no, just a friend.

At every visit, Doctor Skeet would tell me that he is going to talk to Tony and tell him that I wasn't well and that I was hiding my depression way down deep inside, but the act I put on, one would have to dig deep to pull me out. He told me that I worried him because I was so full of hate.

When I went to see Harriet at the sanitarium, she surprised us all. She was happy and had lost a little weight. She promised to stay with Tony and me. She promised not to cause any trouble with Brandon. After the doctor and nurse had left the room, I said, "If you have any intentions of upsetting Brandon's life or influencing him in any way, then you had better stay at the hospital."

Harriet said, "Oh no! I know what you're saying to me. I won't say or do a thing." Then she whispered to me, "My doctor has already told me that Tony would take me out to the ocean and feed me to the sharks if I caused any trouble."

I said, "Good, now we understand each other."

I arranged for her release and left for the gulf. We no sooner got into the door when, Sandra handed me a big brown package from Courtney.

I should have found time to stop by to see her when I was there to get Harriet. I'll look at this later and call her tonight.

I looked into the other room and to my amazement, Harriet ran into the other room and was playing with the boys and Brandon was lit up like a light bulb. This didn't bother me. I wanted the child to love his Mom and I would never lose him. I could tell my little man was happier and even though I hated sharing him with Harriet, I was thankful that I had brought Harriet home for him anything to give him a perfect life.

Sandra said, "You better hurry. It's almost time for dinner."

I went to my room throwing the package on the bed. It would just have to wait. I had to have a bath. I didn't even get myself dried off when Sandra came knocking on my door.

"Miss Drucilla, do you know a Mr. Phillip Jemez?"

"Yes, why?"

"He's on the telephone. He wants to talk to you."

I picked up my phone and with all the love I could muster said, "Where the hell are you?"

Phillip said, "Drucilla, I'm in town for a few days and would like to talk to you."

"Yes, I can see you tomorrow, the next day and the next. How long can you stay?"

"Like I said, I'll only be here a few days. I won't take up much of your time."

Hanging up the phone, I silently knew I must be ready to deal with Phillip and I would. Knowing darn well he was here about the Hallmarks. Yes, I'll deal with that. What a joy it had been!

Dinner was good and Tony had invited Sam Arturo and had Sandra seated him next to Harriet. The poor fool was drooling. He couldn't take his eyes off of her. Kicking Tony under the table, motioning for him to look, just as Michael reached for Amanda's hand. It was then that I saw the new ring on my daughter's left hand. Jumping up I ran around the table scaring everyone to death saying, "Let me see that ring. What is this all about?"

Michael jumped to his feet saying, "Drucilla, it's about love."

I said, "Amanda, why haven't you showed me this before now?"

I had embarrassed Amanda. She looked me dead in the eyes saying, "We will talk about why tomorrow."

Turning to Sandra I said, "Turn on the music and bring in the best champagne. We have a celebration."

Reaching to hug Michael, I could see tears fall down Amanda's face.

I said, "Come on Tony, let's dance. No! Wait. Call Papa Perricotti and the boys. **Get everybody**! Tell them to meet us at the Love Club at ten. This is going to be a night to remember."

We got to the club and I felt as though ten tons had been

lifted from my shoulders. Papa Perricotti asked Amanda to dance with him. He had accepted her into the family. It was okay that Michael had chosen Amanda.

Papa walked up to Michael taking his chin into his hand squeezing hard while slowing saying, "Boy, you take good care of her or I'll dance with you!"

On the way home that night, Tony and I talked about Amanda. I don't know if I can stand to give Amanda up for marriage. She has just started making good money. I have killed myself bringing her up to work and make a name for herself. It's not that I don't love Michael it's just that I want Amanda to know what living is all about. It's wonderful to see her dressed up like a doll and to see her dancing, dining, and mixing with all kinds of people. That's what I want for her. I can't bear to think of her being a house mouse. She has a mind of her own and I want her to be able to use it."

Tony said, "Michael is my brother and I know he will treat Amanda with all the love and respect she deserves."

"You know Tony some girls are not allowed to even handle the household money. It's more than I can bear, to think that Amanda would be cowed down by any man. Being told when and what to do some men even keep their wives away from their mothers. Brainwashing them to the point they think it's normal to be nothing more than housemaids without pay."

"Dru, Michael would never treat Amanda bad and I will personally see to it that she will have money, if that's what worries you."

"Tony, you can also tell him to let her live a little before he sticks her with a house full of snotty nose kids to break her back. Tony, I want Amanda to have everything money can buy. But money isn't everything. Sometimes after a man marries, he turns into a real louse taking the younger years of life away from her in the name of love and children. I'll be the first to say that I don't want to be a granny."

"If it will make you feel better, we both can talk with Michael. Dru, I assure you, you don't have to worry about a thing in the world because I know that Michael worships Amanda. He told me that himself. Dru, you just remember, Papa will be looking out for Amanda. I assure you he will set any wrongs right. You can believe that!"

It was two forty-five a.m. when I sat on the edge of my bed kicking my shoes off. I saw the brown package from Courtney. I thought, oh well, I've got time for this while Tony is in the shower. I pulled the paper clippings out placing them on the bed. One big sheet had Courtney's letter clipped over it. Her letter began:

Dear Drucilla,

What the hell have you done? You know the law will be on you like stink on crap. Don't you think things are happening too fast? I will be there in a few days with the girls.

The news clipping read:

Two broke legs and one arm, with multiple bruises from falling down his basement steps. Police said, this is a likely story since his front door had been kicked off its hinges. The lady at the house said her husband had lost his keys and he was mad because she didn't have her purse with the other house key, so he just kicked and kicked until he kicked the door down. She went on to say he had too many beers and looking for the bathroom, he had opened the wrong door and tumbled down the steps.

Hearing Tony cut the shower off. I grabbed all the papers, sticking them back into the brown paper bag. Thinking, damn, Topaze and Arturo must not have heard a word I said. They've not even let me know that it was over. The date on the newspaper was the day before yesterday. I wonder just what kind of work Tony was helping Papa with that night.

I was getting ready for bed when Tony came in asking,

"Did you have a good time baby?"

With my soft smile, I said, "Yes, Tony, after thinking about it. It was a better night than I thought."

At nine the next morning, the florist delivered my pink roses, but the card read: Love you, Tony. I found Tony getting out of bed. I took the newspaper clippings out and handed them to him. I said, "Why didn't you tell me Tony?"

A look of disapproval came over his face. Tony hastily replied, "Because people like Percy don't need joking around with, so I did the job right. Now Dru, you tell Courtney that we will get our own newspaper. I don't want anymore of this!"

He handed all the papers back to me as he went out the door.

I was making sure everything was just right for lunch when the doorbell rang. I ran to look in the mirror checking my lipstick. Then as nervous as a cocked gun, I walked out to face Phillip. He was so full of kindness with how good I looked and it was good to see me happy for once.

I knew better than to let my guard down. I knew he'd get around to asking questions. All I could think about was something my Grandmother once told me, stay ahead of all men or they will walk on you. I thought if this fool is here to do some walking on me, he'd better step fast. Pushing our chairs back from the table, Phillip and I walked out to the sunroom. I gave him a tall, cold glass of ice tea and sat down beside him.

Looking dead into each, others eyes, I broke the silence with a smile and said, "You know Phillip, I didn't need all these riches. I just needed someone to love and care for me. I know now there is a God and given enough time. He does get revenge."

Phillip took my hand and said, "Drucilla, would His name be Tony? Would your God be Tony? Did he get revenge for you?"

"Why do you say that Phillip? You know darn well if I had the money years ago, I would have personally got my own revenge. Besides you are forgetting, nothing happens that God doesn't let happen. Phillip, you can't be waiting for me to say I'm sorry about the Hallmarks. You know darn well that I'll never say that. I took twenty-three years off that bunch and the papers said that the fire in that house lasted about twenty minutes. I say, Hell no! I'm not sorry. As a matter of fact, it was the happiest day of my life. And yes, if I had known that a few cans of beer would have broken Percy's legs and arms, I would have bought him a truckload."

"What about sister Harriet? She didn't just get sick."

" Damn you Phillip! You know that, as well as I do."

"Drucilla, why did you get your dandruff up?"

"I am pissing mad! Listen Phillip, I thought this was a social call and if so, I'm glad you're here. On the other hand, if you came as an investigator, you're not welcome. You know damn well that if I could dig DeRoy up and kill him all over again, I would. Just remember investigator or friend, don't ask any questions and I'll tell you no lies."

Phillip stood up and said, "No, you listen girl. I'm here to warn you to keep clean. Things have been happening too fast. Someone just might start digging into this family of yours and you know what I mean. If you're having anything to do with these accidents, you better stop while you can."

**"Get out!** You make me want to throw up!"

When we got to the door, Phillip laughed at me saying, "I know very well you're guilty, but I'll cover for you as long as I can. After what they put you through, there should have been a God to get revenge for you. All in all, you've done a fine job by yourself. Maybe, just maybe, you'll cool off and give things time to die down."

After Phillip left I cursed and kicked things around. I may cool down for a while, but I'm not through by any means. After I had calmed down, Tony and I were talking about Phillip.

I laughed saying, "I know curiosity is killing him as to who did what, you or I. But I'm sure he knows the responsibility is all mine."

Tony said, “I’m sure he will check out both of us.”

“Phillip knew I would have taken care of my problem long before I knew you, if I had the money.”

“Yes Dru, I’m afraid we haven’t seen the last of him.”

“Tony, Phillip will always be a Sheriff, but he will be back as my friend. You just wait and see.”

# CHAPTER 28

"Dru, the club is well underway and everyone is excited. You need to go down to the club and look around. I don't want you to be disappointed with anything there."

Tony said something about Phillip, but I didn't hear a word he said. I was thinking about the day. It was September and I had just bought six acres of land at the edge of Gulf Shores. I knew the club would do fine from June to October. It would just have to bring in enough money in those five months to carry itself through the winter. I wasn't worried about it. I knew that once Fritzie started to work he would bring in the people and the country singers, then without a doubt the club would bring in enough money for the whole town.

"I'll take care of the club, Tony. As a matter of fact, I'll go now and you can come with me. It won't take five minutes."

"So be it. Let's go."

Walking over to where I wanted the bandstand to be, I said, "This is it boys! You knew what I wanted and you've helped make it come true. It's got to be ready by Christmas Eve. I want Gulf Shores to be packed. I'll bring in the best entertainers and no admission charge as a Christmas surprise for my customers. Once they see what we have to offer, they'll be back time and time again."

I was holding Tony's hand as I walked around looking at every crack and corner. I wanted everything to be just right.

"Good Lord Tony, just look at what can be done in such a short time when you have money."

"Speaking of money," Tony said. "I've got to be going. See you at the Love Club."

Tony Tortomasi loved me there wasn't a doubt in my mind. For the first time in my life I could let my husband go anywhere, anytime and never think about him fooling around on me. The very day he came to my door saying, get rid of Richard, I knew he loved me and that I would never have to worry about such things again. Tony had always been wonderful to me. I'll never forget the first time he said that I would make the best Mom and he knew that for sure. He did know.

Tony and I had one little blow up and that was to let him know how much like Uncle Louie I really was. I had gone to meet Tony at the Love Club and as I walked in, I saw a pretty little thing coming on to him. To tell the truth, it made me fighting mad and before I knew it, I had taken a twenty-five automatic out of the back pocket of my jeans and shot the girl's glass out of her hand. Tonnymacker grabbed the girl and went out back. Charlie was at my side before Tony could get to his feet.

Tony said, "What the hell do you mean Dru?"

I laughed and said, "I just showed you my mean side. Some girls flirt, some talk and you better know the difference because the next time I find you lollygagging, I'll shoot you in the face!"

Tony snarled, "Damn you woman! Are you crazy?"

"Don't say that Tony! I'll show you what a crazy woman will do to you."

I turned and walked out to my car with Charlie by my side.

The look on Tony's face said it all. I didn't have to worry about Tony and one thing was for sure now, he would send the sluts on their way. Besides that, Max would tell me anything I asked. He would never let Tony hurt me. He would take care of Tony personally. He had confessed to being in love with me the day Tony told him he had gotten word that Richard had made brags that he was going to kill me. Tony had laughed about Max's loving me, but I knew it was no joke.

Max Tombrello had moved into the house saying he was tired of the rough life. Brandon and Anthony needed him to be closer to them. He had always been loyal to Tony, but Tony gave him to me. I knew he would put Tony away or anyone else at the drop of a hat if I gave the word. Even little Brandon knew that Max loved him best. He had really worked with Brandon and the child was learning so fast that it was amazing. He was doing everything little Anthony was and more. Max had seen to that.

I was just telling Max about what happened at the club when the two boys came in hugging me with arms and legs asking, "Where have you been all day?"

Max said, "Let up boys. She is wanted on the phone."

I asked, "Who is it?"

"Tony," Max said.

I ran to the phone and asked, "What the hell do you want?"

"Do you want to go out tonight," Tony asked.

I said, "Oh well, not tonight. You bring it on home, baby. I'd hate to come get you. I'm mean. That's a joke! I'll open the door in fifteen minutes and you had better be there."

As I was hanging up, I heard Tony tell someone that I was still mad about the girl. He should have sent that bitch on her way. She'll have hell waiting for me.

I screamed out, "Who are you talking to Tony?"

But he had already hung up. Tony was fooled. I went right back to playing with the boys and watching the time. I heard the car door and ran throwing my arms around Tony giving him the hottest kisses he had ever had.

I said, "You're the best Tony, the very best. I know I don't have to worry about you."

"No, Dru, you sure as hell don't, but you do have to worry about that club of yours."

"The Hot Box Club, oh Tony doesn't that sound delicious."

"Yes, it sounds just like you. What you better do is go see your decorators. They're bitching at some of the carpenters. It's just going to slow the work down. You know how men are."

"Tony, have you sent someone to track down Fritzie Rogue?"

Tony hesitated, "Yes, but you won't like what you see baby. He has married a slut of a thing. She is so ugly she would snag lightning and triple thunder."

I laughed saying, "You just send me Charlie Perricotti and Tonnymacker in here tomorrow morning. And Tony, don't you dare go to sleep in that chair. I want you to spend some time with me tonight in the Jacuzzi."

But even as I left the room, I could see that Tony was half asleep. I told Sandra to let Tony sleep while I had a fire lit in our bedroom and that I wanted dinner for two, set up right next to the new white rug I had made for Tony as a surprise. It was a white fur that had been stuffed at least two inches thick. Seeing that everything was ready right down to the champagne, I went to get Tony. Sure enough…Tony was asleep, but not for long.

Later that night I got up. I couldn't sleep for thinking about the new club. The basement was ready. It had the most beautiful apartment for Fritzie you ever saw. Closets took one whole side and it was full of the finest clothes money could buy. I knew he wouldn't need a thing except to lose the weight he had gained and that shouldn't be too hard. The club has the best exercising equipment…just waiting for him. Plus, there was Perricotti and Tonnymacker to see to it that he would eat right and exercise.

The next morning I was in the family room when Sandra came in with Perricotti and Tonnymacker.

"Hello boys. Today's the day. I want you to go pick up Mr. Rogue for me. Tell him he has two choices. One is to come with you and the other is to have his butt planted in cement and dumped in the damn river. As a matter of fact, that's what you can do with that slut he married, unless he agrees to legally leave her behind. I'll tell you boys, Fritzie is as fast as greased lightning and will fight at the drop of a hat, but you bring him here even if you have to fight him all the way! Just to think about him, being married to a, nobody makes me mad enough to kill him all by myself. I know that this boy could be at the top of the charts if he had been ambitious. He was born with class and he can out sing any country singer anywhere. His trouble is he has no confidence in himself. Plus, he's always with the wrong people. What he needs is someone to keep him on the right track and I'm that somebody. Let's get him here and see to it that he mix's and mingles with the right people. There's one good thing…I know he loves to play golf so we should be able to keep him busy. Tell him that his job is to run a new club called The Hot Box. Tell him that its pure luxury decorated in black and silver and that even the chairs are done in black velvet."

I laughed out loud. "He may be mad as hell at first, but just wait until he sees all the luxury, then he'll be like a wet hog in the sunshine. Well boys, I hope he doesn't give you any trouble, but bring him back anyway you have to. I don't want you to tell him who I am or where I come from. Just that I said, he'll make better money than he's ever seen."

I gave Perricotti the keys to Fritzie's new apartment. I saw them to the door and said, "Oh yes, Charlie, why don't you two take a few days to do some Christmas shopping while you're in Birmingham. If I were you, I'd fly in and go straight to the Galleria Hotel that's part of the new fantastic mall and shop there. I'm going there myself in a week or two. I'll have to sweet talk Tony into going with me of course, but I want you back here first. You know to call me as soon as you get back."

I walked over to my desk picking up the keys to the new Porsche I had bought for Fritzie. I walked over to the sofa and sat thinking how sad he seemed the last time I had talked to him. I knew that his biggest trouble, is not loving himself. I was sorry for the way I had talked to Fritzie the last time I saw him. I had told him that I didn't care about him and that I had just used him to make Richard jealous. I could tell by the sound of his voice that he was hurt. It had all been a lie and I knew it now, but I also knew that I had always held him close to my heart. I knew I would do everything I could to make his life easier. Mr. Rogue may be big and tough, but what myself and many others had forgotten, was that he does have a heart and most of the time it is a big chunk of gold. I knew it didn't take much to make him happy…just money in his pocket with no one leaning on him. Flipping the keys up in the air, I said out loud, "Boy, will he be surprised when he sees me."

Just then Amanda came through the door and said, "Who will be surprised Mom?"

"Fritzie Rogue," I said, "You do remember him?"

Amanda said, "Yes."

"He's coming here to manage the club. But gosh, I didn't realize I had been talking out loud."

I quickly changed the subject. "Come on over here and let me see that ring again. Amanda, what about your apartment in New York? What about your job?"

"Mom, there's nothing much happening right now and I've been thinking about Julie, my roommate. She wants my apartment by herself. So, I may just have her ship my things here. I've really not been very happy there for months."

I stood up saying, "Why not? You make good money. You have anything you want. Why haven't you been happy?"

"Mom, it's Jeff. He won't leave me alone. He has called saying you were wrong about us and that you had no business keeping us apart and all kinds of things. He has had me so upset for weeks and now I'm really worried because he is here."

I felt faint. "Here? Where baby?"

Amanda replied, "He's working for that man named Bob Tosti as a laborer at the club."

My heart was pounding as I asked, "Amanda, why didn't you tell me before now?"

Amanda said, "Because I thought that after he saw that I was engaged he would leave me alone. But he won't. He's just out to cause trouble with Michael. Mom, I don't want my life with Michael to start off bad."

I was pacing the floor. "Amanda, Jeff doesn't want you and he never did. He just wants a fight from me."

"But Mom, you always say that and it doesn't make sense!"

Then I strongly said, "Think about it Amanda. He has had everybody in his family bowing to his every whim. But when he met me. I didn't bend for him. He started out to show me what a big man he was by taking you knowing I'd rather die than see you with him. Well, he made an ass out of himself and he's still an ass! I tried to tell you when he was doing all those horrible things to me, but you just went on and on that it was because his Mom and Dad were divorced or he hadn't grown up yet. Just like I said, he knew what he was doing then and he knows now. I'll just tell Bob to fire him and he won't be tormenting you or me!

Do you remember when he said that I'd change my feelings for him when you two had a baby? I swear I could have died. His damn Daddy is sick in the head, not to mention his redheaded Mama.

I knew it the day we went to their house to talk to them about Jeff coming to the house drinking. But, don't you worry Amanda, he is a coward and he won't do anything. Just avoid him all you can. It's for sure he won't be calling here to harass you. If you ignore him, maybe he'll go away.

Do you remember when Jeff called that night and Richard answered the phone and heard him say, I'm coming, I'm coming. It made you so mad when Richard told you it was Jeff and you know a lot of those other calls were him also. I couldn't make you understand that he was tormenting me to death, laying on my sofa all day everyday, pretending to be helping me in the garden and with the canning. He was just staying away from his Daddy so he wouldn't have to work. He's just like DeRoy and that's who I saw every time I looked at him especially the day he poured that tea all over me. That's when I should have killed the bastard. But I kept thinking that you would put him on the road. Time just went on and on with me hating him more and more with everything he did to me. I tried being good to him and that backfired.

Amanda, remember when I went to the races with you two and I told him not to drink anymore? What did he do? He went right back to the concession stand and got another beer and smiled in my face. He knew I'd get another ride home and I did. That should have opened your eyes to the fact that he is a sick bastard. Not wanting you to do the dishes or to change little Brandon's diaper. Remember the fight we had when he wouldn't let you stay at the hospital with Brandon. He said he hated Brandon and Harriet and that your Daddy and I shouldn't love anyone but you and him. He wasn't my son and I didn't know what in the hell he wanted from us.

All he wanted was to keep a battle going between us and that you were the one that was being hurt most of all. I knew I had to talk you into going to New York the day I came through the house from the garden and found him on the sofa masturbating and I told him to get out and he just ignored me. I've never been so embarrassed in all of my life! That's the day Harriet came in and all hell broke out. Amanda, you were so young."

"Yes Mom, I knew how bad Jeff hated you. What made him hate you the most was telling him he couldn't drive my car. You didn't want me giving him money and he couldn't come back in the house again. I tell you Mom, it liked to have killed him when you said he couldn't come back into the house."

"I well remember that! He wasn't just mad, he was crazy as hell he bided his time until he brought you home on New Year's Eve. That's the night he ran into the bedroom saying, get up and come out here. Amanda's real Daddy is out here. He said your Daddy wanted to see me. Amanda, Jeff knew that your real Daddy, as Jeff called him, died in a car wreck years ago. There's one thing for sure, he knew that I would kill him and that's why he left his car running with the door open. He knew I was running for the gun and he ran like a scalded dog. You know I'm still surprised that he had enough sense to run."

Amanda pleaded, "Please Mom. Let's not talk about him anymore. I just want him out of my life. I'm thankful that you were strong enough to live through it all without hating me."

I was gritting my teeth. "It's okay baby, don't worry about it. That's all behind us now. I'm not surprised. I knew what Jeff was doing. I knew what Richard was doing. But now DeRoy, he was another story. The bed and the pearls had me wondering because there wasn't anyone in the house but your Daddy. It sure didn't make sense that your Daddy would do anything that would cost him money. Just think I paid two hundred dollars for the answering machine. There again, only Jeff and your Dad were there. As soon as it started to mess up, I knew it was Jeff that came into the house to call you while I was working in the yard. No one was in the house but him and he squirted hand lotion all inside my answering machine. But what looked bad was your Daddy didn't stop Jeff."

Tears ran down Amanda's face as she said, "I'm sorry Mom. I was afraid of Jeff and I didn't know what he would do next."

"To tell you the truth Amanda, I had forgotten about Jeff. I didn't even talk to Dr. Skeet about him. Amanda, I've got to go to the beauty shop. Do your best to put Jeff out of your mind. Be thankful that you know him for what he is…a schizophrenic son-of-a-bitch. He'll meet his match some day."

"Mom, tell Sandra that I'm going to the pool if anyone needs me."

Amanda started to leave, stopped and turned around. "Mom, I am thankful and I'm even more thankful that I have you."

I went to find Max. I told Max all about Jeff.

I said, "Max, could you find that fishing slough that you, Tony and I went to last September?"

Max smiled as he said, "Sure, I know just where it is."

I said, "Tell Bob Tosti to get Jeff ready for a fishing trip then stop at Papa Perricotti's and call me. Tell Bob to be careful. No one is to know about the fishing trip. He is to tell everyone that he had to fire Jeff because he wouldn't ride in the work truck with the windows down because it would mess up his hair and that the other boys said it was too hot to keep the windows up. Oh, and Max, that did happen one time, believe me."

I went to the beauty shop and then to see Papa Perricotti. It is on my way home. And I didn't stay long I was waiting on the phone call.

Bob carried out the orders except for the fact that Max came along on the fishing trip. They went right up to the mouth of the slough where a big log had them blocked out. Jeff wasn't about to go up there and said that it was a beaver dam and too much work to move the log.

Max said, "So be it. Let's go on up to the next slough. There should be good fishing there."

Even Bob knew Jeff was a nut when he asked if he could take a radio with them. Bob had shook his head saying, "Boy, you know damn well that the noise will run the fish off."

It was about eight-thirty that night when I got the call from Papa's place. Saying I'd be right there, I was thanking God that Tony was gone for the evening and Amanda was off with Michael. This night was mine. Max was waiting for Papa and me. As they took the elevator down to Papa Perricotti's basement, Papa started to say something.

"No, Papa. This is my night. Max just do what you have to do to get us there."

We didn't have far to go. When the elevator doors opened. There was Jeff with a beer in his hand. One look at me and he knew that he had had a bad day. The elevator doors closed taking Bob and Papa upstairs. That left me, Max and one stupid looking asshole Max elbowed Jeff in the neck, put a knee in his groin and jacked his jaw. When Jeff woke up, he was back in the boat not far from the slough.

He tried to stand up but Max had a Three Fifty-seven Magnum in his ear saying, "It might as well be now as later."

I was filled with hate. You could hear it and see it. I said, "Take time to think Jeff. Remember all the bad things you have done to me. Remember, I said I would never bend for you and that someday you would push me to the limit. Today's that day Jeff I want you to know its pure hate and five kids wouldn't change my mind! You do know that Amanda has woke up now. As a matter of fact, she woke up when you put the lotion in my answering machine."

We had come to where the log blocked the slough. I picked up a rope with a big hook tied on the end. Throwing it over the log, I said, "Back it up. Let's pull it out just enough to get the boat in."

Jeff began to shake and cry as the boat made its way into the slough. It was bigger and deeper than I thought at first. The weight on the fifty-foot rope hit bottom at twenty-three feet.

I said, "It's plenty deep Max. What do you think? Has he had time? Do you think he's prayed up by now?"

This made Jeff look up and he started to say something, but I stopped him.

I said, "Save it you bastard! You well remember all you ever did to me and I should have killed you long ago. You just couldn't stop could you? Your people couldn't see what you were. They couldn't see that you are really crazy. **No, Jeff!** You wouldn't leave Amanda alone. But it was a taste of me you wanted and now you have **me!"**

I reached into my boot and pulled out a knife that was sharp enough to slice a hog. Then I nodded my head at Max.

Max placed the handcuffs on Jeff's hands behind his back and at his feet.

I said, "I'm not like you Jeff. I'm not a sneak. I'm going to tell you what I'm about to do. You can let it run through your mind and your eyes if you're so brave."

I did tell him and after giving him time for his life to flash before his eyes.

I nodded for Max to hit him just hard enough so he couldn't move around. Then I leaned over him taking one long hard cut coming from his chest bone all the way down to his very own little fishing worm. I knew I had to cut deep so his dead ass would stay on the bottom of the slough.

Richard's Uncle Slim had told me a few years back what to do with people that keep getting under your skin. He said that if you open their stomach up they wouldn't ever come to the top.

Now as Max was dumping Jeff out, I was taking off my rubber clothes and stuffed them into a big plastic bag. On our way out not a word passed between us. We put the log back in place and were on our way. We worked fast at Papa Perricotti's house putting our clothes into the incinerator and washing down the boat. Bob and Papa came down and I went up in the elevator and out the front door toward home.

# CHAPTER 29

I was just getting out of my bath when I heard someone at my door. I asked, “Who is it?”

“It’s me, Harriet. Can I come in?”

“Sure. Get in here and talk to me.”

Was I ever shocked? Harriet did talk. She told me all about her seeing Bob Tosti while she and Sam were at the Love Club.

Harriet gasped, “Drucilla, seeing him scared me half to death. I don’t want to start dreaming those crazy dreams again. Bob came over and talked to me and said he was here working on your club and that he would love to see me again. Sam didn’t have much to say, but I know he didn’t like me knowing Bob.”

“Don’t worry about it. Now that he saw you with Sam, I’m sure he will leave you alone. Oh yes! How did Anthony and Brandon do at the water slide today? Did they have fun?”

“We all had a good time and Drucilla, I’m glad Brandon has Anthony. Oh! Listen, I’ve lost ten pounds!”

“I’m thrilled! I can see the weight falling off you and you better get it all off. You’ll never guess who’s coming here to run my club.”

Harriet gave out a few names with me shaking my head no, and then I told her who was coming.

Harriet said, “No! You wouldn’t bring him here. He’s a nobody.”

“Oh hell yes I am. When I’m through, he will be somebody. You wait and see! Now get out of here. I’ve got to get some sleep. Tomorrow I’m going to the beach and stay all day. Harriet, you do remember we are going to have Courtney and the girls here for a few days don’t you? I want you to be sociable and help the girls have a good time.”

“You don’t have to worry about me Drucilla. I’ll be fine.” And with that Harriet was gone.

I was asleep before my head hit the pillow. When I awoke, Tony had me wrapped up tight saying, “Woman, why can’t I keep up with you?”

I was moaning and groaning turning over in his arms kissing and hugging him. I said, “I know how you can keep up with me for a while. You can take me to Birmingham to shop for Christmas.”

To my surprise Tony said, “When do we leave?”

“Oh Tony. I want to go in the car so we can really shop. Let’s see, this is Wednesday, let’s wait until Sunday to drive in. By that time Charlie and Roger should be back with Fritzie. I want to know he’s settled in before I go off. I hope he’s not as fat as you let on. He only has twenty-one days to get it off. My Hot Box is going to open Christmas Eve…fat or not!”

“The hell you say. Your Hot Box is going to open right now!”

Later Sandra was knocking at the door. I said, “Go away, go, away. What do you want? Don’t you know it’s too early to get up?”

“Yes, Miss Drucilla”, but Courtney wants you on the phone.”

I picked up the phone. “Hello Courtney. Don’t give me excuses or lies.

Oh, that’s fine. See you in two weeks.” I hung up the phone.

"Come on Tony, let's get up. All we do is sleep. I'm going for a walk. Don't you want to come with me?"

"I'll take a rain check on the walk. I have a million things to do." Then Tony asked, "Why can't we go to Birmingham this Sunday? We can be back and rested before Courtney gets here. Besides we will have friends coming and going every day until the club opens. We need to go now and you need time for some advertising."

"Okay, if I hear from Charlie, we will go Sunday for sure. Tony, would you like for me to send you some coffee?"

"No thanks. I'm right behind you."

As soon as I was out of the house, Tony told Sandra to get everybody into the kitchen so he could talk to them. Amanda, Harriet, Anthony, Brandon, Max and Sandra all sat around the table and listened as Tony told them the house was completely ready and he needed all the help he could get. It had to be planned and carried out right so I wouldn't know a thing.

Tony said, "Sandra, I will have the movers here on Monday. You get everyone busy packing and be at the new house, finished unpacking by the time we get back from the trip. I'll stay as long as I can and I'll call you. You shouldn't have any trouble. All the utilities are on."

Brandon was clapping and squealing, "When can we tell her?"

"Yes, Daddy," said Anthony, "When can I tell Mama, now?"

Tony said, "No. We have waited this long and this way you can be at the house to surprise her when we get back."

"Alright Amanda, will you help?"

"You bet." Amanda said, "It will be fine Tony. I'll see to it that you have all the help you need."

Tony said, "I can't wait to see Dru's face. I know you all won't let me down."

He was sure proud of the new house and he was happy as he left knowing everything would go as he planned. Everything was perfect and this would be the best Christmas in years.

I came back in early saying, "The wind has turned cold and I'm going to listen to the weather. Just maybe we can have a fire tonight."

I couldn't keep my eyes off the boys. They were so happy. I said, "Get over here you two. Tell me what you want for Christmas."

Believe me I just thought I wanted to hear from them. They had a list a mile long.

Brandon said, "Mam Maw, we have a surprise for …."

Anthony jumped up shouting, "Shut-up Brandon. Don't you tell! Daddy will have your hide."

Brandon ran to Anthony screaming, "You shut-up. You don't know what you're talking about. This is my Mam Maw and I can tell her anything I want to. Do you hear me?"

Anthony backed up yelling out, "She is my Mom too."

I looked from one child to the other.

Brandon said, "I'll tell you Mam Maw. It's about Amanda. She took some of your songs from the piano seat and she sung them so she can sing them to you."

Anthony had squeezed his little fists so tight they were white, but let them go as he heard what Brandon had said. Anthony said, "That's all Brandon, let's get out of here."

Leaving me to wonder why Amanda would take my songs, I hadn't heard Amanda singing at all lately. Speaking of my lovely Amanda, I pray she doesn't ask any questions about that idiot Jeff. No one would ever know what I have been through for Amanda and Richard. Oh my Richard, what you put me through. Now like Jeff, you will pay too. I sure do wonder if your new puss has found you yet. Max said he gave the bitch Richard's address. She was to have car trouble and ask him to let her use the telephone. I can still hear Max saying, don't worry Drucilla this girl is a paid hooker. She knows how to work her way into a man's bed. I thought **Work!** It doesn't take work to get into Richard's bed. Just the wiggle of an ass is all it takes. Without a doubt he would screw a squirrel if he could catch one. Now he can have this piece with my blessing a steak and potato girl…one that's well educated. I even bet she goes to church. Oh my dear Richard. Will you believe her when she tells you she got gonorrhea off a church pew? Lord, will he be surprised when he finds out that this girl's best friend gave him syphilis. That's life Richard. You should have known that hookers believe in sharing their men. Just think he will get two for the price of a few drinks. Only this time, he'll get some puss he can't wash off!

It had taken Max awhile to find those girls and had cost me twenty-five hundred dollars each, but it was worth it. I just wish I could see Richard's face when the doctor diagnoses his troubles. Now, I'm sure from all the talk about AIDS, it want be any trouble at all to find a dying AIDS person that needs money enough to do anything. By the time I'm through with Richard, he'll know the fear of venereal disease. Even more so than I did all the years I lived with him. I know damn well that this is how justice should be brought about. To hell with the law!

When the telephone rang, it scared me half to death. My nerves were still shot. It was Sandra on the phone.

Sandra said, "It's Charlie, Miss Drucilla."

"Put him through Sandra."

I was on my feet. "Hello Charlie. You know best, but I won't be here next week. Don't you remember? We're coming there to shop. Just do what you can. You say Fritzie didn't give any trouble at all?"

Charlie replied, "That's right Mrs. Tony. The best part is he said he doesn't have a wife any more. She left with some fuzzy face guy and filed for divorce last week. He said this job was God sent because he needed to get away from here."

"For goodness sake, bring him on before something happens and changes his mind. Gosh! I never dreamed it would be so easy to get him here. I know he's never worked in Gulf Shores before, but I do know he'll love it. And Charlie, whatever you do, don't tell him who I am! Just bring it on home! Thanks!"

Hanging up the phone, I was beside myself. Thank God. I know Fritzie will be happy here which means he will give my club his all. Yes sir. I am going shopping. I will buy the prettiest clothes possible. The next time Mr. Rogue sees me. I will be a blonde bombshell.

I remember the last time I was on stage with him. I had been so scared…but never again. This time will be different. The stage will belong to me. I had made up my mind that he wouldn't know who I was until I came out onto the stage.

I had to get out of the house and do something. My mind was going ninety to nothing. Just as I started out, Sandra came back in.

"Mrs. Drucilla, Papa Perricotti is here to see you."

Looking Papa Perricotti dead in the eyes, I said, "Yes sir. Why are you so concerned?"

"I want to know how much money you want this Club to make? Is it a playhouse or a business?"

I laughed. "Now Papa, you must be joking. You know I want to make all the money in this world. I can't tell you how much the club means to me. You must know it's a dream come true. Somehow it's got to work year around. I'm glad you came to see me Papa. I know you have a lot on your shoulders, but if you could help me take care of the business part and handle Mr. Rogue, I feel sure my club will go over big. I wouldn't want to be left out of a thing, but I do know I need some help. This is much more than I anticipated. I guess I'm trying to say I know more about playing house than running a club. I know that Rogue can manage the everyday cash flow, but I don't want anyone's hands in the big money …if you know what I mean.

I am going to appear and entertain on weekends. I tell you Papa the young people need a place like mine for entertainment. There won't be any trouble and it will always be spotless. Max has hired guards because I want everyone to feel safe coming here. That way they will be back time and time again. This new dirty dancing will go over strong for a good six months and that should give us time to make a name for ourselves. You will see Papa, Fritzie will see to it that we have the very best in music. I have no doubt about that."

Papa spoke up, "Drucilla, you haven't had to convince me about anything. It's me that's here to make you a deal. I love your club. Especially the way you arranged the seating. The different levels and that dance floor twenty by fifty is great. I have another plan laid out at my house. I want you to come home with me. I'll show you the real way to make a dollar!"

"Hell fire Papa, what are we waiting for?"

Papa Perricotti's driver was leaning up against the limousine. That is until he saw Papa. Ross opened the doors and asked, "Home sir?" As if he already knew the answer.

When we got to his house, Papa had me by the hand like some little girl. Papa said, "Come on doll, we have to go downstairs."

But when the elevator stopped at the basement, Papa took out what looked like a charge card sliding it into a slot, then to my amazement, the elevator moved on down to another floor. When the doors opened, Papa said, "Step out and tell me what you think about my club."

"Damn you Papa! You've had this hid from me all this time."

I tried to act mad as he watched me walk from table to table. "You said it! People have to spend money for me to make money. Papa, I bet you think I'm one dumb puss. Oh Papa! I want you to teach me how to gamble. I'm so excited I can't wait."

"Drucilla, we'll see, but first things first. Come on over here and let me show you something. These are the plans. Here is your club, The Hot Box, and around the corner is where we are now. Now, I know that when we're up on the road it seems like it's farther away, but if we build a tunnel from the basement of your club to this place, it will only be about one mile."

"Hell Papa, people won't walk that far."

He laughed, "You're right. That's why we'll have transportation for them. But you do know we are very careful about who knows what."

"Okay, we can put in a secret elevator at your place. It will sure help us both." Papa took me by the shoulders turning me to face him, "Now Drucilla, I want you to have all the pleasures life has to offer, but I had rather you not play house at your club. It would be too dangerous. I've seen you turn a few heads and you keep in mind that this is no place for mischief."

"Now you wait a minute Papa. Maybe you misunderstood me. I didn't say I wanted to be a gambling nut and I wouldn't ever cause you any trouble. You know that! I'll never even talk about this place. For that matter, I'll leave all that up to you. It looks like you've done a fine job so far. Damn you Papa, I can't believe you have this place!"

"I know you're mad at me, but you won't be mad when all that money starts pouring in. Let's go up and celebrate this deal with a good glass of Black Velvet."

We went upstairs and put business aside. We talked and got to know each other better. "Talk to me Papa. Tell me about Mama Perricotti."

The old man settled down in the easy chair and a sad look came across his face. He said, "She was a lovely lady, fun loving, happy, and oh how she loved to cook. She fed everybody that came around. We had the biggest fish fry's you ever saw. But her dream was to go to Italy to see her two sisters and I knew that Tony's Dad and Mom were planning a trip. I bought Mama tickets to go as a surprise. I tell you, I changed my mind two times about letting Mama go, but then Tony's Dad said, old man, let my sister go. I'll take care of her and you can keep Tony and little Michael here for us. I did just that and they wrote me saying what a wonderful trip I was missing. Then, the next thing I knew their plane had gone down taking them away from the boys and me."

"Papa, you did a fine job raising Tony and Michael. Papa,

Tony's a fine man and I'll always be a good wife to him. I pledge my trust to you Papa. You can count on me. Papa, if you will excuse me for a minute, I've got to powder my nose."

The old man had to know he could trust me. I may be soft, little and smelling like I just fell in a perfume barrel, but after what Max had told him, and he knew I was pure gold with a will of iron.

Tony had told Papa that I beat all he had ever seen. I just do whatever I have to do, then put it out of my mind. Papa had told Tony to do anything that I asked, but not let me go to Italy.

Coming back into the room, I said, "Papa, I hate to leave good company, but I must go pack. Tony is taking me to Birmingham. Is there anything you need or want? I tell you what I'll do Papa, I'll bring you some good cherry smoking tobacco."

Giving him a hug, I asked, "Papa, what would you really like for Christmas?"

"Oh my! I'd like a blonde…just like you if that's okay."

"I don't know if you know what you're asking for, but I'll do my best to find her Papa."

Then out the door I went to find Ross. After watching me leave, Papa poured himself another drink and got back into his easy chair to sleep the afternoon away.

Ross drove me around by the clubhouse to see if Tony was still playing golf. I had to get home to rest and help Sandra with the packing and make a grocery list. A piece down the road, I noticed Ross was looking at me in the mirror. He asked, "What are you thinking about Mrs. Tony?"

I smiled at him, "Would you tell Papa if I told you?"

"Yes, I probably would. I tell him everything. There's no one that has a secret from Mr. Perricotti!"

"In that case Ross, I'll keep my thoughts to myself."

Now I was thinking that I could walk home on Ross's lips. He looked like a big Duck. I said, "When you get back, tell Papa I want him to come to my house for dinner. Tell him I'm going to make beef stew and cornbread!"

Going straight for the kitchen, I pulled out the pots and pans. It wasn't long until you could smell the aroma of the stew.

Sandra said, "I can do it all by myself. It isn't right for you to be in the kitchen."

I quickly said, "Will you shut-up and just help me. Tony will be here in a minute. Go get Amanda and my boys. Tell Harriet to get in here. Papa is coming for supper."

Tony came in the door asking, "Now how do you know that Papa will be here?"

"Because Mr. I sent word of what I'm cooking he'll be here, just you wait and see. Now get out of here and I'll be right behind you as soon as I get the cornbread out of the oven."

Papa came in just as we were sitting down at the table. Papa said, "Damn Ross, he almost made me late, but I could smell this stew for miles."

I winked at Tony and said, "Late or not Papa, you'll always have a place at my table."

After dinner everyone went in different directions. Tony and I went to bed for an early start to Birmingham the next morning.

# CHAPTER 30

As Tony and I pulled into the hotel, I believed I was going to be sick. Being this close to Shady Grove had upset me, but I thought that once I got settled in my room I would feel better. This place shouldn't bother me, but it did.

I said, "Gosh Tony, if you don't mind, we will do the shopping in Pensacola from now on."

"Dru, maybe you're just hungry. Maybe if you eat a bite you will feel better. I'll call room service and let them bring us something. You can rest and we can shop later this afternoon."

As Tony watched me, he knew we shouldn't have come to Birmingham. But Lord, he didn't want me to know about the new house. Laying his head next to me he said, "Please forgive me. I will never bring you back here again."

Deep down, I was hurting I prayed to be able to understand why the people I loved couldn't love me. I said, "Tony, could we take time to see a doctor?"

"Of course we can take time."

He was sincere now. He had never seen me like this. I had become weak and white. Tony was walking the floor. He asked, "What can I do? Do you think driving down to your old place would make the feeling go away?"

Sitting up I said, "No Tony. I will feel better in a minute. I'm sorry. It's just being away from Brandon and Anthony. I should have let them come with us. I've never been one to leave home and besides, I love the gulf. I feel so safe there."

I knew I had lied like a dog, but I couldn't let Tony know that I was dying inside. I would give anything to see the home that I had killed myself to build. I had fought Richard and everyone tooth and nail trying to be happy and keep my home together. If only the memories would go away. The hurt of Mama Marselle and that blubber lip Daddy still living right where I left them. They still couldn't love me even though DeRoy had been dead for months. I grieved myself into a deep depression because I couldn't understand it. Here and now I was making myself sick just remembering.

Washing my face, I decided to call Courtney and let her know that Tony and I would come by to see her. There was no answer, so I called Jerry and talked to him for a while. It was good to hear Jerry's voice. He was the only good person that I had left in the Grove.

Tony had been right about eating. I did feel somewhat better thinking, God if only you will let me live to get away from here I will do my best to keep Shady Grove and Mama Marcelle off my mind! I walked over to the window and looked out over the city. I thought, Oh God! Richard, why did you let this happen to us? I never loved anyone but you. I turned, running for the bathroom with Tony by my side.

Tony said, "What's wrong baby? Why are you so sick?"

I began to cry. I said, "I hate this place. I can't ever come back here. Do you hear me? This place makes me sick!"

Tony held me until I had cried out. I said, "I'm sorry Tony. If you would get me something for my headache, maybe I would go to sleep and wake up feeling better."

Tony gave me three extra strength caplets and lay holding me in his arms until I was sound asleep. Then Tony called Papa Perricotti telling him he had made a bad mistake by bringing me to Birmingham.

Tony said, “Papa you have to get everyone working on the house. It has to be ready for us by tomorrow night.”

“Just come on. The house will be ready”, Papa Perricotti said.

“I’m bringing her home. I can’t stand to see her like this. The pain she feels from her memories here have devastated her. I must bring her home.”

“Don’t you worry son, everything will be in order.”

The next morning Tony had me at the doctor’s office where he sat waiting for an hour. Tony was on his feet as I came out.

I said, “I feel much better now and I’m sorry. Let’s go back to the Mall and do our shopping. The boys will be disappointed if we come back without presents to put under the tree, and, oh yes, Tony, we must get them a big beautiful tree on our way home.”

Taking my shopping list out I asked Tony, “What would you like for Christmas?”

Tony put his arm around my shoulder and began to walk me to the door as he jokingly said, “I don’t know, but I’m sure I can find something to spend your money on. Are you sure you feel that much better?”

“Yes, I’m fine. You’ll see and I know this is one shopping trip you’ll never forget.”

When I got through shopping, not another package could be put into the car.

Tony said, “All the men working for me want money.”

I laughed. “That’s fine, but Max is special to me so you give money and I’ll do what I want to do. I know what we should have done Tony. We should have gone to New York to shop, but I think we did excellent.”

Tony said, “I really don’t think we could have done any better in New York.”

“Let me see.” Looking down my list, I had checked everyone off. Tony had bought a new movie camcorder and of all things a dog for the two boys. Only the dog would be shipped home.

Walking down the Mall I said, "Tony, if you will take me dancing, I will be fine and we can leave tomorrow. I hate to go back early. Amanda would know that something had happened. Please Tony, I will be fine. I can't let this place hurt me, but I do wish I could set fire to the whole damn town for miles around."

"We'll do whatever you want Dru. I can call Papa back and tell him we'll be home tomorrow."

Tony did call Papa. Talking for a long time while I was in the bath. Papa had told Tony the house was ready just like he said it would be and Tony told Papa that I was feeling much better and that I had decided to stay until the next morning to start back.

Papa said, "Max came in with Mr. Rogue and the doctor had checked him from head to toe and put him on a special diet. He seems as if he's on top of the world. While Mr. Rogue was in the shower, Max went through his wallet. He found six dollars and a picture of Drucilla among other personal papers."

Tony said, "Thanks Papa, we will see you tomorrow."

When I came back into the room, Tony said, "Everything at home is fine. Now, can we go to dinner?"

"Sure, I'm ready. Its eight o'clock and we can have dinner and dance the night away."

Dance we did. We came in at two-thirty in the morning. I was so tired that Tony had to help me undress. Tony was in bed asleep before I could get my face cleaned and get back into the room. It didn't seem like I had been asleep but a minute when I heard the telephone ringing. Tony answered it. The clerk at the desk said, "I hate to wake you sir, but there's a call for Mrs. Tortomassi."

Tony said, "That's fine, put the call through."

I put the phone up to my ear as I looked at the clock. I said, "Good Lord Tony, its three-thirty."

Then all of a sudden I heard Richard's voice. He said, "I

followed you all around town and the Mall, but I couldn't get a good shot at you. I'm going to kill you**! Do you hear me**? You sent those two hookers to give me this damn bad disease."

I laughed out loud and said, "Bastard, you wait a minute! I didn't make you drop your pants. I didn't make you screw around the first time nor the last. Furthermore, if you didn't jump every Gorilla you meet up with, you wouldn't have a bad disease. But remember that I said I'd send you something you couldn't wash off!"

Then I hung up saying, "Tony, call the desk and tell them to hold all calls."

The next thing we heard was the little clock that I had set to alarm at nine o'clock. We were dressed and on our way home by ten-thirty. There was no sign of Richard, but I was a little nervous. I knew he wouldn't make threats he wouldn't carry out. I had pen and paper out working on a new song.

Tony asked, "Do you know what kind of car Richard is driving now?"

"No, why is something wrong?"

Then I got up on my knees looking out the back window. I saw a black Trans Am coming fast.

"Tony, what will we do if it's Richard?"

"It may not be, but if it is, you get in the floor board okay?"

"I will. Where are we? I'll call for help."

By this time Tony had reached under the seat and pulled out a Three Fifty-seven Magnum. He looked around and then at the mileage. Tony said, "We are about ten miles out of Montgomery. But it's to late to call."

Tony didn't say another word to me until the Trans AM was about three car lengths away. He hit the gas telling me to get down at the same time. Richard was beside us now. Tony saw Richard's gun as the shot rang out. Tony hit the brakes sliding for what seemed like half a block. Tony told me to stay down. Richard had slowed just enough for Tony to shoot out his back tires. Coming up beside Richard, Tony shot out the front tire, and then sped back up to eighty miles per hour.

Tony said, "Its okay now baby. He won't hurt you now."

"**No, hell no.** Not now, but he will Tony, he will. If I don't get him first."

"Wait a minute, Dru. I'll take care of this myself. I want you to stop this! I let you do what I thought you should do to get yourself back on the right track, but now it's too dangerous. I won't have you hurt. Do what you can at the club and at home, but let me take care of him. Do you hear me Dru?"

"Yes Tony. You're right. At least I do know those girls earned their money and I'll have to give Max a bonus."

Nothing else happened the rest of the way home. Tony was so excited about the house that he could hardly keep from telling me about it as we passed the road we normally would have turned onto.

I said, "Tony, you missed your turn. Where are you going? I'm too tired to go to Papa's and I look awful!"

Tony said, "When I stop up here to get the Christmas tree, you can fix your face. I just need to stop and show you something. A minute more won't hurt you I know."

We stopped at a place that sold Christmas trees and sat in the car and looked around.

I said, "Oh Tony, just look! I want that big tree on the end."

To please me Tony moved the car, pulling right next to the one I saw first.

Then I said, "Oh no! That one's bigger!"

Tony said, "I tell you what Dru. Let's get out so you can make sure and I'll have the man deliver the tree for us."

Tony had written out the address while I picked out the tree. Gosh, was I happy. I had put Richard behind me and there stood Tony watching me. He knew I loved Christmas better than any child.

As we drove up this long driveway with moss hanging from the big, twisted oaks I asked, "Tony, where are we going? Who lives here? I've never dreamed that there was such a place here at the gulf."

After we got out of the car, I turned around and around.

Turning to look at Tony, he was putting a key into the door lock.

I ask, “What are you doing? Do you know these people?”

Tony said, “Yes I do. Come on in.”

He came back and all but pushed me in the door. I said, “Tony, just let me stand here and look.”

He picked up a remote control and turned on the lights all over the house. For the first time in my life, I couldn’t say anything. Then I noticed.

I said, “Tony, all this furniture belongs to us!”

# CHAPTER 31

Little Anthony and Brandon ran out screaming, "Merry Christmas! Mama this is your surprise! Uncle Tony wouldn't let us even touch the moss in the trees! Mama, why are you crying? Don't you like this house?"

I wiped the tears from my eyes and saw Papa along with the whole family. Everyone was here to welcome me home.

Tony said, "Come on baby, let me show you your new Christmas Home."

As he walked with me through the house, I couldn't say anything but Gosh! I couldn't believe all this. We came to my antique kitchen and I was so surprised I couldn't hold back the tears.

I said, "Tony, if only Mama Marselle could see this. This whole house is fascinating. Tony, is this where you've been working all those days that I couldn't keep up with you? To think my little boys had to keep this a secret. I don't know how they did it."

Tony said, "I don't even know how I did it! Let's get back to the others. I think I hear music."

Going into the family room Tony said, "This room is

thirty by fifty feet! I hope you like it."

"I'm thrilled to death. **It's wonderful**! Oh Tony, this is a dream come true."

At that time Anthony ran around the corner. "Daddy, the man is here with our tree. Tell Max to let us help. We want it in here now. Aunt Amanda said she would help us."

Looking at me, Tony said, "Tell Max to let the boys help put the tree up."

Anthony shouted, "Oh boy!"

I took Tony by the hand and said, "Come on slow poke. Let's find the music and some food. Then, I want to see the rest of our house."

I heard the door chimes. Sandra came to announce that Mrs. Courtney was waiting in the foyer. I was visibly mad. I said, "Sandra, don't you ever let Courtney wait! She is my family. Do you hear me?"

The blood drained from Sandra's face. She turned to leave with me on her heels. I entered the foyer. I said, "Courtney, don't you ever wait in this home. It is yours as well as mine."

Courtney burst out crying, "I hope you mean that Drucilla because I need a place to stay. Dan has left me taking the girls and has moved out leaving me alone."

I replied, "Yes, and you think the world has come to an end. It hasn't, so dry your face and pull yourself up by your bootstraps and be thankful it's over. Besides, nothing is ever as bad as we see it the first time it hits us. Come on, we'll get you settled in your room. Can you believe this house? It has six bedrooms upstairs and four down here on the ground floor.

I'll put you next to Amanda and Harriet. Sandra's room is just off the kitchen. Don't hesitate if you need anything. You can rest or join us in the family room.

Now Courtney, you were coming here in a few days in the first place, so just try to forget about Dan. He'll be ringing this phone and the girls will be back when their money runs out. Besides, look what I found here on the beach when my world was coming apart. Who knows, it may be you that won't have

Dan back in a few days. I'd love to have you here. If you let your hair down and have a good time for once in your life, you wouldn't ever leave the gulf. Don't sit around here feeling sorry for yourself. Go down to my club tomorrow and tell Fritzie Rogue that Mrs. Tony said......"

Courtney's mouth flew open, "Say what?"

"That's what I said Courtney. It's Rogue. See, being here won't be so bad after all. Now freshen up Courtney and let's go look over this new place of mine."

I went on talking and told Courtney all that had happened with Richard and that Tony had guards outside. There was no need to worry. Tony wouldn't let anything happen to us.

I hugged her saying, "Now, you pull yourself together and help me decorate this new house for Christmas. Oh! I know something you need to do if you will? As you know the Hot Box will open Christmas Eve. I don't want Fritzie to know that I own the club, so I can't go down there. What about it? Will you decorate the club for me?"

Courtney said, "Sure, but you will have to help me."

"That's a deal. We can go to the florist and order most of what we need tomorrow. I want a big tree and big red bows all over the place. I know you'll do a fine job."

Just as we got up to leave, Harriet pushed the door open and said, "You two better get out here. You're missing all the fun. Amanda is dancing with Papa. Courtney, you better take him away from her. Michael has threatened to grind Papa into hamburger."

I said, "Let's go. I want to see this. I just hope Anthony and Brandon are through with the tree."

As I came in, Tony hugged me and Brandon was saying, "Look Mam-Maw, this is the biggest tree I ever had."

Max and Sandra had brought in all the gifts from the car and put them under the tree. I said, "Gosh, I can't believe we had all of those boxes in that car!"

Max was putting the Angel on top of the tree while Sandra was turning off all the lights in the room. Sandra said, "Are you ready? I'm going to plug the tree lights up now."

The two boys came to stand by my side and the bubbling lights came on, it was a breath taking sight. Amanda, who had never gotten excited in her life, was ecstatic. She grabbed Brandon up kissing him. Amanda said, "Just look! Do you think Santa will find you here and what about you Anthony?"

Michael wasn't about to be left out and said, "I have a map to give to you boys to send to Santa, just in case he can't find this new address."

Papa was trying out his new Cherry pipe tobacco. I gave everyone time to wind down and then went to find Courtney.

I said, "Courtney, come with me. I want to show you the rest of this house. Did you know that Tony and the boys were keeping this a secret from me? I couldn't believe Brandon had known. He's always told me everything. I've never known him to keep a secret big or little."

"This is a mansion," Courtney said. "Just think Drucilla, last Christmas you were in Shady Grove with a broken heart."

"Yes, you've got that right Courtney. I wasted my life with brain dead people. People that were not about to love me you should see a lesson in all that and learn to love yourself first. Look around you Courtney you or I never thought I'd have this. I tell you, if you'll give those girls a good taste of this cold world, they'll be better people. Don't go running back. You're forty-five years old and been married all of your life. You can be free now, if that's what you want. If Dan wants you, he'll find a way, but speaking from experience, you should not give him the time of day!

Let's walk out to the pool. I want you to see the statues Tony had shipped from Italy for me. They're all full size Courtney and I love them."

As we stepped out the door, Charlie stood up and said, "Miss Drucilla, you can't come out here tonight. The wind is too cold. Why don't you wait until tomorrow?"

I said, "Okay, we will Charlie."

As I turned, Max was at my side. I said, "Courtney, I'm

going up to bed. After today, I'm ready for some rest."

I lay in Tony's arms for what seemed like hours thinking back over the years with Richard. Life had been hard. He had told me that he was ashamed to take me out among the people he knew what a joke that was just pure bull crap. I had stayed there a prisoner for days, weeks and months. Yes, eight years. What a fool I had been for staying there thinking he was just too tired to go off with me and a bigger fool for not making him get out. After he said all the things he did, I remember being mad and telling him, yes, Richard, you love me as long as I don't ask you to take me anywhere and not accuse you of anything. Oh yes, as long as I didn't make waves and didn't ask to go anywhere. I guess I should count my blessings that DeRoy hated me or I might have stayed around long enough for Richard to kill me. Oh! Richard…now, I wait for the dirt to be thrown over your face. Then and only then will I be happy! I'll tell Tony in the morning that I won't stay inside hiding from you. No big boy! I'm not afraid of you anymore. You can't play with my mind anymore. I finally hate your sorry butt and I'll get you out of my life for good!

I did go to sleep, but it seemed as if I had dreamed all night. Tony was up getting dressed. He said, "Hello sleepy head. I'm glad you're awake. Now you can have breakfast with me."

I said, "Tony, I must tell you I'm not going to stay locked up because of Richard's threats. There's too much to do at the club and I have to practice. Besides, I need to stay busy."

Tony gave me a big smile saying, "You're going to be busy all right! Michael and Amanda are going to have you planning a wedding. I mean soon!"

"How do you know that Tony?"

"Michael asked Papa about a New Year's wedding. That's what Amanda wanted and he didn't want to wait until next New Year's Eve."

"That's alright, if it's what she wants but don't you encourage them. Do you hear me Tony?"

Tony laughed, "She's the best catch Michael will ever find. She'll make him toe the line."

One look at me and he knew. We said it together, "I know like Mother like daughter."

I said, "I don't know about that Tony. I've led a lot of people to water, but I couldn't make them drink."

Tony said, "That was before you met me. Now, the one's that don't drink, you can drown, you don't have any trouble with that do you? Don't worry about Amanda. She is like you and she is wise at a young age."

The whole time that I was getting dressed, Tony was pushing the wedding. Tony said, "You know that Papa wants them to marry. It's time Michael settles down and has a family."

I said, "Now Tony, I will not encourage Amanda and you better not! I'll do what I can if I'm asked, but right now a wedding is the last thing on my mind. Courtney and I are going to the florist and I'm going to practice. Tony, about us all meeting out at Wolf Bay Lodge, you can bring Papa and I'm sure Harriet and Courtney would enjoy a night out."

"That's fine with me baby. We can take them all there and the two of us can skip out. For safety's sake, you and I will come home!"

"Damn you Tony! You skipped me right out of my honeymoon for safety's sake and if you think you can take me away from Wolf Bay Lodge for a piece of ass, you have another thought coming.

Oh, Tony, while I'm thinking about my honeymoon, we have a cruise planned for the last two weeks in January. And yes, Papa knows all about it. He is the one that's making all the arrangements."

"That's great baby. I'll have you all to myself."

Courtney was waiting at the breakfast table when we came into the kitchen. She asked, "Do you still want me to decorate the Club?"

Tony spoke up, "Yes, she sure does and she will run you to

death by saying do this and do that! She's got a one track mind and that's the Hot Box."

I said, "I'd talk if I were you."

Tony, shut up and left the room. I said, "Come on Courtney. Tony's the one with a hot box on his mind and it's not my club. We will go to the florist and then you can find me over at the Love Club. Please do come and tell me all about Mr. Rogue. Max said he has lost ten pounds. See what you think about him. I don't think he'll remember you. Didn't you say he just saw you that one time?"

"Yes, and that was years ago."

"Oh yes Courtney, Tony is meeting us at Wolf Bay Lodge for dinner. Tell Charlie to make sure Mr. Rogue is busy at the club. I really don't want him to see me before opening night."

Courtney had gotten a phone call and Sandra had stopped us at the door. I went back to the table for a second cup of tea. Amanda came and sat beside me.

"Mom, I know you're busy with Christmas and the opening of the club, but Michael and I want to get married on New Year's Eve."

I didn't know that Tony came into the kitchen right behind Amanda. I looked up to see Tony smiling from ear to ear. I turned to Amanda hugging her saying, "Baby, you can have the biggest and best wedding that this town has ever seen. Tony was just talking about you and Michael this morning. He said for you and Michael to have the best of everything. We can fly to New York and buy your dress next week."

I had not taken my eyes off Tony's face. It was all I could do to keep a straight face.

Amanda said, "Papa will be the one to order the wedding cake, so I'll tell him to do it now. He knows what I want."

"Amanda, you can go to the card shop and get a rush on the invitations and get them sent out soon. Do that today and then take care of anything else you can."

Just as Courtney came back in Amanda said, "Mom is it okay with you if I marry Michael?"

Looking my daughter straight in the eyes, I said, "Little girl, do you remember what you said to me before I married Tony?"

"Yes Mom, I do."

"Go look in the mirror and ask yourself that same question and if you can't handle the family, then you go to New York and stay. I'm your mother and I'll be happy if you're happy. Only be sure what that happiness is."

I had gotten up to leave stopped and said, "One more thing, don't make me a grandmother for a long, long time. Is that clear?"

Tony was smiling again. Walking over to kiss him, I said, "I'll knock that smile right off of your face if she gets screwed up Mr."

That sure brought on the laughter. Even Sandra giggled spilling Tony's coffee.

I said, "Let's get out of here Courtney."

Max and Courtney were at my side as I walked over the new yard while waiting for the car to be brought around. I said, "Just look at the moss and the Azaleas. They're so big they look fifteen years old. You were right Courtney this is a mansion! I'll have to live up to all this. Tony is so good. He didn't miss a thing. This house is a dream home."

Max opened the car door for Courtney and Charlie was waiting inside the car. Charlie said, "Hello Miss Drucilla. You don't mind if I tag along with you and Max, do you?"

I said, "You're an ass Charlie. It wouldn't do me any good. So I guess not!"

Max pulled into the florist parking lot where all four of us went in. Max hurriedly walked in front and Charlie tagged along behind me. The owner was beside himself as the order began to mount up. Courtney asked the owner, "May I stay and help with the bows and the packing? I don't even want a wrinkle in the bows. We need fifty large pots of red Poinsettias."

The owner said, "Yes'um, Yes'um, it would be best if you stayed."

I said, “Do what you have to Courtney. I’ll see you later today.”

I turned and the owner hurried to open the door.

He said, “Thank you, Mrs. Tortomassi.”

I said, “Mr. Russo, I didn’t think you would remember who I am.”

“Yes’um, Yes’um, I know, I will give you my best.”

“Yes Sir, you always have.”

We left and headed for the Love Club.

# CHAPTER 32

Charlie said, "All the musicians that Mr. Rogue hired are to meet me here at the Love Club. We made arrangements to use the club and I think you will know these guys. I think they have been with Rogue before."

"Yes," I said, "I know they have. I've sung with them before. If they need to work, they won't talk."

The band was all set up and ready. Max was surprised to see such a reunion. J. B. Brown played the piano. I was thrilled to see Jerry, Pam and Bobby. I had been so busy talking that I hadn't noticed that Max was going to be the drummer. He hit the drums saying, testing, testing.

Max could see the surprise on my face. All I got back was his sweet smile and then we worked until I knew I had it made in the shade. We had gone over and over my songs. As I stepped off the bandstand, I heard Jerry say, "I can't wait to see Rogue's face!"

Pam asked, "Drucilla, why didn't you continue with the band in Nineteen Seventy-six? That song you wrote and sung brought you a standing ovation."

"Pam, that song was stolen from me and at the time Fritzie

intimidated me. But let's keep the record straight. It wasn't all Fritzie's fault. We were young then and we jumped at the chance to make a dime. Remember the night of the big blowup when Fritzie said that I would never be a singer and that Richard would be running my life forever. Richard doesn't run my life and Fritzie doesn't intimidate me anymore. The best part for you is that he's not even your boss, I am!"

Turning to talk to them all, I said, "I want to see your wives here tomorrow. Pam, your husband, of course."

When Courtney came in, Jerry said, "I don't have a wife."

I said, "Oh yes you do and Courtney has a husband that's bigger than you."

Jerry was backing Courtney into a corner when Charlie came in and saved her by saying we had to get going. J. B. came over and hugged me and said, "It's good we can all be here. This is the way it should have been. I just hope Fritzie has mellowed. He was mean to us back then."

"Yes," I said, "I want you all to forget the past. Fritzie has mellowed all right. I've been told that he is nice and he'll know just how lucky he is in a few days. Okay, Charlie, I'm ready now."

Courtney walked up beside me and I told her, "Don't give Jerry the time of day. He has screwed half of Alabama. I love him Courtney, but the truth is the truth! Now, tell me about Mr. Russo and Fritzie."

"The club is beautiful. Mr. Russo will work there Sunday. The old fellow called in two girls to help him. Everything will be fine. I helped him order what we needed to work with. Most everything will be silk. I'm going there Sunday afternoon to make sure things are right, but as far as I can tell, the club is ready.

The liquor truck was there, so Fritzie hardly noticed me at all. But Drucilla, he is just as he was the first time I ever saw him, a doll, just a walking doll. Don't you think that Tony will be jealous of you and him?"

"Courtney, are you crazy? Have you been wearing

blinders? Tony has no reason to be jealous of Fritzie. Besides that, I think it's you that's jealous. But don't be. If you've got the hots for him, go to it, sister!"

Max spoke up, "Now, Drucilla, it sounds as if she's made you mad!"

I said, "Hell no! I'm not mad, but I don't want anybody planting a seed of jealousy in Tony's head. I love Fritzie, but not in the way some would like to think. I'll tell you all, you better be careful what rag you pick up. You never know who washed what with it."

Charlie had been quiet, but he couldn't hold back the laughter. He said, "Damn you Drucilla. You say the damndest things."

Courtney said, "Yes she does and I didn't mean a thing except that Fritzie is a hunk that would make any man jealous."

I said, "Shut up Courtney. You'll have me so curious that I'll go see for myself. Tony told me that Fritzie was fat and looked terrible."

I turned to Max. "Will you see who's going to Wolf Bay Lodge? I need to rest before we leave, but I want everyone there on time."

As we drove through the big oaks, I said, "Just look Courtney. I sure have come a long way. Gosh, every trip that I made here I would pray that I wouldn't have to go back to Shady Grove and now I don't. I can hear a bath and bed calling me."

Max said, "Drucilla, don't you know sleeping is a form of death?"

"Yeah, but I'll come alive in time to go to Wolf Bay Lodge!"

As we were going in the door, I whispered to Sandra, "Let me die until seven p.m."

At the club the next day I didn't want to practice, I just wanted to talk and to make everything clear between the band and me. I was told that Pam's husband is new to this life. Bobby had a new wife and I'm sure the band knew each other better than I know them, but I wanted my club to be the best. All of you must understand that it takes mixing and mingling with the people to keep them coming back. You have to make them feel good about being there. If they don't enjoy themselves, they won't be back. I insisted that they move from table to table, joke and laugh with the good and the bad. It keeps the money coming back and if we don't have a good name, we won't be able to stay open in the winter. I didn't want any fighting in my club caused by jealousy. This can be a happy way to make a living, once you learn that mixing and mingling is the trick to keeping a crowd happy. Fritzie hired you. He is the manager, but I can have the last say and if you ever need me, say so, but don't cause me trouble. I don't know who wants to work or who doesn't, but if any of you need a job, I'm sure one can be found. I assure you there's plenty to do when school lets out. This place will be butt too butt and bumper to bumper. I gave them the rest of the day off.

I told Max to come on. I've got to go take care of some things at the house. I had told Sandra that we would have some extra help two weeks before Christmas and two weeks after. She had said her Mom, Beth wanted to help and they would be waiting for me along with all the groceries for baking and candy making.

I ran in, changed my clothes and came into the kitchen. The recipe books were out and the ingredients had been set out on the kitchen table. Sandra and Beth were anxious to begin. Beth was a lovely person, clean and ready to work, and work is what we did for the next three days. Even Amanda and Courtney helped, but Harriet made the excuse that she would gain her weight back if she even smelled the goodies.

Later in the day I sent Papa a box of chocolates and boy did he love the candy. The phone rang within thirty minutes.

Papa said, "Drucilla, send some more coconut bon-bons."

I said, "No! Not until Christmas, but I will send Sandra and Beth."

When Beth heard this she backed toward the door saying,

"No way. I'm not going to his house!"

Sandra said, "Don't worry Mama, Mrs. Tony's just joking with Mr. Perricotti."

I said, "Beth, if you had good sense you would find your way into Papa Perricotti's Christmas stocking."

Papa was still laughing when we said our good-byes.

This caused Beth to pout for a while, but she seemed better when the work started up again. Amanda reminded me that we would leave for New York on Wednesday and come back on Friday.

I said, "That's okay Baby, I've taken care of everything. I'll be ready, don't you worry. I've been meaning to ask you, where have you been going these last few days?"

"Mom, I could ask you the same."

"Yes, but I asked you first."

No one had time to answer. Tony came in and took me away, saying he wanted to show me what he had been doing for the boys. I couldn't believe my eyes. I was more surprised over their tree house than my own new house.

I said, "I don't believe you built this Tony."

At the same time, two little familiar voices said, "Yes he did! We saw him."

Anthony said, "Daddy's been working for days!"

The tree house was twenty feet high with two windows, a full size door and a porch with rails all the way around it. There was a swinging ladder to climb up plus, the steps. But what the boys loved the most was the firehouse pole to slide down if they were in a hurry. The little house was built to last.

I said, "Tony, it's too big to be a tree house."

Tony said, "No, No, it's just ten by ten. I just hope they don't break an arm coming down that pole!"

Then I made the mistake of asking about curtains. Brandon spoke up, "Mam-Maw, do we look like sissies? You know our house ain't going to be girly! Do you get that?"

I looked at Tony. He said, "I think I heard you say that a time or two. Let's get back to our house."

Walking back, I asked Tony, "Are you going to New York with me and Amanda?"

Tony said, "I wish you wouldn't ask me. I'll miss you but why not take Courtney?"

"I will. I'm sure Amanda will run us to death and you do need to help Papa get ready for the holidays. Tell Papa that I'll see him in a day or so and remind him that I'm leaving for New York so he can let me know if he needs for me to bring anything back."

Later that evening it turned cool. Tony and I were alone in the den.

"Tony, I'm cold. I wish we could have a fire."

Tony said, "That's a deal my lady. You get some hot coffee and I'll light your fire."

I went to the kitchen and got our coffee while Tony made a beautiful fire. We sat quietly on the floor and the next thing I knew we were waking up at the break of day.

I said, "Tony, can you carry me upstairs? I doubt that I can walk after sleeping here."

"Come on Dru, I'll help you up, then we can help each other up the stairs."

"Tony, do you even remember the last time you slept in the floor?"

"Oh gosh, Baby, I don't want to remember. Baby, let's put the **DO NOT DISTURB** sign on our door so no one will get us up!"

But the ringing of Tony's private phone woke us. Tony was out of bed in a flash, pulling on his pants. Tony hung up the phone and said, "Get up Dru. Ring Max and Charlie to bring the car. Papa's been hurt!"

I had gotten Max before, Tony had gotten the words out of his mouth. Knowing that Max would be at the front of the house by the time we could get down stairs. I threw on a jogging suit and with shoes in hand, I was at Tony's heels with him saying, "Baby, you should stay here. I don't know what we will find!"

"Hell no! I'm going to find out how Papa is!"

Max had the car door open and the car was moving before Tony was all the way inside saying, "Move it Charlie. I don't know how bad Papa's hurt. Tonnymacker just said he had been shot."

We pulled up into Papa's driveway. The car was still rolling, but Tony was out and running. The ambulance was backed up to the front door. Thank God the guys had enough time to bring Papa upstairs. Tony and Charlie had knelt beside Tonnymacker who was at Papa's side. As they put Papa into the ambulance, I heard Tonnymacker tell Tony it wasn't as bad as he thought. One shot had grazed his head and the other shot got him in the left shoulder.

They pulled out for the hospital with Max and me following the ambulance. Tony and Tonnymacker rode in the ambulance with Papa.

"What in the hell happened?" asked Tony.

Tonnymacker said, "A Dr. Shane had come in with two of the Friday night regulars and since he was a friend of Mrs. Drucilla's, Mr. Perricotti was showing him a good time. The doctor had won a good bit of cash and Michael had been looking out for Mr. Perricotti. Then a group came in from the Love Club and he had to help them. You know old man Leopard is there every weekend. He said he heard two in that group talking about how much money the place was taking in and before Leopard could work his way over to Michael, the shots were fired. One of the guys had pulled a knife on Mr. Perricotti. When Mr. Perricotti swung at him, the other guy shot him. Papa then pulled his gun and shot both of them. We've got them both upstairs, one with a bullet in his heart and the other with a bullet right between the eyes. They'll never try to rob anyone else."

The doctor came out of the operating room all smiles and said, "Mr. Tortomassi, we are very lucky. Mr. Perricotti is awake and asking for you. He insists on going home. We both know he needs to stay here, but if you sign all the papers and he has a doctor around the clock, I'll let him go."

Charlie and Michael came in as I was just coming out from seeing Papa.

I said, "You can bring the car around Max. Papa is going to our house! Michael, did you take care of everything at Papa's house?"

Michael's smile was sweet as he said, "Sure did. I don't know why anyone would rob Papa, but I'm sure glad he proved to be too much for them. The police said they both were from Dothan. They said there have been a lot of robberies lately between here and there, but I think Papa just stopped them!"

Tony came out looking worried. Everyone asked, "What's wrong? What about Papa?"

Tony hugged me saying, "Don't worry, everything is going to be fine."

"Then why do you look so worried," asked Michael.

Tony said, "Hell boy, Papa being shot at his age, shook me up!"

I said, "Michael, you ride home with Papa and we'll go on ahead and get a room set up for a doctor. Let's go Max."

Papa had insisted that I take the trip to New York with Amanda. He was better and would be fine. Little Anthony and Brandon were telling me to go and that they would take care of Papa. The way they put it, Papa would help them get into all the presents under the tree.

I turned and winked at Max. I said, "I tell you what Max, if you find one package tampered with, I want you to skin them both."

"Yes Mam," Brandon said.

"Now Anthony, you know we can keep Papa busy playing games because I don't want you to be skinned."

Max jumped at Brandon and both boys ran laughing.

Courtney wasn't going to New York now. The shooting had scared her and she was going home. This wasn't the life for her and she said she would be back for the opening of the club.

I said, "You don't make sense Courtney. It's just two more weeks! Why don't you tell the truth? It's Dan. Has he called here?"

Courtney dropped her eyes, not saying a word.

I said, "Damn you Courtney. When are you going to stand your ground with him? He's been running his trips to Montgomery and back, for that so-called newspaper for years, or has he just told you that? What have I told you time and time again? If you don't respect yourself, no one else will!"

Courtney finally spoke up, "All right Drucilla. I'll stay here with Papa, but I'm not going to New York. I don't know anything about that place!"

"That's damn well and fine Courtney, just as long as you don't go running back to Dan. You don't have any little girls now, so you don't have to put up with the likes of him!"

Turning back to Papa, I said, "I'm sorry for the screaming Papa. Love the boys for me. They must have gone out to the tree house. Sandra has set out fruit and goodies all over the house, but if you would like anything else, you tell her, okay?"

With a hug, I was gone to find Amanda. I found Amanda all right .... having words with Max. Amanda said, "Did I hear you say you are going to New York with us Max?"

Max answered, "Yes, I asked Tony and he said fine!"

I could tell that he was really pissed at Amanda so I said, "Its okay Baby. I'll feel safe if Max is with us."

As hateful as hell Amanda said, "All right, but he should have asked us. It's our trip, not Tony's."

I said, "Wait just a minute Amanda. Tony has the last say in whatever I do."

"Yes Mom and so did Daddy for twenty-three years and that's why you're here."

My temper flew. I said, "Hell yes and your Daddy is the reason for Max going. The bastard tried to kill me on the way home from Birmingham. Now Tony is worried that he'll try again and if you think he won't just because I'm with you, you're mistaken. He will get me if he can. Now are you going or not, if so lets load up!"

Max and Amanda were at the door at the same time. Tony had walked in with Papa. Tony said, "Wait a minute everybody!"

I said, "For what? What's wrong?"

"Well," said Tony, "Harriet was arrested last night."

All of our mouths flew open and I said, "Tony, you don't mean that."

"Oh yes," Tony said with a wicked smile and laughing. "She was arrested on drug charges. When the police stopped her and looked under her dress, they found forty pounds of crack!"

Everyone bent over with laughter. I said, "What a joke! Take care of him Papa. I know he's full of bull! We'll see you soon. **A forty pound crack!"**

By the time we were out the door, Papa had Anthony and Brandon playing Black Jack and Five Card Stud.

# CHAPTER 33

We had gotten home late Sunday night from our trip to New York. We were so tired that I didn't do much talking. It took almost all day Monday to tell about the shopping trip.

Sandra and I were alone in the kitchen the next morning.

Sandra said, "Papa was a joy to have around. I believe I heard him tell Mr. Tony that he would stay on until after New Years."

I was thrilled to death that Papa was going to stay. Amanda had just come down and was gleaming from head to toe. You would have thought she had been away from Michael for a month.

Courtney had made sure the Club was ready. Mr. Russo had done a fine job. Every table had a mini-love bouquet on it, made with small red poinsettias. Fifty big, red pots of Poinsettias were all around the band platform. The tree lights were all red. Everything else on the tree was silver, just like I wanted. Courtney swore to me that my club would be beautiful! There are advertisements all over town. Fritzie told her that ads had been run in all the papers everywhere. The phone at the club had rung from morning until night. The place would be packed for New Year's Eve and without a doubt, opening night. That was wonderful, but I was a little worried about opening on Christmas Eve.

After Tony and I had gone to bed, he said, "I wish you had been at the club Friday when the band started up. You're right about him Dru, he is good I think I do like your friend."

"I'm glad you do Tony. I just hope Fritzie will be happy once he finds out who I am! Oh yes, Tony, earlier today Max asked me about Fritzie's car. I told Max to give the keys back to me and I would give the car to him for Christmas, if he agrees to stay after he sees me on opening night. Max also said that Fritzie has lost all the weight he had gained and I'm proud of that."

We were quiet for a minute and Tony asked, "What are you thinking about baby? Are you happy here with me and Anthony?"

"Why do you ask that Tony? Do I give you the impression that I'm not happy? If so, I'm sorry. I am happier than I've ever been in my life. Your family has been wonderful to me. Tony, you're the best! Sometimes if I allow myself to think back, it hurts me. I know it's not important that the people back home love me, but it still hurts. I still find myself wishing they did, but we know wishing is a waste of time and I've wasted enough time, right?"

I fell asleep in Tony's arms, thinking about my new pink leather suit that I would wear opening night and remembering Amanda was going to wear her white one. She will be beautiful, that's for sure!

The next morning Tony was up before anyone and knocking on Max's door. "Get up Max. I need to talk to you about Dru. Let's go play nine holes of golf and talk. Charlie can take care of things here, we won't be gone long."

Tony waited until they were on the golf course to talk. He wanted to make sure he would not be overheard.

Tony said, "Max I want that psychiatrist friend of Dru's

checked out again. Remember Dr. Shane that came to Papa's place? You know he was there the night Papa got shot. He came here to get me word that the psychiatrist thinks maybe Dru's in trouble. That maybe we should watch her close if she starts showing signs of being sad. He believes she had buried the hurt deep inside and it may surface at any time. That bunch hurt her much more than she lets on. Dru gave into depression when we got to Birmingham. I couldn't believe the shape that place put her in. Dr. Shane told Papa that Dru is a survivor, but he wonders if she is putting on a good act this time. He said she told that quack if the dreams and hurt come back, she would take her life and that she'd rather be dead than have the hurt. We all know she can do it! We know it doesn't take a crazy person it just takes a person with guts enough to do it and a reason. I love her Max. I don't want her out of your sight when she's not with me. Until we know for sure that it's all behind her, we will have to watch her."

Max said, "You can count on me Tony."

Tony said, "You know she told me to burn that place of hers to the ground, but at that time, she was hurting when we were leaving. I didn't think she meant it. Now, I wonder if maybe I should have. I've been over all the sessions she had with that Dr. Skeet. Everyone could plainly see that she fought Richard and the others trying to keep her home happy, until her health and started slowing her down. When the bastards saw she was getting weaker, they all ganged up on her. I know she couldn't help but give into depression. The things that kept her going, was the love and respect she had for herself, plus being desperate to find out who Richard's woman was. You know Max that just may be the key to this depression. I feel sure it is."

Max asked, "What makes you think that?"

"This same thing happened to her the first time Richard had an affair. He had that slut for nineteen months before Dru found out about her. This was three years after they were married and it took Dru three more years to find out who she was. You see, even though she knew what he had done, she didn't divorce him until after she found out who his slut was. She divorced him and married him back two months later and went on with her life. It's just a repeat! Think about it. She's taken care of DeRoy, Percy, Jeff and Harriet. Now what's holding her up? Why hasn't she done away with Richard? She's got to have the answers. That's why! Who was his girlfriend and why? Then and only then, will she be able to put it out of her mind.

Let's think about this Max. We know for sure he had that ghost girl, as Dru called her the one that worked in the construction department and out of the same building as he did. Richard talked about the garage slut and the cable repair girl that worked in his group. Richard had told Dru that the cable repair girl was so ugly that all the men called her Gorilla. Dru said she would bet her life that the Gorilla was his woman. Richard would not find her and Richard's supervisor would not give Dru any information on the girl. I'll tell you one thing, that Yankee doesn't know how lucky he was that Dru didn't tell his wife why he was spending his Saturdays at the East Lake Plant. To tell you the truth, Max, I'm surprised that Dru didn't tell and she may yet! Anyway, we have got to find that Gorilla, at all costs. Just maybe, it will help Dru just to know who and where she is. We know the Gorilla, had four or five children and for sure one is a boy. Dru said, the boy kept calling her. He would ask if Richard was home yet and Dru would tell him no, but he could call back. What I want you to do Max is get some men in Birmingham and tell them to look under every rock and not to stop until they find them. Richard had said when he married her back that he wouldn't go inside the homes to work and would never work with women again. Max find out. This is when they almost killed Dru."

"Tony, I already have men in Birmingham. I personally guarantee that they will find her."

"We know that all male whores protect their women and the phone company does too. Richard said he felt sorry for a test board girl she had headaches from hearing the phones ringing all day. This woman may very well be the one. You know very well that Richard couldn't tell the truth, because it not only meant his job, but his woman's job as well. He told Dru, that he felt sorry for the ladies, that their men had left them with kids to care for all by themselves. It's hard to work all day then try to take care of a house and kids. Just like Dru said, Max, he would have killed her and almost did. The man is just a male whore. The fool had told Dru about his whore in a dozen ways or more. Just like the feeling sorry bit. Dru knew that Richard wasn't a bleeding heart for anyone!

Max, you tell the men to get on this and that it's the most important job they will ever have. Tell them there's a bonus for the man that finds them all. I'm betting it's the **one** on the test board. I believe they were moved from downtown to East Lake."

"Tony, I'll have them on it as soon as I can get to a phone. I feel better now. Maybe I can win this round of golf."

When Tony had started talking about Dru, Max had pulled their golf cart up under a big moss covered tree. As they pulled around to the first hole Max said, "You don't worry me man. Remember, I saw Drucilla beat you!"

Tony played a good game, but Max won.

The next few days flew by. I was so busy it seemed that I didn't have a worry in the world and by rights I shouldn't have. The little Shih Tzu dog had been delivered and Brandon and Anthony were thrilled beyond words.

On the twenty-third, I gave a dinner party. All of Tony's men plus J.B., Jerry, Pam, Bobby and their families were there. J. B. was at the piano and everyone was singing Christmas Carols. Papa had asked me to come and sit by him, just as I started across the room, a shot came through the window. I had fallen to the floor. More shots were fired, but they were on the outside. Max and Charlie had been taking turns patrolling the house. Max came flying in the door just as Tony was going out.

I said, “Did you stop him, Max?”

“No! He got away on a dirt bike! Is everyone alright in here?”

Tony came back into the house to assure everyone that things were fine. Tony told Max the shot was meant for me and if I hadn’t tripped over the dog, whoever it was would have shot me. Tony moved everyone to another room and the party went on. Tony told everyone to just party, have a good time and that everything was being taken care of.

The party was over about one-thirty. Tony had given money to everyone for Christmas and that was fine with me. I knew most of them needed the money, but I was giving Max a gold nugget ring. Tony would have to wait until Christmas morning, for his three-carat ring. I knew that Tony had rings, but not from me. Oh and for Papa, I had taken a five by seven picture of his wife and had it enlarged to an eleven by fourteen and had it put into a beautiful frame. The five by seven was a black and white, but the large picture was in color. I could hardly wait, but like Tony, Papa would wait.

I knew Tony was worried to death about me. That shot was too close! He got all of his most trusted men together and gave them instructions.

Tony said, “First of all, I want the Hot Box surrounded. We can’t let anything happen. Topaz, you and Sam take care of the doors. Michael, Charlie and I will be at a front table with Rogue. I want every available man outside. Bob Tostie will blend into the crowd, but be in reach of me. Max, I want you to replace Rogue on the drums. I will explain to Rogue that you being on the drums will be just a one-night thing. He will be free to enjoy the night.”

It was plain to see that Tony wasn’t taking any chances. He had it planned for Max to be on stage with me. No one was about to take my life.

Max had made his calls to Birmingham, but Papa had sent some of his own men out to find Richard. With orders to bring his behind to Pensacola and then call him. Even though Papa wasn't well himself, he wasn't going to sit back and let harm come to me.

I didn't know how in the world I was going to get into the club without Rogue seeing me. My worry had been wasted because Rogue would be with Phillip Jimez.

The excitement was building. Tony, Tonnymacker and Charlie had searched the club using a trained dog. He looked in every crack and corner to make sure there were no bombs or booby traps of any kind waiting for me.

I was dressing when the private telephone rang. Tony said, "My Lord, it's only eight o'clock!" Turning to me, he said, "Baby, the club is packed. Max said they would have to turn some people away because of the fire code."

Amanda knocked on our door. "Mom we've got to be going. Harriet and Courtney are ready."

I said, "I'm on my way, Amanda. Just as soon as I see what Papa wants with me."

Tony was off the phone now and he took me in his arms saying, "You're a doll, a lady and you're mine."

"Yes, all yours. Oh Tony, do you think Amanda will be surprised that I'm singing?"

"I'm sure she will baby. Now, you listen, you and Amanda must stay behind the curtain until time for you to sing. When you get through, then step down to my table. I know for sure that Richard can't get inside. I don't want you to worry about that, but I don't know who he may have sent. I have men all over the place."

"I don't know what to think about you Tony. You're the one that's worried but just keep Rogue at your table so he will be sure to see my face when I step onto the stage and I'll be fine."

"I'll do that and baby, your club is pure luxury. I think you covered everything."

I went downstairs and met with Papa, he handed me a velvet box saying, "Merry Christmas." I tried to get him to wait until Christmas morning, but no way. It had to be opened now. As soon as I opened the box, I was taking off my earrings so I could put my new ones on.

I said, "Help me. Papa, put the pendant on my neck while I put the earrings on." Turning them over and over in my hands, I said, "Papa, I don't deserve all the good things you have given me."

Amanda ran in saying, "Come on Mom, you're making us late."

I said, "Look Amanda. Papa gave me my Christmas, to wear tonight! Aren't they beautiful?"

Papa spoke up, "Yes, they were Mama's! She would have given them to you herself had she been here. She would have loved you Drucilla the same as Tony and me."

Amanda had forgotten about being late for the club. She said, "Good Lord, these must be five carats. Are they Papa? Do you think Michael will ever love me that much?"

Papa gave Amanda a hug and said, "I'm sure he does and will for a long time baby."

I stepped back beside Amanda and asked Papa, "Would Amanda and I win a beauty contest?"

Papa didn't have time to answer because Tony came in and I ran to show him what Papa had given me. I said, "Tony, you came in just in time. See what Papa gave to me."

Tony said, "My Lord, Papa, you're doing your best to take her away from me. You made me forget what I came here for. Oh yes, Ross has Papa's limousine waiting and we're late."

I stopped dead in my tracks. Amanda asked, "What's wrong Mom?"

I gave them a big smile and said, "I just want to remind everyone that it doesn't matter if I'm late. I'm the boss!"

Tony said, "You're right, but what about Rogue?"

I said, "I guarantee you that Phillip will call before bringing him back." I laughed. "But, I'm ready. Thank you Papa. You're the best Santa Claus a person could wish for."

Tony said, "What about me Dru? I gave you a house."

I said, "Why Tony! I'll not even talk about that. At your

age you should know that diamonds talk loud and clear."

Ross pulled the limousine right up to the front door. Topaz and Sam were waiting. They walked halfway down the aisle with us and turned back. Max was behind the curtain with Amanda and me. Amanda was so excited.

She said, "Just look Mom. Peek out this side. Courtney and Harriet are having the time of their lives. Here he comes Mom! **Look!** It's Fritzie, strutting his stuff!"

All of a sudden I thought I would throw up. **No... No** I can't be sick! I could still see him. Tony had stopped him and Phillip. I could hear Tony tell him that they were to sit at his table.

Pam was on stage singing Christmas Carols and Max had to insist that we move away from the curtains.

Amanda said, "Okay, Okay." Yet, she was pushing him back saying, "I love the people. Just look. Have you ever seen so many beautiful clothes in one place? Everyone is dressed in red, silver and gold."

I interrupted and told Amanda to sit down. She was making me nervous. I ask Amanda to tell me, if I looked okay.

Pam was taking her bows and I said, "Listen! It's Pam." I looked at my watch. "She's right on time, it's ten o'clock."

Amanda and I looked at each other. Amanda asked, "Mom, are you going to sing? Why Mom, you are! I can't see you from in here."

She jumped up and ran for Tony's table just as Max and I ran onto the stage.

# CHAPTER 34

The crowd was on their feet as my loud sounding voice boomed, "I am Drucilla Tortomasi. Welcome to my club, the **Hot Box** and **Merry Christmas.**

Now let me brag because I know without a doubt we have the best band in all of Alabama. We have J.B. Brown on piano, Pam Sides with her tambourine and vocal, Jerry Williams on lead guitar, Bobby Bar on electric steel and Max Tombrello on the drums. Max is sitting in for Mr. Fritzie Rogue this evening. Stand up Fritzie. By the way, Fritzie is the manager of the Hot Box and my friend! Now, let's take just another minute because I want you to meet my family. Standing at this front table is Papa Perricotti, my husband, Tony Tortomasi, my daughter, Amanda Hallmark, and her fiancé, Michael Tortomasi. I don't think Michael and Amanda will mind if I tell you they will marry, this New Year's Eve. Won't that be great, my brother-in-law will be my son-in-law? He may not know how lucky he is tonight."

With a wicked look from Amanda, I started to sing.

## I SORTA MELT

We've never cheated and we've never lied
We've always been together side-by-side
We both said our vows and wear wedding bands,
But we get together every time that we can, and
I sort of melt at the touch of your hand.
It's O.K. if you wear a wedding band
I still melt at the touch of your hand
It's O.K. if you wear a wedding band............

The dance floor was full. I told the crowd one more and I'll turn this over to someone that can sing. This is a message from all of us gals to all of you guys and I sang:

## BOARDING HOUSE BLUES

This is a special bulletin
Are you listening man?
I'm closing you Boarding House down.
All you do is run around and
I've got the Boarding House Blues
Yes, I've got the Boarding House Blues.........

The crowd gave me a standing ovation. Pam handed me a piece of paper. I know she could see the surprise on my face. "Well folks, this note tells me that our next guest is my very own, Amanda Hallmark."

I handed Amanda the microphone and stepped off the stage. Max said, "The word is scrumptious!"

I couldn't believe my ears. Amanda was wonderful. It was as if she had been on stage all of her life. She had the people eating out of her hands.

I asked Tony, "Did you hear that? Just listen to her!"

I hadn't even given Fritzie, a second look. I couldn't take my eyes off Amanda.

Michael said, "Just listen!"

Amanda had started her next song. She asked, "Do you want to dance? Do you need a dancing partner?"

By the time her song ended she had more partners begging for a dance than she knew what to do with. Backing up as far on stage as she could, she said, "If you're single and want a dance, put your names in a hat and at one o'clock, I will draw one name for a dance."

After singing a special song for me, she said, "Now, here is your real band leader, Mr. Fritzie Rogue."

As I watched Fritzie, I thought how handsome he is in his new black velvet jacket with silver roses. I wondered why I was doing this for him. He was one of the ones that had kicked me in the teeth when I needed help. My wheels were rolling. Just think, Amanda should have been a star and could have been if only that fool had cared about us and had faith in himself. Just you wait Mr. Rogue. I have a lot of hell raising in store for you.

Turning to tell Amanda how proud I was of her, I was surprised again to find her on the dance floor with Tony.

Papa said, "Don't say a word. He asked you, but you were in another world, so he asked Amanda."

I said, "That's alright Papa. Isn't she wonderful? Papa, I wonder if this is the life she wants. If it is, we can make her a star. She has what it takes if only it's what she wants."

When the music stopped, Amanda walked over to me and said, "Are you surprised Mom? Even after Brandon told you that I had been into your songs?"

I said, "I do remember him saying that and Anthony had been so relieved. But I thought that he thought that Brandon was going to tell me about the house. Baby, this is a wonderful Christmas and I'm so proud that the club is packed and jammed. I've never seen so many people in one place. Just look Amanda, a lot of them we know. They've come in from Birmingham. I wish I could read their minds!"

Time was passing so fast, it was unbelievable. It was one

o'clock. Time to draw the name out of the hat. Amanda was on stage and she took time to mix, bounce and shake the hat. Doing her best to make it a real time of suspense, but to everyone's surprise she pulled out Papa Perricotti's name. The younger men moped back to their tables to cry in their beers.

Tony asked, "Do you think that's fair, old man?"

Papa said, "Heck yes! She said single men, didn't she?"

Papa turned toward Amanda and shouted, "Come on baby. Do you need a dancing partner? Here I am."

Papa had everyone applauding and Amanda promised she would draw another name later.

I had no doubt about my club making it. I knew it would be fine. I was the happiest I had ever been.

I turned to Tony and said, "Just look at Harriet and Courtney, they have danced with everyone from the Mayor too Ross the chauffeur."

Michael said, "The band is the best I have ever heard. I heard one of the girls working tables say that she had made two hundred dollars in tips."

Amanda had been back on stage singing with Fritzie and now he wanted me to take over so he could have a break! Stepping up on stage, I handed him the car keys with a red ribbon saying, Take these and whatever car they open outside in the parking lot here will be your Christmas from Santa!

It was almost closing time and I had sung my last song and all of a sudden Max grabbed the microphone and said, "It's my turn to sing and I have a surprise for Drucilla. This is a song she wrote back in September of Nineteen Eighty-seven when, a group of people were trying to take our Confederate flag down from the Capitol building. So here you are folks!"

**BE PROUD YOU'RE A SOUTHERN MAN**

I'm living in Dixie Land. Yes, I'm a Southern man.
I'm a rebel through and through.......................

The crowd went wild and it was then that I heard a fight. Everyone was moving and shuffling around. Max ran over and stood in front of me.

Charlie shouted from the back, "It's all over back here. Say your goodnights."

Max gave me back the microphone. I said, "Merry Christmas and sorry for the disturbance!"

Before leaving I told Fritzie that I loved him and hoped he would be happy at the club promising to stay out of his hair as long as the Hot Box was his first love. He was invited to my home for Christmas dinner. He pulled me over to the side and said, "Baby, I read in the paper all about DeRoy. I'm sorry."

I snapped, "Are you? Don't baby me!"

Then remembering he had never accepted any invitation to her house before, I said, "One more thing Fritzie, if I invite you to a s`eance, you best show up." Then in a low whisper I said, "When you start that car, you've been bought and paid for. See you tomorrow."

I walked off leaving him standing there with his mouth open. I was looking for Tony, when I ran into Max.

I said, "Let's get out of here Max. I've got to find Santa Claus and make sure that Sandra, has that ham in the oven."

On the way out Papa said, "You see my girl. Tonight tells us just how successful you are. Just think...with your entertainment adjacent to my gambling, we can't lose. And let me tell you, Amanda was the star of the show"

"I know Amanda was good Papa and not just because she is my daughter. She is tops! Fritzie is the veteran and he's been working steadily for the past twenty years or so."

Then I stopped to read the huge sign.... Come on into our **HOT BOX**. Our band will appeal to all ages because of their versatility. We play everything from big band, Dixieland too today's Pop and Top Forties...**GRAND OPENING TONIGHT**.

Out of the corner of my eye, I saw Ross motioning for Papa, but by that time Harriet and Courtney had came up. Max opened the car door telling Papa, that he'd take the ladies on home. I hadn't taken my eyes off Papa's limousine. I knew something was going on! Tony, Charlie, Sam, Bob and Phillip were standing at the car.

I said, "Max, let me out of this car!"

Max drove on as if he didn't even hear me.

I said, "Damn you…**stop this car**!"

Max still drove on as if he didn't hear me.

I said, "Where are Michael and Amanda!"

Max said, "They're right behind us Drucilla. Tony told me not to stop for anything."

I said, "Stop this damn car or I'll stick this gun in your ear!" Courtney let out a scream. I said, "**Shut up**! We've got to find out what's wrong back there!"

Max said, "We will. Just let me take the girls home, then you and I will come back and get Tony!"

Getting the girls out of the car wasn't any trouble. The minute the car stopped, they ran for the house. Max said, "Now you listen Drucilla. What you want is for my butt to end up in that slough. I can't take you back there! I was given orders to get you the hell away from there and I did! You're right about something being wrong. The scuffle at the club tonight was a man about twenty-five years old carrying a Mac Ten to kill you! Bob wrestled him to the floor and with Sam's help they got the gun and locked the man in Mr. Perricotti's limousine. It's my guess he's the same fellow that took a shot at you last night. I'm sure Tony is trying to find out who he is and why he is out to get you."

I said, "Listen Max. Just take me back. We all know that Richard has hired him to kill me, and just maybe I'll know him, if he's from Birmingham. Let's go. I'll take full responsibility for this."

Max obeyed reluctantly. I stepped out of the car saying, "Tony, I made Max bring me back. I want a look at this guy myself!"

As Tony moved over to let me in, my mouth flew open and I popped his face saying, "His name is Davey Ray. Now

Davey you tell them why you're here."

Davey just sat there staring straight ahead. I said, "Davey, is Richard paying you to kill me?"

The young man nervously glanced up and then began to cry saying, "I couldn't let you tell my wife!"

Tony and I walked over to my car. I said, "Tony, I will tell you how I know Davey. When I had the investigators on Richard, they were watching Richard's truck and Davey just happened to be meeting his lover at a motel everyday at lunch. Richard was laying up with his woman on a week's vacation while telling me he was at work. Davey was driving Richard's work truck the week the investigator was following the truck. When they burst into the room to get some pictures, they got some all right, of Davey and his gay co-worker. I used up all of my money and this idiot is all I got."

As we walked back to Papa's car, I said, "You're a fool Davey. They gave you the pictures and the negatives. I wasn't going to tell your wife, little boy. But you are now! You have one week to tell her. **Do you hear me**? Now, you take your butt back to Birmingham and tell the others at that plant that if they don't find out who Richard's woman is, that I'm going to tell on them all."

I turned to Max. I said, "I'm ready to go home now Max."

As I was walking off, Davey said, "Richard is going to kill you!"

I jumped back toward Davey and grabbed a hand full of hair…jerking his head around so I could look him in the eye and said, "Listen fool, Richard killed me a long time ago. Now why don't you do your wife a favor and shoot yourself!"

Then I asked Tony, "Will you just let Davey go?"

Tony and I were still in bed watching television when the seven o'clock news, Christmas morning, came on saying that Davey had been found dead. He had taken my advice and shot himself in the head. I felt no remorse. That's what he should have done long ago.

Fritzie was at the house at nine o'clock that morning. He

had been driving his new car all night. When he came into the living room, we were all around the tree.

Fritzie said, "I was afraid if I went to sleep last night, this morning when I woke up the car would have been a dream."

I said, "You better be worth it or it will be a nightmare!"

Brandon spoke up, "Mam-Maw, you know your bark is worse than your bite."

Everyone laughed except Max, Tony and Fritzie. They knew better.

Anthony and Brandon had been all over the beach with their new four wheelers. The boys were having the time of their lives. Anthony ran to me, kissing and hugging me.

Anthony said, "This is the best Christmas because you're the best Mom."

That's all I had to hear to make tears run down my face. I turned to run before anyone could see me cry. Why did I still hurt so badly? Other people lose the people they love and get over it. Why can't I get it into my head that I never had Richard? I went to my bedroom to be alone. Looking into the mirror to put my lipstick on, I saw my new earrings and pendent that papa had given me last night. My being sad, that's nuts! I have everything to be happy about. Telling myself that I should have been an actress, I went back into the family room singing.

Max had found his package on his nightstand with a note saying, Thanks for teaching me to swim and for being a friend. A wink from across the room had said it all.

Tony said, "It's too cold this time of day."

I said, "Cold or not, I've got to hear the waves. I want to go for a walk." We walked for a while and then I said, "Isn't it beautiful? Tony, I can't come up with words enough to tell you how much I love you, or how much I love the gulf."

We walked and talked awhile and then Tony said, "We'd better get back. Michael and Amanda will want to talk about their wedding plans."

# CHAPTER 35

As we were getting ready for bed, Tony said, "Amanda is worried that Jeff might spoil her wedding. Tell me about Jeff."

"Tony, it is hard for me to believe that at one time I loved Jeff the way I love Michael. I tell you, Jeff didn't have a darn thing to offer Amanda. The boy had wonderful grandparents, but they passed away long ago, leaving him with no money of his own. I thought the world of them and it's beyond me how Jeff ended up so warped. Being so jealous of what Amanda had made him crazy! He did everything he could to cause trouble in our home. He wanted Amanda to move out into the poverty world he lived in. I just couldn't imagine her being with his people…being a freeloader. But of course Jeff had been a freeloader all of his life so he thought it was a normal way of living. Thank God she eventually saw through that fool!"

Tony said, "I guess it's good that you have already solved the problem."

The next morning Tony looked out the window and said, "Just look Dru, there's Michael's car. I knew he'd be here."

Sure enough, Tony and I found them sitting at the dining room table with plans laid out everywhere.

As I entered the room Amanda said, "Look Mom, I think we have everything ready. The church is ready and Mr. Russo has all my flowers ready.

He will decorate everything himself. He was so nice and he said that he would make it the most beautiful wedding in the world, just for me. Father Raymond is helping. He is calling in some volunteers to help hang the flowers."

I looked down the list. Eight bridesmaids to walk in pairs, carrying two pieces of garland, to the communion rail where it would rest for the wedding mass.

Amanda said, "Mom, I hope you don't think I'm copying you. I'm sure glad that Sally volunteered to give us our reception at the Mayor's Mansion. We know it will be elegant. She is one lady that never does anything half way. Michael has the photographer sitting on ready and my bridesmaids will be here Wednesday with all of our wedding party here by Thursday. There will be twenty-six in the wedding party alone. Don't you worry Mom I have everything under control. With Father Raymond, Mr. Russo, plus Sally, I'm not the least bit worried. Mom, I know it seems like a big wedding, but honest, it's what I want."

Amanda looked over at Michael and said, "A wedding is a serious thing. I want it to be with gracefulness and tenderness. We know it will be filled with joy."

Tony squeezed my hand and said, "You kids know that a Catholic ceremony is the most beautiful of all weddings."

Then, reaching in his back pocket, he pulled out everything they needed for a honeymoon at Paradise Island, a tiny island across the harbor from Nassau. Handing the papers to Amanda, he said, "My dear, this is the most romantic place I could find for you. All your transportation has been planned as well." Amanda was hugging Tony and I was at a loss for any words. Tony went on to say that they sure didn't have a thing to worry about. Papa had the cakes on their way and he had sent enough champagne to the Mayor's home to float a ship.

The next few days went by so fast that I didn't have time to rest. All I heard was rehearsals and departure times. Thank goodness Amanda had let Father Raymond select the organist and the special music for her ceremony. There was no worry that Father Raymond wouldn't handle everything perfect, since he knew that Father Andrew would be there also. Amanda had given Fritzie a list of their favorite pieces to be played. He knew just what to play, when she was to enter the reception, cutting of the cake, the first dance and the throwing of the bouquet.

Tony knew that I was getting more upset as the days passed. He stuck with me like glue. We went to the beach to sit until we were frozen. Once, while he was in the shower, I had Max and Sandra help me hang a quilt up on the frames. Somehow quilting calmed my nerves. Tony ran all through the house looking for me Then it dawned on him to look in my private kitchen where he found me quilting the most beautiful quilt he had ever seen. I looked up with tears in my eyes.

I said, "It would be hard to give her away to anyone, not just Michael."

"Baby," Tony said, "I assure you, she will be well taken care of all of her life."

"I know Tony, and tomorrow is the big day. I'll be fine. You'll see. At least, in here, Amanda's friends won't see my sad face."

"Can you believe there are so many people in this house? I had to call Beth in to help Sandra plus one of her sisters. Tony, it's beyond me how Amanda and Michael got Brandon and Anthony to be in the wedding."

Tony laughed at that. "I know Dru. Papa bribed them. Now, why don't you come along? We have to be at that dinner party at eight you know."

Amanda came into the room as I was going to change. Amanda said, "Mom, I must talk to you. I just got a call from Grandma Marselle. She and Gertrude are here with Grand

Daddy and some of the others from the Grove."

I said, "Amanda, you don't mean here…not right here…do you?"

Amanda said, "Oh no Mom, I mean here at the Gulf. Really…they are down at Fort Morgan."

I said, "Okay Baby. That's all right, it's your wedding and if you invited them, that's fine. They're here for you. That doesn't mean that I have to deal with them. I think it's wonderful that they've come to see you and Michael marry. I'm glad you came to tell me. I do love Mama Marselle even though she sure did all of us kids wrong. I guess I'm the only one that couldn't deal with what went on. I hope you let my life and theirs, be a lesson to you Amanda. I want you to be a good wife to Michael, but don't ever bow down to him. You already know there are people in this world that cruelty comes perfectly natural to, as natural as breathing. These people are born without compassion. To some, it's fine if their mates are living dead zombies that just take orders. Now Amanda, I don't want you to fall into a trap of not having a mind of your own. I hope you have made it clear to Michael that you are your own person."

Tony came into the room saying, "Mama, Mama, let your baby go!"

Tony and I laughed. Amanda assured me that Michael knew she would come back from their honeymoon to work at the Club and even continue to do some modeling. This brightened me up. I went over to my dresser and took out my necklace of pearls and gold beads and a beautiful lace handkerchief that had been given to me by a dear friend in Mississippi.

I said, "Amanda, I would be very proud if you would wear these in your wedding. Did you give Papa the charms for your cake?"

"Yes Mam and good night." Amanda turned to leave, stopped and turned back to say, "Don't you worry Mom, I'll make you proud."

The wedding party left the house with Tony, Papa, Amanda and me all riding in the limousine. Eight cars followed the police escort. The wedding was filled with excitement and emotion. Michael and Amanda exchanged vows, beneath a bower of wedding flowers, in the sanctuary of the church. The eight bridesmaids were dressed in gowns replica of Amanda's own wedding gown, except for the fact that theirs were knee length and her gown was full length. The headpieces were of sweetheart rosebuds as was the bouquet, which I was thrilled to see that Amanda's bouquet was large with the ivy streaming almost to the floor. I never saw so many little pink and white rosebuds in my life. The church was full of hundreds of friends and family members. It was so elegant and I found myself having a wonderful time. I had calmed down after seeing that things were moving right along.

On the way to the reception, I asked, "Tony, do you believe that Harriet has lost fifty pounds? She looked nice and did you see how Courtney was looking at Fritzie?"

After arriving at the mansion, Michael came to me and said, "Will you come with me for a moment, please? Amanda says she needs to talk with you. It will just take a minute."

I almost ran to find out what was wrong. I was relieved when Amanda asked, "Mom, do you know what happened to Jeff? I have lived in fear all day that he would cause trouble."

I said, "No Amanda, Jeff won't ever cause you any trouble, not ever again. After Bob fired him, he went back home raising hell, playing his sick games with his own folks and they put him in a mental institution. I saw one of their neighbors at the beach one day. She told me all about it. So, I know for a fact that he will never come back here."

"That's funny Mom. His folks are telling everyone that he's missing."

Courtney came in at that time and said, "Amanda, let's get out of here. Fritzie can't start the music until you and Michael come in."

Courtney turned to me and said, "We have the most

elaborate cocktail buffet and a fountain with flowing champagne is waiting for us, not to mention the dancing. The band is playing the most romantic music and sending everyone into a love mood. Just look what a fine job Amanda has done. Everyone in her wedding is matched perfectly. You're her Mom. Did you know she could do this in the short time she had."

I laughed at Courtney and thought to myself, she is a nut after a few drinks and then asked, "Have you been in the champagne?"

Courtney said, "Wow all these men make my blood run hot. Just look how handsome these men are. They are all dressed in tuxedos and sparkling patent leather shoes. Their pink cummerbund matches the pink rosebuds to a tee."

My ears sure perked up when Courtney said, "Just look at Fritzie's band. Can you believe how handsome he is?"

"Yes Courtney, but I believe it's the rose pink accented tuxes that make him so handsome. Courtney! It's true! You do have the hots for Fritzie. Oh my, now you'll be dirty dancing. Dan can kiss off now! Thanks to Amanda's wedding, you're hooked Courtney. Come on you nut it's time for them to cut the cake."

As I stood looking at my daughter, I just knew her wedding dress must be the most beautiful that New York had to offer. It had a low cut front with long tight sleeves fitting like a glove. The bodice flared out at the knees and it had a full, long train. The designs with the beads and all the handwork were magnificent. Amanda was beautiful from her headpiece to her satin shoes.

Papa Perricotti had come to stand beside Tony and me.

Papa said, "My dear, this cake is a jewel in more ways than one. I have made arrangements for the bottom two layers to be carried to my house after the party is over."

I ask, "Why Papa? Is there a reason for that cake being so big?"

Papa just smiled and looked back at Amanda. The cake had

eight layers, each three inches high with the two top layers upon pedestals. It was frosted in pink with rosebuds and eight pink ribbons that had been carefully arranged to fall gracefully down the sides of the cake. Amanda's small charms had been attached to each ribbon.

I stood silently, as Amanda called one bridesmaid after another to pull a ribbon, each claiming one charm that prophesied her future fortunes. This ceremony for the bridesmaids had to be performed before Amanda and Michael could cut the cake. Amanda had disassembled her very own charm bracelet, to do this.

I said, "Tony, isn't this a beautiful ceremony?"

Tony said, "Yes, I believe everyone is thrilled. Everything has been wonderful."

After the cutting of the cake was over and done with, the party was in full swing. Michael had the first dance with Amanda and then Papa next and then Tony.

Tony came back to me and asked, "Baby, did you know that Papa has given Michael, Mama's ring to give to Amanda? I tell you, I don't know what's got into that old man! He has always been as tight as a banjo string. Now, just look at this wedding. I bet it set him back thirty grand."

"What do you mean set him back Tony? This wedding is going to set you back."

"That's what I thought, but Papa said no way."

"Tony, you and Papa will have a rude awakening if you think thirty grand will touch this wedding. I know one thing for sure Amanda will be thrilled to have Mama's rings. Isn't she the most glorious bride you ever saw Tony?"

Tony said, "Just a younger version of my bride."

Tony was so thankful when the party was over. He wanted to go home and pass out. It seemed as if we were on a merry-go-round for weeks. We kissed Amanda, wishing her and Michael a safe trip and the best honeymoon ever. I heard Papa tell Amanda to come to see him as soon as they returned home. As Michael and Amanda drove off, Tony and me were not far behind.

Tony said, "I know why Papa wants to see them when they get back. He wants to turn his home over to them if they will just let him live there. He talked to me about that and said that he was tired of being by himself."

I asked, "Do you still wonder what's got into Papa, Tony? It's a new life, new hope for his name."

Max and Charlie were like live wires in the front seat. They were trying to talk their way into going on the cruise with Tony and me, but after Tony said they would have to draw straws because only one of them could go, they got quiet.

Max said, "That's good. We'll just do that as soon as we get home."

I said, "Listen you two, I don't want to see anyone for two weeks. I'm so tired that I think I may die tonight. Tony, did you notice that Mama Marselle and the family didn't even look our way at the wedding. They were gone before we got out of the church."

I over heard Max tell Charlie that Fritzie would be bringing Harriet, Courtney and any other guests back to the house that needed to stay the night. He also heard Courtney, tell Harriet she was going home for a few days. I thought, just maybe to file for a divorce. Let's hope she is happy with whatever she does.

I said, "Well boys, I will place bets on her and Fritzie. I do believe Dan had a tiger locked up. We will soon see."

As Tony and I walked through the house, I stopped in the family room and said, "Look Tony, Amanda forgot her note that Michael sent on her love bouquet. I want you to read it."

Tony took the card from my hand and began to read out loud.

Baby, I have satin smooth love for you.
You can have satin smooth dreams with me.
I'll marry you as sure as light of day cause
I've been yours forever and always.
You're like the morning star.

You shine so bright and clear.

Your beauty's like the rose and I love you dear.
Pure as snow is white and you're special with a
Heart of gold and you'll be mine tonight.

Superb entertainment…first class accommodations
I have the best waiting for you.
Snuggle up beside me and you will see,
I'll treat you warm and tender and hold you close to me.
Think about it baby, I have satin smooth love for you.
Now you can have satin smooth dreams with me.
I'll marry you as sure as light of day, cause
I've been yours forever and always.
You're like the morning star
You shine so bright and clear.
Oh, how I love you dear.

You're warm like a summer breeze
I'm in love with you.
You're natural as the leaves in fall
You're pure as snow is white
Think about it baby, you'll be mine tonight.
You can have satin smooth dreams with me,
Cause I have satin smooth love for you and
I'll marry you as sure as light of day!

"Man," Tony said, "I wish I had written that for you, but you knew that was the way I felt, didn't you?"

"I suppose so. Now, let's go to bed."

We went off to bed alright, but Tony was too tired to sleep. He rolled around for a while and then got up to find Papa still up watching a movie.

Tony said, "I'm glad you're still up Papa. I wish you would tell me why you love Dru so much and why you show your feelings to her when you have never showed affection to anyone."

The old man's temper flared as he looked around making sure that I wasn't coming into the room, not knowing I was sitting just outside in the hall.

Papa said, "You listen young man and you listen good. There's nothing wrong about my love for Drucilla. That little girl took a big worry off me. You boy! You have been moping around here for the last few years. I couldn't make you understand that your wife died. You didn't die. Don't think I didn't see you sitting around with the old men on their dead dick bench while you watched Anthony play. Heck, I was beginning to worry about the business until Anthony found Drucilla. She put life back into you. Put a spring back into all of us. I sure as hell do love her! And like she would say…you get it."

Tony was at a loss for words. Finally he said, "Now Papa, don't get me wrong. I'm proud you love Dru. I just couldn't stop thinking about how generous you have been. I'm thankful you care so much Papa."

Papa said, "Boy, I'll tell you just like I told Michael. Beautiful women need beautiful things. You need to remember that diamonds show other people just how we do love our women."

Papa lit his pipe and sat back in his chair next to the fire. He said, "Besides that Tony, she may be yours, but I do get to look at her and I'm proud to see her sparkle with diamonds. I guarantee you others take a second look. Do you see any reason to keep the diamonds locked up in a vault?"

"No Papa, Did you ever get around to telling Dru what was shipped in the bottom half of that wedding cake?"

"No, I didn't. I thought I'd let her see for herself tomorrow. I'm going to bed now."

# CHAPTER 36

At lunch the next day, Papa, Tony and I were sitting at the kitchen table and Papa asked, "Tony, did you forget about the Hatchery? You know that I've got good money in those cocks. I had Bob to go down and check on things. He tells me they're sure killers and there's a fight on for ten o'clock."

Tony never said a word. Papa asked, "Do you think Drucilla would enjoy going?"

Papa could see the disapproving look on Tony's face.

Papa said, "Come on Tony, let the girl come along. You know good and well her own Daddy used to let her go every Sunday. Besides it would break the hectic pace around here. Come on Max will drive us."

Thank God Papa won. I had the time of my life. I won three hundred and thirty dollars. One thing was for sure I had an eye for the best. Tony and Papa had gotten so involved with their betting that I slipped away. When Tony found me, I was helping a breeder named Jake trim the spurs down to attach artificial spurs to the gamecock's legs. Getting them ready to fight. After that Papa couldn't watch the cockfights for watching me saying that I was a better show than the fighters. I had watched as the two men held the beautiful roosters and allowed them to peck at each other making them as angry as the Devil is mean. I told Papa to look at the one that had a small head. He has all the power and courage…watch him. He is faster than lightning. After the cocks were released, it was just a matter of minutes until their spurs had ripped and torn each other apart. One must die for the other to win. I thought maybe that's the way it should be. While Tony and Papa placed bets, I was talking fast. Old Jake was a breeder and trainer, so it only took me a matter of minutes and I had bought myself a pair of fierce fighting roosters. Jake would keep them trained at the hatchery and the pair only cost me twenty-five hundred dollars. When I told Tony and Papa about my new roosters on the way home, all hell broke loose.

Tony said, "Papa, see what you caused!"

Then for the first time Papa really saw me mad. I didn't give Tony time to get a word in edgewise.

Papa and Max cracked up with laughter when I said, "Oh no Tony, the only time you want me to see a chicken is when it is laying out in someone's plate with people saying grace over it. It's a lot of crap Tony and if you think you're going to the fights with me staying at home. Then Mister you've got another thought coming."

Tony said, "Now you listen Dru. It's because I love you. I think there are some things that are just for men. Game fighting is sure one of them. You're mine and I don't want you there as a game fighter and you won't be, even if it means that I don't go!"

Then I shocked Tony by saying, "I'll sale my rooster. I just got caught up in all the excitement anyway. I'm sorry if I upset you Tony. To be honest, I don't even care about going to Atlantic City in June, but I'll tell you this…you better put your money on that bigger guy because he will have a knockout in the first round."

I turned toward Papa. I said, "You have a birthday in two

weeks. You can have my roosters now happy birthday to you and good riddance to my cock-a-doodle-doos."

All Papa heard was what I had said about the fight in Atlantic City. He asked, "What makes you think it will be a knockout in the first round Drucilla?"

I said, "Too much money Papa. Two of the biggest names in boxing no one has to be hurt when that much money is being paid. Papa, you know darn well it's just a joke like a lot of other things. I swear, sometimes I believe most people are a joke on themselves. Ninety percent are gullible. They make me sick! All this big money being poured into these boxers and take a look at the ballplayers, they get this big money because they know people are going to keep coming and pay the price of those tickets."

Tony said, "We sure have made a lot of money through people being gullible Dru, but they call it having fun and being good."

I said, "Oh yes, I know that Tony. But it's still sad that people never seem to wake up. Just look how some people dress, looking trashy from head to toe saying this is a fad or that's what's in now. The parents fall right into the trap with their children. It's got to be brand name this or that. It's pure stupidity. Only the people can put a stop to it all. Tony, you and everyone knows it's the parent's fault that children in this world have turned out to be dope heads, dropouts and runaways. We, the parents, didn't put a stick on their butt and teach them what no means. We, the parents, sat back and let their education be brought down so low that it gives them brain damage just to go to school. And why? Just because the parents are too busy living too fast to see what's going on with their children until it's too late. I've never believed that there would be an end of time, but with most people being so sorry, I don't see how the world can stand."

"Damn," Tony said, "We should build you a church!"

I laughed and said, "Go to hell Tony!"

Papa had been listening, not saying a word, just a grunt

now and then. He finally said, "Drucilla, I'm proud to say that all of my money came from gambling and like your Daddy making moonshine, it's all I ever knew. So, I'm not sorry. I'm glad my outfit had been drug free, but you're right girl, the children have been crippled and it sure didn't help when about eighty-five percent of the women went to work just to stay away from home. A little bit of trouble in their marriage and they give up. It really does cost them more to work than most of them bring home."

Max spoke up saying, "I'll tell you what's disgusting. It's all these children that's been separated from their brothers and sisters and being raised under different names. Men have been leaving bastard children in every state.

Now who's to say that brothers and sisters won't grow up and marry?

Honestly, not knowing any better. I have heard stories that when brothers and sisters have children together or first cousins marry, their children turn out to be idiots. It's as bad as sleeping around today with all this AIDS. How in the hell do you know who has it and who doesn't. I'll be the first to tell you that if you don't want AIDS, you better keep your pants up. The only thing that will save the children is for families to pull back together and live decent. Most of all, if a woman has a child, she should be made to stay home and put some discipline into this world."

I said, "You're right! If they didn't want to raise them, they shouldn't have had them. I guess you're right about me Tony. I do have the answers to some of the world's troubles. Lady Liberty needs to put a lock on the Gate of our country. We have let in more aliens than we can stand. A big part of our national deficit is freeloading people. It should be stopped. I want someone to get the message across. Government money comes out of the hands of the hard working people. I have seen it happen over and over. The people will work like dogs getting a candidate voted into office on a promise that he will see to it that our tax money is to be used for the improvement of the country and not for the special interest groups. **Bull**, then they get into office and fill their own pockets with the working people's money laughing all the way to the bank while giving the rest to every kind of freeloading sham that comes through Washington. They should be giving out a pick, shovel, some seeds and assign a spot of land to everyone that's on food stamps and able to work. Make them grow their own food. What they don't freeze or canned could be sold. I'd just like to know…where all these bleeding hearts were, when I was a child. We were cold and hungry, but the government didn't give us a damn thing!"

Max said, "When there is no one to hand out food, then and only then will most people get off their butt and do for themselves."

I said, "Take a look at prisons. All full and from fourteen thousand dollars to forty thousand dollars a year to keep just one! If I had the say so over them, I'd issue orders for every prison in the United States to be fumigated at three in the morning with deadly gas. I'd let this world cry for a few days, then maybe they would rejoice."

"Now wait a minute," Max said, "I have a lot of friends in there. Let's not get carried away."

I said, "There's one thing for sure, no one would be eager to get into prison for fear of the same thing happening again. It's pure bull that the hard working people have to keep up prisons."

Tony said, "Dru, you sure do get worked up."

I was quite for a minute and no one else said a word. I get mad when I think about how hard my father worked and we still starved, but the taxes were taken out before Daddy got his money. After that it's tax for this tax for that over and over again.

I said, "The truth is that the leaders of this country have let our laws go to hell because they didn't and still don't have a backbone. There's only one thing that's going to help our country and that's for people to wake up and get to know who they are voting for! Just maybe by the time AIDS gets through with this world, people will get back on the straight and narrow, but I doubt that they will."

Tony had given me several wicked smiles all during our talk.

I said, "I know what you're thinking Tony."

Tony said, "Yea, what?"

I said, "That if I'm so lawful, why am I so hellish. I won't try to justify any wrong I've done. I'll be the first to tell you that if I had been big enough, I would have boxed many ears and jacked a lot of jaws years ago.

Max, won't this car go any faster? It's taken us a lot longer to get back than it did to get there."

Max said, "Drucilla, you were just all excited and now the excitement has dwindled away."

Papa said, "Why can't we go to my house and take care of that wedding cake?"

I said, "Yes sir… and talking about your house! Now, Papa, I've had time to think about what you want to do and I'm telling you that you are not moving my daughter in there. That little security box could break open any day and my baby's not going to be in it!"

Tony said, "Dru's right Papa. Michael has a home and you need to come live with us. Let Charlie have that place. He can take care of the visitors from out of town, the way you've always done. Think about it Papa, don't you think that would be best for us all?"

I could see Papa's house up ahead, so I began putting my shoes on. I said, "Tony, I'm sure tired, but I had a wonderful time and the least you can do is let me go back sometime…just to watch."

As soon as the car stopped, I said, "Hurry up Tony, let me out. I can't wait to see what the joke is with that cake."

Papa took us to the basement. Charlie was waiting so it didn't take them long to lift the heavy cardboard up to show that the whole bottom layer of the wedding cake was fake, three feet in diameter and three inches deep. My mouth flew open when the top came off. Tony and Papa reached in to pick up one of the guns.

I said, "My Lord! No wonder you wanted to order the cake. I never dreamed that a baker could cook up things like this!"

I had started to count them just as Tony said, "All twenty are here."

I asked, "What kind of gun is this? Why didn't you just buy them?"

As Tony held the gun out, he said, "This is a Mac-ten and they can be bought but with a lot of red tape and besides the serial numbers have been filed off of these. It's past time for my men to have real guns. You never know when all hell will break out."

I was excited about the guns, but it had been a long day and I was tired. I said, "Tony, please tell Max to get the car. I'm dead on my feet and we've got to go home."

I said, "Papa, I can't believe all this. This is the life I used to dream about. I should have been with you all of my life."

On the way back home, Max said, "Charlie told me that Richard had slipped right out of their hands the night before. They hoped to get him tonight."

The investigators that Max had talked to in Birmingham had said even money couldn't get the people at that phone company to talk. All they would say is that, it was so long ago or I can't risk losing my job to help you. I was so mad. I could have bit a ten-penny nail into. I said, "No, them jerks won't talk about each other. One day I will spill my gut's about them all."

Max said, "I'll tell you Drucilla, Richard had everyone thinking that you two had the perfect marriage and that he loved you the best in the world. He also has some thinking that you were an invalid."

I said, "Oh yes, he even fooled me some of the time. I was an invalid. I had a crippled brain. He would be so wonderful in front of people. Help with anything and be so good, even opened my car doors, called me baby and gave me enough money to run the house and then stabbed me in the back."

"Gosh," Max said, "I almost forgot. Charlie did say something about a woman rookie that had worked with Richard."

I said, "What about her?"

Max said, "The men called her the Gorilla."

I said, "The Gorilla! I'll be damn, do you mean…he had her on his truck everyday, all day.

Max, when I look back to all that happened to me, it's the very reason I say make Anthony and Brandon dig into their schoolwork and get an education. If that damn bunch that raised me had sent me to school, I wouldn't have had to stay with Richard. There was no way that I could pay my hospital insurance and utility bills. I had to stay in hell until Tony found me."

Tony had me all hugged up and said, "Don't think about him. I promise we will get him. For now, just think about me."

I said, "I love you for helping me Tony. I know the timing has to be right to pick him up, but I want his ass."

Tony said, "Dru, I want you to stop worrying. Tonnymacker's got this old surgeon over in Pensacola that's helping to take care of some AIDS patients in the basement of an old drug store. That's where Richard will get his blood transfusion."

I said, "Let's not talk about it. Just tell me when it's done and over with."

Before I went to sleep that night, I lay thinking that it didn't matter that my new family was Mafia. I loved them for trying to set things right. There's one thing for sure, I want to be like them. They take care of things the old way.

Take Percy for instance, his hard head made him a jerk. It's a lot like raising a child to the tune of a hickory stick. It only takes one nod of the head for that child to hear the music. One thing is for sure, the Mafia is a business and everything is handled as a business.

The next thing I knew, I was standing in a small cemetery. Charlie and Max on each side of me holding the new Macten's. I couldn't believe it. Jeff's deranged old Daddy had finally died. It has given me the best opportunity in the world to kill the whole bunch at one time. The few friends that had gathered around his grave were leaving now. Only the family was left. Yea! They were walking closer to the grave, placing flowers here and there. What luck? Even Jeff's old red headed mother was there, wiping her tears away. She hated the old bastard as much as I did, so why the tears. I couldn't wait any longer. I told the boys to come on. I've been waiting on this for years. We started running toward them. I fired first, than all I could hear was gunfire and screaming. When the last one fell, I shouted **Hallelujah!**

I was shaking uncontrollable and I could hear a voice far off. "Dru, wake up! Dru, wake up!"

Tony was shaking me hard.

I said, "Stop Tony! What are you doing to me?"

Tony said, "Dru, you must have been dreaming about a church. You were shouting out loud Hallelujah over and over again."

I said, "No Tony, it was judgment day and I was carrying out God's punishment. Go back to sleep. It was just a dream. A wonderful dream."

# CHAPTER 37

Anthony and Brandon woke me up. It seemed as if I had just gone to sleep.

Brandon said, "Come on Mam Maw. We want you to have breakfast with us in the tree house."

I said, "You're a joke. I guess you want me to slide down the firehouse pole too." Anthony's laughter got to me. I said, "If it will make you happy."

I was surprised to see the homemade table with a complete breakfast waiting. After two hours of card games, the boys let me go, but only if I would slide down the firehouse pole.

The days had gone by so fast. Sandra was helping me get my things ready for the cruise that Tony promised me. I had never been so excited. When Tony came in that night, I hugged and kissed and made over him. Tony loved every minute of it. Later that evening we were talking.

I said, "Tony, you have made all my dreams come true."

Tony said, "Dru, I'm glad it was me."

I said, "Have you seen Courtney today?"

Tony said, "No, but you were right about Fritzie and Courtney. Fritzie wants you to have lunch with him tomorrow.

He wants to hear it from you that it's alright to see Courtney."

I said, "Tony, he's a fool. Sure it's alright. She's just what Fritzie needs. There isn't a jealous bone in that girl. Let's see if Fritzie and Courtney want to go bowling with us. We can take Brandon and Anthony too. Do you think that Papa will let you off? The boys need to have fun. It'll get their mind off school. What do you say Tony? Can we go or not?"

Tony said, "Dang it Dru. You could charm a hobo out of his clothes in the middle of winter. What about Harriet?"

I said, "You can count Harriet out. She and Sam are going to the car races in Pensacola."

Later that night I heard Tony talking to someone in a loud voice. I slipped out of bed and headed for the voices. I just knew something bad had happened. I entered the room and Max and Tony were looking at a map.

I said, "What the hell is going on?"

Tony took me by the arm and said, "Now baby, let's go back to the bedroom."

Max looked scared to death. He said, "I'm sorry Mrs. T."

Tony cut in and said, "I'll tell her Max."

Tony took me to the bedroom and we sat on the love seat. I looked at the clock. It was eleven p.m.

I said, "Spit it out Tony. Has something happened to Papa? What is it?"

Tony said, "It's Brandon."

I felt like a Mack truck had hit me in the face.

Tony said, "Max took Brandon and Anthony to the movies. As they were getting into the car to come home, someone hit Max from behind. Max was only out for a minute. Anthony said there were two men. They hit Max and grabbed Brandon and ran off. By the time Max came to, the car was out of sight. I have been out looking everywhere. We'll find him and he'll be alright."

I screamed, "Get everybody out! Get you ass out and find my baby. You know damn well who has him!"

Papa ran in and said, "What the hell is going on in here?"

I said, "I'll tell you what's going on. It's that sorry bunch you have in Birmingham. I never did believe they were doing what you were paying them to do. Now you see how good your men are. They let Richard get my baby while everyone was pussyfooting around."

Papa came over and sat beside me and said, "Drucilla, wait a minute. It may not have been Richard."

Tony had just dialed a number, but hearing Papa, he hung up the phone without listening to see if anybody answered. He said, "What makes you say that Papa?"

Max jumped to his feet and said, "You don't mean that bunch from Dothan do you?"

Papa said, "Yes I do. Old Clyde came into the club with a couple of thugs just the other night. He wanted to buy in with me. Go half and half he said. His half always ends up more like three quarters. We had a few words and he left. Do you remember Tony? This isn't the first time Clyde made his offer."

Tony said, "That's right Papa. He was here on the Fourth of July. I heard him tell you he would change your mind. Maybe this is his way of changing it. Max, call around and find out if Clyde has been seen."

Max started for the phone and Papa said, "Hold it Max. Tony, I already know he's here. Topaz told me that he saw Clyde this morning."

Papa reached for the phone to call his house. Sam answered and Papa told him to find Tonnymacker and Topaz and for all three to be there in ten minutes.

Tony had fixed me a stiff drink with Black Velvet.

Papa said, "I'll bring Brandon home even if I have to take the whole damn town apart."

It only took Papa fifteen minutes to find out Clyde's whereabouts and only five more to kick in his door. Clyde and three more were sitting around a gambling table. The first thing Papa did was to shoot Clyde's ear off.

Papa said, "You big illegitimate thieving bastard. Where is my grandson?"

Old Clyde fell to his knees saying, “Please Mr. Perricotti, I beg you, please don’t kill me.”

Papa said, “Then tell me about my grandson.”

Old Clyde said, “Please, Mr. Perricotti, I don’t know anything about your grandson.”

The other three men had their backs against the wall. Tonnymacker had one of the new Mac-ten’s stuck up the nose of one of Clyde’s men.

Tonnymacker said, “Speak up or I’ll blow the top of you head off.”

The man said, “**No**! We didn’t get your little boy. I swear we didn’t do it.”

The man had a puddle at his feet. Tonnymacker was known for being a killer and he would leave their dead bodies all over the place with just a nod of Papa’s head.

But Papa kicked Clyde over in the floor. Papa said, “Get your bony ass out on the street and find my boy or I’ll kill you all.”

Before Papa was through talking, Clyde was crawling out the door on his hands and knees.

Everybody was out looking for Brandon everybody but Max. Tony would not leave me by myself and I wouldn’t leave in case Brandon called on the phone. Tony had called me several times. Harriet and Anthony were crying. Not me. I was mad as hell. After Papa said he didn’t think it was Clyde, I knew it was Richard. He knew this was the only way in this world to hurt me. Time was dragging and by daylight, I was nauseated to the point of being sick. At five the next afternoon there still wasn’t any word from Brandon. I had insisted that Max bring in the map and show me every ball field in and around the Gulf.

Tony had his men running in and out of every business with pictures of Brandon. Even in Pensacola, people were looking. Then about a quarter to ten that same night, the telephone rang. I ran across the room.

Brandon said, “Hello Mam Maw, can you come and get me?”

Max saw the gush of tears. I tried to speak, but nothing

would come out. Brandon kept saying, "Mam Maw, Mam Maw."

Holding me in one arm Max took the telephone in the other hand. Brandon had been left at an ice cream parlor. Max helped me to the car. In two minutes I had Brandon in my arms swearing to kill Richard.

Brandon said, "But Mam Maw, Pa Hallmark just wanted to play ball with me. Pa said you would be mad, but he missed me so much that he didn't care if you were. And Mam Maw, Pa said he was sick and he may never be back. He just wanted me to know that he was sorry that he caused trouble and made us leave. He said you wouldn't let him see me, so he had to steal me from you. We had a good time Mam Maw. Please stop crying."

I said, "I can't help it little man. They are happy tears. If I could get my hands on your Pa, I would put his lights out."

Max was on the car phone calling everyone in.

Courtney walked into the kitchen looking young and happy. She said, "My divorce will be final in sixty days. I will stay here with Harriet if that will be all right."

I smiled and said, "It sure is Courtney. You know that my home is your home. Will you be Brandon's Godmother?"

"I would be honored," she said.

I said, "I tell you Courtney, last night almost put me away. I've got to know for sure he has someone that I love to take care of him if anything should happen to me. I know Brandon loves you. Courtney, will you always be near him and watch over him the same way I would?"

Courtney said, "Of course Drucilla you know I will. I swear to you, I will always treat Brandon as if he belongs to me but what about asking Amanda?"

I said, "Speaking of Amanda, she and Michael will be back next week. Now Courtney, let's keep this talk just between us. At least until I get back from this trip. You and I know that Amanda would do the best she could with Anthony and Brandon, but she is young. Besides, Brandon will have to stay here with Tony. I just need to know that Brandon will have a special eye watching him."

Courtney said, "Am I supposed to be reading between the lines of this talk?"

I said, "No! Just sometimes things happen that can't be helped and I do know that you and Fritzie will have a good life here. You will be happy. Children need happy people in their lives."

Thank God, I was saved. This conversation had gone as far as I wanted it to go. The boys ran in and Anthony was so glad to have Brandon back that he put a play gun in his back pocket. He said, "Mama, I won't let anyone take Brandon away ever again."

Brandon asked, "Are we really going on a big ship Mam Maw?"

I said, "Yes we are. For two weeks. Don't you think that will be fun?"

The boys were happy and jumping with joy. Courtney kissed the boys and went out, but it wasn't long before Tony and Papa came from their rooms looking like two old tired dogs.

It's a day to hang around the house, I thought. I have sure caused this family a lot of trouble. Tony had just poured us all some coffee when Sandra came in and said that I had a visitor. I was surprised to see Doctor Skeet waiting.

I said, "My word, what brings you here? Come on in. We can sit in the sun room."

As we were going to the sunroom, I told Sandra to bring us some Brandy. I turned back to hear him say that he had a brother in Pensacola with four children, so he had left the noise to come to see me.

I said, "That's wonderful. I sure need a good talking to. You're the only one that gets away with talking back to me you know."

This brought on laughter because we both knew that I only tell him what I want him to know. He was here again to tell me that he was sorry about being wrong and that he was just young and not as experienced as he should have been. We talked for a long time before Tony came in to join us.

I asked, “When is the last time you saw Doctor Shane? I sure do love him. He’s been good to me all of my life. I’m going to Birmingham one day just for a visit with him.”

Doctor Skeet said, “He’s doing fine. Just kicking around the hospital. I’m sure he’d be glad to see you.”

We talked for hours I was beginning to think my friend wasn’t ever going to leave. He did stay until after dinner…leaving with a promise that he’d be back soon.

As soon as the door was closed behind the doctor, I said, “Tony, I know he has an ulterior motive for coming here. I can feel it.”

Tony said, “I’ll put a man on your doctor and see what he is up to.”

As Tony and I lay in bed talking that night, he said, “Dru, I know you’re not completely happy, but I wish you were. I wish you could put all the hurt away and be happy for me and the boys.”

I said, “I’m trying as hard as I can Tony. I guess it will just take time.”

I lay awake half the night thinking and just like many nights before, I always came back to the same conclusion. I hated lying to Tony, but I didn’t want him worrying about me. The only way I’d ever get it off my mind would be to kill my brain. The memories will never go away. I had been hurt too bad to forget. I had been through the good, bad and the ugly and still didn’t feel any better. All the money didn’t take away the hurt. Taking care of Harriet, Percy, DeRoy and Jeff hadn’t helped me. So, I couldn’t help but wonder if killing Richard was going to help me, or have I been fooling myself?

Here I am, unhappy as hell. I’ve hurt another family Tony loves me, and Lord, little Anthony, not to mention Brandon. I know they will all forgive me if I get to the point that I can’t take it anymore. If they could only know how hard I’ve tried to make the hurt go away. I wanted my family to love me. I wanted Richard to tell the truth. I couldn't right all the wrongs and I can't make the memories go away. It's my brain. It won't turn lose of the hurt. I know with all my heart that I have tried everything. There is no way out but death. Turning over, I kissed Tony's back saying, "Thank you for being so good." And with that I fell asleep.

I spent the next few evenings at the Hot Box. It was good to hear Fritzie's band and to watch the people dance and have a good time. Going out was the one thing I missed most. Richard had said he was ashamed of me and didn't want to be out among people with me. Especially people that he knew. No one will ever know how bad it hurt to hear him ask me why I thought he had kept me at home. I was just getting up to leave when Fritzie came to my table. I brushed the tears from my face and sat back down.

Fritzie asked, "Drucilla, why can't you talk to me? You have been avoiding me the whole time I've been here at the Gulf?"

I said, "Fritzie, I think you have always had the wrong thoughts about me. I was never your woman and I never wanted anyone to think that. All I wanted from you was friendship. I was lonesome as hell living in those woods and besides that, I needed someone to help me with my songs. **But no!** I couldn't say a word to you about that because you made me feel like a bimbo that needed to be home."

Fritzie asked, "Why don't we go for a ride? You haven't even been in my new car."

I said, "Not tonight Fritzie. What about tomorrow? Better yet, why don't we play a round of golf?"

"You're on," he said, "I'll see you at eight in the morning. Drucilla, be sure to bring your money."

This gave me something to smile about. I said, "You be sure to bring your money too."

Max had driven home slow and as we pulled up to the new house, he said, "Mrs. Drucilla, you haven't said a word all the way home."

"No, I've sure been thinking. You know, I should have won an Oscar for the performance I've given over the years, my life in Fool's Paradise…what a story that would make."

Leaving Max looking bewildered, I walked right on through the house to the bath. I started my bath water and then walked over to the mirror. I beat the image I saw with my fist screaming, "Why, why do you have to know? Why can't you just be happy? You already know the truth! Why can't you just hate Richard to the point of not caring?"

I had gotten to the point that I hated for night to come. The dreams were back and I couldn't stand them. They were torture and I knew my nerves couldn't take much more. I would tell myself just to love Tony and stop dwelling on the past and I'd be fine. I thought sure, just like before. You're a fool. It's the hurt, the hurt makes me dream and I sure don't tell myself what to dream. Not having the answers to Richards's part in it all. Twenty-three years is a long time to be in a fool's paradise.

I stepped into the bath crying. I had been in this shape many times. Once in Nineteen Eighty-four at two in the morning, I had taken a thirty-eight, caliber pistol out of my purse and went to sit in the bathroom floor by the window knowing the only way to get peace of mind was to die. I thought I was ready, but then a car came down the road with its lights shining in my eyes and the lights somehow brought me out of the state I was in. I remembered saying to myself, I have as much right to be happy as Richard. There are places to go, things to do and people to be with. I can't let him keep me a prisoner here any longer. I put the pistol up and went to bed, but I couldn't go to sleep. I cried all night like many nights before. When the alarm went off, I begged Richard to stay home with me. To please take me somewhere, just get me away from there. What a fight we had. This is when he said he was ashamed of me and I let him know I wasn't anyone to be ashamed of. I told him it was **him** and that he was afraid his slut would see him with me. I knew I wouldn't go off with him anymore, but it was because I was ashamed of him now. I really know it was because he didn't want her to know that I wasn't an invalid. I went on to tell him that I had might as well take a gun and blow my brains out. Richard was standing between the bed and the dresser. After listening to what I had to say, he reached up to the top of the dresser and brought down an automatic pistol, cocked the hammer back and leaving the gun lying in arms reach of me, he left for work. What a silent message of good riddance.

I shook from the bad memories and got out of the tub and dried off. I knew that Tony wouldn't be in until about two o'clock, so I picked up a poem book on my way to bed and read myself to sleep.

I was in a whirlwind going around and around. Richard was standing in front of me laughing and laughing. I could hear him saying, you wouldn't know the truth if it hit you in the face. I was kicking flowerpots off the porch, dancing, laughing, and crying. I answered the phone to find no one. His shoes were dancing on the floor. Richard called to say, hello, I've got to go. Get away get away, what's that awful odor. It's disgusting! Please take me out of these woods, I begged. Richard was smiling, shaking his head no. I could hear him say, I have to work. All the phones ringing and ringing all my past was flashing before me. The whirlwind went around and around.

I woke myself screaming out, "I have got to know the truth!" Sitting straight up in bed, I was wet with hot sweat so thick that I vomited. Ringing for Sandra to help me, I knew I couldn't tell anyone about my dreams. I had to find a way to shake these feelings. Sandra helped me to the bathroom. She cleaned the bed and was gone only a minute to bring me some hot tea. I was lying in bed when she returned.

Sandra asked, "Are you sure you will be all right?"

# CHAPTER 38

I was at the Club House ready for a good game of golf and a good game it was even though Fritzie beat me so bad that I was ashamed. I snatched the scorecard away from him tearing it into a million pieces.

I said, "No! Mr. Rogue, I could never let you show this to anyone."

Fritzie said, "Come on. I'll buy you lunch down at Wolf Bay Lodge."

I turned to Max and said, "You can go back home or do whatever you want. Fritzie will bring me home."

Max said, "I can't do that Drucilla. Tony said not to let you out of my sight."

I said, "Max, you go tell Tony that I sent you home. Tell him that I will be fine and that Fritzie will have me back no later than four o'clock."

Max left me reluctantly. He couldn't stand for me to be with Fritzie. Not even for a golf game, much less a lunch date.

Our lunch was wonderful and I did enjoy Fritzie's company. He made me laugh telling me tales from his childhood. I listened to him thinking that it must have been wonderful to be brought up in a big house with plenty and everyone happy.

As we started to leave, Fritzie said, "I can read your mind Drucilla. I know what you would like to do."

I stopped in my tracks. I said, "Oh yea. Tell me, are you getting bold or just stupid in your old age?"

This sure brought the laughter from him. He said, "You're a dirty minded old woman Drucilla."

This broke the ice between us and he did know what I wanted to do. He drove to the beach and took a blanket out of the trunk of the car to wrap around my shoulders so we could sit on the sand and talk.

Fritzie said, "Just listen Drucilla. How many times have I heard you say, I've got to go to Gulf Shores I can hear the ocean calling me."

"Oh yes," I said. "Many, many times, I love it here."

Fritzie took my chin in his hand and looked dead into my green eyes and said, "Yes! You love it here, but something is really wrong Drucilla. You can fool some, but you can't fool me. I know that when you're happy you have sparkles in your eyes. There's no sparkle and I know why Drucilla. You've got to wake up. You can't let Richard kill you and yes, I remember the very words you said to me years ago. Are you listening Drucilla?"

"Yes, I'm listening and you had better butt out of things that are none of your business."

"I'm making it my business whether you like it or not. You said that Richard hated his Daddy. Yet he was doing you the very same way that his Daddy treated his Mother. You said that Richard's Mother was a wonderful person just like you and that his Daddy had fed her a pack of loving lies while he was whore hopping around until she died young from grieving. I don't understand it Drucilla, you have never let anyone get the best of you. You're an extraordinary person. You've got to forget the past and live for today. You're letting this sorrow get you down. Tell me what it is you're looking for. Why can't you take hold of what you have? Drucilla, you have it all!"

I yanked away and said, "**No! Fritzie**. You don't understand. You or anyone else."

Fritzie said, "Well then make me understand."

I screamed, "I've got to know who his whore was. I've got to know who has tormented me from Nineteen Eighty-three until now. You listen Fritzie. It was **me,** all alone having the strength pulled from me. A puzzle that couldn't be put together because I wouldn't face the truth and you, your memory must not be too good because I asked you to help me. **But no**! It was a family matter. I'll tell you what I want. I want to know who Richard's whore was and why he stayed with me wasting my life. That's all I want Fritzie. That's why I'm here. Richard wouldn't tell me, so I left my home. Yes, Fritzie, just like his Daddy did his Mother and he **is** making me grieve myself to death. I was all, alone and believe me the pines that surrounded that house didn't talk back. All I wanted was someone to love me."

"Did you hear what you just said Drucilla? For someone to love you, that's what you've missed. You just need to **let someone love you**. No, you're not going to get better until you know in your heart that Richard never did. Doesn't now and never **did**. You said that he wanted you to die and be out of his way. You've got to accept it. Do you hear me Drucilla? People have to do what they have to do to survive. What about me, and Brandon? We depend on you. And the dead can't take care of the living! You can't take care of us if you don't take care of yourself. Do you hear me? Say to hell with Richard and stop torturing yourself. Please Drucilla, pull yourself out of this hold he has on you."

Then with a light kiss Fritzie said, "I'm sorry that I wasn't there when you needed me."

"No! Fritzie. No one was there. I won't forgive you or any of the rest. All the ladies that I ever met hated me. I was talented and stayed busy doing fifteen different things at one time while they were too lazy to pull their girdles off at night. I was a beauty and knew it. I flirted with their husbands if I knew they were jealous of me and I loved doing it. But why was I so talented Fritzie? No one ever stopped to think about that. But I had to stay busy or I would have gone crazy. I'd just like to see all the people that I know just sit in those woods… day after day week after week…for as long as I did. All by themselves!

Yes Fritzie, after Richard hurt me the first time, I partied and I had a wonderful time…got it out of my system. I divorced him and married the fool back so he could do the same thing to me again. Yes, Fritzie, everybody loved Richard. He was one fine son-of-a-bitch. It was me that was always bad. I was the bitch. I was asked many times, why can't you look over what he does? He brings home a good payday.

I was the one that was lonely, so lonely that I cried many a day while Richard read himself to sleep. I prayed that I wouldn't wake up the next morning. Everybody thought I had it made in the shade, that I had everything. I did!

Everything that money could buy. No, Fritzie, money can't buy love. All I ever wanted was Richard, but Richard didn't want me. So, I was left alone in the country with nothing but pine trees that surrounded my home and believe me, they don't communicate. Yes, I was guilty of being lonely while Richard had his head up every skirt he could find. I stayed Fritzie and I was a good girl, just like you and everyone wanted me to be. Not understanding why I was rejected, but I stayed and stayed in hopes that someday I could live in peace. But, here I am. Still looking for answers."

We sat silently for a long time. He could tell that I was getting upset. He asked, "Will you sing at the club tomorrow night? You know Drucilla, you are happy when you're on that stage. Maybe you should consider really helping me. You could sing every weekend."

"I don't know Fritzie. I'll think about it, but you're right about the stage. Oh, how I love it, that and climbing through the window of a racecar. Lord, there's nothing like it. The only thing wrong is, I can't sing all day and I'm too old to race, cars! Now, please take me home. I'm about to freeze to death."

I had forgotten how cold the beach could be in January. I was so mad that I wouldn't have felt the cold anyway.

I could visibly see the relief on Max's face when I walked in. Laughing at him, I said, "See, I'm back in one piece. Now what about you Mr. Max are you ready to cruise around the ocean?"

Max's face lit up like a light bulb. He said, "Sure am. Everything is packed and I'm ready to leave. Sandra helped and I have all the papers. So look out St. Thomas, here we come."

Tony called saying that he would be home early and that he was tired and not to plan anything. I laughed saying to myself, not me honey. I'll sure let that man rest because we are going to party for two weeks. If he's tired now, he'll be dead before we get back.

I made sure that Sandra had packed my jewelry and when my mind had been set at ease that all was ready, I took paper and pen to the Sun Room. I needed two new songs for singing at the Hot Box and by the time Tony came in, I had written three songs.

I said, "Tony, I'll be right with you. I want to call the club."

Fritzie answered the phone. "Hello Drucilla. Have you thawed out yet?"

"Yes, thank you. Max is on his way with some new songs. Tell J.B. to put me some simple music to them for tomorrow. Just enough to get by then he can work with them later. Plus, I have more. Call me when he gets ready for me to practice."

"I'll tell him right now."

We said our good-byes. Tony walked into the room just as I was hanging up.

"Oh gosh," Tony said. "Can't you smell that spaghetti? I'm calling Papa and the boys in. Sandra will call us to dinner any minute."

Sure enough she did. I sat back watching my family eat. Lord did they eat…spaghetti, French fries and salad. Not me I was so afraid I wouldn't fit into my new cloths. I wouldn't have anything but plain salad.

After dinner Sandra came to me and asked, "May I have an advance on my pay? My Mom is making my sister and brother-in-law leave. I know that my sister doesn't have a dime."

I gave Sandra the money she asked for and said, "This isn't a loan. It's a gift, but you let this be a lesson to you. When you marry, be sure you marry with your mind and not your heart. I know what I'm talking about girl. My sister married a rambling man and there is truth in the saying, a rolling stone gathers no moss. Men can turn a woman into a tramp in a matter of minutes."

Tony came in asking, "What are you two talking about?"

"Men," I said, "Sorry men. Free loading men like that sorry DeRoy that was married to my sister. I remember Gertrude telling about them going from state to state. She would work on the big farms picking fruit and vegetables trying to get enough money to get back to Alabama.

Once she told us how they tricked people across the country to get home. She said that DeRoy would drive until the gas in the car was almost gone, and as soon as they saw a gas station, he would get out and walk. He would walk right past the station just far enough to be out of sight. Gertrude would drive the car into the gas station and beg the attendant for a tank of gas telling him that her husband had run off and she couldn't get home without help or some other made up story. Then, she'd pick DeRoy back up and this would work until they pulled back into Shady Grove.

So see, Sandra, the best thing your sister can do is kick his ass out and get herself a job taking care of number one. I'll tell you this, as long as you and your folks keep giving handouts, your sister is going to tag along with that sorry thing. Sandra, you can tell her what's right, but you can't change her. You, yourself, need to learn to help those who help themselves and let the others root hog or die poor."

"Yes Mam. I'll have a good talk with that sister of mine."

With that, I took Tony's hand and went out. I said, "Tony, will you and Papa go with me to the Hot Box tomorrow night? We don't have to stay late. Has Papa started the construction on the tunnel yet? I was wondering if it would be finished in time for the summer crowd."

"Yes, we will go with you. Yes, Papa has started on the tunnel and yes it will be finished for the summer crowd. Remind me to get a pencil and piece of paper."

"Why do you want a pencil and paper?"

"You ask so many questions at one time that I want to write it down so I won't forget."

"You're a nut. I know one thing Tony, Papa was thrilled that the gambling laws were passed. Lord, I'm glad we bought those twelve acres of land when we did. I don't think anyone ever thought that law would be passed here. Did you Tony?"

"No but after the lottery passed in Florida we had to have something exciting to draw the people here when they would come to Pensacola to get the lottery tickets."

"Tony, I think that Papa may be a little pissed at me for saying what I did about his men in Birmingham." Just as I said, "I don't give a damn," Papa walked in. I went right on talking. "Papa, I'm glad you're here. I want you to stop pouting. I can't leave on my trip with you mad at me. I was scared to death that that fool might hide Brandon. You know that your men should have found Richard."

"Don't you worry Drucilla I'll get him I promise you that!"

"I don't care anymore Papa. Honest, I don't. It won't help me to kill Richard. The only thing that will help me is time. I'm learning to pity him along with a lot more. I just don't want you mad at me for what I said about your men."

Papa said, "I was never mad at you baby. I was ashamed that they let him get away. Besides, you were right about that Birmingham bunch. They didn't mean business. They were just looking for an easy dollar. I've got some real men in there now. I know who Richard's last woman was."

I jumped up. "Who Papa? Was it that one he was working with…the Gorilla?"

"Yes," Papa said.

"Papa that's hard to believe, she is too ugly."

"Drucilla, you never fail to amaze me. When are you going to learn that with some men pussy is pussy even if it's on a cow? And you can believe it is the Gorilla."

I got quiet. I had a lot of planning to do.

Tony asked, "Papa is your shoulder all right?"

"Yes it will be fine. At my age, it takes time."

Tony asked, "How are the new gamecocks coming along?"

I said, "That is a sore subject with me. I'm going to see the boys and then I'm going to my room to soak in the tub."

I found Brandon and Anthony playing with ships and talking about what games they would play once on board the cruise ship. I finally got away after answering fifty questions.

After my bath I lay down to read. I stopped reading when Tony came to bed. Tony said, "The boys sure are excited about the cruise."

I said, "I hope the boys aren't the only ones excited about going. Tony, don't you think that while we are on the ship we can have someone look after the boys so Max can enjoy the trip? You know we run him to death and he never complains."

"That will be fine baby. Whatever makes you happy."

"Oh Tony. Did you remember to ask Papa about going to the club?"

"Yes Mam. We are going, but we can't stay late. Dru, I didn't tell you about Papa sending Ross to bring the eleven by fourteen picture of Mama over here so he could hang it in his room. Papa said that was the best gift he could have gotten. This man beats all I have ever seen in my life. I've never known him to show his love to anyone the way he does you. Papa said you saved his family."

"Yes Tony. I know he says that, but we know it's a joke. I

brought a lot of hell here and I'm sorry."

"Well now. Papa didn't say anything about the hell. He said you brought a lot of fire and saved me from the dead dick bench."

Tony had slipped up behind me and picking me up in his arms, he said, "I love you lady. Let's see what kind of fire you can conjure up."

Now, I don't know who lit the fire, but I do know it was hot and after things got cooled off, Tony and I lay talking about Harriet. She had told Max that she didn't like me taking Brandon without asking her and she didn't like not being included in the plans.

I said, "I have ignored her Tony hoping she wouldn't talk to me about it. We both know that some things are better left unsaid. You and I know that I would snatch the Devil out of hell and throw him around her neck over Brandon. I pray that she leaves things alone."

"You want me to have a little talk with her?"

"No, I guess I'll do that later."

I had told everyone about the cruise and the whole gang was at the Hot Box. It was a night of pure fun and as I looked around me, I wished that I could take them all with me. Tony made me go home saying, we have to be rested for the flight tomorrow.

# CHAPTER 39

Max and the boys were so nice on the flight. They talked about the sea and ships asking every question they could think of. Then Anthony asked if they would get to see sharks?

I said, "Oh! Tony let's go back. I didn't think of the sharks!"

Brandon said, "No way, we are going. Tell Mam Maw Anthony."

Anthony said, "That's right, we have read all about this trip and we won't let you be afraid."

The ship's accommodations were fabulous. Anthony and Brandon checked out all the activities. Tony and I watched them, in their white suits with caps to match, talking to the captain.

Brandon asked, "Sir, are you the Master of this ship? If so Sir, we need to talk to you."

They did talk, the poor Captain almost never got away from them. Anthony asked, "Is this cruiser like a warship? I mean a battleship?"

"Well," the Captain said, "It is just a little bit. This is a pleasure cruiser. Just good times, but the cruiser that you're talking about is a fast warship and it's smaller than a battleship."

Max pulled them away saying, "I will tell you boys all about it for the tenth time. I'm sure the Captain has to get back to the bridge."

The next few days were pure heaven. The gentle breeze, the turquoise blue water and St. Thomas were a dream.

The tropical foliage was breath taking and we looked and shopped until I was ready to holler uncle. It was so exquisite.

I said, "Just look Tony, Amanda will love all this gold and I sure do. I can't believe the prices."

I had bought necklaces and bracelets for Amanda and me. Tony had gotten some things for Brandon to give Harriet. He would look at me saying be nice, be nice. After getting back to the ship, Tony wanted to eat. Eat that's all the people do here is eat. I've never seen so much food in my life. I must say it was excellent but I couldn't eat. I told Tony to go ahead. I needed to get all dressed up for the night.

Tony couldn't take his eyes off me. I was a doll and knew it. My dress was dark green satin with green satin shoes to match and they were beautiful. I was putting on my pearl earrings while Tony fastened my bracelet. He turned me around to face him.

He asked, "Do you remember what you told Michael about dolls?"

We both burst out laughing and at the same time we said, "Yes, they're to dress, undress and play with!"

The entertainment was superb and the ship had the friendliest staff we had been around.

After a night of pure pleasure, Tony and I lay in bed and talked and talked about the people from Oklahoma, New Orleans, Louisiana, Missouri and Fort Worth, Texas.

I said, "I love the couple from Greensboro, North Carolina but the ones from Kentucky were very sophisticated, don't you think?"

Tony surprised me by saying, "Hell no! I think they're the two best actors on this cruise."

Walking around the ship the next morning, I was the happiest I had ever been. I said, "Tony, I forgot to tell you about someone. Mr. and Mrs. Green, I have invited them to come from Birmingham to visit us."

"I'm very proud of you Dru. I didn't think you would want a friend from there."

Tony and I walked on, talking and playing hard all day. The last night of the cruise was going to be a wonderful night. I had taken a nap to be rested. I didn't want Tony to feel that we had to leave a good party and I knew I wouldn't want to leave until the last tune was played.

My dress was long, black and silver, covered with sequins, off one shoulder and slit up one side. I don't mind saying I was beautiful. I was so proud to have the diamond earrings and bracelet, not to mention my eight-carat diamond that Papa had given me. Oh, Gosh, I thought, just look at Tony in his single breasted suit with the Shaw collar. He really is a Golden God, and he is mine! Then as I was thinking about Tony, Max walked up.

He said, "Hello Doll, can I have a dance?"

I looked at Tony. He gave me a nod yes. Max was a wonderful dancer and could he talk. But tonight I had him beat. I asked, "Who's that hussy you're with? Don't let her take my place. Do you hear me?"

Max had come to a stop. Looked straight into my eyes and said, "No one will ever take your place."

"I was just joking Max. I want you to have a good time tonight and always."

I had just gotten back to my seat when the Captain took the floor. "Friends," he said, "I have two fine young men on board that tell me they have a Mom that's a knockout on stage. I promised them that I would ask her to sing for us. Now what about it, Mrs. Drucilla Tortomasi?"

The people wouldn't take no for an answer. I went on stage

not knowing what I would do. Hoping the band knew something I could do without making a fool out of myself. I couldn't believe it when the leader of the band handed me the sheet of paper. It was one of the songs that I had written a few days before we left for the trip.

The man winked saying, "We've got good music and you will do fine. Your little boys gave us a tape of you. All you have to do is sing."

I took the microphone and said, "Hello everyone, I'll sing you my favorite song, Angels Do Cry."

Anthony and Brandon had been standing by the door smiling from ear to ear. When my song ended, the Captain let them out. Everyone wanted one more. So for fun, I sang.

**I NEED A MAN**

**I need a man to play week days**
**But I won't play on holidays**
**I don't need any night callers**
**All I need is day time dollars.............**

Hours later I could still hear someone singing, I need a man. What a night to remember. I loved it all.

It was so late the boys were asleep. Kissing them, good night, I said, "Sweet dreams my babies."

Then it dawned on me that I hadn't dreamed at all while on this vacation. Knock on wood and please Lord, don't let me dream.

Tony was standing at the mirror when I came into the room. I went over and stood beside him asking, "Aren't we the most Tony? We make the best, looking couple in the world. You're so handsome and I am proud to be with you."

"Now Dru, if you can't believe all you hear, you should at least believe all you say."

"You can believe me Tony. I know we're the best."

The next morning, I asked Tony, "Guess when the best time to do something is?"

Being dumfounded, he couldn't guess.

I said, "It's between yesterday and tomorrow."

"Why Dru, you're right and that's right now."

Tony jumped up and ran around the table, but he was too late. I had already made it to the door. I was in the boy's cabin before he caught up with me.

He said, "How dare you trick me like that."

After socializing around the ship, we all went to the pool, playing with Brandon and Anthony.

The day flew by and I was dead tired. Tony went to get the boys so we could all rest before dinner. I knew if we didn't get them in the bed early, they wouldn't have a good day tomorrow. The ship was scheduled to dock late and we could wait until the next morning to get off.

The next few days were long days, I didn't like Miami, but I could feel that Tony was trying to keep me there as long as he could. He had planned this and that until I had enough.

I said, "No Tony, We are going home! We have sand in our own back yard and I'm going with you or without you. I'm tired and I'm sorry, but I want to go home."

Hugging Tony, close to me, I told him the cruise had been a dream come true and I loved him for being so kind, but I had to leave. Tony was out the door to find Max and the boys. When he returned he said we would leave for home in the morning.

"Now baby" Tony said, "If you want to rest, I will go play blackjack with Brandon and Anthony."

I said, "That would be nice Tony."

After I had my bath, I called Papa Perricotti on the telephone. I said, "Papa we will be home tomorrow and we had a wonderful time. Please tell Amanda and Sandra, that we will be home soon. Tell Sandra to cook some black-eyed peas I'm starved to death."

Papa said, "You come on baby. I'll see to it that she cooks a feast and Drucilla, you and I can have a good talk."

I laid down wondering if his talk had anything to do with Richard. An hour and a half later I awoke wringing wet with sweat and crying. In my dream, Richard was telling me that he wasn't any of my business from the time he left me to go to work until he returned at night. He belonged to the telephone company and that a lie wasn't a lie unless you could prove it was a lie. I could hear him so plain when he said I don't have to give an account for the money I spend. Just rerun after rerun of the same old things. I lay there wondering why. Why was I letting Richard make me sick? I would be better off dead than to let him make me live in fear of even going to sleep. I wished with all my heart that I hadn't got Tony involved in my troubles and little Anthony. He loves me, it would be bad to hurt him, but I didn't see any other way out. I cannot take anymore of this torment. I know Lord I have said this week after week for years but maybe, just maybe someday I'll get the guts.

At least Papa had found that slut and found out that Richard had lied about riding with her. The rookie and the whore hopper, I started to laugh and laugh. Richard was only right about one thing. That she was a gorilla.

Papa didn't tell a lie. The family was all at home and a feast was waiting. Fried pork chops, cold slaw, corn, black-eyed peas with cornbread and iced tea. Tony was looking across the table smiling.

I said, "Tony I know what you're thinking. No you'll never get the country out of me. No, I'll never be a steak and potato girl."

Papa said, "Tell'em Drucilla, tell'em."

Later that night Brandon and Anthony begged to spend the night in their tree house.

Tony said, "Let them, I'll have Topaz and Tonnymacker stay the night to watch after them."

Jumping with joy, they ran out to get the toys they wanted.

Tony said, “Let’s go to bed early ourselves.”

After giving Tony time to be sound asleep, I quietly got out of bed to find Max. As usual, he was watching a movie. I asked him to come to the garage with me.

# CHAPTER 40

"Max, do you know how to use a drill?"

"Yes, Mrs. Drucilla."

"I need you to help me make something. Before I do, I want you to listen very carefully to what I have to say. Don't ask me any questions and I'll tell you no lies."

I turned on the hot plate and put the lead into a pan to melt while Max dilled what seemed like a million small holes into two baseball bats, plus drilling an eight inch deep hole in the big end of both bats. We poured the melted lead into the end holes. After it hardened, I drove nails into the holes. Max cut the heads off all the nails with a pair of nine-inch wire cutters. He cut the heads off at an angle so it would have a sharp point on each nail. As soon as Max was through cutting off the heads, I would take the bat and wrap friction tape on the small end so my hand wouldn't slip when I swung it.

After I finished the first one, Max just stopped and said, "Drucilla, in all my life, I've never heard of such a weapon."

"No, and if anybody asks, you still haven't. My Uncle Louie told me how to do this. He also said that after you use it, burn the bat and drive the nails into a wall here, there and everywhere.

Let's get through so we can get to bed. I want you to take me to Birmingham tomorrow. I'll tell Tony we'll be gone for the day, then I'll call back saying we had car trouble and that it will be the next day before we can get back."

Max asked, "What about the boys?"

"I've talked to Charlie about that. So ask me no more questions. Charlie will watch the boys and you will be with me."

The next afternoon Max and I were waiting as the Gorilla drove up at the South Side Work Center. After waiting about thirty-five minutes, she drove back out. It was 5:30 p.m. and almost dark. Hopefully, she would go straight home. Lucky for me she lived in the country. There wouldn't be any problems finding a deserted stretch of road. I didn't want any mistakes. We followed her and when she got onto the old road, we made our move. Driving right up to the side of her car, Max backed off and with just a tap of the bumper's her car was off the road.

I said, "Okay Max, we can't screw this up. It cost Papa two grand to find this tramp. Do just what I said."

Jumping out of the car, Max punched her in the face just enough to stun her he pulled her out of the car snatching her up by her heels and while standing on both her arms, he pulled her legs apart.

I screamed at her, "Look at all these nails! How many times did my husband nail you?"

That's when I swung the bat and nailed her right between the legs. Max turned her loose. She fell to the ground with the bat still stuck between her legs.

I picked up the other bat and hit her in the stomach tearing her stomach open. Then with one more swing, I nailed her right between the eyes.

Stepping back I said, "I feel good Max! She could be the one that was driving the white car but it looks as if Richard had two at the same time.

Something tells me that we should get the test board operator."

We got the bats and wrapped rubber rain suits around them,

the same rubber suits that we had worn so we wouldn't get blood on our clothes and put them into a plastic bag and then into the trunk of the car.

Then driving off as fast as the old road would let us, Max asked, "Where in the hell are we?"

"This is the backside of Alabaster. Now get us away from here and home as fast as you can."

"Damn," Max said, "If I ever find a woman to marry, she will never meet you! I'll take her out of the country. I pray Tony never steps out of line."

"Get me to Papa's house so we can burn these suits and bats. Good Old Uncle Louie, he said the bats were good weapons."

Max and I stayed at Papa's club until almost daylight. I went home about five a.m. Getting into bed, I told Tony we were able to get the car fixed sooner than I thought and we had stopped at Papa's club to play around. I know I slept better than the dead.

I was all smiles, when I went to find the girls. I gave Amanda, Harriet and Courtney the gold chains and other gifts I had gotten them and we talked for hours about the cruise.

Before Papa went to bed he left word with Sandra for me to meet him in the kitchen at six a.m. the next morning for a walk on the beach. I said to myself, Papa has important news and it's not about the club or he would have told Sandra.

I was in the kitchen at five a.m. with a bad headache from dreaming all night. Papa came in at five thirty looking for coffee and was surprised to find me there so early. He knew I wasn't a morning person.

Papa said, "Hello, my honey bun. I'm glad you're up early. I can help get your day off to a good start."

"How's that Papa?"

"I want you to know that you don't ever have to worry about Richard Hallmark again."

That statement sort of cleared my head. So I asked, "What makes you think that Papa? I'll be the first to tell you that

Richard will go down fighting. He's one that doesn't believe a thing until it happens."

"He believes it because it did happen. I wasn't going to let him hurt you anymore so I got some real men as you suggested. They took him to the basement of the drugstore and gave him a blood transfusion from a dying AIDS patient, then took him back to Birmingham. Is that what you wanted Drucilla?"

"Yes sir, it is. He doesn't have to live in fear of getting it like I did. He has to live with it. Maybe now it'll dawn on him just what he put me through."

Papa said, "He may live two months, but I doubt that. One thing's for sure Drucilla, if I had ever laid eyes on you. I would have gotten you away from that family. I'd never let you be used so badly."

"It was my parents fault…at first Papa, then as the years passed, it was my own fault. I was too much of a coward to try making it on my own. I stayed to have the crap rubbed in my face. It hurts to know I was nothing more than the keeper of a boarding house for a lying man that couldn't keep his pants up.

Let's take our coffee and walk Papa, I wish I could walk out off the past and be happy."

"If I could help you baby, I would. I would do anything for you and Tony. Just keep holding on. I'm sure you'll see that you don't have to be afraid of the future."

Papa stopped and looked at me. He said, "You do know that's what's wrong don't you? You've had to worry about what's going to happen next for so long that you dread or, I should say, fear each day. Believe me, baby, when he's gone, your fears will be over. You can trust me Drucilla, I know all about fears."

"I know you're right Papa. I'll never be free until Richard is dead. It's hate that's eating me up. I love you Papa. Thank you for all you have done."

The next few nights were bad on me. I was worn out and had to rest during the day. If I wasn't dreaming about snakes, I was going back over and over all the things that Richard had done to me over the years. It was unbearable. The thought hit me. Just maybe if I go back to Shady Grove, see the house and walk in my yard it would help set my mind at rest.

I eased through the house looking for Max. He was in the shower. Tony had left early and the others were in the bed. Courtney's keys were the only ones I could find and they were in her car. Jumping in, I flew out of the yard, knowing that if anyone saw me they would never let me go by myself. I knew I could drive to Shady Grove in five hours and that would give me plenty of time before dark.

I pulled into the yard about six. Getting out of the car, I slowly walked from the front yard to the back. There I stood looking at the willow tree thinking about the song I had written so long ago.

The willow tree is flowing; it's dancing, in the yard
The roses on the fence are sparkling from the morning dew
I lean against the doorframe watching you
You leave for work, but you don't say, good-bye.
Like you use to do

Oh! Richard, how I once wished I could call back the love of yesterday. But there had been no love to call back. I had only been a maid. I walked on saying to myself, still it's a good song…for those who did have love.

As I put the key into the lock, I was surprised when the door pushed open. I was even more surprised to see Richard lying on the floor.

Walking up to where he lay, I said, "This is a fine homecoming."

I could feel the adrenaline pumping. It was as if a tornado had been turned loose inside me. All of a sudden I was mad enough to kill him, just like many times before. I stepped back, telling myself to calm down.

After a minute, I said, "I'm sure glad you're here. You

ought to get up and look in the mirror, Richard. Oh hell, I forgot, men like you never really look in the mirror. You don't dare see the real you. Not your type Richard. You're the real vampires. Men like you that suck the life out of women with you fake, upstanding way. I'm glad you're dying here, what should have been our happy home.

Now get up Richard. If you can't get up, then crawl, but take your ass to the bathroom, shave and put on your best clothes. Put on you fake smile. Turn on all that fake love you turned on when company came, or when you were around other people with me. Get up, dig way down, find some energy, I guarantee you this will be the last episode in our lives. Just think about it Richard, I turned the tables on you, didn't I? Oh yes, you jerk, you need to be dead. You've tormented me so bad that I don't know how to be happy. So bad that I can't even learn to be happy."

Stepping up, I kicked him screaming out, "**I hate you**, I hate you for what you've done to me! Remember all the years, all the hurt, all the tears and all the begging? Remember all the good lunches, the grapes, cakes, pies and melons, the best sandwiches. Remember how I begged you to call me during your lunch. But **oh no**! You couldn't call me because you ate lunch at eleven so you could have that slut at twelve. You bastard, I can still smell all that homemade bread. My mind almost died from being here seven days a week, twenty-four hours a day. You enjoyed sucking the life out of me, didn't you Richard?

I wish I had brought a gun with me. I would kill you **here and now**! How could you? I was the best wife this world had to offer. You just used me!"

I kicked him again. "You were always a good for nothing bastard. You were ashamed of me. Isn't that what you said, Richard? You weren't ashamed of me! I wasn't anyone to be ashamed of."

I started laughing, "You handled me right, didn't you Richard? If I had been you, I wouldn't have wanted to be seen with the keeper of the boarding house either. That's all I was to you **the keeper of your boarding house.** I did a fine job, keeping your house, but I couldn't keep you. I tried hard Richard. Twenty-three years is what I call trying hard for us to be happy in this place. I remember so well, begging you to help me keep a happy home Richard. How many times did I say that we should live out our lives right here? I tried so hard to let you get by with it all. I tried not to make waves. But when the talk of AIDS started, I made waves all right, so damn high that you wanted to kill me.

**Look at the fool**, the fool that stayed with you anyway. Thinking everyday that you would stop hurting me, but you didn't. You couldn't love me. You never did in the first place, did you?"

I didn't think that Richard was going to say a word. All of a sudden he screamed, "**No, No, No**. I never loved you! I could blank you out of my mind, even when we were in the same room."

"I know that's true Richard. I hate myself for living with you as long as I did. I'm only sorry that someone didn't take me away long ago. I'll tell you one more thing Richard. I let you embarrass me and ruin my life to the point of wanting to die. But today as I leave, it's the best good riddance I've ever known."

As I turned to walk off, I said, "I've got to hurry. I know that Tony will be worried to death about me."

As I stepped out onto the porch, I heard Richard whisper, "Stop, I've got to tell you something, come back."

Then I saw the pipe flying through the air.

# CHAPTER 41

Tony was half crazy with worry. His men had combed the whole Gulf area. He told them that I had played golf with him and Papa early and I didn't want to stay and have lunch with them. He dropped me off at the house and I was supposed to be resting. Or was that yesterday. Tony was so worried he could not remember.

All the cars were accounted for except for Courtney's and she must be with Fritzie. Fritzie was the only one that Tony hadn't heard from.

Max had said over and over that I must have left the house when he was in the shower. I had told him that my head hurt and I was going to lie down for a while. That was about ten o'clock.

Tony and Papa had come looking for me at one, but I was nowhere to be found. Thinking I would run in the door any minute, Tony jumped at every noise.

At the first sound of the telephone, Max jumped for it, listened for a second, then handed it to Tony and ran out the door to bring the car around.

Fritzie was on the phone. He said, "Tony, I talked to

Drucilla about nine forty-five and she said that she would give anything to see her yard. There were plants in her yard that she wanted and I just wonder if that's where she is."

"Where is Courtney?" Tony asked.

"Courtney is with me, Tony. She left her car there with the keys in it."

Max ran in all excited. He said, "Tony, the car is ready."

"Okay Max, but first, we have to know for sure that Dru is there. I have called Phillip Jimez and he is sending a car to see if she is out there."

Tony paced the floor waiting for Phillip to call back.

"Damn!" Papa said. "I wish I hadn't told Drucilla about the bastard. I thought she would feel safe and be happier knowing she didn't have to live in fear of him."

Tony said, "Papa, maybe she did feel safe. Maybe she felt safe enough to go back to her house."

The ring of the phone made Tony turn white. Phillip had called back. Tony put the call on the speakerphone so everyone could hear.

Phillip said, "Yes Tony, Drucilla is here and there is an ambulance on its way here now. She has been hit with a pipe. Tony, I don't know how bad she is hurt."

Tony said, "Okay Phillip, call Dr. Shane. I'm sure he will do all he can for her, and Phillip, if you see Dru, please tell her that I'm on my way."

Hanging up the phone, they ran for the car. Max set a record time getting to the airport. Tony had been surprised to see Papa in the back seat of the car waiting for them. The old man said he had been waiting in the car from the moment Phillip had called back.

After the plane was in the air, there wasn't a word spoken between them. It was a two and a half hour flight. Papa had one of his men waiting for them at the hanger.

Tony told the driver to go as fast as he could and be even faster.

Phillip was waiting in the emergency room for them. When

he saw Tony running up the hall, his smile let them all know that I would live.

Phillip said, "Dr. Shane and his son, Dr. Bob, are with Drucilla now. She was found just outside the door. She had been hit in the head with a pipe. She was out cold, but you know she is hard headed. We think Richard threw the pipe, but he was too weak to crawl out the door and finish the job."

It wasn't long until the two doctors came out. Looking at Tony, Dr. Shane said, "I believe that Drucilla told you to burn that house."

Tony was shaking his head, "Yes, yes she did. The dreams and that telephone ringing tormented her so bad. But now she's got so much to live for and we all love her. I thought with time she would get over being hurt so bad."

Dr. Shane wouldn't let anyone in to see me. He said he would send someone to get them after I was put into a room.

Six hours had passed before I was able to answer Tony's questions and I asked if Richard had been brought into the hospital with me.

Tony said, "No Dru, you must have been hallucinating. No one said anything about Richard."

"Oh no! He's the one that hit me and it's his last time! Papa has done a job on him."

Tony met with Dr. Shane to see when I could go home. Tony told Dr. Shane that he would personally keep an eye on me if he would release me to go home. Dr. Shane told Tony it was fine, but he would have to keep both eyes on me because if he let me get hurt again, he would operate on him.

After getting settled at home, Tony and I talked for a long time. I told him that no matter how stony the path I had always forged ahead. I didn't know why I had been dumb enough to go back to Shady Grove. Papa was right. The future did scare me because the past had been so bad.

Tony said, "The future is me. Dru, you and I have responsibilities. Brandon and Anthony depend on us. Besides that, I love you. I'm not like Richard. Dru, my love is real."

Tony didn't get that out of his mouth good until Father Raymond walked in. But before he could get a word out, I said, "Don't you come in here giving me any crap Father. We both know that religion is a cloak used by some people in this world who would be warm enough without it in the next world."

This brought a smile to the old man's face. He said, "I believe you're going to live Drucilla, but God's going to straighten you out someday and I feel like doing it by bending you over my knee."

After they had left, I lay thinking how unfair I had been to Tony's family and friends. Richard had caused all this. He had married me when I was no more than a child and ruined my life. He thought he was a Saint because he was selective in his sins, but all he had been was a bad sneak. To hell with Mr. Hallmark he has just played his last part in my life!

There was a knock on my door. Max quietly walked over and asked, "What in the hell do you mean doing me this way? Don't you know that Tony was ready to kill me for letting you get away from me?"

Without cracking a smile I asked, "Were you really afraid of being put in that slough?"

"Hell yes, I was."

"I'm sorry Max. I was just thinking of myself."

"Why can't you see that you've made it to the top of the ladder?" Max was shaking his finger at me.

I said, "Now, now Max, your temper is a valuable possession, so don't lose it."

"I'm getting out of here so you can rest, but I won't be far away. Do you hear that Drucilla? I won't be far away!"

# CHAPTER 42

Weeks went by with me working hard at the Club. I had gotten over my little trip and was happy until Max came into the kitchen and gave me the news about Richard. I couldn't help but cry. I had been with Richard all my life. I looked at Max and he was giving me a strange look.

I said, "I'm glad the bastard is dead. You can stop looking at me as if I've lost my mind. Max, don't tell Tony that you've told me. He has talked me into going to New Orleans for a riverboat ride. I think it will be good for us both."

"I'm sorry if I upset you Drucilla, but I knew you would want to know."

"Think nothing of it Max. I'm glad that you look out for me."

Tony wasn't about to let me hear about Richard. He had given orders that no newspapers were to be brought into the house and no one was to tell me. He kept a straight face through it all. He walked me on board the riverboat and I had never been happier. For that matter, I was speechless.

I said, "Oh Tony, how did you know I wanted to do this? All of my life, I've wanted to ride the Mississippi River Boat."

Then it dawned on me that we were being photographed.

People were nodding their heads, as if to say, Hello, Hello.

Tony said, "That's one thing about being a gangster. You hit the news with a blast and it seems that they know more about us than we know about ourselves."

As we stood looking out across the water, I couldn't help but think of the night before. I had written Tony a song and Fritzie was going to let me sing it. I stood waiting and thinking how handsome Fritzie was and that he was the best singer and drummer in Alabama. He had his head in the clouds and didn't have any confidence. How I wished I could have found a way to make him see that I could have made him a star. I do believe he thought that I was just another groupie following his band looking for someone to dirty dance with. Fritzie broke my train of thought when he called me to the stage. I announced this is a special song tonight. It was especially for, Tony my loving husband.

**MAGIC SPELL**

You put a magic spell on me baby, you've enchanted me
A miracle of all miracles, you've made me see.
You bring delight and pleasure; I have made up my mind
I surely love you baby, I love you all the time..........

Tony was thrilled with my song and of course Papa had asked, what about me? With a hug I told Papa, you know I love you best! As the night wore on I got a little moody and often staring into space.

Tony brought me back to reality. Tony had his arm around me saying, "A penny for your thoughts."

"Tony, I think that Richard must have died. I have this empty feeling that hurts. I feel sorry for Richard. Why is it Tony that revenge is so sweet but it leaves, such a bitter taste?"

"I don't know baby, but let's not talk about all that. We are here to have a good time."

It was going to be a beautiful trip. Tony had been lucky to

get the canceled tickets and, of course, it was someone else's misfortune. Gosh, I was happy for the first time in my life. Papa had been right. I didn't have to fear the future. I didn't have to fear what would happen next.

As Tony and I were standing on the deck and the stars shining all around, I whispered, "Not the first raindrop. There isn't an Angel in heaven that cried for Richard."

"No Dru, he didn't know how lucky he had been to have you. I have never known a woman like you. Richard was just a fool. There's one thing I know for sure. Someone up there is looking out for me. You are an Angel, Dru."

Tony never asked how I knew about Richard and I never said. As we were leaving the boat, I asked, "Tony, did you know that I would have traded the cruise for this trip?"

"Say what woman? You mean I spent all that money and you would have been just as happy on this boat?"

"That's right!" I laughed and said, "I would have told you miles down the Mississippi, but I was afraid you would throw me over the side."

Tony pulled me close and said, "I will never hurt you and I will never let anyone else hurt you."

When I returned home, Amanda and I talked for a long time. Amanda had gone to see her Daddy without me knowing anything about it.

She said, "Mom, I'm the one that helped Daddy get the house livable. He talked to me for a long time telling me not to gossip. It just caused trouble and that you called it, ear pollution. He told me to listen to you."

"Like you should have many times, Amanda."

"I know it now, Mom. Daddy also said that loose conduct sure can get you into a tight place."

"Just take a look at your old Daddy, you'll see it for yourself. Amanda, he was all I ever wanted, but he couldn't make himself be true to me. There are only a few men that inherit a good reputation and even fewer that can keep it."

"Mom, Daddy said that you had overlooked the

unbecoming, understood the unconventional, tolerated the unpleasant, overcame the unexpected and outlasted the unbearable, which was him. He admitted that his family got him off on the wrong foot. He did love us when he married you, but he saw that he was losing all his family because of us and it caused him to change, then things got worse and worse."

I have sat and listened to your every word, Amanda. I don't care what he said. I'm here to remind you that he, was twelve kinds of a liar. The one thing I hated most about him was that he was a gutless liar. His family was sorry as crap and he knew it. He never had anyone making him do the things he did to us.

No one has to tell me how good I was and I don't want you to ever breathe his name to me again. Anytime you want to tell me something about him, you just remember the time he left you outside in the car so he could go into his slut's house to be with her. I'm glad the fool's dead, Amanda. What does that song say about a desperado riding in to steal you away? I prayed for just that and Tony came for me. What more can I ask?"

We heard Harriet laughing out in the hall. Amanda got up to leave.

Amanda said, "Mom, I will call you tomorrow, and Mom, Harriet is riding back into town with me. She and Sam are going to bowl the night away."

"Amanda, one more thing. Where was your Daddy when the ambulance picked me up?"

"Mom, he said when he heard the ambulance coming he crawled to the barn to hide until everyone was gone."

"I'm glad he's dead. Living with him was shame on me. That's not the way the police will tell it. I just wondered what the lying bastard told you."

Harriet opened the door and said, "Let's go, I'm late."

"Good-bye Mom, I'm gone this time."

The girls were gone, leaving me with my thoughts. I don't feel sorry for him. I feel sorry for me and I'll have to be brain dead to forget all he put me through.

Brandon came tiptoeing into the bedroom. I sat up on the side of the bed.

Brandon put his arms around me and said, "Please Maw Maw, don't get hurt and die. Please don't leave me. I heard Mother tell Sam that if anything happens to you, that she will take me back to Grandma Marselle's in Shady Grove. Please promise me Maw Maw, that you won't let her do that. Maw Maw, do you promise?"

I sat listening to him. He was all I had lived for him and Amanda. I could feel my blood boil. I would send that fat idiot to the fat farm as sure as I was living.

Holding him close to me, I said, "Yes Brandon, I do promise. I won't ever leave you and you will never go back to Shady Grove. So help me, I promise you Brandon, you and I will never be apart. Would you like to sleep in my bed for the night?"

"Oh no Maw Maw! Anthony would never stop laughing." As he was running out the door he said, "I'll see you in the morning."

Papa Pericotti and Dick Rizzio had been family a long time. Papa had moved Dick's family out of Birmingham and into Chicago. Setting him up with a cleaners on one of the business streets. Ever since then the two men had a bond that couldn't be broken. This time Papa needed Dick's help.

Dick arrived in town the next day. First they looked at the movie film of Richard's funeral. Papa explained that he had fool proof evidence that four of the women had been Richard's sluts.

Papa said, "They all live in the Birmingham area and work downtown." Papa handed Dick a map and said, "Does this look right to you boy?"

"Hell Papa, this would be sweet revenge and easy done."

"Then do it, but get the men you need out of Chicago. I don't want this to haunt my family. Is that clear?"

"That's no problem. For you I get the best. Consider it done."

Dick Rizzio had been fired from his job and his worst

enemy had stepped up the ladder into his place. There wasn't a thing about the gas lines in Birmingham that he didn't know.

Dick left to get it set up and was back with a map in a short time. On the map the key spots had been marked for the gas mains. It shouldn't take but three, two men crews to go out with jack hammers and drill holes next to the mains and just leave a crack for a small amount of gas to leak.

Rizzio said, "I know there's no worry about getting caught. There's no one in that whole damn town that knows what's going on and no one knows who's supposed to be doing what."

Papa said, "Just make damn sure they do a good job and get out as fast as they can move."

Dick said, "I will have the time bombs under cars at each location of the map. They will be set so all of them will go off at once. My men will have plenty of time to get out."

"I don't want a damn thing left but smoke and for sure, they've got to go off no later than two in the afternoon."

"Don't you worry Papa, I'll get Joe Pecchioni to help me. That way I know there won't be any screw-ups."

On Dick's way out, Papa hugged him and said, "Damn you boy, I wouldn't recognize you myself with you all made up like you are."

"Don't you worry Papa, you will hear from me on the late night news in a week or two."

Two weeks later Tony, Papa and I were listening to the ten o'clock news. A special news flash came on. The cameras were on people in the newsroom. They were running back and forth. You could tell the newsmen were trying hard to keep calm. The one in charge said, "We don't know how to go about reporting this, but we will give you what we have. We have news that all of downtown Birmingham has exploded and is on fire. Our information said it looked as if someone would have had to open all the gas mains to cause such a fire, and that Arab terrorists were seen in the vicinity. As of yet, no one has claimed responsibility. Please don't call the station. We are giving you all the information that we have. Our news is coming in from all around the outskirts of town thanks to HAM radio operators. One of our callers had reported that Birmingham is in real trouble. The fire is so hot that help can't get in."

Asking Papa and Tony to excuse me, I left the room long enough to get three glasses and a bottle of Champagne. Coming back into the room, I handed the Champagne to Tony.

I said, "Please help me with this. It's time to celebrate." Holding up my glass I said, "Here's to the burning of the largest whorehouse known to man. So large it didn't have a top."

Papa gave me a smile and a nod with his glass. An hour later the florist delivered two, dozen miniature pink roses mixed with baby's breath and a note that read… With love Papa.

Tonight was my night. I wanted to go to the club and dance the night away. I walked into the Hot Box with Tony on one arm and Papa on the other. Everything was beautiful and Fritzie had just started singing his number one hit, **Satin Smooth Love.** I had turned loose of Tony and Papa, looking around at all my friends from Birmingham. My eye caught Doctor Shane's table. I stood very still, looking at each and every one. I could hear Fritzie singing, Baby, I have satin smooth love for you…

Then over and over, I heard myself screaming. "Where is Doctor Bob? Where is Doctor Bob?"

# CHAPTER 43

"Mrs. Hallmark, Mrs. Hallmark, wake up! My name is Duke. I'm your nurse. I'm going to shine a light into your eyes."

I could hear people moving around me and I felt as if I had drunk too much. Feeling a warm strong hand rubbing across my forehead, I heard myself say, "Tony." Then fear gripped me. I couldn't talk or move. The warm hand had moved here and there until it was holding my hand.

I heard someone say, "Hello Mrs. Hallmark. I'm Doctor Bradley. I'll do my best to take care of you and I'll get you out of here in no time at all."

Oh no! It was all coming back to me now. To hell with this, I wished I could tell this Doctor Bradley to please let me die. Please don't send me back to those people. I can't take anymore. If only I could scream out, but tubes filled my throat. I prayed, please God let me go back to sleep and not wake up! You know Lord that my life has been hell with no way out. This is my only chance to get out of Shady Grove. You know Lord that I'm not loved. I beg you to take me now, but please take care of Brandon.

A familiar voice broke my train of thought. I opened my eyes to see Doctor Shane. My head was clearing now as Doctor Shane started to explain that Doctor Bradley had saved my life. He said that I had been in the operating room for six hours and in the Intensive Care Unit for three days so far. Doctor Bradley would continue to take care of me. I could hear Doctor Shane being paged.

He said, “Don’t worry Drucilla, I’ll be right back.”

Then all of a sudden Doctor Bradley took charge. He began taking the tape from around my face and out came the tubes. He said, “Mrs. Hallmark, can you talk to me? Do you want to see Richard? He has been here constantly.”

Doctor Bradley looked puzzled when I said, “Please put me back to sleep. I want to see Tony. Please don’t send me back to those people.”

He stood there looking at me for what seemed a long time. He was looking at me funny, but I couldn’t remember what I had said. I could feel myself drifting back into sleep.

Doctor Bradley spoke up saying, “Now, I don’t know anything about your situation before this happened, but this is no time to deal with it. So, we are going to think of only one thing and that’s getting you well.”

With every day that passed, I loved Doctor Bradley more. I knew that he knew more about my situation than he let on. I listened to his every word. He was so kind. He told me that the bullet DeRoy had shot me with had zigzagged between the main arteries in my back, then chipped a piece of bone off my spine and to top it all, a piece came off the bullet and cut my small intestines in two.

Looking into his beautiful powder blue eyes, I was wishing he could be the Tony in my dream. I thought, oh why did it have to be a dream it was all a dream, my Tony, the Gulf and little Anthony…was all a dream.

Doctor Bradley said, “You listen to me lady, you are a miracle. We really didn’t expect you to live! Mrs. Hallmark, do you understand me?”

"Yes sir, but it's you that doesn't understand. I had rather be dead than to go back to that place."

"Mrs. Hallmark, many people have died with a lot less injury than you have."

I softly said, "I want to die. You can believe that. I hate the trap I'm in."

The doctor had been standing at the window listening quietly, but he turned with a furious look on his face. He said, "I am not going to let you die!!! Do you get that Mrs. Hallmark? Do you?"

A few days had passed and I was cursing him again. I said, "Oh yes, you want me to live, but you are starving me to death. I want some food. Do you hear that?"

He was quiet. Just standing there, looking at me. I wanted to say, go ahead and get me well so you can send me back to the wolves. I made the mistake of looking into his eyes, oh, those eyes.

Doctor Bradley said, "You've been so busy bitching at me that I've not told you everything. The bullet hit your small intestines. I had to take out six inches of your intestines and it's no joke. You can't eat. We have to go slow and allow it time to heal. If I allowed you to eat, it would pull the stitches out and I would have to operate again."

I was quiet as he went on to show me the tubes coming out of my stomach and telling me how I was being fed.

He finished talking and said good-bye, turned and headed for the door. Just as he got to the door, I said, "I still want some Jell-O, just a bite."

He stopped in his tracks, turned his head and said, "People in hell want ice water too."

I said, "Speaking of water. I want my hair washed. I can't stand looking like this."

His smile broadened and as he turned to leave he said, "Okay, that you can have."

I heard him tell the nurse to get a hairdresser for me.

The day before I was to go home, Doctor Bradley came

bouncing into my room. He said, “Okay, little girl, let us have a look at that stomach this morning.”

I said, “Hell yes, you look. It looks as if you cut me from stem to stern. I look like Frankenstein’s daughter.”

He said, “What are you bitching about. You’re still alive.”

While each hand mashed inward on my sides and punching here and there. I thought warm hands mean a warm heart. Knowing better, I looked into those eyes and surges of heat spread over me like never before. As sick as I was, I wanted to ask him if he knew what dolls were for. Dolls are made to dress, undress, and play with. But no! I never said a word. I just turned my mind loose to do a lot of wishful thinking. As he was leaving the room, I heard myself say, “Lord this Doctor makes me crazy.” I grabbed a pencil and wrote a song.

**Powder Baby Blue Eyes**

He bounced into my room all dressed in white
Gosh, oh gosh, what a sight!
One look into those eyes makes my temperature rise
But gosh, he’s got the cure,
He’s got those powder baby blue eyes.................

I had just finished my song when Amanda walked in. She said, “Mom, a penny for you thoughts.”

“Okay, but make it a dollar. It’s worth it.”

“You’re on Mom, now talk.”

Amanda blushed when I said, “I was just thinking about that Doctor. He’s sweet as a peach in spring.”

Amanda burst out laughing. “Mama. You fell in love with Doctor Shane twenty-six years ago.”

“Yes, little girl and I still love him. You best remember never continue to go to a doctor that you can’t love. It may be bad for your health. But this Doctor is something else.”

“Mom, let’s get serious.”

“I am. I don’t want to be shot again, but Lord if I could just look into those eyes everyday, I know without a doubt I would never have another sick day."

"Now Mom I want to know if you're going home to Shady Grove."

"I'll tell you, it's funny. Richard, Harriet and now you have asked that question. I didn't answer them, but I will tell you. I've not had the first thought about going home."

"Are you going to give up you home?"

"I'll never let anyone run me away from my house."

"What are you going to do about Daddy?"

"When Doctor Bradley tells me I can go home, I'll have Richard's butt put out and I'll get on with my life."

"But Mama!"

"Don't but me! You know Richard has a slut. I gave him a second chance. I don't intend to let him hurt me anymore. All I ever wanted was a man that could keep his pants up. One that didn't care if I stayed home with my hobbies one that wouldn't be ashamed to take me anywhere to dine, dance, or whatever. I know I'm a beautiful person and I won't let myself be locked in prison any longer. Your Daddy looked over me, under me and around me, but never at me!

Amanda, you be sure to spread the word that I'm coming home meaner than ever. I was shot in the gut. I didn't have a heart transplant."

Amanda didn't answer. She turned and left.

That afternoon I started having muscle spasms in my lower back. I was scared and crying. I didn't know what was happening. I rang for a nurse and in a matter of minutes Doctor Bradley came running. He had concern written all over his face. He took care of the pain and explained what had happened.

He said, "Don't you worry. I'll do the worrying for you. Now that I have you settled down, I want to talk to you."

"What do you want to talk about?"

"Tony. You may not remember, but you talked about him in I.C.U."

"I had a dream about Tony, but he's not real."

"Tell me Drucilla. Is he a secret of yours? Come on. This is off the record.

Is this Tony your lover?"

"Now Doc I'm too sick to laugh, but I wish with all my heart that I could say yes. My Tony was just a dream. A dream that I had while I was out, so to speak. If you have time, I'll tell you my dream."

"I'll take the time, tell me."

"Doc, you may think it's gross. Personally, I wish it had been true."

It was one-thirty in the morning when I finished telling him about my dream.

Doctor Bradley said, "You're right. That is the damndest dream I ever heard."

He stood up to leave and said, "See you about nine on my rounds. If you need anything, call a nurse."

Doctor Bradley was late. He had made it a point to stop by Doctor Skeet's office with a you better be listening look on his face.

Doctor Bradley said, "Just in case you don't know, Drucilla's dream came from her subconscious mind. You couldn't deal with her conscious mind, so I'm telling you to fade out of her life and I do mean now."

Doctor Skeet said, "Now just a minute. That's for Drucilla to…"

**"No**! Don't you get it? She damn near didn't have a life because of you."

Doctor Skeet just stood there with his mouth open. He never uttered another sound as Doctor Bradley left the room.

It was ten o'clock in the morning when Doctor Bradley came bouncing into my room.

I said, "Doctor Bradley, you are a wonderful doctor. I'm proud that you can save people, but saving me was a bad mistake."

"Drucilla, what makes you think that?"

"Now that I've killed DeRoy, I sure will be hated in Shady Grove. I tell you there is, no one to take care of me when I get home."

"That's what private duty nurses are for. You won't need too much help. I'll have you fit as a fiddle."

"I've been told that my sister, Gertrude, breathed a sigh of relief when the last shovel of dirt was thrown over DeRoy, but Mama Marselle has taken to her bed. You can believe me when I tell you that Mama Marselle will never let me live in peace."

"Drucilla, you can deal with peons like them. It's my understanding that you always have. Enough of this I have something else to talk to you about."

"Alright Doctor Bradley, what's on your mind?"

"Now tell me, would you know this Tony, the one in your dream if you saw him?"

"Yes! You say I'm a miracle. It really would be a miracle if you could put me back in that dream. I would know that Tony anywhere, anytime, and I would never let him go."

Then it dawned on me. This fool is making fun of me.

I said, "Doctor Bradley, get your happy ass out of here. You're just making fun of my dream."

"Oh no I'm not! I have another patient down the hall and I want you to look at him. His name is Tony Tortomasi."

Without thinking, I rolled out of the bed pulling the IV out of my arm. I didn't even realize the blood was dripping off my fingertips. Doctor Bradley caught me took me in his arms and put me back in my bed and cleaned my arm and stop the bleeding.

Doctor Bradley said, "I have not been able to understand it. I've tried my damndest to find out how you two are connected. Your family said they didn't know him. I don't know how you did. I don't even know if it's possible. You were at deaths door when you came into the Trauma Unit. Tony Tortomasi was in the Trauma Unit at the same time. He also had a gunshot wound. He is from Gulf Shores and it is said that he is the Mafia. I want you to see him. I want to know if you recognize him."

"This is beginning to sound phony. You had me going for a minute Doc."

"I'm telling you the truth."

"I'll have to see him to believe it."

Doctor Bradley pushed the button and asked the nurse to come in with a wheelchair. I thought this Doctor is as full of crap as a crippled Coon...that is until he rolled me into a room down the hall.

Tears poured down my face. A little brown-eyed boy with coal black hair walked across the room with his hand out.

He said, "It's nice to meet you. My name is Anthony."

I couldn't talk. I just sat there thinking, oh God. I'll get revenge and it won't be a dream!"

**THE END**

www.ingramcontent.com/pod-product-compliance
Lightning Source LLC
Chambersburg PA
CBHW051551250626
47157CB00001B/258

* 9 7 8 0 9 7 7 0 3 0 3 2 3 *